THE CHASE

by

Jonas Saul

PUBLISHED BY:
Imagine Press Inc.
Ebook ISBN: 978-1-927404-48-5
Paperback ISBN: 978-1-998047-44-4
Hardcover ISBN: 978-1-998047-45-1

The Chase
Copyright © 2017 by Jonas Saul

The Sarah Roberts Series

The Decoy (Thirty-Three)
The Disappearance (Thirty-Four)
The Whole Truth (Thirty-Five)
Alex (Thirty-Six)
Parkman (Thirty-Seven)
Darwin (Thirty-Eight)
Aaron (Thirty-Nine)
Remains To Be Seen (Forty)

The Jake Wood Novels

The Immortal Gene (Book One)
The Immortal Target (Book Two)

Standalone Novels

'Til Death Do Us Part
The Drowning
The Woman in the Woods
The Threat
The Specter
The Mafia Trilogy
A Murder in Time
Frequency of the Dead

Co-Authored Novels

Collision Course (Written with Gary Ponzo)
There Will Be Blood (Written with Rania Stone)
The Soulless (Written with Rania Stone)

Short Story Collections

Twisted Fate (Tales of Horror)

Twists of Fate (Tales of Hope)

Chapter 1

THE RUSH OF THE chase, or as Vincenzo "Baby Face" Balzano called it, *the hunt*, was what brought him back every time. It wasn't the blood. It wasn't the murder. That was the culmination of the hunt, the necessary part at the end.

The adrenaline rush was in the chase. Maybe that was why he was so good at it. After a decade of hunting targets, the killing was a boring afterthought. Everyone dies eventually. How they die wasn't of consequence—well, maybe sometimes, as clients might often request a message sent through a specific act. But it was just a job for Balzano, a job he had no moral or religious attachment to. It made him money. He performed the task.

Then he was good for several months until the bosses needed another job done.

Upon contact and contract, Balzano would initiate the chase again, each time altering his patterns. Mindful of the authorities, but more so of his enemies, each target was someone of importance, a protected person. Some had armed bodyguards. Some armed themselves. Regardless of the target's abilities or those around him, Vince's job was to root out the exterior, home in on the target, and execute with extreme prejudice.

He flicked his cigarette from the open window of the black SUV. The tiny red tip brightened as it danced with gravity. It bounced several times, lost its battle in the air, then settled on the concrete, rolled left, then right, then stopped, the red heater dimming.

Would the cancer stick kill him before someone else did?

He wasn't long for this world. A man like Vincenzo never retired or expected to see himself playing cribbage in an old age home. A man like Vincenzo never left the business. When it was his time to go, it would be an order. Another contract is written for someone else, someone younger, stronger, faster, to execute. All that would happen when he wasn't useful anymore. Until then, he would remain useful.

Keenly observant, cunningly deft with weapons, Vincenzo would go on for years without worrying about his usefulness or the toxins—cigarettes, drink, whores—he used to enjoy life.

Without regard for his sleeping partner in the passenger seat, Vince lit another cancer stick and inhaled deeply. Idle, while he surveyed Marty Fermosa's home through the vehicle's mirrors, he exhaled the smoke in tiny rings, watching as several rings violated their cousins.

He wasn't more than a hundred yards from the Fermosa abode. He'd parked with the rear of the SUV facing the home, the vehicle dead center between two streetlights where darkness was the thickest. Not that it mattered up here. The homes were spaced hundreds of yards apart, and traffic was almost nil at this hour. No one walked by, and no cars had passed in the previous hour. Most of the people on this street were either asleep or about to be. His lips offered the hint of a grin in the rearview mirror as he dragged on the smoke again. The people on this street would wake in the morning to police cars and ambulances, red and blue lights strobing throughout the area. By morning, it would be a murder scene.

Marty Fermosa's life was worth only two hundred thousand dollars. At least, that was the rumor. As an enforcer—hitman—for the Toronto mafia, Vincenzo was issued a contract on Fermosa three days ago. Vincenzo had heard of Fermosa while playing blackjack at the Calto Social Club on Ellesmere. Every once in a while, someone spouted off his mouth and got beat down. Disrespect wasn't tolerated at the Calto. But Fermosa was a made man, high up in one of the seven families that ran Toronto. He answered only to the Board of Control as head of one of the 'Ndrangheta clan, or as they're known on the streets, *locali.* Marty Fermosa had entered the Calto one night, about two weeks ago, and talked to Mancuso Corrado about a betting scam he had in place. According to the rumor, Fermosa assured Corrado he couldn't lose. Corrado had said he would be good for two hundred large.

Three days ago, not only did Mancuso Corrado lose the two hundred thousand dollars on the *sure thing*, he lost it to Marty Fermosa. Now word on the street is that Corrado wasn't prepared to pay. Instead of taking the issue to the board and working out the details independently, Mancuso

Corrado took matters into his own hands—and swiftly—as the money hadn't changed hands yet. With Marty Fermosa dead, Corrado would never have to pay on a bogus bet everyone felt Fermosa had set up in his favor to begin with.

Tonight, this random Tuesday evening in August, was the last night Marty Fermosa would draw breath. Balzano didn't care what the dispute was either way. He was the hunter, the chaser, the killer. Corrado would pay him his fee, and the matter would be dealt with.

Fortunately, the garbage trucks had come through the area earlier. During Vince's surveillance of the Fermosa home yesterday, Mrs. Fermosa carried a heavy white garbage bag to the bin. That afternoon, the garbage truck came, and the Fermosa bin was emptied. Shortly thereafter, Vince had Vito, his sleeping partner in the passenger seat, take a small explosive device filled with a gas similar to tear gas and place it in a white garbage bag. They covered it with kitchen garbage and sealed the bag. Once that was done, Vito nonchalantly placed the white bag in the Fermosa garbage bin. It was risky, but without neighbors close enough to see what they were doing, Vito's work went unnoticed.

After the supper hour, Marty Fermosa returned to his wife and daughter and wheeled the garbage bin inside the garage without looking inside it. The garage door slid down and locked their small explosive device within.

Now they were set for the kill.

Vince and Vito had waited outside Fermosa's house most of the night, hoping the wife and daughter would leave, but they didn't. He checked his watch and decided to wait until after midnight. If the women weren't going to leave, he would at least wait until everyone was sleeping so their response to his intrusion would be somewhat dimmed by fatigue.

In the passenger seat of the nondescript Chevy Suburban, Vito Romero, his sometime partner, breathed deeply in slumber. Vincenzo dragged hard on the cigarette, the heater glowing bright red, as he watched Vito. The man was ten years his junior but nowhere near as smart or crafty. He never got his own contracts and worked as a bouncer for one of the strip clubs the 'Ndrangheta ran. Vince had brought him along for a couple of odd jobs where the risk proved higher than Vince was willing to encounter on his own. Whether Vince knew he wasn't long for this world or not, the risks he took were calculated. If the risk was too high, then Vito was his man. He worked for peanuts and did what he was told. If he was too dumb to see the big picture, how was that Vince's problem?

After another long pull off his cigarette, Vince tossed it out the window, where it landed among the half a dozen butts littering the ground a mere six feet from him.

He smacked Vito's arm. "Wake up." He smacked him again. "Job to do."

Vito stirred awake, grunted something, then blinked rapidly as he sat up.

"What'd I miss?"

"Shut up."

Vito nodded slightly, then knuckled his eyes, blinked several times again, and cleared his throat.

Vince had to be strong with Vito. He demanded respect and got it. For Vito, this was an honor to be out on contracted hits. But that wasn't the only reason Vince came across as rude. Vito was known for his puns. He could make, create, or recite a pun or a saying for almost every situation. It was the kind of thing that drove anyone mad within minutes of being around Vito. Letting him sleep on the stakeout: no problem. Telling him to shut up throughout the day: not an issue. Letting him talk freely: madness.

Vince slipped his weapon out of his inner pocket and checked that he had a bullet in the chamber. One more look in the mirror confirmed all the lights of the Fermosa house were off, but the one on the side where the main bedroom was. The daughter, he was sure her name was Arabella, was fast asleep and would hopefully stay that way until Vince could conclude his task. The contract was for Marty and Marty alone. The wife and daughter were to be left untouched.

"You have the detonator?" he asked.

Vito nodded.

Good. He wasn't talking yet. Better that way.

"You ready?"

Vito nodded again and turned his wide, sleepy eyes to Vince.

"You gonna collect the butts?" Vito asked.

"What?" Vince spun around in his seat. "Why would I do that?"

"Cigarettes are like hamsters. Perfectly harmless until you stick one in your mouth and light it on fire."

Vince jerked back, surprised. "Are you trying to tell me to quit smoking? Or is that another saying of some sort?"

Vito stared out the windshield, his eyes slit with the weight of sleep. "This being our third job, and the smell of smoke in this car." He shrugged. "I'm just saying that those butts outside your window have DNA on them." He adjusted himself in the seat and met Vince's gaze. "It's not cancer that concerns me. It's the cops."

"Fuck you. Don't ever preach to me. I leave those cigarettes because they'll be looking for a smoker of that brand. I hate that brand and only smoke it on the job. The cops don't have my DNA, so they can't match it to me. There's nothing here for you to judge. Just shut the fuck up and do your job." He smacked Vito's arm harder this time. "Can you do that?"

Vito nodded, his head bobbing twice, chin to chest, head to headrest. "I need to stop questioning myself. Right?" He rummaged around by his lower leg and came up with a gun. Checked it, then dropped it inside his jacket. He ran a hand through his hair. "You know you're getting old when all you exercise is caution."

"Is that another wise-ass remark?" Vince asked. "Another cliché or something?"

"No. Just saying." Vito placed a hand on the door's handle. "We going?"

Vince nodded. "You got the device?"

"I do."

"When we get to the side of the house, blow it."

"Got it."

They exited the SUV and started for the trees on Vito's side of the road. All of it came down to the next ten minutes. Enter the house. Locate the target. Execute. Then leave the premises and drive home casually. It seemed easy enough, but something almost always, invariably, went wrong.

At the last tree before they would be exposed and in the open, Vince grabbed Vito's arm and held him back. They waited like that for half a minute. The street was empty. The only sound of vehicles was on Highway 407 in the distance.

"Okay," Vince whispered. "We're good."

He led the way across the street and beside the garage, Vito keeping close. The darkness beside the garage was almost absolute. A faint amount of light from the gibbous moon was enough for Vince to see Vito's glistening eyes.

Vince leaned in close, placing his mouth next to Vito's ear. "Give me one minute. Then blow the smoke bomb."

"Got it." Vito popped one earbud into his right ear, then slinked away to watch the house from the back living room window, which had an unobstructed view of the hallway leading to the garage.

Vince began working on the locked side door of the garage by feel. He'd done it many times in the past for generic door knobs like the one on Fermosa's door. All he needed to do was jimmy the keyway back and forth until he felt it give. Twenty-five seconds later, the door unlocked.

He also popped an earbud in his right ear and tapped the phone button to call Vito. Seconds later, they were connected.

"We good?" Vince asked.

"Solid. No movement on the lower level of the house."

"Door's unlocked. I'm ready. In position."

"Blow it now?"

"Do it."

Not a second later, there was a thump on the other side of the garage door. Vince retrieved his weapon, aimed it at the grass by his feet, and waited. He gripped the unlocked door handle and listened intently for Vito to give him the go-ahead. Not a single car passed on the street in front of the house.

Something banged on the other side of the door. Vince

leaned closer, listening. Vito hadn't warned him anyone was coming. Then two more successive thumps.

What the hell?

He was tempted to open the door and start blasting away.

"Someone jumped off the stairs," Vito said.

Someone?

"You can't see who?"

"No. They ran toward the front of the house."

"Man or woman?"

"No idea. Only saw a wisp of white clothing, like a robe."

The front of the house? Were they leaving? If so, this hit would be aborted, which had never happened to Vince.

He moved away from the garage door and strode along the brick wall toward the front.

"Someone's entering the garage now," Vito whispered urgently in his ear.

"Fuck," Vince cursed, then retreated toward the garage door. "Who?"

"Can't tell."

"Flying fucks in a bowl of soup. I need to fucking know!"

"Can't tell. They're inside now."

The gun aimed upward, Vince steeled himself as he gripped the knob, then tore open the garage door. Before anyone in the garage could react, he jumped inside to the right, the weapon up in front of him. A small light illuminated a tall woman, broad-shouldered and wearing a white silk robe.

"Who are you?" she asked. "And what are you doing in my garage?"

No scream at the sight of the gun. No fear any other regular homeowner would exhibit. The wife of a made man felt protected as the years waned, especially the wife of Marty Fermosa.

"I'm here for your husband," Vince whispered.

"You're what?" Vito asked in his earpiece.

Vince ripped the earbud from his ear.

"He's not in," Mrs. Fermosa said, an air of indignation creeping into her voice.

She wasn't afraid of the man in her garage with a gun. She was irritated with him. *Un-fucking-believable.*

"He's home." Vince coughed as the smell from the covered garbage bin reached him by the door. "I watched him bring that bin inside."

"Then come walk through the house yourself," she said, gesturing at the door beside her that led inside. "Here, come on." She stepped up and opened the door.

"Wait," Vince shouted.

Before he could react, Mrs. Fermosa disappeared inside the house, the door slamming behind her. Before Vince got two steps, the deadbolt thrust into place.

"Fuck. Shit."

He retrieved his earbud and placed it in his ear. "Vito? You there?"

"Yeah. Who were you talking to?"

"The wife. She's locked me out of the house."

"Why'd you let her do that?"

"I didn't"—he ground his teeth—"let her do anything. She just did."

"Nothing happening back here."

"This is taking too long. Armed reinforcements could be

on their way. I'm going in. You should, too."

"Hey, what kind of guy lets his wife check out the disturbance in the house?" Vito asked.

"Shut up. Just get inside and pin Marty down if you get to him before me. Do not kill the wife or the daughter. Hurt them if you have to, but do not kill them."

Vince strode across the garage floor to the door, placed the tip of his weapon against the handle at an angle, turned away, then fired twice. The knob disintegrated on the second shot. He stepped back and kicked at the door, the sound reverberating around him, but the door didn't open.

It wasn't supposed to happen this way. The small device's noise and smoke were meant to lure the man of the house—Marty Fermosa—to the garage. He would gag at the smell and open the garage door to air it out. Vince would take the shot with Vito in his ear, telling him what was happening inside the house just beyond the garage door.

But none of that happened as planned, and now he was fighting with the door that led into the house while the occupants were probably either running down the street, calling for backup, or waiting for him to come barreling through the door into a waiting barrage of gunfire.

But Vince had no choice. He had been contracted to hit Marty Fermosa. The hit had to happen tonight. After three days of planning, Vince thought this would be an easy hit. He did not account for how wrong he would be in his thought process.

After the fourth kick near the knob, he shouldered the door open. Balance lost, Vince dropped inside the house and slammed onto the linoleum floor. A grunt escaped his lips. He swung left, then frantically swung back to the right.

A voice jolted him. Vito. In his ear.

"Someone just came in from the garage."

"Oh, my fuck," he whispered through a wheeze of breath, his jaw tight. "It's me. Didn't you see me fall? Quickly, which way did she go?"

"What?" Vito said. "You're whispering."

His anger boiled over as he clambered to his feet.

When this is over, I'm going to kill Vito.

A remote light came from the upstairs hallway. It was enough to let him see which way the hall went, but nothing past the next alcove. Two doors led off to the right, with a staircase to his left. Marty or his wife—he was pretty sure her name was Patricia—could be behind any door, any darkened recess, a loaded hand cannon ready to send him to the next life.

He melted into the wall as far as he could, his weapon leading the way, and slinked along the corridor toward the stairs. The beating of his heart in the deadened silence made it hard to hear even the subtlest sounds. Why was he so freaked out on this job? Could it be his last hit? Was this the one that got him killed instead?

Usually, the hit was easier than this. He'd walk into a restaurant, place the gun behind his target's ear, and end a life. He'd done it so often that the extermination part was not only effortless, it had become mundane.

He rounded the edge of the staircase and peeked upward. Not a single soul was evident, nor did he hear the thump of a footstep, the careful click of a weapon, or the subtle movement of a jacket or other piece of clothing. The house was as silent as a graveyard in the wee hours before dawn.

Most would assume he would climb the stairs. Others

might assume he would continue his search through the house, examining closets, looking under beds, and going room to room searching for his target. But Vince didn't do what most hunters did. The one thing he hated was stealth. It drove him insane, waiting for a sound, trying not to make one himself. So he turned to the doorway behind him, stuck the weapon just inside the darkness beyond, and fired blindly three times, sweeping his hand left and right.

He jumped across the doorway, lunged in front of the next access to another cavernous room, windows slightly lit by a streetlamp outside, and fired wildly three more times.

He spun around and slammed his back to the wall, breathing hard.

"Vito, you there?"

He received no answer. Vince frowned and looked back down the hallway toward the rear of the house. He could barely make out the window that Vito would have used to watch the garage door but couldn't make out if his partner was still there.

"Vito?"

Fuck it. The Fermosas had to be in the house. He had watched them enter. Marty was the one who brought the garbage bin inside. His wife had attended the disturbance. And now he had fired his weapon half a dozen times, and no one responded.

They were waiting for him. There was nothing else to it. They were prepared. Marty probably had a shotgun and was just now waiting for him at the top of the stairs. Or worse, he might have an automatic weapon of some kind. But where was Vito?

He studied the end of the hall, scanning the windows,

seeing nothing.

"Shit," he mumbled under his breath.

The contract was a solid bond. He had no choice in the matter. Once accepted, the job was considered complete. If he walked away to wait for another chance, his reputation would take a hit. Or they would put a contract out on him. None of that mattered because Vince was not leaving the Fermosa house until Marty was dead.

After three deep breaths, he steeled himself for what had to be done and started up the stairs knowing the entire time he was a sitting duck. There was no cover on the staircase and no retreat. Halfway up, all he could hope for under a hail of bullets would be to turn and jump, probably breaking an ankle or, worse, a leg. And then what? Lie there on the floor and get shot like a wounded horse? Fuck that. He would jump, but he would empty his gun into his pursuer before they took him out.

Encountering no one and nearing the top of the stairs, he slowed and peeked over the edge. The immediate hallway closest to the top of the stairs was empty. This was where the light shone bright, illuminating the closed doors.

Concentrating on his surroundings, he gave little thought to what had happened to Vito or where he was. Staying alive was first and foremost. Executing the contract was second. After that, he could determine the fate of the man who was supposed to be covering his ass.

The master bedroom was to the rear of the house. Would Marty and his wife hole up there? Any weapons in the house would most certainly be stored in their closet, on a top shelf, far from the groping hands of their child.

Perhaps Marty and his wife had armed themselves and

were just now hiding in their child's room, hovering over her, protecting her with their bodies.

Vince reached the top of the stairs and leaned against the wall, trying to decide his next move, when something thumped from the floor below. Could that be Vito? Or was it Marty and his wife?

Or maybe Marty's protection had arrived.

If that were the case, then this hit was about to get certifiably insane because of the waves of bullshit several families would have to wade through to find peace. A mafia war would erupt, to be sure. And all because of Vincenzo "Baby Face" Balzano's mistake.

This needed to end, and it needed to be over ten minutes ago.

He rushed to the door on his left but didn't waste any bullets. Keeping low, he flicked on the light and jumped to the side. The room was a small den of some kind. Bookcases lined the walls. Centered on a large carpet, four plush chairs surrounded a cherry oak table with several decanters filled with amber liquid.

Vince spun around, reentered the corridor, and hopped to the next door. When his free hand twisted the knob, his body jerked in response to the thunderous clap of a weapon discharge.

He jerked his head left and right but was alone in the corridor. A warmth of some kind slithered down his arm.

Blood.

He glanced at the wound. His gun arm had taken a hit.

Something metallic clicked from behind the door he hadn't opened. A series of holes in the drywall were scattered near where he had been standing when he gripped the knob.

If he had remained beside the door instead of in front of it, his chest would have taken the brunt of the shot. Luckily, his gun arm had only been grazed. It looked like nothing more than a burn slash that the tip of a cigarette would give him if applied to the skin.

Whoever was behind that door had reloaded in the precious seconds he took to deduce his predicament. In a manic craze, standing in the open corridor, Vince placed the tip of his gun just inside one of the holes in the drywall, aimed indiscriminately left, right, and straight ahead, and emptied his gun at will.

There was no return fire.

When he ceased firing, the silence was deafening. Ears ringing, he stepped aside and reloaded his weapon without looking. He prepared his weapon and waited, unaware he'd been holding his breath. He let it out slowly, then inhaled through his teeth, only to release it again.

On a positive note, he was more than pleased to not hear sirens in the distance yet. Whoever was in the house with him had no use for the authorities, which suited him just fine. Soon enough, the coroner would be called to the house, and either his body or Marty's would be toted from the premises.

Gun fully loaded, the pain in his arm rising slightly, spurring him on, he stepped back and made a running charge at the door. It burst open without much resistance but cost Vince his balance. He tumbled inside and stopped abruptly against a solid piece of furniture.

Rousing himself from the floor with his back to the wall, Vince saw who he had shot under the glow of a bedside lamp.

Mrs. Marty Fermosa—Patricia—had taken two of his

bullets to the face. Normally he would pride himself on the luck of that particular hit as he had shot her blindly through a wall, but not this time. He would have to leave town with Patricia Fermosa dead and Marty still alive. Vince was as good as dead unless he got to Marty in the next few minutes.

Upon quick examination, Patricia took one below the left cheek, which had bled profusely, leaving streaks of red that, at first glance, could be mistaken for paint. The other was in her right eye, leaving a gaping hole where her optical sphere had been plucked from the orbital bone. The previously attractive woman wore a grotesque expression found only in a clown's demented funhouse.

Taking out the wife was regrettable. Waves would be stirred through the families. He would need to contact Mancuso Corrado at the Calto and inform him of this error before doing anything else. A story might be needed. Or worse, the daughter may have to be hit to make it look like something other than a professional job—besides, it had lost that feeling back in the garage.

Vince moved for the hallway. He needed to search the entire house. Marty Fermosa was here somewhere, and Vince was determined to find him.

At the threshold, with one foot in the hallway and one foot still inside the room with Marty's dead wife, another gun fired as Vince's step carried him into the hall. In that briefest of moments, before he could retreat into the room, he glimpsed Marty Fermosa five feet away, a large handgun held waist high.

Another bullet entered the wall. Then another. Vince screamed with each shot. Startled and forced back into the room, he had nowhere to hide.

Marty stepped into the doorway and fired before Vince could raise his own weapon.

The bullet missed. Marty jumped inside the room, then moved to the side.

Vince tried to raise his gun again, but his arm didn't respond.

What the fuck?

He looked down. His hand was covered in blood. It dripped off his knuckles and pooled at his feet. A quick glance back up brought him eye-to-eye with Marty's gun.

"Burn in Hell!" Marty shouted, his voice hoarse with rage.

The gun fired, the sound deafening in the room.

Marty Fermosa's eyes widened as he slid to the floor in front of Vince. Blood seeping from his mouth, Marty tumbled sideways and rolled onto his back. His sightless eyes stared at the ceiling. Vince gasped when he saw Vito Romano standing in the doorway, a gun in his hand.

"Thought you could use some help." He shrugged. "Hey, since I took out Marty, do I get some of that contract money?"

Vince had a whole-body shiver as he realized how close he'd come. A second ago, he was a dead man. Vito saved his life with mere seconds remaining on the clock.

Maybe it was time to retire, even though he didn't think that was possible.

"Can you mend a flesh wound?" he asked Vito in a monotone.

"Sure can."

Vince started forward. "We need to clear this place. Get far from here." He pushed past Vito and started for the stairs.

"Once you've tended to my wound, we will discuss your pay structure on this hit."

"Good news abounds."

Vito sounded too happy after what had just happened. Not ten minutes ago, Vince had considered killing Vito. Maybe he still should. It would give the authorities a body and Vito's gun—a murder weapon—for this hit. Not to mention the contract's lucrative pay structure would be divided by one. He could tell Mancuso Corrado that Vito shot the wife, so therefore, Vito had to go.

Inside his jacket, Vince's phone vibrated. Answer the phone or shoot Vito? He chose the phone. At the ruined garage door, he placed the earbud in his ear and answered it.

"Yeah."

"Our package is arriving."

"Now?" he asked.

"Now. You have one hour to get there. Remove her boyfriend from the scene. I understand there are friends with the boyfriend."

"One hour? What time does the flight land? Remove the boyfriend? His friends, too? You mean take him out?"

"Whatever you choose. Just make sure you're there to pick her up. She can't leave with anyone other than you. She lands in sixty-five minutes. She might be traveling with someone. I don't care what you do, but bring the girl alone, unharmed."

Vince and Vito exited through the side door of the garage. "The boyfriend teaches martial arts. He'll be hard to deal with in public."

"I'm sending three men to meet you there. They will cause a disturbance. This will slow the authorities' response time if you run into trouble. This is your job, though. My men will help if needed. Follow the boyfriend into a bathroom stall and knock him out. I don't care how you do it. Just take the girl. This is a must. You cannot let her leave that airport unless it's in your vehicle. When you have her, call me back for the location. Then deliver her promptly."

Vince nodded. "There was a complication tonight." No one heard him. The caller had hung up. "Shit."

"What's up?" Vito asked.

"That girl is coming back from Kelowna. She's landing in Toronto in about an hour."

"Great. Another job."

"Yeah, but this one we don't kill."

"What? Why not?"

They reached the Chevy Suburban unaccosted. The night was still quiet. No sirens wailed in the distance. Vince shrugged before opening his door. "I have no idea. But we will follow orders because we already fucked this up tonight." He jerked his head toward the Fermosa house.

"How did we fuck up?" Vito asked. "Marty Fermosa is dead. That was the hit, right?"

Vince hopped up in the SUV. Vito followed on his side. Once they were rolling away from the scene, headlights off, Vince's wounded arm cradled in his lap, he turned to Vito.

"I killed Patricia Fermosa. Wasn't supposed to do that."

"Oh shit. What about their kid?"

"Arabella?"

"Yeah."

"Didn't see her anywhere."

"She was home. We saw her go in earlier."

"Maybe she was asleep."

"With that many guns going off?"

Vince slammed the wheel with his hand. "I don't fucking know."

They rode in silence for a few blocks, then Vince turned on the headlights and started for the highway. The 407 would easily take them across the top of Toronto at this late hour, and then they could drop down the 427 to the airport.

"Hey, didn't the Fermosas make their money in the meat packing and butcher business?" Vito asked.

"Yeah, as far as I know. Why?"

Vito shook his head and grinned. "I can see it now. When Marty the butcher introduced his wife, he would say, 'Here, meet Patty.'"

Vito slapped his knees and laughed uproariously.

"Can you shut the fuck up with your puns and jokes and shit? I'm trying to think."

He realized too late that he should have killed Vito back in the Fermosa house. He was sure of it now. It was a missed opportunity. One he wouldn't forgo if given another chance.

Vito Romano had to die.

Chapter 2

JOHN WHITMAN PLACED THE coffee cup on the table before him and swallowed the meager amount in his mouth by sheer will. The grimace on his face did not go unnoticed.

"Are you ever going to like our coffee?" Spencer asked him.

Whitman shook his head. "Can't say that'll happen."

"Then why do you always agree to having one?"

"Because I love coffee and, as a rule, never refuse it." He licked his lips and swallowed again to rid his mouth of the taste. "Maybe one day you guys'll get it right."

"Fuck you, Whitman. I love our coffee."

"I have to remember there's stupid and there's ugly, and you can't fix ugly." He pointed at the offending cup. "That shit's ugly." He looked up. "Nasty too."

"Can we get on with our briefing, coffee expert, esquire, extraordinaire?"

"Don't let me stop you. But I will need a drink of some kind."

"Oh, for shit's sake." Spencer released the manila folder in his hand and pushed off the table to stand. "What'll it be, sire?"

"A healthy dose of fuck you, a side of you're an asshole, and a dash of go lick yourself." He smiled at his own inventiveness, then added, "Oh, and a cup of your finest tea, my manservant."

Spencer dropped back in his seat. "Get it yourself with that attitude, fucktit."

Whitman rose from his chair, meandered over to the back counter where the coffee and hot water pot were still warm, plopped an Earl Grey tea bag into a cup, filled it with water, then returned to his seat.

"You're a bit crusty this evening," Whitman said. "Or is it morning already?" He checked his watch. "Yup, almost one in the morning." He sat down and stirred the tepid water with his finger. "What's got you fired up?"

Whitman and Spencer had a unique history. John Whitman used to be Drake Bellamy, but Drake had dangerous enemies, and a name change—an identity change—was necessary. It had started with an ex-girlfriend wanting to frame him for murder and then kill him. It ended with an international human smuggling ring wanting him dead because several of that ex-girlfriend's family members were discovered to have falsified documents that could lead the authorities to them. Instead of being killed, Drake killed himself and reinvented himself as John Whitman.

Sarah Roberts had saved his life at a baseball game several years ago. Shortly after that, Drake Bellamy died, and his body was found in Lake Ontario, and John Whitman was born.

Detective Spencer took him on personally. Trained him, sent him to the right schools, and got him field-ready. As unorthodox as it seemed, Spencer's superiors liked what they saw and allowed Whitman to come on board after a series of rigorous tests. His results were outstanding. His ability to stay alive when being hunted by hardened criminals had surprised even the most jaded agents in the Toronto Police drug task force. Against staggering odds, he'd survived his murderous ex-girlfriend. Spencer had witnessed the entire ordeal.

Under Spencer's tutelage, Whitman even helped Sarah when she was in Mexico and fighting for her life. Now, entrenched in Toronto, working with Spencer's team, they were preparing for an assault on drug smuggling factions that were using the Toronto harbor as a means of entry from New York State.

Spencer opened the folder and dispersed sheets of paper and photos, sliding several of them toward Whitman.

"Recognize any of these faces?"

Whitman dragged the photos closer and examined the faces of three men. To the right of their images, birth dates, facts, statistics, known aliases, and current city locations were listed for each.

"Lorenzo Falcone," Whitman read from the first sheet. "What's his story?"

"The three men you're looking at are bosses of three different mafia families in Toronto. Each man reports directly to their Board of Control that represents all seven families in the area."

"The 'Ndrangheta group?" Whitman asked. He sipped his tea, found it had cooled too much, set it down, and shoved it away.

"Don't like the tea either?" Spencer asked.

"Too cold." Whitman avoided adding another barb as the conversation had gotten down to business, which he preferred even though he liked harassing Spencer.

"Yes, the 'Ndrangheta group. As you know, these seven families run the Toronto and Hamilton-area mafia. They're called the Siderno Group, which are linked to families based in Calabria, Italy."

"Lorenzo Falcone, Antonio Lombardi, and Martino Fermosa." Whitman looked up from the papers and studied Spencer's face. "Why am I looking at these men?"

"Some of this started as far back as 2002," Spencer said as he leaned back in his chair. "The Van Gogh Museum in Amsterdam was robbed back then. Fourteen years later, two of the stolen Van Gogh paintings were in the home of an Italian international drug trafficker when the local police raided it in Castellamare di Stabia. It's near Naples."

"And this affects us how?"

"We believe these three men are tied to that organization. The Italian authorities are forwarding us intel that's supposed to reveal how the narcotics are still reaching Toronto via New York. During one of their investigations, these guys' names came up."

"What are we to do?"

"Assemble a task force, although it's supposed to be small, and investigate these guys to the point where we know what their bowel movement schedule is."

"Oh great. Okay. I'll handle their grocery list

investigation." Whitman raised a finger. "Wait. I'll even go so far as to commit to examining what they throw out. I, myself, will root through their garbage. You handle the other shit. So to speak." He suppressed a laugh. "Deal?"

"What's with the comedy routine? This is serious."

"You're right, I know. I know. So how about this? I'll be serious when you get serious."

"Come again?" Spencer did that lean-back thing again.

"You didn't bring me into the office for a midnight meeting to brief me on three Italian drug lords in Toronto. This isn't about setting up a task force. Something else is going on. Spill it. What's up?"

Spencer looked away. He pulled the papers closer, lifted them, smacked them down on the table to align the pages, then neatly filed them back in the manila folder. After a moment's hesitation, he turned his attention to Whitman.

"I'm retiring."

Whitman jerked his head back, eyes wide, brows arched. He felt like he'd been shot in the gut.

"What?"

"Retirement. You know, like when you collect a pension and golf until you die."

"You don't fit the requirements."

"Requirements?" It was Spencer's turn to be surprised. A half smile played across his lips. "What requirements?"

"Well, first, you have to be old."

"I am old. Too old to be doing this shit anymore."

"And you have to want out. You're good at this shit. You couldn't possibly want out."

Spencer glanced away, shaking his head as he stared down at the closed folder in front of him. "I want out,

Whitman. More than you know."

Whitman grabbed Spencer's wrist and gripped it tight. "But you can't. You're the only one who really knows me here. We have history."

Spencer rose from his chair, dislodging Whitman's hand. "You've got others here. Don't give me that. I can't stay for you. I'm sorry. I have to do what's right for me."

Whitman stuck a finger in his mouth and nibbled on a jagged nail. He swung his chair around and faced the window.

"You're right," he mumbled. "Of course, you're right. It's just, they don't treat me the same as you do. I came up in this department a different way." He gazed at Spencer. "I didn't use the normal channels. They think of me as your pet project. With you gone, I'll fade into the shadows."

"Not true. And do you know why?" It was Spencer's turn to raise a finger while making a point. "Because you're going to bust this wide open"—he slapped the folder twice—"and get recognized in this building as someone to be reckoned with."

"You're not going to help?"

"Oh, I'll help, but this is your case. And you've got one month to deal with it."

"One month?" Whitman gasped. "That's not enough time to investigate these guys. Operations like this take time. You know that."

"We haven't got time. I retire at the end of September. That's why I pulled you in tonight. I want to take you down to Toronto Harbor and show you around. We have an informant down there. You will have eyes on boats coming in and out. We already know one of Lorenzo Falcone's ships is docked there. Cargo was unloaded last night from *The Carolina*, an American-registered vessel. It's empty now. *The Santa Maria* is also Lorenzo's, an Italian-registered vessel. If we can nail this down fast, make an arrest—a public arrest—then you're our new golden boy."

Whitman shook his head. "It's not going to happen."

"Why not?" Spencer's tone sounded impatient. "Don't be such an arse crack. We can do this."

"How can I expect a department to do well, things to go right, when your guys can't handle making good coffee?" He met Spencer's eyes with a straight face. "Not going to happen."

"Fuck you, Whitman. You're going to do this with good coffee or not—" Spencer's phone interrupted him. He answered and turned toward the window.

"Spencer here." A pause. "Oh, Buck. Nice to hear from you." Another pause. "I've got John Whitman with me. Yes, that's it. No one else." Spencer nodded. "Okay, one sec." Spencer pulled the phone away, then clicked a button.

"You're on speaker. Go ahead."

"Whitman," Buck said as an introduction.

"Casper," Whitman responded, using Buck's nickname.

"Gentlemen, we've got a verifiable source claiming the mafia families in the Toronto area are stirred up about something."

Whitman and Spencer exchanged a glance.

Casper continued, "Chatter has come back with several names. Family bosses. Meetings with the 'Ndrangheta board. We haven't seen this much chatter since the families went after that kid and his wife."

"What kid and his wife?" Whitman asked.

"You know, Darwin, Sarah's friend. The Fuccini family chased him from Toronto to Rome and then back to Toronto. They lost a lot of men. Then the Gambinos went after him in Florida. Finally, the Russian mafia, the Bratva—brotherhood—took a shot. They all missed that guy and his wife. Then Darwin disappeared. Not since then have we seen these many meetings and this much action in the Toronto and Hamilton area."

"As much as I appreciate the call, Casper, and don't get me wrong, it was great to work with you in Mexico, why call us about this?"

"Because Sarah's name came up. Since you guys are in Toronto and she'll be there in roughly," a rustle of linen came through the speaker, "one hour, I thought you'd want to know."

"Sarah's coming to Toronto in one hour?" Whitman almost shouted. "I thought she was in Kelowna."

"Her plane lands at Pearson in an hour. I'm en route to Toronto, but I won't be there until tomorrow."

Whitman's mind raced through scenarios. Sarah is in Toronto. The mafia mentioned her name. Why? Had she ever wronged them?

"What do you want us to do?" Spencer asked.

"Meet Sarah at the airport. Bring her in and keep her safe until I get there. Just the two of you. No big scene. I've got questions for her—ones only she can answer. Can you guys do that?"

"We're on our way," Spencer said as he snatched the phone off the table and started for the door.

Whitman grabbed Spencer's arm and hauled him back around before he got to the door. He leaned in close to

Spencer's phone.

"Casper," Whitman said. "Why would the mafia be interested in Sarah? Is there anything in that chatter of yours to indicate motive?"

"We're not sure." He cleared his throat. "That's why I want to talk to Sarah. Together, we'll get to the bottom of it."

Whitman leaned back, his stomach dropping. Spencer finished with Casper and hung up. Once in the elevator heading to the lower parking level, Whitman faced Spencer.

"Why would Casper lie?" Whitman asked.

"He lied?"

"When I asked about the mafia's interest, he said they weren't sure. That he would talk to Sarah to discover the motive." Whitman ran a hand through his hair. "He lied."

"We can deal with that later. After we get Sarah safe."

The doors opened, and they jogged side by side toward Spencer's unmarked cruiser. In minutes, Spencer got them out of the underground parking and onto the Gardiner Expressway. Then he hit the lights and dodged the few cars on the road this time of night, hitting speeds of a hundred and forty kilometers an hour.

Whitman retrieved his cell phone. "I'm going to call her boyfriend."

"You're calling Aaron at this hour?" Spencer asked, his voice louder than normal.

"Of course. Aaron's probably gone to the airport to pick her up."

On the third ring, Aaron answered.

Whitman filled him in.

Chapter 3

IN ORDER TO HEAR Whitman better, Aaron Stevens moved away from the crowd of weary travelers as they emerged from the luggage claim area and met with their families and friends.

"And how did you hear about this?" Aaron asked Whitman.

"Casper."

Aaron rubbed the back of his neck. He found an empty chair and plopped down too hard. "I recently had an altercation with several Italian men at the new dojo."

"What kind of altercation?" Whitman asked.

"They came to the dojo we're renovating and asked about Sarah. I told them nothing. They came back, five strong, and asked again. The second time wasn't so polite."

"Anyone get hurt?"

"No, short of pulling weapons, they weren't about to

attack a crew of black belts."

"Makes sense. Look, Aaron, we're on our way. We must escort Sarah downtown and keep her safe until Casper rolls into town tomorrow. We'll figure out what's happening and go from there."

"Sarah's not going to like that. She's just coming off a hard week in Kelowna. Almost got herself killed."

"Aaron, I understand, but we can't take any chances here." The engine revved through the phone. "Casper believes the information to be credible. Sarah's got to come in with us."

Aaron faced the crowd, scanning for his men. Daniel, Benjamin, and Alex were scattered around, watching for Sarah at different locations just in case the Italians made an appearance. Aaron didn't want to take any chances after their two encounters at the dojo.

"I'll leave you to tell her then. But I go where Sarah goes."

"No issue there. You can come, too."

"I'm in terminal three, waiting by the gates for WestJet."

"We should be there in twenty minutes. Maybe a little more."

"Okay, hurry. The board says Sarah's plane is coming in early. If you're not here, I'll take her out to my car and wait for you there so she's safe. But be prepared. She's not going to like this."

"We'll be there shortly. Watch for us."

Aaron slipped the phone into his pocket, got to his feet, and studied the crowd. Even at this late hour, men, women, and children gathered around the doors where travelers emerged, standing wherever there was room. He spied Daniel to the far left, leaning against a pillar. Daniel shrugged at Aaron in a who-was-that gesture. He waved Daniel off. No point in exposing their positions. The teachers were there to back up Aaron if the Italians showed their faces at the airport. Walking up to Daniel would reveal his presence.

Aaron moved closer to the doors, easing through the crowd. He saw Benjamin a minute later, watching everything from a side window, keeping an eye on everyone coming and going. From his vantage point, he could see the doors Sarah would come through as well, everyone standing near those doors, and to his left, the sliding doors that led outside.

After ten more minutes, Aaron was unable to locate Alex. He'd melted into the crowd too well. Alex would be seen when he was ready to be seen. Aaron had to wonder who'd taught Alex those techniques because it certainly wasn't Aaron.

He checked the time on the board. Sarah's flight would land in less than fifteen minutes. That gave him time to grab a coffee. It looked like it might be a long night, and the coffee at the police station sucked. He got to the small beverage stand before they closed for the night.

After getting an extra-large in case Sarah wanted some, he moved to the huge windows that looked out onto the traffic. The taxi line was long as other flights let out from another set of doors. Sirens wailed somewhere, and Aaron frowned. Sirens in the city were normal, but sirens at an airport made him think of terrorism.

He sipped from the coffee, then stepped outside to see if he could locate the sirens. By the time he got to the taxi stand to glance down the length of the roadway, two cruisers raced by, their red and blue lights flashing, sirens screaming.

"What the fuck?" he whispered to himself. "This better not be related to Sarah."

Anger rose, suppressing his fear. Couldn't everyone just leave Sarah alone? She needed a break, and he wanted his girlfriend back. Would it be too much to ask for three months alone, maybe six?

He waited several more minutes, drank more of the coffee, then reentered the terminal and took up a position by a square pillar where he could see most of the area. The arrivals board said her plane was eight minutes out. He took a deep breath, exhaled, then inhaled again. It would all work out. Sarah would exit with Parkman. They would be tired. Aaron would take them to his car, wait five minutes for Whitman and Spencer, then either head home or to the station. But everything would be okay. It would all work out because if it weren't supposed to, Sarah would know about it.

Wouldn't she?

To his right, someone gasped and spoke loudly. "I couldn't believe it." A man and a woman, dressed casually, walked toward Aaron. The woman was talking, a hand over her heart. "The guy hit the other guy's car on the access ramp to arrivals here." The man nodded briefly. "The vehicles skidded to a stop sideways." The couple walked by Aaron, four feet from him. "Then they started fighting and chased each other away."

"What? They just left their cars parked in the middle of the road?" the man asked.

The woman nodded. "Two SUVs totally blocking access to this terminal. The only way in is to enter the parkade." They were almost out of earshot now. Aaron tried to follow to hear more. "That's what I did," the woman added.

"That's why you were late," the man said.

They entered a restricted access area and disappeared. Aaron stopped and looked around for Daniel. He had been watching him, a concerned look on his face. It was time to fill Daniel in. If they got separated, at least Daniel would know what was happening.

At Daniel's side, Aaron told him about Whitman's call and about the access road being blocked to their terminal.

"Sounds deliberate to me," Daniel said. "Of all nights, Sarah and Parkman are about to land, and we've Casper concerned for her safety, two cops are coming for her, and a blocked access road." Daniel shook his head. "I don't like this. We need to let Alex and Benjamin know, too."

"Agreed." Aaron searched for Benjamin as he wasn't sure he'd find Alex before Sarah landed.

Not ten feet from Daniel, as Aaron walked around the crowd, he spotted two men he thought he recognized. Two Italian men. He slowed to watch them closer. The group of people waiting was so thick he could only see from the men's shoulders and up. Neither one had looked his way yet. Aaron clenched a fist, unclenched it, and stared.

The Italians talked to themselves as they walked closer. Fifteen feet from Aaron, they turned toward the exit doors. The crowd thinned in that area, offering Aaron a glimpse of their side profile. The smaller one was pulling a suitcase behind him.

Maybe he was wrong. He hadn't seen them before. The short one had probably just landed, and the taller man had been at the airport to pick him up.

Aaron released the air he'd been holding and walked toward the area where Benjamin was last seen. He couldn't look at every Italian man and suspect him of being a threat or associated with the mafia somehow. Not only was that ludicrous, but it was also counterproductive.

But he couldn't shake the feeling he'd seen the tall one before.

And it looked like his sleeve had been wet recently. If it was wet and not just stained, it was something other than water because it hadn't rained in Toronto for days.

His phone rang again. Call display came up PRIVATE NUMBER.

"Who's this?" he said harshly into the phone.

"A friend," the voice said. Aaron recognized Darwin's voice immediately. "You safe to talk?"

"Yes. Go ahead."

"Do you have Sarah yet?"

How does everyone know about Sarah? As soon as he thought about it, he remembered he was talking to Darwin. The man had survived an attack by multiple mafia organizations years ago and was forced into hiding in Italy. Since then, the man had built a respectable intelligence-gathering base in the hills of Umbria, where he lived with his wife, Rosina. After meeting Sarah when she was working in Italy, Darwin had tracked her whereabouts for years, monitoring whether she needed help or not. He'd shown up in Toronto, Mexico, and recently at a Danish airport when Sarah was trying to leave the country after being placed on a no-fly list. Darwin got her out. This call would be a surprise to anyone else but not Aaron. Darwin Kostas always knew where everyone in his immediate family was at any given time.

"I don't have her. Plane's landing within minutes."

"Are you alone? Or did you bring the boys?"

"I've got my boys. Four of us in total."

"Shit."

"What?" Aaron asked. He moved to a side window to be as far from strangers as possible. "Why is that a problem?"

"Four men is not enough."

Aaron waited. It seemed there was something else Darwin wanted to say.

"Are any of you armed?" Darwin asked.

"We've got Alex."

"No guns? No knives?"

"Just our hands."

Aaron wasn't sure, but he thought he heard Darwin cursing under his breath. He glanced around, suddenly anxious.

"Hey man, tell me what you know," Aaron said.

"Look, Aaron, just get Sarah and leave the airport as fast as you can. But watch your backs."

"Why? Who am I looking for?"

"Hitmen. Mafia executioners. Hardened criminals. The worst kind. Think cartel executioners. Two men, three, maybe four. Could be a small army. I just don't know. Maybe even authority figures. Don't trust a uniform."

A coolness swept over him, and he shivered. "Authority figures? What are you talking about? Cops?"

"Yes, cops. Or airport security. The mafia is tied in everywhere."

"Holy fuck," Aaron whispered into the phone. "You got this on good intel?"

"Solid. Guaranteed going down right now."

"You close?"

"Not close enough."

"They planning on a hit tonight?" Aaron asked, trying to keep the waver out of his voice.

"The word is Sarah lands from Kelowna and doesn't leave the airport. She's supposed to disappear. And anyone who gets in the way doesn't make it to the hospital. They are to disappear, too. I'm sorry, Aaron, this is fucked. Watch your back."

"You're telling *me* this is fucked."

"Aaron, just get Sarah. Find a back way to your car. Or better yet, leave your car. Take a taxi or hire a limo. Just do whatever you can to get her out of the airport in one piece. Aaron, listen to me. Do *whatever* you have to do, but take care of her. We're all counting on you. I'll be in touch."

The phone clicked.

Aaron slipped it away, his hand shaking. He scanned the crowd in search of Benjamin or Alex. Dodging people, suitcases, and laden-down carts, he ran through the throng of people looking for his dojo teachers. Before finding Benjamin, he glanced up at the board.

Sarah's flight had landed.

Chapter 4

Vito had done a decent field dressing on Vince's flesh wound. They'd cleaned up as much blood as they could, but the light summer jacket he wore couldn't be helped. The sleeve retained some of the blood. At least on the arm of the green jacket, it didn't look like blood—more like he'd leaned on something wet and soaked his arm. Overall, the bullet barely touched him. It just opened a big enough path in his flesh to make him bleed out well.

Once parked on the second level of the parkade, Vince grabbed a small suitcase out of the trunk.

"What's that for?" Vito asked.

"You. To any casual observer, it'll look like I came to pick you up. The guns go in the suitcase. No bulges under the clothes." He pointed down at the suitcase. "In arrivals, everyone assumes these things have gone through security at whatever city you flew in from. No one will suspect our suitcase is armed."

"Brilliant," Vito said. "And you thought this all up on your own?"

Vince slapped him in the face. He didn't pause. He didn't think about it. The regret of not having killed Vito at the Fermosa house stung like a wasp in the gut. He'd warned Vito about his sarcastic remarks, but the guy wouldn't stop.

Vito held his cheek a moment. A stupid grin creased his face. "I guess I deserved that." Vince waited to see what Vito would do. The trunk of the car was still open. Vito's grave waited. He could easily slip a knife into Vito's heart and stash him in the trunk.

"I'll watch that in the future," Vito added.

Vince slammed the trunk closed. "Follow me. There's not much time."

As they entered the terminal, Vito tugged on his sleeve. "What are you going to tell the girl?"

"I'm not going to tell her shit."

Vito leaned away from him as if he'd just said something astonishing. "Then how you gonna make her come with us?"

Vince moved to the side and waited for a family of three to walk by. He faced Vito and lowered his voice. "Just follow my lead. We see the girl, we follow her or whoever has come to pick her up, and we nail them in the parkade before they get in their car. The weapons are to convince anyone with her that it's not worth the fight. Remember, we're here to pick up a package. Nothing more. We don't kill or hurt this one."

"Okay, but what if no one is here for her, and she walks out and hops in a taxi?"

"Then we grab a taxi and follow. But that's unlikely."

"Why is it unlikely?"

Vince looked around but saw no one paying attention to them. "It's unlikely because this girl is well-liked. There'll be someone here for her." He pointed ahead to the large crowd assembled by the gates Sarah would exit within a half hour. "See, even at this time of night, there's got to be a hundred people waiting for planes to arrive. Someone will be there for Sarah."

Vince pushed off the wall and started toward the crowd. He detected Vito catching up with him by the sound of the small wheels on the luggage Vito pulled.

"Act casual," Vince said. "Like we just saw each other again after years apart."

"Got it."

As they neared the large group of waiting relatives and friends, Vince headed for the exit doors. He studied people quickly, watching as many faces as he could in the time before he turned from the area. He was looking for the guys from the martial arts gym he'd visited last week. They had not been helpful. Instead of answering his questions about Sarah, they'd wanted to know why Vince was asking about her. Most businesses wouldn't be so protective. Pushes clientele away. So he came back with more men. That didn't solve anything.

Then his boss got a tip from some informant in the Toronto Police Department that Sarah Roberts was in Kelowna, British Columbia, and would be returning to Toronto within days.

Vincenzo was told to be on call. At any moment, he would be required to go to the airport, snatch the girl, and deliver her to an undisclosed location. His boss knew where Sarah was supposed to be delivered to, but he wouldn't tell

Vince until he had cleared the area and had Sarah with him. Telling him early jeopardized the location in the event Vince got arrested. Not only was he familiar with the process, but he could also have written the mafia handbook if there ever was one.

Vince made a hard left and stepped out the sliding doors with Vito close at his side. The instant he turned at the door, a man moved from the crowd of people and stared at them. Vince caught the movement with the corner of his eye. He couldn't risk a look over his shoulder, so he used the second set of glass doors in front of him to catch a glimpse of the man in the reflection. It was no use—the sliding doors opened before he could see him.

"Keep up," Vince said. "Look natural. Laugh as if I said a joke."

Vito laughed, his head tilted back. "That's so funny," he said, loud enough to be heard by someone passing by. "Haven't heard that one since the days grandma would—"

"That's enough," Vince snapped.

They cleared the doors and stood by a concrete divider. The man who had watched them exit couldn't see them unless he came outside.

"Someone was watching us in there."

"What? Who?" Vito scratched his head, the look of bewilderment giving his face a comical appeal. "Wait, who even knows we're here?"

"The boss's men know. He didn't just send us. We're the delivery guys. He also sent some muscle in case we need help. They're supposed to cause a disturbance."

"That must be what's happening near the terminal entrance. I saw airport security heading that way."

"Must be. Look, we're supposed to deliver this girl by herself. No boyfriend or anyone else. I only got a glimpse of the guy who was watching us, but I think it was that asshole from the martial arts place."

"I heard about him. Tough talker."

Vince thought about it a moment, then decided.

"We need to go in and hang back. We need to watch the crowd and wait for the girl to come out. We can't fuck this up. If the boyfriend is in there and he sees us and comes to talk to us, we'll deal with it then."

"You want, I can deal with him myself."

"Vito, the guy's a black belt in karate. He teaches other people how to be black belts. Unless you're shooting him, you can't *deal* with him yourself, and you won't be able to get inside that luggage for a weapon before he breaks several of your bones."

Vito patted the pocket on the inside of his jacket. "I've got my hunting knife. If he tries anything, I'll slice him up."

Vince was too preoccupied to respond properly. "You do what you want with the boyfriend and anyone else associated with this girl. I don't care. But we don't hurt the girl. And we don't hurt our chances of snatching her tonight."

"You already said that," Vito said. "Don't hurt the girl."

"Come on." Vince started toward the doors again.

Why would the boss send the same guys to the martial arts gym and the airport? Of course, the boyfriend would be at the airport to pick up his girl. And, of course, the boyfriend would recognize Vince since he had antagonized the guy to learn of Sarah's whereabouts. That caused another layer of complications.

At the doors, he grabbed Vito's arm and jerked him back.

"Wait a moment," Vince said as he pulled out his cell phone. Seconds later, the boss answered.

"What?"

Vince cleared his throat. "Seems to me I remember you had a *friend* here at the airport. Someone in their security detail."

"And if I did?"

"You might call in a favor."

"What kind of favor?"

"The boyfriend's here. He might have friends. I'm waiting for our package. I think the boyfriend remembers me from his place of business."

"And you want the boyfriend detained momentarily to avoid an issue while picking up the package."

"If it's possible. Would make things go smoother."

There was a pause on the other end of the line. Then, "Just wait for the package. Call me when you have it. Everything else has been handled."

The line clicked dead.

"What'd he say?" Vito asked.

"That we have nothing to worry about," Vince said, not feeling the reassurance of those words.

Outside, amid the constant sound of cars, taxis, and airport shuttles with the occasional horn blaring in the arrivals area, Vince didn't feel at all reassured that everything would work out. Mrs. Fermosa was dead. He had a bullet wound to his arm that still seeped blood and a black belt in hand-to-hand combat.

Vince shook his head, and on a deep breath tainted by gas fumes, he steeled himself for what must be done and stepped through the sliding doors, reentering the Toronto airport with Vito at his side, glad he hadn't killed him yet. He may need him a little longer.

Chapter 5

AARON STARED AT THE arrivals board. Sarah and Parkman had landed. He wondered what she would think upon hearing that Spencer and Whitman, *and* Darwin were all concerned about her welfare based on intel that the Toronto mafia was interested in her. Aaron didn't have much experience with organized crime, but he knew Darwin did. It was times like these when Aaron wished he'd wired his three men so they could talk among themselves wherever they were. Alex still had no idea what was going on. Only Daniel knew about the Whitman call.

"Shit," Aaron muttered to himself as he planted a fist into his open palm.

It would take time to deplane and gather luggage. He estimated he had ten to fifteen minutes until Sarah and Parkman walked out into the public area. At that time, he could at least update Daniel and Benjamin and attempt to locate Alex.

Aaron turned away from the arrivals board and almost bumped into two men.

"Excuse me," he said as he attempted to maneuver around them.

"Hold up," the tall one said.

Aaron stopped and faced the men. Two airport security officers blocked him. Darwin's words echoed in his head, *Yes, cops. Or airport security. The mafia is tied in everywhere.* With Sarah deplaning at that exact moment, they were making their move.

"What can I do for you guys?" Aaron asked.

They exchanged a glance. The smaller officer appeared less sure of himself, easing his weight back and forth from one foot to the other.

"Our cameras picked you out of the crowd," the tall one said.

This was a setup. They had to be a part of what was happening tonight. It was no coincidence they would attempt to delay or detain him at the exact moment Sarah would be deplaning.

"Why would your cameras do that?" Aaron asked. "Have I done something wrong?"

Behind the tall one's shoulders, two more airport security officers approached.

"Who are you waiting for?" the tall one asked.

Aaron looked for name badges, but they didn't have any. He turned left to see if he could spot any of his men. Only seconds had passed by the time he looked back at the officers in front of him. The smaller one had crossed his arms, his face tightened, lips pursed.

"If you plan on detaining me, you're going to have to tell me why," Aaron said. "Otherwise, I'll be on my way."

"Hold up," someone else said. The other two officers had stepped in close enough to hear, one of whom had a unibrow that was hard to ignore. "We're only going to need ten minutes of your time. If you would follow us, please?" Unibrow turned sideways and extended his right arm. "This way."

Aaron took each one in slowly, watching their eyes, gauging their resolve. The short officer didn't like this part of his job. The tall one stood closest and enjoyed the thought of intimidation. Unibrow seemed to outrank the others, and the fourth man he arrived with stood back to keep the public away from them. Were they actually trying to stop him from picking up Sarah?

The doors to the outside, roughly ten feet away, slid open. The Italian man Aaron thought he had recognized came back inside the terminal with his shorter companion alongside him, pulling that small carry-on suitcase.

They saw each other, eyes locking for a moment. In that look, Aaron recalled everything. He was the man who came to the dojo looking for Sarah. He'd arrived with several large Italian men. There was enough testosterone and tension in the dojo that Aaron felt it prudent to contact Sarah while she was still in Kelowna to warn her, culminating in him picking her up personally. But he had underestimated the mafia's reach, their power.

The Italian man—Aaron even recalled his name as Vincenzo—offered him a sly grin as he passed behind the wall of airport security men.

"We haven't got all night," Unibrow said. "We would

hate to have to force you along."

If they'd watched him on camera, then they knew about Benjamin and Daniel. Alex would be off their radar. No one would know about Alex.

Shit, most of the time, I don't even fucking know about Alex.

Aaron nodded. "I'll go." He raised his hands to calm the tension. "But I want to know why I'm being detained. My girlfriend has landed, and I've done nothing wrong unless roaming back and forth, talking on my phone, and looking agitated is a crime."

Unibrow lowered his outstretched arm and stood up straighter. "We observed you enter the terminal alone. You then approached a man by that railing and had words with him. You took several phone calls, then made eye contact with another man, all the while searching the crowd as if looking for something. I understand it doesn't amount to much, but it certainly looks odd, considering you're the only one here acting in such a manner. These are times of heightened security, and you're not acting like anyone else waiting for a loved one." He wiped his brow. "We only want a few words with you, if you please."

Aaron tried to catch a glimpse of Benjamin or Daniel but couldn't as the arrivals board blocked his view. He had three qualified men waiting for Sarah, not to mention Parkman, and Sarah's abilities far outweighed an average person's range of alertness and preparedness. Everything would be okay. It would all work out.

He would go with them. Talk it out. And maybe he could get Spencer to tell them why Aaron was so antsy when Spencer and Whitman arrived, and Aaron would be sprung from airport security in a flash.

He stepped forward, and immediately the group of four officers fell in place, surrounding him as they led him toward a door in the wall marked Security Personnel Only.

Once inside, they placed him in a sterile white room with only three chairs along either wall. The door shut and clicked.

"Fuck," he muttered to himself, then said a silent prayer. *Sarah, you've got my boys and Parkman. Just make it out of the airport in one piece. That's all I ask.*

What he couldn't shake was the lopsided grin on the face of that Italian man who had come to the dojo looking for Sarah. Aaron wondered if it would be Alex or Sarah who would wipe that grin off his face before the night was over.

He clasped his hands together and tightened his grip until the door opened five minutes later.

"We're ready to speak with you," Unibrow said.

Chapter 6

"THAT HAS TO BE the boss's men," Vince said. "I told you this girl was important. No way would that many favors be called in for some skank." He checked the board and saw the plane had arrived. "We're right on schedule, and the boyfriend is out of the picture."

"Hey Vince, let me ask you something while we wait."

"Sure. Go ahead."

Vito faced him and held his hands out to the sides. "Where does the white go when the snow melts?"

"Aww, would you fuck off with the joking around."

"No, seriously, why do they drive on a parkway and park on a driveway?"

"Vito," Vince said through clenched teeth. "Not now. We have to pay attention. This is important." He grabbed Vito's jacket and tightened his grip. "If we fuck this up, it's our heads." He released the jacket.

"Okay, okay," Vito said, brushing the folds where Vince had held him. "Take it easy. I'm just fuckin' around."

Vince ignored Vito's apology as he surveyed the crowd. Where to stand? At what place would the best vantage point be?

Airport security brushed past the two of them, clearly intent on someone else in the crowd. He eased back against the wall to watch what was happening. Vito followed close, his mouth shut, which Vince thought was good for his health.

The officers surrounded a tall man in the far corner and gestured for him to follow them. Another man standing twenty feet from Vince was escorted away. This one he recognized as a friend of the boyfriend. Vince was sure he'd also seen him at the martial arts place.

He smiled to himself. The boss had made this possible. But not just possible; he made this easy. Sarah Roberts would enter the terminal after gathering her luggage and walk right into Vince's arms.

"What do you think is going on?" Vito asked.

"Just follow my lead. The girl will show at any moment. She's as good as ours."

Chapter 7

Unibrow led Aaron into an office where Unibrow sat on the other side of a desk. The taller security guard leaned against the door.

"We watched you on the cameras," Unibrow said. "After we received a tip that you were speaking into your cell phone."

"My cell phone?" Aaron sputtered. Nothing these guys had said made any sense. Sarah would walk out into the terminal at any moment, and he wouldn't be there. He struggled with the warring urge to bolt from the room. Staying seated for the moment seemed like the only option, but unless they gave him something concrete, he would have to call Spencer back and raise this debacle to the next level. "Is that why I'm here? Because I spoke on my cell phone?" He fought to keep the fury out of his voice.

Unibrow leaned back in his chair and crossed his arms,

the smug look of a confident man, sure he held all the cards.

"You want to enlighten us on who you were talking to on the phone earlier?"

"How is that any of your business?" Aaron asked, his anger barely contained now. His missing finger itched at the phantom knuckle.

"We have the Toronto police en route. We have zero issues with you waiting for them, but at this hour"—he made an exaggerated effort to look at his watch, then back at Aaron —"they may be awhile."

"I'm a Canadian citizen on Canadian soil," Aaron stated, not really thinking it through. "I do not have a plane ticket. I am here to pick up my girlfriend. That's it. So, since you have nothing on me except I talked on my cell phone, which is not against the law, I will be leaving to go meet her."

Aaron stood and approached the door. The tall officer moved a foot to the left to block his way.

"I wouldn't do that if I were you," Aaron whispered, hands raised off his sides slightly.

"Mr. Stevens," Unibrow said.

The use of his last name startled him. He turned back to face the man.

"How do you know my name?"

"Sit down. You aren't going anywhere."

This had to do with those two Italians and the people looking for Sarah. He knew it, and they knew it.

"How much are they paying you?" Aaron asked.

"Excuse me?" Unibrow blinked, his hairy eyebrows lifting as one, then dropping.

"The mafia. The Italians. I don't know. Whoever orchestrated this shit, is it a lot of money? Career-ending money? Because you'll be out of a job and up on charges when we're through." Aaron shot a look back at the tall guard. "You too, fucker."

The tall one stepped closer. Aaron dropped into his zenkutsu dachi, a Shotokan Karate front stance, which made the tall one falter and stop.

"Come on, fucktard." He waved his fingers in a come-and-get-it gesture. "Let's see what you're made of."

"Now hold on," Unibrow shouted.

Aaron eased out of his stance and stood to his full height. Unibrow had gotten to his feet.

"What the hell is going on?" Unibrow shouted again. "We aren't being paid off by anybody. This is our job. You were witnessed on camera, talking on your phone and covertly meeting with several other men in various places in the terminal—"

Aaron cut him off. "And how is that illegal? Or even suspicious?"

"We received an anonymous tip from two sources that while you were on your phone, you were overheard uttering the word *bomb* at least twice."

"I *what*?"

"That's what we have, and that's why you're here."

It all came to him in an instant. There was a ring of truth in Unibrow's voice. The man was only doing his job. Following up on a tip. Knowing he didn't say the word *bomb*, Aaron could only surmise that the Italians called in the anonymous tip while outside that exit door. Even though he thought he recognized that guy, to his chagrin, he'd let it go.

"Shit," he muttered under his breath, slamming a fist into his open palm for the second time that evening.

"Did we foil your plans?" Unibrow asked.

"No. Someone else did."

The guards exchanged a knowing glance. "And what plans were those? Where's the bomb you propose to use?"

"My plan was to get Sarah Roberts out of the airport safely. I don't need bombs."

"Sarah Roberts?" Unibrow frowned. "Why do I know that name? And how were you proposing to use bombs to get her out?"

"There are no *fucking* bombs," Aaron yelled, frustrated at his confinement and lack of action. "For fuck's sake. Someone is after Sarah, and I've had two phone calls this evening from reliable sources telling me I need to get her clear of this place as soon as possible. Your *anonymous tip*" —he used air quotes to emphasize the words, even though he hated when people did that—"has me detained and unable to get her out of here safely."

He dropped back into his chair hard, bumping his elbows, consoled by the notion that Daniel, Benjamin, and Alex were still out there, watching for Sarah and Parkman.

"Tell me," Unibrow said as he followed suit and eased back into his chair behind the desk. "Who called you with the information about Sarah?"

"The police," Aaron said. That was all he would say. No one would get Darwin's name from him.

That was the second time Unibrow's eyebrows rose halfway up his forehead, then lowered slowly.

"So the police warned you that your girlfriend might be in danger at this airport, and they don't have officers here to guarantee her safety? Not to mention, we've heard nothing of this by any authority." He exchanged another glance with the tall officer. "Somehow, I find that slightly dubious." He placed his elbows on the desk and tented his fingers. Aaron noticed the lack of a wedding ring. "So, explain to me why you were talking to the *cops* about bombs while in our airport."

The anger spent, the frustration mounting, Aaron kept his cool and answered in a monotone voice.

"I. Did. Not. Use. That. Word. On. The. Phone."

"But we have tips that you did, in fact—"

Aaron slammed the back of his fist on the desk. "I fucking didn't."

Someone walked by the window to the office. When he turned to see if the police had arrived, he locked eyes with Daniel. Then a moment later, Benjamin walked by, both his friends surrounded by multiple airport security officers and two uniformed Toronto police officers.

Only Alex remained on the outside. Sarah was walking into a trap without any backup. His only hope was Vivian had seen this coming and would alert Sarah in time.

He shot to his feet. "I demand to be charged or released. I will not stay here a moment longer on a *tip*."

"I'm afraid you have no choice, Mr. Stevens. You will talk to the police, and they will advise when you can leave."

"Then I'm calling the cops right now." He retrieved his cell phone from his pocket.

"Fine by me," Unibrow said. "But you don't leave this room until the authorities say you can."

Aaron turned away and dialed Spencer's number, all the while telling himself it would all work out. Everything would be fine. It always worked out. Didn't it?

Chapter 8

Sarah Roberts snapped awake when the plane hit the runway. After a rough few days in Kelowna with the bruises to prove it, she nodded off when the plane departed the Kelowna International Airport. She rubbed her eyes and blinked a couple of extra times as her stomach rumbled like an empty cavern.

"Where are we?" she asked, feeling slightly dazed.

"Toronto, sleepyhead." Parkman grinned. "Just taxiing to our gate."

"Good. I need to see Aaron, and I need sleep." She stretched, arms above her head, and yawned. It felt good to be home. It was all over. No more prophecies. Nothing recently from Vivian. This was downtime, rest time. A chance to reconnect with Aaron and see the sights of Toronto. Maybe Vivian would give them a week, maybe a month before she assigned Sarah to something dangerous.

She opened the window shade and peeked out at the darkness. "I'm happy to be here. Would love to take a break, catch up on some reading."

"I hope you get that chance." Parkman fished in his carry-on. A moment later, he popped a toothpick in his mouth. "Aaron was pretty freaked out about something when he called."

"Oh yeah." It all came back to her. "Shit, and here I thought we could chill for a while."

"You probably can. It was something about Italians visiting him twice to locate you. Could be they just want to solicit your help for something." He gave her a cocky smile.

"Yeah, right. They want *my* help." She shook her head and glanced back outside as the plane came to a stop at the gate. "It's more like I did something to one of them, and they're coming to exact revenge."

"Vivian saying anything about it?" Parkman asked.

"Nothing. She's been quiet. But I don't mind. I really need a break." The plane lurched once more. The interior lights splashed the inside of the plane so brightly she had to squint. In a hurried bustle, passengers got to their feet and reached into the overhead bins.

"Parkman." She rested a hand on his forearm. "I've been at this a long time, and I've been very lucky. It's time for a break." She met his gaze. "I'm not quitting. In fact, I'll probably never quit. But I could use some me time. Whatever these Italians want, we'll deal with it, but then I'm out. Aaron and I need time together. Maybe start a family one day."

Parkman seemed to mull her words over, his lips pressed tight to a white line. Then he nodded. "I agree. And I wish that for you. If anyone deserves it, it's you, Sarah. Besides, my P.I. business in Santa Rosa is pretty well dead. When I get back, I'll have to restart. Which won't be too hard, but the slower pace of chasing cheating spouses and working online searching for long-lost relatives will do wonders for my health."

She smiled back at him. It was settled. Deal with the Italians and take a vacation.

She rested her head back as the crowd slowly moved up the aisle toward the front. "Then it's settled. Find out who these Italians are and take a break." She inhaled, then let it all out in an exaggerated sigh. "Sometimes, as much as I love the rush, the fight, I do get tired of the game. You know, I get tired of the unknowns. Doesn't that sound ungrateful? I've got Vivian in my ear and dead people gesturing at me, but I get tired of the unknowns." She laughed to herself.

"It's the unknowns that can kill you. Those people who show up offering you clues aren't God. They have their limitations, too. I know exactly what you're talking about."

She looped her arm through his. "Take me off this flying tube and into the arms of my man. Then I want a shot of whiskey and a bed."

"Deal."

Parkman eased out of his seat, grabbed his bag, and offered a hand to Sarah, who didn't take it. She pushed his hand away and got up on her own.

They followed the last of the passengers out of the plane and onto the ramp that took them into the main terminal. Her butt ached from sitting for so long in the same position. She stretched again, another big yawn, and her eyes watered.

It seemed like the Toronto airport was designed to make the incoming passengers walk the Boston Marathon before claiming their luggage. It was at least a full fifteen-minute walk to the carousel where their bags would come out.

Sarah and Parkman stayed off to the side, leaning against a wall, until the buzzer announced the bags were coming.

"Wait here," Parkman said. "I know your bag."

He sauntered off to stand by the carousel. Sarah brushed at an errant piece of lint on her pant leg and thought about what had happened in Kelowna. It led her thoughts back to before Kelowna when she was in Toronto last and dealing with a guy named Ben who had been a computer whiz. It seemed all she did was travel from one city to the next, dealing with lowlifes while trying to stay alive. One day, one of those lowlifes would just raise their gun and shoot her, and she would be dead. What would Vivian say to that? But Sarah didn't feel Vivian at the moment. She hadn't felt her presence since before heading to the airport in Kelowna.

Sarah raised her head as she realized the reason. The last time Vivian wasn't present was because she was being blocked. This time was no different.

A man wearing an expensive-looking suit watched her on the other side of the carousel. His dark complexion and slicked-back hair made her think he was of Italian descent. She stared back at him. He pointed at his watch.

In time.

His outstretched hands, held at shoulder height, pleaded with her that everything would be okay. Then he nodded.

A man's voice echoed in her consciousness. At first, it was gibberish, just like the first time she heard something similar in Kelowna, but then the sound formed barely perceptible words.

Intime itllbeeokayyy Illbeetheretoo.

She repeated the words to herself. *In time, it'll be okay. I'll be there, too.*

Be where?

Close movement to her left gave her a jolt. She stood up straighter and turned to face two airport security officers, one unshaven and the other too young to shave.

"Excuse me, ma'am," the unshaven one said. "But you're going to have to come with us."

She pushed off the wall. "Afraid not," Sarah said and started toward Parkman, who had his back to her while looking for their bags.

The unshaven guard grabbed her arm. Sarah stopped moving and looked down at his hand. Now knowing everything would be okay as per the guy in the expensive suit, she turned all the way around and glared at the guard.

"Have you ever had a broken finger?" She shook her head and frowned. "Hurts like a bitch. How about five broken fingers?"

The guard's hand tightened on her arm at the inferred threat.

"You explain nothing to me," she said. "You say I have to come with you. Then you grab my arm. No mention of a reason. Just this," she pointed at his hand on her arm. "I've got you on assault and forcible confinement without cause." She hoped that sounded legit enough. "My advice: release my arm before I break your hand in several places. It'll be *you* up on assault charges, not me." She leaned close to the guard, prepared to beat on his face if he held on.

"What's going on here?" Parkman asked.

The guard's hand dropped away.

"We're here to bring Miss Roberts in for questioning."

"Questioning?" Parkman asked. "Regarding what?"

"We have an Aaron Stevens in custody. Apparently, he was waiting for Miss Roberts while plotting some kind of bomb attack on the airport—"

"That's ridiculous," Sarah blurted. "We're getting our bags and going home."

"Afraid not, Sarah," the guard said, casually using her first name.

More guards watched them from afar. She caught them do a double-take to see what was happening.

"Can we at least get our bags so they aren't left out here when everyone's gone?" Parkman asked.

"Go ahead. You can, but Sarah stays with us."

Parkman met Sarah's eyes. She nodded, and he trotted off to collect their belongings. While they waited, Sarah looked for the Italian man with the slicked-back hair and nice suit, but he'd disappeared.

Parkman was back two minutes later. The guards led them into a restricted area, then down a long corridor, their luggage wheels reverberating off the walls in the long hall. A sign pointing the other way said the security office was behind them.

Vivian? Anything?

Because of the Italian man in the suit, Vivian remained blocked. When random entities dropped in on Sarah, she hadn't yet nailed down how long it took to begin hearing her sister again, but she guessed it to be at least ten minutes.

What could these guys want? They didn't appear to be professionals of any kind. Aaron had said Italians had visited him. These guys weren't Italian.

Parkman shuffled along close behind. When Sarah

looked back at him, he gave her an I-don't-know-what's-going-on-either shrug.

She watched color come to the cheeks of the young guard. His hands shook as he walked. Something was wrong with this scenario. They were not taking them to the security office. This meant they were leading them somewhere they didn't want to go, which would piss Sarah off. She was tired. She wanted to see Aaron and go to his place and sleep.

Steel double doors loomed up ahead. The unshaven guard used a card in a reader to the right of the doors to unlock them. The noise of jet engines rushed in when the unshaven guard pushed them open.

Sarah held up a moment. "Wait a sec. The security office is back that way. Where are you taking us?"

"This is a shortcut."

"I don't think so."

The younger guard eased back and out of the way. She felt something was about to happen and didn't need Vivian to tell her she wouldn't like it.

"Parkman?"

"I'm here."

"We need to leave. These guys are bogus."

"Agreed."

The unshaven guard released the door and produced a gun in one fluid motion.

"You're not going anywhere," he said, the gun pointed at Sarah at point-blank range.

The younger guard whimpered and shuffled his feet as he backed up farther.

"I didn't sign on for this," he said. "We were just supposed to walk them outside. That's it."

"Get back here, Milton. You don't want to defy these guys."

Milton turned and ran back along the corridor as if his ass was on fire.

Sarah remained calm. She felt surprisingly relaxed. She was so relaxed, in fact, she didn't see this coming until it was too late. She should have been studying the guy for weapons. She should've asked why they walked right by the hallway that led to the security office.

"Defy what guys?" she asked.

"Nothing to do with you." He motioned with the weapon. "Let's go. Outside."

"You know, you surprise me."

"No more talking. Outside."

"That was bold to kidnap us right at the baggage claim. And with other security guards watching." She shook her head. "That's why they took a second look—to see who you were and what you were doing."

"That's a lot of talking for someone without the gun." He motioned with the gun once more. "I won't repeat myself. Both of you, outside."

"And if we don't?" she asked. "Are you man enough to use that gun inside an airport terminal?"

"Absolutely. I have no other choice. I'm dead if I don't deliver you."

The unshaven man aimed his weapon slightly behind Sarah—toward Parkman—and pulled the trigger.

Chapter 9

Vince studied the doors as each passenger entered the area where family and friends waited for their arrival. More than eighty percent of the people crowded around had dispersed with their loved ones as the passengers of the plane carrying Sarah exited the baggage claim doors. A few stragglers were left behind to wait for a random piece of late luggage.

Vince rubbed the back of his arm with his good arm. The wound grew increasingly sore as the evening wore on to early morning. Where was she? Could she have known they were waiting and exited elsewhere?

"I have something I'd like to share," Vito said.

Vince grunted in reply.

"Did you know sharks only attack you when you're wet?"

Vince frowned, took in what Vito was saying, then got it. He almost drew his weapon from the suitcase and emptied it into Vito.

"I thought I told you," Vince took a calming breath, "to shut up with the jokes and shit."

"What does it hurt while we wait? And who knows, maybe that's useful information if you're ever in Australia or Hawaii."

He stepped inside Vito's personal space, feeling lightheaded with blood loss and the anger flowing through his veins. "Do you see me heading to Australia anytime soon?"

He pushed himself away from Vito before he decked him and started toward the doors that let the passengers out from the baggage claim area.

Where the fuck was that Sarah girl?

A skinny blond-haired kid watched them with an unreadable deadpan expression as they neared the doors.

"What are you looking at, kid?" Vince asked.

The kid didn't flinch, didn't move at all. Vince ignored him and tried to catch a glimpse of what was happening beyond the doors. Half a dozen travelers lingered by the carousel, none of them Sarah Roberts, as far as he could tell.

"Shit. She's gone."

He turned back and scanned the immediate area. The skinny blond was gone.

"What now?" Vito asked.

"Let me think."

Vince wandered toward the exit doors. Maybe they missed her, and she was waiting just outside the doors. If they didn't find her and make that call to the boss, perhaps he would need to head to Australia after all. He could buy a ticket and leave the airport bound for the outback within the hour. That would be the only way to stay alive.

Outside, the usual line of taxis and limos and people pulled up to the curb to collect weary travelers, but no Sarah. He headed back inside.

"We can't keep going back and forth," Vito said. "Gonna catch someone's attention."

"I know." Vince stomped his feet when he stopped. "Let me think."

He surveyed every face he saw. He studied the people, the two security guards wandering by, one with a Tim Horton's coffee cup in his hand. Nothing was unusual, nothing out of place.

Then where the fuck was Sarah?

Maybe she wasn't on the plane. That would explain it. That had to be it. She wasn't on the plane.

"Maybe she missed the flight," Vito said. "Thought of that?"

Something like the sound of a firecracker popped somewhere to their right.

A gun. In the airport.

"Was that what I think it was?" Vito asked.

The two guards—one with the coffee—bolted toward a secure door, the one without a coffee retrieving a white key card from his breast pocket.

"C'mon. We're going to find out what that was."

Vince ran after the guards. They entered the door marked Airport Personnel Only and left it to close on its own. Vince made it with less than a second to spare. He jammed his fingers between the door and frame, winced, then pulled it open and peeked down the length of the hall. Within five feet, the hallway hit a wall. The guards either went left or right.

Vince entered the corridor with Vito close behind.

He leaned back to whisper, "We check it out. If it's Sarah, we escort her out of here. If it isn't, we simply got lost looking for security."

"Why were we looking for security?" Vito asked.

"We only have one bag." Vince pointed behind Vito. "Mine was lost by the airlines. We were trying to find someone to make a claim."

Vito shrugged. "Sounds good to me."

Vince led the way as he started down the corridor to the right.

Chapter 10

AARON GOT SPENCER ON the first ring. Before Spencer could say a word, Aaron blurted into the phone, "How far out are you?"

"Ten minutes. Maybe less. Why?"

"Airport security picked me up. They've grabbed Daniel and Benjamin, too."

"What?" Spencer shouted. "Why?"

"Trumped up claim that I allegedly said the word *bomb* on the phone when I was talking with you earlier."

"That's bullshit. Have you got Sarah with you?"

"No." The frustration oozed out of Aaron's every pore. "That's the thing. These guys yanked us before we could meet her."

Spencer gasped. "But the plane had to have landed by now."

"I know," Aaron said, his voice raising with each word.

"It has."

"You're being set up. Put whoever's in charge on the phone. I want to speak—no, wait, put it on speakerphone. I want everyone to hear me."

Aaron pulled the phone from his ear and hit the speaker option.

"Go ahead, Spencer. You've got two airport security guards in the room with me. They're waiting for Toronto police to attend."

"My name is Spencer. I'm with the special investigations unit, narcotics division, metro police. I'm en route to your location with credible information that Aaron's girlfriend—Sarah Roberts—may be in danger. Aaron and his friends were tasked with retrieving her from the airport and getting her out of there by any means possible. Are you hearing me?"

"Yes," Unibrow said. "Loud and clear. But none of that is my problem. This isn't a narcotics thing—"

"Listen," Spencer bellowed over the phone. It was so loud his voice came out distorted on Aaron's cell phone speaker. "I will be there in less than ten minutes. I can vouch for Aaron and the others he is with. They are doing nothing wrong. Whatever you heard or think you heard is a mistake. I demand you release them at once."

For a moment, the three men listened to the sound of a revving engine on Spencer's side of the conversation. Unibrow rose from his chair and shook his head back and forth slowly. He exchanged a glance with the other guard at the door.

"Afraid I can't do that. We're following up on a credible lead ourselves. Once the police get here, we'll see when Aaron can leave—"

"I *am* the *fucking* police, and I'm telling you to release him immediately!"

"Hang up the phone, Aaron," Unibrow said. "You can't call a friend at home to get you out of this. There are no lifelines in this business. We will discuss the situation with the *proper authorities* when they get here. In the meantime, hang up that phone and take a seat—"

"Okay, Aaron," Spencer cut in. "Do whatever you have to do to get out of there. I don't care what the fuck you do, as long as you don't kill them. Get to Sarah and get her out of that airport. Send the rest of them to the hospital. Do it now. I got your back. GO!"

The phone died as Spencer hung up.

The tension in the room thickened. A wave of heat enveloped Aaron. He slipped the phone into his back pocket as the guard at the door uncrossed his arms and turned slightly into a defensive posture.

"Now, guys," Aaron said, his hands up chest high. He wanted to appear as non-threatening as he could. "We can be reasonable, can't we?"

Unibrow remained on his feet. Only his eyes moved, roving back and forth from Aaron to his partner, then back to Aaron.

"Whoever you called," Unibrow said, pointing toward Aaron's hidden phone, "was a phony. There's no way an officer of the law would say what he just said. He can't get you off an assault and battery charge—or worse—just because he's a cop. That's bullshit." Unibrow pointed at Aaron's chair. "Now, I need you to sit down and sit tight until the *real* authorities get here."

Aaron eased closer to the desk. The guard at the door was

just behind him and slightly to the left, the perfect spot for Aaron to catch him with a backward roundhouse kick.

Aaron nodded and smiled, offering Unibrow a moment to feel relief, to lower his guard. He was sure the man at the door felt relief, too. Their body language told him they were anxious but didn't think Aaron would try to fight them.

"Boys, I think it's time I go get my woman."

"Wait," Unibrow shouted.

Aaron spun on one foot so fast that the guard at the door had no chance to defend himself. The heel of his right foot planted itself in the guard's sternum, smashing the man backward into the closed door, which vibrated upon impact. Before the guard hit the floor gasping for air, Aaron leaped onto the desk and took a page out of Alex's gymnastics book. From the desktop, he flipped over and around Unibrow to land behind the man. During this feat, Unibrow crouched and put his hands up in front of him in some form of defense that revealed his lack of skill in any martial arts arena.

Aaron wrapped his right arm around Unibrow's throat and brought his left arm around from the other side to grasp the elbow of his right, his right bicep over Unibrow's Adam's apple. He pulled backward until his shoulders rested on the wall, and Unibrow was off balance.

"Now," he whispered in Unibrow's ear. "When I flex my biceps like this"—he flexed, choking him, then relaxed—"you can't breathe."

"You can't," Unibrow was able to sputter, "do this."

"Go to sleep. When you wake, this will all be over." He adjusted his arms to the sleeper hold and tightened his grip. Unibrow was out in under twenty seconds. Aaron eased him down to the floor and let him go. He grabbed the keycard off

Unibrow's belt and jumped from behind the desk.

The other guard was breathing better and attempting to regain his feet.

"Get up." He glared at the guard. The guard eased sideways, allowing access to the door. "I said, get up." Aaron leaned down. "Or do you want to die on the floor?"

"Die?" the guy's pitch was as high as a ten-year-old girl's. "What?"

"Sarah's in trouble. Cops are coming at this very minute to protect her. Because you guys pulled us out of the waiting area, Sarah has been left exposed. If something happens to her, it's on your head. But if you get up," Aaron grabbed his arm and half hauled him to his feet, "you can tell the other guards that we're being released, and it was all a hoax." He leaned in closer, and the guard eased back, his eyes filled with fear. "Tell them the anonymous tip was someone's idea of a joke."

A gun fired down the corridor.

Sarah!

"Go," Aaron shouted, ripping open the door. He shoved the guard out into the hall and almost lost him to gravity. "Get up," he shouted, then forced the man to his feet. They jogged two doors down to where a door opened, and a guard stuck his head out.

"What was that?" the new guard asked.

"It was a hoax," the tall man beside Aaron said. "Let them all go."

"What?" the guard with his head out the door looked bewildered. "How do you know it was a hoax?"

With no time to lose, Aaron grabbed the guard in the doorway and shoved him to the floor. He stepped over him and grabbed the other guard's wrist. He spun in a full circle, the wrist an unwilling victim as he windmilled the guy until his feet left the floor and he landed on his back, a huge puff of air expelling from his lungs.

"Come on, guys," Aaron shouted into the room. "Let's go."

Daniel and Benjamin jumped over the guard on the floor, skirted the tall man Aaron had brought with him, and ran behind Aaron as the trio sprinted toward the gunshot.

Chapter 11

SARAH JERKED AND JUMPED back into the wall when the weapon fired. It all happened so fast that she didn't have time to process the insanity of her actions. One moment, the weapon fired. The next moment, Sarah lifted her leg and kicked at the hand that held the gun. The toe of her shoe connected with the guy's wrist. He bellowed something incoherent, his mouth wide. In the aftermath of the gunfire, her hearing was all white noise with a ringing sensation that sounded like it was echoing off the inner walls of a cave.

The guy's hand reflexively opened, and the gun flew into the air.

As her foot hit the floor, she moved her weight forward onto it. With her left hand, she grabbed the back of the man's neck and jerked him forward while her right arm twisted into place in a windmill action from behind her. In a graceful move resembling ballet, the guy shot forward, and her right arm clotheslined him, knocking his head backward upon impact.

The fake guard dropped to the floor hard like a heavy sack of coal, eyes fluttering. The door he'd held open closed slowly, then latched. Sarah started breathing again and looked back along the corridor to see what had happened to Parkman.

He had flattened himself against the wall. He held up the suitcase for her to see. It sported a new hole.

Sarah shook her hands to release some of the tension. "What the fuck was that?" she shouted. Since the proximity of the gunfire dulled her hearing, she assumed Parkman would be going through the same thing.

"Whatever that was, thanks."

"Thank me later. Let's get out of here. But not through that door."

The fake guard at her feet was stirring. He rolled to his side and shook his head.

Sarah retrieved the gun and placed it in the back of her pants.

"Help me here," she said to Parkman.

Together they got the guy to his feet. He leaned heavily on Parkman's shoulder, giving his head another shake. She opened the door behind the fake guard and shoved him outside. He stumbled twice, tripped over his own feet, and dropped to a knee. Sarah slammed the door shut and watched it latch.

After slapping her hands together a few times, she turned to Parkman, her hearing already coming back. "Let's go home."

How many times had someone threatened her with a

gun? How many times had she been thrust willingly into high-tension situations? Life and death situations? Whatever the number, a part of Sarah never got used to it.

They ran back along the corridor and slowed near a corner. Someone was coming. Multiple someones. Parkman held up a hand for her to wait, then he peeked around the edge.

He released a sigh of relief. "Oh, thank goodness."

"What?" Sarah whispered.

"It's Aaron."

Sarah stepped out into the corridor and almost slammed into her boyfriend. She wrapped her arms around him and buried her head in his chest.

"Am I ever glad to see you," she said.

"Was that gunfire we heard?" Aaron asked.

Sarah pulled away to look behind Aaron. Daniel and Benjamin led half a dozen officers. They all crowded around behind Aaron. A man with one thick eyebrow suspended over both eyes pushed his way through to stand directly behind Aaron. The man's neck was bright red.

"Some jerk just tried to kidnap us," Sarah said. "He had a young guard with him named Milton."

"Milton started here last week," the guard behind Aaron said.

Sarah eased away from Aaron and faced the guard with an imposing eyebrow. "These your guards who shot at us?" She stepped closer to him. He eased back. The red splotches on his neck looked as if someone had recently tried to strangle him. "You want to tell me why your guards wanted to take us out that door against our will at gunpoint?" She gestured back toward the door where they had just tossed the guard out.

He glanced down the corridor, then turned back to her.

"Where are they?" he asked.

"Milton ran away. After the other guy—didn't catch his name—shot at us." She stepped aside to show the hole in Parkman's suitcase. "I clotheslined him, and we shoved him out the door at the end of the corridor."

The guard frowned. "That door leads to the tarmac. Why would he take you out there?"

"Why have a gun on us in the first place? What the fuck, man? We just landed and want to go home."

Vivian's presence entered her consciousness like a soft breeze. She whispered apologies for being blocked, then added a piece of information.

"The anonymous tip you guys received was fake," Sarah said, not knowing who she was talking to exactly but repeating Vivian's words anyway.

The guards looked at each other, Aaron, then Sarah.

"How did you know about the tip?" the guard asked.

Sarah closed the distance to stand inches from the guard with one long eyebrow. "What's your name?"

"Ruben Turner."

"My name is Sarah Roberts. I'm tired. I've been very busy in Kelowna, and now I'm leaving this airport with these men." She cleared her throat. "Someone called in an anonymous tip that Aaron was on his phone and said a bad word when in fact, he didn't. The tip was meant to pull Aaron and these two," she pointed at Daniel and Benjamin, all the while wondering where Alex was, "out of the way so that Milton and his friend could deal with us." She pointed at Parkman. "You will find the guy you're looking for out that door, and you can deal with Milton on your own time. We're leaving."

She started forward, but Ruben grabbed her arm.

"That's the second time tonight someone's done that," she spat the words out in a rage.

Ruben released her as Aaron crowded him.

"I can't let you leave," Ruben said. "This is an active investigation, and Aaron assaulted me and my other guard. We're going to press charges." He addressed his men piled up behind Benjamin. "No one leaves. Call for backup."

Aaron's phone rang.

"What now?" Ruben asked. "More cops?"

Aaron answered it. "Yes." He listened, then met Sarah's eyes. "Yes. She's with me. But security wants to hold us here." He paused. "We're in a secure area—well, not so secure—behind the security offices." Aaron nodded. "Right. Come to the security offices. We'll leave you to deal with these bozos so we can go home." He ended the call and put his phone away.

"Spencer and Whitman," he said to Sarah and Parkman. "They're here. Headed for the security office now. We leave in ten minutes." He pointed at the assembled security guards. "These guys will be here all night."

"Okay, fun's over," Ruben said. "Let's go and meet these all-powerful narcotics cops who feel they supersede our jurisdiction."

"Not so fast," someone shouted from another corridor behind them.

Everyone stopped moving as a group. Sarah whispered to Ruben, "You guys armed?" Ruben shook his head. "Shit."

A tall, well-dressed Italian man stepped into view from

around the corner fifteen feet away, a semi-automatic weapon in his hands, leveled at the group.

"Nobody moves," he said as he edged closer.

One man armed with a weapon could severely hurt or kill at least half of them before they made it down the hall and around the corner. Sarah raced through her options, not liking any of them.

"What kind of airport is this?" Sarah asked. "How the hell are so many heavily armed assholes just walking around the back hallways?"

Ruben shrugged as if Sarah was actually looking for an answer.

The Italian stopped about five feet from Parkman and Aaron.

"All I want is the girl." He jerked his head back once. "Send her my way, and the rest of you can walk the other way."

"Yeah," Sarah said. "And all I want is a whiskey and my bed, but we don't always get what we want, do we?"

He raised the weapon an inch, glanced at it, then offered them a grin that matched the insanity in his eyes.

"But I've got the most powerful negotiator."

Sarah's hand eased back to the gun she'd taken off the last guy who tried to kidnap her just minutes ago. She had to be a sure shot. There would only be one chance at this.

"Why?" she asked, hoping to delay the inevitable. With Spencer and Whitman close, this could only end badly for the Italian. "Just tell me why I should go with you. Convince me. Maybe I'll come willingly. Like, do you have chocolate?"

"Shut up," he yelled. "This isn't a negotiation. Now come on. I'm not waiting. We have to leave fast."

Her hand gripped the butt of the weapon at the small of her back. The odds were against her. She allowed doubt to cloud her judgment.

Vivian? Anything here?

A man stepped out from behind the guy with the semi-automatic. The same well-dressed man from the baggage claim. Of course, Vivian was gone. She was being blocked again by the dead guy gesturing that everything would be okay.

"Of all the fucking timing," Sarah said. "Get out of here. I'm trying to talk to my sister."

She felt the eyes of every man around her turn her way.

"Your hand," the Italian barked as he stepped closer and leveled the weapon in his hands as if to use it. "Show me your hands."

There was no use. Nothing she could do with a handgun. Pulling it now would be reckless and probably get half the people in the corridor mowed down.

"You heard the man," someone else shouted from behind the group. Another Italian-looking man, a bit shorter than his semi-automatic-toting partner, walked up behind the guards with a large weapon.

"Just the girl," he said.

"Everyone, start moving down that corridor. Sarah, come my way. There will be no more discussion."

Aaron turned to Sarah, his face rigid. She shook her head in a don't-try-anything gesture. "They're too heavily armed," she whispered.

Parkman moved first. Then Aaron. Several of the airport security guards followed, everyone moving around Sarah. Daniel and Benjamin stood sentinel by each corner until everybody was out of the hall, leaving the Italians and Sarah alone.

"So, where are we going?" Sarah asked.

"For a ride," Semi-Automatic said. "Someone wants to talk to you." He waved a hand. "Let's go."

"Wait!" the smaller partner yelled behind Sarah.

Everyone froze. The partner moved toward Sarah, his gun up so he could aim using his eye. At any moment, a bullet would leave his weapon and kill her. She was sure of it. The man looked that ready.

The ghost had sauntered off down another corridor or through a wall, Sarah didn't know. This meant Vivian could be back in time before she left the airport.

Aaron moved up and stood between his teachers.

The air seemed to have thickened. Sarah breathed in small pants, her mouth tight, her mind racing.

The short Italian got to her and yanked the weapon from her waistband.

"Oh shit," she said. "And I was going to kill you guys with that."

Semi-Automatic lunged forward and used the butt of his weapon to smash Sarah in the cheek. She spun sideways with the blow but remained standing. Blood filled her mouth where her teeth cut the inside of her cheek.

Aaron and Benjamin were closest to Semi-Automatic. They lurched toward him, but he got back into position fast enough to place the tip of the weapon under Benjamin's chin.

"Back up, asswipes."

Stupidly, both men held their position. Sarah spit blood onto the floor. "It's okay, guys. Don't get killed over one hit in the face. Don't worry about me. I got this." She spit again, a bloody line of drool clinging to her lower lip.

After a maddening few seconds, both Aaron and Benjamin eased back. Semi-Automatic lowered his weapon and addressed Sarah.

"How could you have a gun on you?" the guy asked, sounding manic. "You just got off a fucking plane. Didn't they check you?"

Semi-Automatic was frazzled for sure, as if nothing was going his way tonight. Sarah noticed the wetness on his arm and figured it was blood.

How the hell was he wounded? Vivian, what the fuck is going on?

"You're having a stellar night, aren't you?" she asked, then spit one more glob of blood. "Remember something for me." She moved the last few steps to stand in front of him. "Whatever happens going forward, this night was what caused your death. Remember that on your last breath. The wound in your arm. Nothing. Holding this gun on my friends. We could let that go. But taking me wherever the hell you're going to take me will be the death of you."

"Fuck off," he said and smacked her again, this time on the other cheek. "You're just talking shit. You bleed like anyone else. When this is over, I walk away. You don't."

The second smack to the face wasn't as hard as the first. They were too close for him to have any chance to wind up.

Her cheeks were numb from the abuse, so when she smiled at him, showing her teeth—no doubt covered in blood —the edges of her mouth felt like they were pushing against deadened flesh on each side.

"Take me wherever you're taking me," she said, wanting to get him alone and away from everyone else. "Let's go have our fun. Then I want to go home and get some much-needed sleep."

He pushed the semi-automatic into her side and started her down the hall back the way he'd come. At the end of the hall, he turned around. His partner was sauntering along, watching Aaron and Benjamin, who had eased out from the other corridor that hid all the security men and Parkman.

"Vaffanculo," the shorter man shouted as he raised the handgun he'd taken off Sarah and began firing down the corridor. Aaron and Benjamin jumped back out of the way. Sarah shouted and lunged forward, but Semi-Automatic jerked her back so hard she fell into the wall and dropped to her butt. The magazine emptied in the man's hand, the silence deafening. The weapon must have fired five or six times. People shouted down the hall. Sarah's ears rang in her head. She had sudden pangs of fear that Aaron was mortally wounded. She tried to stand, but the man beside her kneed her back to the ground. His weight was too much a match for her to counter in her crunched-up position. She grunted and pushed but to no avail. Dazed, she stared along the length of the corridor, hoping to see it empty, hoping to not see one of her men hit.

In her lap, blood covered her hand, and for a moment, she didn't know why. How could she have been shot? Then she remembered. Her mouth was bleeding. Blood, always blood. Everything was blood. Her world was blood. Scarlet. Crimson. Death.

The empty weapon dropped in front of her. The oppressive knee came off her back. A hand grabbed the shoulder of her shirt and yanked. Another hand wrapped itself in her hair and pulled. Involuntarily, she screamed at the pain, letting her frustration out, her anger at being so defenseless at the moment when her friends needed her the most. These men would pay for what they had done. She would tear out their tongues, castrate them, hang them upside down, and slit their throats when this was over.

They shoved her along the hallway toward an exit. A lone suitcase rested by the door, the top open like a hungry maw. At the suitcase, their weapons clanged inside, and the shorter Italian dropped to his knees to zip it closed. The door was shoved open, and the two Italian men escorted her across the tiled floor and out an exit leading toward the parkade, the small suitcase trailing behind them. No one was around—the airport seemed deserted. Outside, several cars came and went, but most of the passengers had been shuttled out or picked up by family and friends.

She thought about calling out for help. She thought about spinning around and fighting them one on one. But if she lost, their weapons were close at hand. Who was to say either one didn't have another weapon stashed somewhere in their clothing?

The ringing in her ears had subsided a notch. They guided her toward an elevator. Close quarters. That could work for her to take both down.

A man and a woman walked by, staring at Sarah's face. She imagined the image she portrayed with the blood that came from her wounded mouth and swollen cheeks.

The elevator door opened. They entered as one.

As the tall man hit the button for the second floor of the parkade, the short one withdrew a long knife, showed it to her, then jabbed left and right, cutting at the air in front of her face.

"I'll slice you up," he said as the elevator slowed, then stopped on the second floor. "Try anything, and I'll slice you up real good."

The door opened.

They stepped out onto the second-floor parkade and almost bumped into two large men. Both men lifted their jackets to display weapons.

"What's this?" Semi-Automatic asked, easing back.

"Falcone sent us. Your boss knows. We're to escort you to the harbor."

Semi-Automatic shook his head. "I'm supposed to call in for a location to deliver her."

"Not anymore. Not after what just happened in there. When we get to your car, call the boss. It's all been arranged."

"This is a lot of men for little old me," Sarah said, her voice deep.

Semi-Automatic shoved her. "Just get moving. And shut the fuck up."

Sarah started walking, her hopes of taking out the two men on her own dashed at the sight of their backup.

Chapter 12

"No way," Benjamin shouted. "Not again, for fuck's sake. I think I'm going to lose my mind."

"Take it easy," Aaron said as he wrapped his belt around Benjamin's thigh.

"I'm done. Every fucking time, I'm the one who gets shot. I'm spending half my life in hospitals hanging around you guys." He gritted his teeth and jerked his head back when Aaron squeezed the belt. "Holy fuck. Why do I always have to be the one to get shot?"

Aaron got to his feet. "Ruben. Can you get my friend to medical? I need to go get Sarah."

"You're going after those guys?" Ruben asked, his face a blanched mask of incredulity. "That's insane."

"Parkman?" Aaron called.

"Right behind you." Parkman pushed past Ruben and around Benjamin's sprawled legs. "Sorry, man," he said to

Benjamin.

"Just go," Benjamin said. "Get those bastards. I'm done." He pointed at the bullet wound that was no more than a surface scratch. The bullet hadn't entered his leg, just sliced a groove in his thigh. "I'll be at the hospital getting more stitches to add to my collection."

Aaron started up the hall with Parkman close behind. At the corner, he slowed, saw the empty hall ahead, and bolted to the door at the end. Once through the door, they were standing in one of the main corridors of the terminal. It was mostly empty.

"Which way, Parkman?" Aaron asked.

"Outside. Either they had a car waiting, or they're in the parkade. They wouldn't risk staying in the terminal."

Outside, Aaron looked at as many vehicles as he could. Parkman ran a few feet left, then right, looking inside the vehicles closest to them.

"Now what?" Aaron asked, feeling defeated. It wasn't supposed to be like this. He had recognized the guy from the dojo but didn't pursue it. The bastards had called in a fake tip about a bomb threat to get Aaron out of the way. They even tried to get Sarah before she left baggage claim. When that didn't work, the guy with the large weapon and the short friend who shot Benjamin was the backup plan. These guys were organized, smart, and determined. The word mafia kept filtering through his mind.

"There," Parkman said, pointing upward.

Aaron followed Parkman's arm. On the second level of the parkade, Alex gestured for them to come up. Aaron took off across the road so fast that a shuttle bus had to slam on the brakes to keep from hitting him. As he entered the parkade, he searched for the stairs. Once there, he vaulted them two at a time. It never once entered his mind what he would do when he caught up with the guys who had Sarah. They were armed; he wasn't. All he had was a determination fiercer than theirs and a will to fight, motivated by love and loyalty. Fighting for a paycheck was never equal to fighting for love, and Aaron was fighting for Sarah.

At the top of the stairs, Alex waited. He grabbed Aaron's shoulder to steady him and then pointed at four men surrounding Sarah beside a black Chevy Suburban five vehicles away. They forced Sarah inside the rear seat as one of them, with a phone to his ear, the guy who hit Sarah back inside the airport, walked around to get in the driver's seat.

"No time to waste," Parkman said between gasps for breath behind them. "They're getting in. Both of you, go. Hide. Pop up out of somewhere like you always do. I'll distract them."

Parkman walked away before Aaron had a chance to stop him. What he was proposing was a suicide mission. They would kill him on sight. At this hour, there were virtually no witnesses in the parkade.

Aaron waited until the men noticed Parkman. Their attention diverted, Aaron turned to Alex, but he was gone. He didn't waste any time wondering how the little fucker did it. He just ran for the nearest car, dropped behind it, and crawled toward the rear of the SUV.

"Come on, guys," Parkman said. "What's this all about anyway? Let the girl go."

Aaron crawled faster. As he came behind the car parked beside the Chevy, he lowered himself and examined the feet. Parkman was in front of the car he hid behind. Two men were in front of the SUV. Sarah was inside the SUV with the other two men from the back corridors of the airport.

"Should we kill 'im?" someone asked in a heavy Italian accent. They discussed Parkman's life like he was a spider under one's boot.

Aaron eased out and rolled until he was under the bumper of the Suburban.

Where the fuck is Alex?

Aaron swiveled his head to study the feet again. Parkman had taken a step back.

"Listen, I'm just here for the girl," he said.

"Yeah," one of the men confronting Parkman said. "We should kill him. He knows our faces now."

A car turned a corner, its tires squeaking on the parkade surface. The pair of men stepped closer to the SUV. Parkman stayed where he was.

Aaron had no plan and no idea what to do. Unarmed, any movement was asking to be shot. But he had to do something. He couldn't leave Parkman exposed and on his own like that. He got into a new position and leaned against the bumper of the Chevy.

"Be reasonable," Parkman was saying. Aaron was proud of the sacrifice Parkman was making for Sarah. Parkman's voice didn't crack or waver. His voice revealed no sign of fear. Just a regular guy asking for his girl.

The car moved closer. This had to be the best time. Their weapons would be hidden until the car drove by. Aaron rose to his feet and peeked in the back of the Chevy. Sarah was in the back seat with a man beside her. It looked like it was the shorter man who had shot at them. The taller guy who had held the larger weapon was in the driver's seat. He still had the cell phone at his ear.

Aaron eased out enough to see the two guys addressing Parkman. When something moved above him, he looked up. Between the concrete bridging of the parkade roof, Alex edged along four feet above the roof of the SUV. He was pressed inside a row of separated concrete, edging along, his feet and arms extended fully, forcibly holding himself up. At that moment, Aaron couldn't be prouder of him. Alex continued moving inch by inch until he was suspended directly above the two men talking to Parkman. When Alex glanced back at Aaron, his face was crimson with the effort.

Their eyes locked on one another. Alex offered a barely perceptible nod.

The car had drifted by. The man in front of Parkman displayed a small caliber weapon. Parkman raised his hands.

"Okay, guys," he said. "Just tell me where you're taking her."

Alex dropped from above, landed perfectly on the guy with the weapon, wrapped around the guy's neck, and drove both feet into the face of the other man. With Alex on top and in control, both men dropped to the concrete in a heap. Before Aaron could run up the side of the Chevy and open one of the doors, Parkman had jumped into the melee on the ground, fists and arms flailing.

Sarah shouted inside the Suburban.

Aaron ripped open the back door and lunged at the short guy beside Sarah but was stopped short by a long knife. As Aaron reached for him, the knife slid cleanly through the center of Aaron's right hand. Stunned, feeling nothing at first, he retreated, his eyes on the imposing blade. Sarah screamed louder and pummeled the man in the seat beside her. The engine revved. It all happened like in a dream. The SUV lurched forward and then stopped. Alex, Parkman, and the other two Italians were still in front of the vehicle. The driver didn't seem to care.

Aaron stepped back as the rear door slammed shut. Sarah's rantings were cut off, now only a muffled scream from the outside. The vehicle shot forward again, bumping up over the bodies on the ground. It got stuck, reversed, then jerked forward once more.

Parkman had jumped out of the way and reached for the handle of the SUV. The vehicle cleared the bodies on the ground and took off before Parkman could open the door.

He ran after the fleeing vehicle calling Sarah's name. Aaron stumbled out toward the bodies on the ground.

"Alex," he managed to shout, despair filling him. "Please, no." His eyes watered. "No." He had to wipe at his eyes as they clouded over. Blood began to seep from his hand wound. He'd survive this. He would meet Benjamin at the hospital, get his stitches, and then hunt those men down until the day he died.

"Alex," he shouted, not able to see him yet.

Like a jack-in-the-box, Alex popped up on Aaron's left. He must've rolled away from the two men on the ground when the engine first revved. From where Aaron had been, he wouldn't have seen him.

"Oh, thank God you're okay."

Aaron's step faltered. The adrenaline was seeping away, and his legs were weakening. It was that, or he was going into shock as he looked at the large blade protruding from the center of his right hand. The same hand that was missing the index finger courtesy of the Enzo Cartel.

Somewhere on the level below them, Parkman yelled Sarah's name. Aaron leaned on Alex's shoulder to stay standing.

"That Parkman," he managed to say. "Gotta love that guy." They started toward the elevator. "That took balls. What he did for Sarah. Standing in front of the SUV. Talking to those guys like that …" his voice trailed off.

Alex only nodded.

Once in front of the elevator, Aaron put more weight on Alex.

"Sorry, man," he muttered. "Not feeling so great."

His consciousness wavered. He managed to think about Vivian. Where was she during this mess? How come Sarah hadn't been warned?

Somewhere in the distance, a man was repeatedly screaming Sarah's name.

Aaron's eyes blinked rapidly before he dropped to the ground, Sarah's name on his mind and in his ears.

Chapter 13

P ARKMAN HADN'T SLEPT A wink. The sun rose in the east, and Sarah was still gone. Aaron and Benjamin had been taken to the hospital. He hadn't been updated on the extent of their injuries. Would Aaron maintain the use of his right hand or get partial use back? He hated to surmise but hoped for the best.

Shortly after the Chevy Suburban disappeared from the parkade at the airport, Parkman met Alex at the elevator and helped carry Aaron to a police car. Spencer and Whitman had made it into the airport minutes before the parkade situation and were directed to their location by airport security. Spencer had called for police backup and several ambulances. Whitman's words were, "They're trying to kidnap Sarah Roberts. Bring a lot of ambulances."

The black SUV that took Sarah was still at large. The plate number Parkman memorized was an empty lead. It belonged to a Mazda.

The guard named Milton had been rounded up and was one floor below Parkman in an interview room being questioned by eager detectives but was proving useless. All he knew was what his partner had told him. Meet a girl—his partner and trainer, Mark Conway, had a picture of Sarah—at baggage claim and direct her outside. Milton knew something was wrong when he saw Mark carrying a gun. In addition, the direction they had taken her wasn't right. He became suspicious when Mark said he would be paid a thousand dollars at the end of his shift if he kept what they were doing a secret. Mark Conway, Milton's partner, had not been located. A BOLO was put out for him.

The other guards, Ruben, and his men, discovered the reality of the situation after Spencer briefed them. Ruben did not want to press charges against Aaron for attacking them. As far as he was concerned, Aaron and Benjamin saved their lives in that corridor.

When they found the time, Spencer had briefed Parkman on what Buck Schaffer had said on the phone. Buck, aka Casper, was supposed to show his face soon. Something was going down, and it was big, but no one seemed to know anything other than the Italians, likely organized crime, were interested in Sarah, and now they had her.

Parkman smacked the arm of the chair he sat in. He closed his eyes and pressed his fingers against them in a fury. Every minute of the last few hours, people talked, gave statements, and surmised about Sarah's whereabouts but did nothing else. She was out there with her kidnappers; only God knew where. Parkman could only hope Vivian was with her. He refused to believe this was the end of Sarah. They had come too far, done too much for this to be the end, yet nothing promising was coming out of the talking and debating.

Outside Spencer's office, Parkman waited, the smell of freshly brewed coffee wafting to him from inside the office. Spencer, Whitman, and two other men from the organized crime squad were gathered in Spencer's office to *guess* where Sarah might have been taken. Parkman suspected nothing would lead them to Sarah, and they would have to leave her to fend for herself. The kind of men they were dealing with wouldn't make it easy to locate Sarah. She was gone, and no one knew where. He felt as helpless as a newborn tossed overboard in the middle of the Atlantic.

"Shit," he blurted out to no one in particular. He got out of the chair to pace the floor outside Spencer's office. A window at the end of the hallway shone bright with the morning sun hitting it directly. He wished he could feel an ounce of that brightness in his soul, but he felt only darkness with Sarah gone.

He was the one who landed with her. He came to the Toronto airport on the same plane. She had slept most of the way, sometimes her head on his shoulder. This was *his* Sarah. The same girl he'd researched back when he was a cop. The same girl that mystified him with daring feats of heroism and seemed to have more lives than a cat. He had been there when she was taken captive by Armond Stuarts's men, back when she was healing from trichotillomania. He'd seen Dolan Ryan killed, Esmerelda and entire street gangs destroyed because of Sarah. From Rome to Umbertide to Amsterdam to Athens, Parkman had traveled with Sarah and loved every minute of it. Even when he faced certain death in

Mexico, Aaron came up with the idea that freed them. Some way, somehow, this little team always figured it out. They always made it. Sarah would make it, and he would be there when she walked away from the Italians, every last one of them dead at her feet.

Thinking of dead Italians, he remembered the two men the SUV had run over in the parkade. They had been taken to the hospital. One died of his injuries as the SUV's front tire had crushed his larynx, and the other was in surgery to stem internal bleeding. Until he awoke from surgery, they couldn't question him.

The helplessness overwhelmed him. He stopped pacing and dropped back into the chair. He needed some of the coffee on the other side of Spencer's office door but was told he couldn't attend the meeting. The anti-mafia squad guys had intel that couldn't be shared with a civilian.

He ran a hand through his hair and waited. Less than a minute later, Spencer's door opened.

Parkman shot up out of the chair. "Got anything?"

"Come in," Spencer said.

Parkman followed him inside. The smell of stale cigarette smoke filled his nostrils, making him wonder how he'd never seen Spencer smoke. It was so intense that it overrode the smell of fresh coffee now that he was in the office. No ashtray was present, and no one else noticed the stale, even sweaty, smell of two-day-old wet cigarettes.

Parkman walked by Spencer, filled a white mug with coffee, and took a drink. It was tepid but decent. The smell alone gave him a perky rush. He turned back to the four men in the room and nodded at Spencer. He was ready.

"You like that shit?" Whitman asked.

Parkman looked at the coffee. "Why? What's wrong with it?"

"Don't pay him any attention," Spencer said. "You'd think he was some kind of fucking barista."

Spencer made the introductions. Parkman had known Whitman since an international human trafficking gang had tried to take a shot at Whitman while he watched a baseball game in Toronto, back when his name was Drake Bellamy. The other men Parkman didn't know but was informed they were the central part of an organized crime task force set up to monitor the 'Ndrangheta. When the thinner of the two, a tall, lanky guy, shook Parkman's hand, he saw the man's yellow-stained fingers—the smoker. He virtually reeked of the shit. His gray hoodie even appeared to have cigarette stains and looked like it hadn't seen the inside of a washing machine in a decade.

His partner was almost double his size and had an obvious distaste for Parkman. He eyed him suspiciously and refused to shake his hand during the introductions. Parkman couldn't care less. Sarah was what was important and not some poser's inflated ego.

"We've got a problem," Spencer started.

Parkman's stomach dropped further, if that was even possible. "What?" he asked, afraid of the answer.

"Martino and Patricia Fermosa were executed tonight. It happened sometime before the airport incident. We've got a team of investigators at the murder scene now, bagging evidence and taking pictures."

"Who are they?" Parkman asked. "Why is that important, and how is it pertinent to Sarah?"

"Major players in the organized crime world," Husky

Ego answered.

Parkman already forgot his name. The man's shoulders were the thickest in the room. They hunched down and forward, giving him the look of a brawler, someone Parkman would expect to be a bouncer at a ritzy club downtown.

"How does this relate to Sarah?" he repeated.

"The guy driving the SUV," Spencer said. "Your description, as well as Alex's, matched that of the Fermosa's daughter's description."

"Their daughter?" Parkman asked. "You mean the killers left a witness?"

Spencer nodded. "We're assuming they didn't know she was there. Hid in her room and watched them leave. Said one of the guys was holding his arm. Like he got hurt."

Parkman remembered Sarah's reference to the guy in the corridor at the airport as having a bad night. There was a stain on his arm. Possibly blood.

"The driver had an arm wound," he said, his eyes widening at the realization that this connection, however tenuous, might lead them to the kidnappers. He refocused on Spencer's face. "Does the daughter know the shooters? Can she provide names?"

Spencer shook his head.

Husky Ego moved toward the door. "These guys are hired hitmen, contractors. Their only job is the hit. Sometimes the mafia employs private military contractors to do their hits. It's all too discreet for the daughter of a made man to recognize the shooter."

Parkman ignored the obvious show of knowledge. He wouldn't stroke the man's ego, which was exactly what the guy wanted. Every man in Spencer's office knew how the mafia worked. Parkman didn't need an education, but Husky Ego wouldn't know that, and Parkman's ego wasn't about to make something of it.

Parkman glanced at Whitman, then Spencer. "So these guys execute the Fermosas, then head to the airport to take Sarah. You're sure about the connection? Same guys?"

"Pretty sure." Spencer nodded. "Days from now, we can be one hundred percent after ballistic tests are done. We'll check bullets and casings to those found at the airport."

Parkman shook his head. "They didn't use their guns when they shot at us."

Husky Ego moved closer to Parkman, a frown so deep his nose skin scrunched at the bridge. "Whose gun did they use?" he asked.

"The handgun Sarah took from that guard Mark Conway before she shoved him outside onto the tarmac. The same one that put a hole in my suitcase."

"You got shot at a lot tonight," the lanky officer in the hoodie said.

The coffee mug covered his face as he drank the rest of the lukewarm beverage. He set the empty cup on the corner of Spencer's wooden desk and waited.

The room was silent. Other than the rustle of shoes on the floor and someone clearing their throat, no one spoke for a full minute.

He'd had enough. "I'm leaving," Parkman said.

"Wait." Spencer moved around him. "Where are you going?"

"To look for Sarah."

"Where, though?"

"No idea. I'll drive around. I have to be doing something.

I won't find her standing around your office."

"Toronto's a big place. You're not familiar with the territory. You'd be wasting your time."

"Isn't that what we're all doing here? Wasting our time?" He looked around the room. No one answered, but Husky Ego gave him a harsh side glance. "Look, I'm sorry. That was uncalled for. I'm just frazzled, and I feel helpless."

Whitman put a hand on his shoulder. "Me too, man. Me too."

"Maybe I'll head over to the hospital. See how Aaron's doing. Sometimes these guys attempt hits on their victims in the hospital."

"That's only in the movies," Husky Ego said.

"No." Parkman glared at him. "It's not."

Someone knocked. Spencer reached past Husky Ego and opened the door.

Buck Schaffer stepped into the room. "Gentlemen." He nodded at everyone, then addressed Parkman. "I've been brought up to speed on my way over here. I have information. There are three possible sites where they would've taken Sarah. My team worked out a probability for each location. Anyone want to come to crash their party?"

Hope filled Parkman with the newfound purpose. "You mean you have a lead on where Sarah is?"

"I have probable locations. We'll start with the one that's the likeliest."

"How could you know something like that?" Husky Ego asked. This was his territory. Parkman assumed Husky Ego had never met Casper before.

Buck shook his head. "Confidential." He faced Parkman, then turned to Spencer. "You coming to help me get Sarah back?"

"He can't go," Husky Ego said, pointing at Parkman. "He's a civilian. Also, he's Sarah's friend. Could compromise any extraction effort."

Casper acted as if he hadn't heard the man. "You armed?" he asked Parkman.

Parkman shook his head.

Casper reached inside his jacket and produced a Smith & Wesson. "It's fully loaded. You're armed now."

Spencer nodded. "Lead the way."

Husky Ego grabbed Casper's arm. "Hey, wait a second here—"

Casper spun and dislodged the man's arm. "This is my gig, my show. I own jurisdiction on anything Sarah Roberts. In this case, jurisdiction is not limited to geography." He moved closer until their noses almost touched. "Stay here or come with us. It matters little to me. What does matter a whole hell of a lot is that we find Sarah Roberts and bring her home. Parkman is the only man I trust, not to mention he's the only man who saw the kidnappers up close. Have you thought of that? And anyone standing in my way is obstructing justice and, upon my command, will spend a week in a jail cell."

"I'd listen to him," Spencer said in a softer tone. "He outranks everyone in this room. Actually, I think he outranks the whole floor."

Husky Ego was startled enough to take a step back.

"Don't ever touch me again," Casper added. "Or try to thwart one of my decisions. Nothing will stop me or them," he pointed at Parkman, Spencer, and Whitman, "from bringing her home, least of all you."

Casper walked out the door with Parkman close behind.

Parkman felt a hundred pounds lighter.

Sarah, we're coming for you, and we're coming in strong.

He wiped at a leaky eye.

Husky Ego and his tall, lanky partner stayed behind.

Chapter 14

THE ROAD RUNNER—OTHERWISE known as Darwin Kostas—cleaned his sunglasses with a cloth, then eased them back onto his face. His rental Cadillac didn't have satellite radio. Only FM and AM—who listens to AM anymore—and Bluetooth. Normally he had no issue using Bluetooth, as his cell phone had a bevy of albums on it, but today his cell phone was in use inside his suit jacket pocket. It was connected to his three men, each man with an earpiece connecting them to him. They were in Toronto on a job, and until that job was completed, the Road Runner would have to forego any use of Bluetooth for personal gratification.

It was good to be back in Toronto. He'd missed the city. He grew up here, roaming the streets, buying CDs at Sam The Record Man on Yonge Street before the iconic store closed. As a teenager, he would wander the endless rows of books at The World's Biggest Bookstore on Edward Street.

He even remembered when one of the first Walmarts was built in the Square One Shopping Centre in Mississauga back around 1994 when he was a small tyke. Toronto had been his home for most of his life, but as an adult, it had become too dangerous for him to remain.

Ironically, it was the danger that pulled him back to Toronto, the city known for its outgoing and boisterous mayors. Mel Lastman—the first mayor post-amalgamation of the City of Toronto, 1997—who, in 1999, after a rather heavy dumping of snow in early January that virtually closed the city down, ordered the Canadian Forces to help clean it up by shoveling and using some of their army equipment to aid in emergency services maneuverability. He was ridiculed for this move—even laughed at—and spent the rest of his time in office, never living it down. Rob Ford became the Mayor of Toronto for four years and lives in infamy for his controversial drug use and legal proceedings. The Road Runner remembered Rob Ford more for his budgeting ability as a city councilor than for his flamboyant lifestyle.

Regardless of Toronto's reputation, whether good or bad, it was a special city to the Road Runner, and that was something no one could take from him. Even now, sitting in the rented Cadillac on College Street, in the heart of what is known as Little Italy, he watched the morning traffic line the street as a TTC streetcar edged along toward the lights at Ossington. This was his home, and maybe he could spend more time here one day. Probably with an assumed name, perhaps even a new face.

Across the street, the gray, nondescript telephone van parked by a small tobacco shop housed his three men. Without his sunglasses on, he would've had to look away from the van as the sun reflected off its large square side mirror. He checked his mirrors, watching for activity behind the Cadillac. People walked the sidewalks, hurrying to work. College Street was lined with traffic, bicycle couriers already hard at work meandering through parked cars and running red lights when they had a chance. An old video game called Frogger from the ColecoVision and Atari days came to mind as he watched a cyclist dodge a minivan at the intersection behind him.

"All units remain ready," he said into the com attached to the underside of his lapel. "Each unit check-in."

"Charlie here," the first voice came through. The code name for this bald mercenary was the cartoon character Charlie Brown. That was the only resemblance, though. Charlie Brown, the merc, was almost seven feet tall and responded to the name Bruno, but for this operation, he was Charlie. He mostly spoke in one-word sentences and constantly lifted weights. While driving, he'd have fifty pounds in one hand, raising it, lowering it, repeatedly. He walked with weights suspended to his wrists and ankles. The Road Runner had watched as Charlie brought weights onto the plane in his carry-on luggage and commenced to work out most of the eight-hour flight from Amsterdam to Toronto.

"George here."

His moniker was Curious George. He always wanted to be the first to enter a building. He had this insane ability to root out which people were hostile targets or friendlies inside buildings that needed to be cleared simply by being extremely curious. "Hey, what's in there?" was something he said frequently.

"Ewmew hewe." *Elmer here.* The third and last

mercenary on the Road Runner's roster on this trip was labeled Elmer Fudd because he placed the letter W where an R or an L should be. He barely spoke, but when he did, he had an uncanny knack for reminding the Road Runner of Elmer Fudd.

The Road Runner chose his name simply because the people they were after had tried and failed to take him out in the past. The Road Runner just never got caught. The Road Runner remained alive with a smidgen of luck and a small part of wit and ingenuity. Even though would-be executioners receive mortal injuries, more just kept coming.

Today was the first day of ending Wile E. Coyote's life. And not just his life but any others that may seek the Road Runner's demise.

"Final weapons check," Runner said.

After a moment, he received an affirmative in his ear. They were ready for what had to be done.

He examined the front windows of the Il Forno Ristorante. After several years of living in Italy, he translated the restaurant's name to mean The Oven Restaurant, although it was translated backward. In Italian, it would be *il ristorante del forno.*

The dash clock said it was two minutes to nine in the morning. Carmine Fabriano owned the Il Forno Ristorante. As the head of one of the seven Italian clans in Toronto, Carmine ran a tight ship. It took incredible pressure to have the man himself attend the early morning meeting that was supposed to happen at nine. It had to be Carmine, as no one else would handle the kind of money the Road Runner was willing to put on the table. Except maybe two other clan leaders in Toronto, and meetings had been set with them for later in the day.

"One minute to nine," he said into his lapel. "Follow my lead. Let's close this deal. Charlie, exit the van now. Walk to my vehicle and stand on the sidewalk by my door."

The back door of the telephone van opened. The seven-foot monster of a man stepped out and shut the door. Runner watched the van rise on its shocks as Charlie disembarked. He was always amazed at Charlie's size and was eternally grateful that this man was on his side. Pay a man enough money, and you own the man. Pay him even more, and you own his decisions.

Charlie Brown walked between parked cars on College Street, paused for a cyclist, then stepped up on the curb and moved in place beside the driver's side door of the Cadillac. Finding a suit jacket large enough to fit the upper bulk of Charlie's massive barrel-like chest was a challenge. They didn't find one until they hit the last Big and Tall Man store the day before. The Road Runner's chest boasted a forty-four-inch thickness. Charlie Brown's chest topped out at sixty-four, yet the jacket appeared tight. How his inner organs and joints handled the weight, Runner how no idea, but he was grateful to have him on this mission.

The dash clock said it was one minute past nine. Fabriano was late, possibly on purpose. Perhaps he used an advance team to reconnoiter the area to ensure this meeting occurred under civil conditions. They would want assurances that the Road Runner was who he said he was and that there weren't several SWAT teams or some other emergency task force lingering nearby.

Carmine Fabriano was connected. The man had several inroads with the authorities. A simple phone call would offer him all the assurances he would need. The Road Runner's ID would check out. Even the bank account proof to display the ten million American dollars the Runner was willing to use to transport a shipment of cocaine to Piraeus Port in Athens, Greece. The Greeks were troubled people, and a little snow was exactly what the Runner ordered.

He waited, his heart rate at rest, beating calmly, meditatively honed for what he had to do. After living through hell and back, a simple meeting with one of the most powerful men in Toronto was like a high school reunion. Going back was almost fun, a novelty. How fast that novelty wore off would determine Fabriano's life expectancy.

Four men, as inconspicuous as circus performers, walked in a tight group toward the front doors of Il Forno Ristorante. The restaurant opened at eleven for lunch. This meeting was set so it would be completed before the kitchen staff arrived at ten. Even though Fabriano and his entourage were late, the meeting would have plenty of time to take place.

As the group of men approached, the Runner studied them. They were dressed in slacks, collared shirts, and suit jackets. Other than a mild variation in hue, each man looked identical. He picked out weapon bulges on several of them. One man had multiple tattoos on his hands that probably ran the length of his arms.

At the front of the restaurant, one man unlocked the door and stepped inside while the other three turned to watch the street. The tallest man sporting facial hair alighted on Charlie, who stared back. After several moments, the door opened, and the man with the tattooed fingers and hands disappeared inside with the key holder leaving the other two men to stand guard on either side of the door.

"Charlie?" Runner said, his lips barely moving.

The merc beside the door gently bumped the Cadillac's window in response.

"Approach those men and inquire as to the meeting time."

Charlie stepped away from the Cadillac. With a gait rarely seen in men, more readily in the lumbering shoulders of an elephant or a rhino, Charlie drew himself up and strode with purpose toward the men guarding the front door.

"My associate," Charlie said to the men in his heavy accent. Runner adjusted his earpiece, watching them through the windshield. "Awaits."

Oh, Charlie, man of such few words.

The thugs exchanged a glance. The man on the right, the tallest one, stepped forward and looked Charlie up and down.

"Who is your associate?" Fabriano's thug asked.

"Mr. Kostas," Charlie said. "He awaits." Charlie stood immobile like a large marble statue.

"Tell Mr. Kostas that Mr. Fabriano will see him shortly."

Charlie pointed at the Cadillac. "I wait. There." He backed up and started for the car, knowing Runner had eyes on the men behind him if there was a problem.

The entire fifteen seconds it took for Charlie to get back to the Cadillac, both of Fabriano's men watched him with faint curiosity. They were probably wondering what the hell they'd do if Charlie got mad, as he was double the size of either man.

Another minute passed. Traffic on the street lessened some with the morning rush hour thinning along College Street. The men in the van were silent. Road Runner's team waited, knowing what was required of them, and prepared to do it.

The Runner placed a hand on the briefcase resting in the passenger seat. Everything he needed for the meeting was inside. The only negative about this entire operation was that he would have to burn the Cadillac. The moment he left the car, he would not return to it. It would be called in as stolen later in the day, and the extra insurance he paid would cover everything, minus a small deductible. But that was all under an assumed name with a fake ID his wife had set up and designed for him six months before in case anything like this ever happened. Even the credit card—with the false identity —he'd used to rent the car had the money on it to cover the deductible, but that was it. After that, the ID was burned, never to be used again.

The dash clock clicked closer to twenty minutes after nine. Fabriano was pushing the meeting late on purpose. Was he waiting for a meal to be cooked? Maybe he didn't meet with anyone in the morning without his required cappuccinos or macchiatos. Whatever the reason, it wasn't good for business, and the Runner didn't like it. Nor was he comfortable with it.

"All clear out here," he spoke softly into the lapel mic. Two *all clears* came back from the van. Charlie said nothing as he stood at the Cadillac's door, not two feet from Runner.

The restaurant door opened. The keyholder stuck his head out. His mouth moved, then the door eased closed. The tallest thug with the facial hair stepped out onto the sidewalk and waved at Charlie to come.

Charlie tapped the Cadillac's window.

"Time to go," Runner said into his lapel. He grabbed the briefcase, locked the handcuff extending from it onto his wrist, and opened the car door. Once outside the Cadillac, he surveyed the street to the west, looking away from Carmine's thugs.

"George. Elmer. Charlie and I are heading inside. Prepare yourselves accordingly and be ready on my word. This is a go. Repeat. Operation Blade is a go. Prepare my El Salvadorian."

He eased around to face east. After adjusting his jacket, he started toward the two thugs who waited near the sidewalk, their hands clasped lazily in front of their crotches, heads tilted slightly back.

Neither man knew they would die in fifteen minutes and their boss, Carmine Fabriano, decapitated.

Nobody could prepare for a decapitation alert. There just wasn't any training for that sort of thing.

The Road Runner paused for the routine frisk, leaving his sunglasses in place. Fabriano's men weren't gentle like a body search at any airport. These men roughly examined each rounded edge of the thighs to the underside of the armpit. They left nothing to chance. Yet they didn't locate his lapel mic or bother with his earpiece. Runner waited while they frisked Charlie. The door to the restaurant opened. Facial Hair led them inside, with Charlie taking up the rear. The other man waited outside, arms crossed, standing in front of the door.

He would be the first to die.

Today would be a good day to do business in Toronto.

Chapter 15

PARKMAN SAT IN THE front seat as Casper drove, Spencer and Whitman in the rear. They took a nondescript Ford Fusion, probably a rental Casper had procured for the day. As Casper drove them south on Yonge Street, Parkman filled him in on what had happened at the airport as best as he could. Once everyone was up to speed, Casper pulled the car over and parked on College Street.

"Five blocks up is a restaurant," Casper said. "It's almost nine-thirty in the morning. The place doesn't open until eleven for lunch, but the employees filter in around ten to start setting up."

"How is this place important?" Spencer asked.

Casper twisted around in the front seat to face Spencer and Whitman.

"Ever heard of Carmine Fabriano?"

Spencer nodded. He looked at Whitman. "You remember.

It was in the briefing. One of the heads of the seven families in Toronto. Keeps his nose mostly clean. Dabbles here and there in prostitution and money laundering." Spencer looked back at Casper. "Known to frequent the Diavolo Club on Kingston Road in Scarborough."

"What's the Diavolo Club?" Parkman asked.

"Italian-run place," Casper said. "Translates to The Devil Club. It's a small pool hall and bar with a twenty-room motel attached. Their slogan for the Devil Club is that the place is damned good. We're heading there later today."

"We recently got intel on that place," Spencer added. "Whitman and I are working on a narcotics case that involves the Toronto Harbor and a man named Lorenzo Falcone."

Casper nodded. "He runs operations at the docks. Makes sure everything comes and goes smoothly. No interruptions. It's how they get the drugs into the States, by taking it across Lake Ontario."

"Right. Well, we've been given a month to nail Falcone on something. It'll cripple several of the bosses in town. Like Antonio Lombardi, one of the oldest members of the 'Ndrangheta Group and—"

"Carmine Fabriano," Casper cut in. He checked his watch.

Parkman listened as these men recited what they knew as if they'd memorized the mafia handbook.

Casper continued, "Carmine Fabriano manages most of the muscle in town. If Antonio needs something done, like having someone disappear, it goes through Carmine at the restaurant. Carmine sends missives to Lorenzo down at the docks with a driver. All deliveries are made in person with food as if Lorenzo had take-out delivered all the time from

College Street." He shook his head. "But this ensures the control of information. Especially the sensitive stuff, like millions of dollars of drugs in a certain shipment."

"Can't you just nab a delivery guy?" Whitman asked. "Or are the messages encrypted in some way?"

"Fabriano only gives Lorenzo part of the message. Nothing a stranger could decipher. Even Lorenzo usually can't figure out what the message is. But if it gets to his hands unmolested, then a simple call to Lombardi reveals the other part of the message. Listening in on that call gets you nowhere. You must have the part delivered by the take-guy to understand what Lombardi told him."

"Then fill us in," Parkman said. "Why are we here? Does Fabriano have something to do with Sarah? Or are we fishing?"

Casper nodded at Parkman. "We're here to find out what he knows. Martino Fermosa was executed last night, and Sarah was taken—boldly—from the Toronto Airport. A man like Carmine Fabriano should know about events like this in Toronto. Lombardi is probably pulling the strings, and Falcone down at the docks will know something, too. Those are my leads. We visit three places today. One will give us the answers we need."

"And this Antonio Lombardi," Parkman prodded. "If he's one of the oldest members of the board, how come he runs a pool hall and bar? Seems like he would have a higher position."

"He doesn't *run* the operation. A man named Angelo Spinello, known as the *little don*, runs it for him. Same with the Calto Club on Ellesmere in Toronto here. Lombardi owns that but has Mancuso Corrado run that one."

"Are they all dons?"

Spencer shook his head slightly. "Just nicknames."

"Okay, what's next?" Parkman asked.

Casper checked the time again and twisted back in his seat to face the windshield.

"We go pay Carmine Fabriano a visit."

"And if he's not in?"

"They get him for us."

"And if they won't?"

Casper turned on the car. "We wait. We're the authorities. We're armed. They don't want that kind of action in their restaurant. Carmine Fabriano will be dying to see us. If nothing else, just to get rid of us."

"Then what?" Whitman asked. "Ask him questions he would never answer. We can't beat him or make him tell us anything. These guys never rat each other out, and we're cops. How would we ever think Fabriano would talk to us?"

"That's a good point." Casper put the car in gear. "We can't harass the guy because we're all cops in one way or another." He looked at Parkman. "But Parkman here, he can do anything. He's not a cop, and we can protect him from witnesses. Besides, if this guy Carmine knows where Sarah might be, I think Parkman would want to know. Isn't that right, Parkman?"

Casper pulled out into traffic.

"Fuckin' right, I want to know." He slapped Casper's arm. "You're driving too slow. Hurry up. I've got someone's head to crack."

Spencer told Whitman in the back seat, "Shit, I wanted to retire next month. Maybe I'll be retiring early."

Casper hit the gas and passed a streetcar on the outside.

Chapter 16

The tallest of Fabriano's guards—shorter than Charlie but still tallest amongst his own men—led them through the restaurant tables on a meandering course toward the back. A table had been prepared for three people with a set of double doors resembling the front doors of an older-style saloon. His back to the wall, Carmine Fabriano sat at the table, a plate of spaghetti in front of him, a glass of red wine in his right hand.

He motioned to the empty chairs. "Please," he muttered. "Sit." He pulled on the wine glass, swished the wine around his mouth, then sipped again.

Charlie moved off to the right to stand by a pillar separating the main dining area from a small waitress section where coffee and tea were served.

Fabriano watched Charlie as he maneuvered into place. Runner knew that Charlie got that kind of attention wherever he went. The man was so tall that he belonged on a basketball court. People often assumed he was a friendly giant—or at least they assumed that because he resembled a human tank, and they *hoped* he was a friendly giant. Charlie's strength was loyalty. He would be loyal to the Runner and even take a bullet for the Runner because it wasn't about a paycheck. The Runner had taken Charlie in and treated him like a brother. Even the Runner's wife loved having Charlie around the house. An orphan at an early age, in and out of the penal system, Charlie had only known a life of violence. When the Runner met him last year, he didn't just recruit him to solve problems; he brought him in out of the cold and offered empathy and family. Charlie was blood now, and the Runner would protect him as much as Charlie would die for the Runner.

Fabriano's men took seats at two different tables close by so they could watch the proceedings.

Runner sat opposite Fabriano and placed the briefcase in his lap.

"We didn't look inside that case," the tattooed guard said.

Fabriano waved him off. "That's okay." He met Runner's eyes. "We're here to do business." The deadpan expression weakened as the corner of his mouth drew upward. "Isn't that correct, Mr. Kostas?"

Runner nodded. In his earpiece, small sounds came through from George or Elmer outside the restaurant as they exited the van across the street.

Fabriano spun a fork in the plate of pasta, winding the noodles on it.

"Do you know what one piece of spaghetti is called, Mr. Kostas?"

Runner shook his head, then slowly removed his sunglasses. He folded the arms of the glasses inward, then eased them inside his jacket's inner pocket.

Fabriano held up his fork and stared at an errant noodle dangling longer than the others.

"One piece is called spaghetto, while the plural form is spaghetti." His eyes refocused on the Runner. "That's how Italian works. You would not say you have a plate of spaghettos. That's the way English would handle it. Like ordering one cappuccino or two cappuccini." He shoved the wad of noodles on his fork into his mouth, set his fork down, and picked up the wine glass. The Runner waited, his cuffed hand spread out on the briefcase.

After a moment, Fabriano dabbed at his mouth with a napkin, placed both hands on the table, and stared at the Runner.

"Wine?" he asked, nodding at the bottle.

"Another time, perhaps," the Runner said.

Fabriano made a show of checking his watch. "It's almost lunchtime." His hands came back to the table, fingers spread. "Why let the clock guide you in your food and beverage choices? Eat what you want when you want is what I always say."

"Wise advice."

Fabriano picked up the bottle and studied the label. "It's a California wine aged in whiskey barrels. It has a subtle bite to it, hence the name Inferno." He angled the label for the Runner to see, then set the bottle back down. "You must try it sometime."

"I'm sure I will."

Fabriano's tongue rolled around his mouth as he cleared

the pasta sauce, swallowed, then placed his hands on the table again.

"So, tell me, why are we meeting at this early hour?"

"Business."

Fabriano chuckled and glanced at his men, who chuckled obligingly.

"Of course, business. What kind of business?"

"I understand you're the man to discuss a particular shipment with."

Fabriano picked up his fork and dug into the pasta. "What kind of shipment? From where to where? What shipping lines? How much money are we talking? Details. I need details." He shoved another wad of pasta in his mouth and commenced chewing.

"Your ships. Ten million dollars worth of cocaine. The destination is Piraeus Port in Athens, Greece."

Fabriano finished chewing as if the Runner had asked him for an ice cream. He was a pro, playing world-class poker. The stakes were real, and Fabriano gave nothing away. He was either this calm all the time or putting on a show. Fabriano had to be that relaxed to hold the elevated position he maintained with Toronto's mafia. After the requisite dab of the mouth with the napkin and double sip of wine to wash the food down, Fabriano got up from his chair and stepped over to the guard with the facial hair. He whispered something to him, and the guard headed toward the front door.

Fabriano turned back to Runner. "What's in the briefcase?"

"A computer. Prepped and ready to transfer half the money upfront as a deposit. The other half will be programmed to deliver to any bank account of your choice when I hear the shipment is cleared and has docked safely in Athens."

Fabriano gave a tiny nod, then returned to his seat across from the Runner. He moved the plate of pasta forward, pushing it away from him. Fabriano was a small man, no taller than five and a half feet. But his countenance and how he carried himself was of a man double his size. He reminded the Runner of Joe Pesci in the movie *Casino*.

The Runner considered the man's history. He had learned everything about Fabriano from a simple Google search. He was the suspect in multiple murders. The loansharking, human trafficking, and other organized crime-related charges could never stick in court. It was the recent kidnapping of Sarah Roberts that the Runner was most interested in, but he could already tell that a man like Fabriano would rather die than reveal her whereabouts. Knowing that and moving forward with their mission wasn't a mistake. Fabriano's demise would serve as a message to the others the Runner planned to visit while in Toronto. Angering the mafia was his current mission. The more fury they felt toward him, the sooner they'd release Sarah. His plan was weak, but it was all he had, and he was sticking to it.

"I've never met you before," Fabriano said. "How do I know you are who you say you are?"

"You don't. There's risk in everything. But," Runner tapped the top of the briefcase, "once I transfer five million into an account of your choice, I'm sure it'll be the beginning of a budding friendship."

Fabriano laughed in short bursts. This was the second time he deemed something funny enough to almost burp a laugh.

Something felt wrong. Maybe the Runner was too forward, too eager to open the briefcase. Everything hinged on the briefcase being open because that was where the weapon was. Sure, George and Elmer had more weapons for them, but Runner and Charlie were to suppress the men inside before they came barging in the front door.

"I don't want your money," Fabriano said.

Charlie pushed off the pillar he had quietly been leaning against and moved closer to the table.

Fabriano's men got up from their table. The tension in the room tripled.

Carmine lifted his left hand, held it suspended in the air about a foot off the tablecloth, then lowered it. His men eased back.

"Tell your pet grizzly to move back to the pillar."

Charlie glared at Fabriano's men, his eyes unwavering.

"Tell me why my money is no good?" Runner asked.

All sense of friendliness drifted from Fabriano's face. As his eyes hardened, Runner could swear the skin on his face also tightened. Years ago, this would have intimidated him. Now he had to suppress a laugh of his own.

"In my restaurant, it is considered disrespect not to oblige me. Ease your grizzly back, or he doesn't leave this establishment with his legs attached to his body."

On the Runner's left, Fabriano's men took another step closer.

In the interest of keeping Fabriano's goons farther away, Runner nodded at Fabriano.

"Charlie, ease back."

Charlie grunted. From the corner of his eye, Runner saw

Charlie move back to the pillar. A moment later, the goons to the Runner's left eased back to their table. Fabriano drank more wine. The tension eased some.

But they were running out of time. He was supposed to have the briefcase open by now. The kitchen staff could show up at any moment. George and Elmer were waiting outside. He had to speed this up.

"Your money is no good because your identity didn't come through clean."

Runner frowned at the thought that his wife could've made a mistake in setting up Mr. Kostas as a formidable player on the market. Everything was supposed to be in place. A lineage, a timeline of events and places Kostas had been. What he built his fortune from—everything was available for the person willing to take the time and look. The Runner had memorized all of it in case he was quizzed. Perhaps Fabriano didn't look deep enough. Or maybe he had a computer genius look too deep. There was always that possibility.

"How does that make any sense?" Runner said. "I am who I say I am." He laughed like Carmine, a short burst. "That reminded me of Popeye." He half-turned in his chair to face the goons at the table on his left, then crossed his legs. "Since I'm clearly who I say I am, and I'm sitting in front of you willing to transfer millions of dollars for a simple transaction, I'm unclear as to your hesitation."

Carmine leaned forward and scrutinized Runner's face. "I'm not hesitant because I didn't check you out. We wouldn't be meeting face to face if I didn't look into who I was meeting. You'd be dead right now if you were a narc or worked for the authorities. We have the capabilities to erase a human in that kitchen." He twirled a hand in the air beside his head. "You'd be amazed what large walk-in freezers can hide and what kitchen staff can do to meat and bones. But enough of that. You did check out, my friend. All is well."

Fabriano was talking in circles.

"Then why don't you want my money?" Runner asked.

"Because no one pays half up front. At least not that much money on the first date."

Runner hadn't thought of that. Nor had he ever done this kind of a deal before. In fact, there was no actual money to transfer, just a laptop wired to send a signal to his wife, who was waiting to make it look like a transfer receipt was created in the amount the Runner typed in. After several minutes of scrutiny, Carmine's people would detect a problem as the funds wouldn't populate into his account, but they would all be dead by then. They had decided he would offer five million up front because even if they were skeptical, who would refuse that kind of money?

"Then tell me how much you want?"

"You're not listening. I don't want your money."

Runner glanced at Charlie, then back to Carmine. "Then we're wasting our time here." Runner set the briefcase up on the table, his cuffed hand resting on top of the case. "Maybe I'll take my business to Lombardi. I'm sure he can make the arrangements I need." He glanced at Charlie again. "I'm afraid I made a mistake coming here."

Carmine grunted, placed a hand over his mouth, and coughed once. Two men, who appeared to be in their forties, stepped through the kitchen doors and advanced to stand beside Fabriano.

"Is this the man?" Carmine asked.

The men were dressed casually, one unshaven. They looked unsettled like this was something they were forced to do. Both of them stared at Runner. The unshaven man leaned forward and looked into his eyes. Then he turned to Carmine and nodded.

"It's him."

Carmine watched Runner; his face turned toward his men. Runner detected the two goons from the table getting to their feet.

"How sure are you?" Carmine asked.

"Absolutely positive."

Carmine waved a hand dismissively. "Okay. You can go."

They turned back to the kitchen and disappeared behind the doors. After a moment, the doors settled.

"What was that?" Runner asked. Time had gotten away from him. They needed this done now.

"Those men used to work for the Fuccini Family here in Toronto. Do you know the name?"

Fabriano asked the question, already knowing the answer. The Runner had decimated the Fuccini family several years back and had been in relative hiding since. Somehow, Carmine Fabriano had put it all together.

"I'll tell you what," Runner said as he unlocked the case in front of him. The guards by the table moved closer. "We'll do it your way. Tell me how much money you want to interest you in my proposal."

Charlie knew the end was near. George and Elmer would be in place now.

Carmine slapped the table. His wine glass shook, wavered, then settled.

"I said I don't want your money. But I will tell you what

I do want."

"What's that?" Runner asked, the briefcase unlocked in front of him but still closed. All he needed was to slip his hand inside and clip open the false bottom where his weapon was hidden.

"I want you tortured for what you did to my people. Then I want you dead. I want your wife, your family pets, if you have any, and any member of your family and friends destroyed and murdered in the worst possible manner. That's what I want."

"Well." The Runner laughed. "Geez, you don't ask for much."

The second he applied pressure to the lid of the briefcase to open it, the cold tip of a gun pressed into his neck.

"Don't," was the only word spoken by the guard.

"Is that why you took Sarah?" Runner asked. "To get to me?"

The half-smiles were gone. Now a full smile split Fabriano's face like he'd just found out he was right about something after years of being told he was wrong.

A noise near the restaurant's front door made the tip of the gun waver as the guard holding it turned to look.

"Who is Sarah?" Fabriano asked.

"You're going to play with me? In the position we're in?" Runner leaned forward. "This is a *game* to you?" The word *game* came out in a growl.

Another noise at the front door. It sounded like someone grunted.

"Go, check that out," Carmine bellowed.

The gun at Runner's neck moved slightly again. The guard was looking away.

"Charlie?" Runner muttered.

Charlie grunted in response.

"Now."

The Runner jerked forward, away from the gun. He spun around and knocked the weapon upward as it fired. He lifted up and drove into the guard standing over him when the table he had been sitting at seemed to disappear. In that fleeting second, he knew it was Charlie knocking it into Carmine. As glasses and plates clanged to the floor around them, the Runner landed on top of the guard on the floor, both of them wrestling for the gun.

Several punches were exchanged. Runner had his left hand on the guard's wrist, holding the weapon away from him, aimed at the side wall, while his right hand clambered for the guard's throat, the briefcase clattering around at the end of the cuff. A minute ounce of strength on the goon's side had the gun slowly easing toward Runner's face. He redoubled his efforts, ground his teeth together, and pushed outward, but it was useless. The weapon inched closer, the goon's finger on the trigger.

"Need." He gasped. "Help." Another grunt. "Here."

The Runner kicked at the man under him. He shoved a knee upward twice, but the man's weapon continued advancing slowly. Presently, it was aimed at Runner's ear. Then his temple. And finally, his cheek.

The Runner faced the man below him. Their eyes met. If a man could smile with his eyes, the man below him was achieving that feat.

In the millisecond it took for the Runner to realize he may die, a gun fired somewhere nearby. The man below him jerked once. A gun fired again, but by then, the resistance in the goon's arm waned, and the gun moved away from the Runner's face.

The Runner gasped in a large breath, exhaled, and gasped again.

"Whoa, that was close." He panted a moment. "Too close."

Elmer stood over him. "Sowwy we wewe wate, siw." *Sorry we were late, sir.*

Runner got up off the dead man. Elmer had shot the guard in the neck. Blood pooled around the base of the man's skull, but the open, dead-staring eyes told them everything they needed to know.

"Better late than never," Runner said.

"You didn't open the case, siw."

"Didn't get a chance," Runner said as he turned to Charlie.

Carmine Fabriano was alive. Bloodied but alive.

"Where's George?" Runner asked.

"At the do-wuh."

"George," Runner called, keeping his eyes on Fabriano. "All clear?"

"Yes, sir. All three men are down."

"The kitchen?" Runner asked Elmer.

"Two dead, siw."

Runner nodded, then advanced on Carmine. He righted the table Charlie had knocked over, set the briefcase on it, and opened the lid. Charlie had shoved the table aside, drove his meaty fists into Carmine's face several times by the looks of his already swollen cheek and bleeding lip, then pushed him up against the wall. Carmine Fabriano now hung immobile, suspended by Charlie's brute force and overwhelming size. The man's face had gone as red as the wine.

Runner got down on one knee and retrieved the bottle. Miraculously, the open bottle had tumbled to the floor, bounced in a manner allowing it to come to rest against a knocked-over chair, and stood upright, barely a drop lost.

"Will you look at that?" Runner said. He grabbed an unbroken wine glass off the floor, pushed his hair off his forehead, and filled the glass with wine. He tossed the bottle aside where it shattered against the steel side of the waitress stand.

"Bottoms up." Runner took a sip, swished it around in his mouth, swallowed, then sipped again. "You're right. Damn good wine."

Fabriano's face was a red mask of contorted fury.

"You're probably thinking to yourself, how dare these men come into my restaurant, kill my men, and destroy the place." He slapped Fabriano to anger him. "What would you do to us if you had the chance?"

Runner motioned for Charlie to let Fabriano speak. As Charlie's arm eased back, Fabriano's first response was to suck on air. The crimson cheeks instantly began to lose color.

Fabriano spit on the floor and looked back at Runner. "I would execute each and every one of you like the fucking filthy swine you are."

The Road Runner drank more wine. "Of course you would." He raised a hand to hold that thought, then looked vacantly at the floor. "George?"

"Yes, sir," George yelled from the front.

"Still all clear?"

"Yes, sir."

"Door locked?"

"Yes."

"Okay, Elmer, leave through the front. Bring the van around back. George, lock the door when he leaves, then let him in at the back while we talk to Mr. Fabriano here."

"Yes, sir."

"Oh, and bring me the El Salvadorian."

"Yes, sir."

Elmer dodged away. The front door opened, then closed while Runner drank more wine.

"I'm going to have to get me some of this shit." He held the glass up to look at it better. "Charlie, you have to try this later."

Charlie grunted. Fabriano turned to Charlie.

"Don't worry about him. He doesn't talk much."

George strode by and disappeared through the kitchen doors.

"Now, you were saying you would execute us for this offense." Runner waved a hand toward the dead goons.

Fabriano spit blood on the floor in front of Runner's feet. Charlie tightened his grip.

"It's okay, Charlie. I'd do the same."

The door at the back closed. Elmer was back with the El Salvadorian.

"If you see what we're doing here as so offensive that the price to pay would be our lives, then why would you commit this very offense against us? Shouldn't you pay with your life?"

Fabriano frowned. "I don't know you. I did no such thing."

"Lies, lies. Tell them to the Devil when you get down

there." Runner tossed the half-finished wine glass aside. "You know me. If you didn't, you wouldn't have brought those two Fuccini goons to look at my face. You know how to get to me, too. That was why you kidnapped Sarah Roberts. The elusive Darwin Kostas has outwitted the Toronto mafia, and the way to get him out in the open is to take Sarah, who is rumored to know him, and wait until Darwin pokes his head out." Runner shook his forefinger back and forth as if Fabriano had been naughty. "Tsk, tsk, tsk. That was a mistake. Don't you people ever learn? The Fuccini Family and then the Gambino Family were decimated. Didn't you learn after the Bratva paid the ultimate price? Fast forward years later, and you guys, the 'Ndrangheta, want to try again." He met Charlie's eyes. "Insane, I tell you," he said in a half shout. "It's insane. So …" He retrieved a small baton from the briefcase. Elmer and George came to stand beside him. "Tell me where Sarah is."

He handed the baton to Charlie, then extended a hand to Elmer, who placed the handle of the El Salvadorian against his palm.

Fabriano remained silent.

Runner nodded at Charlie, who released Carmine and stood to his full height in front of the stooped Italian. With a flick of his wrist, Charlie snapped the baton. It extended as the collapsible baton was supposed to.

"One unanswered question is free," Runner said. "Don't answer again, and Charlie gets upset. Don't answer several times, and you get to meet my friend here, the El Salvadorian." He looked at the eighteen-inch blade of the deadly weapon called The El Salvador Machete. "I've loved this model since it came out in 2004." He looked back at

Fabriano. "And you know what, I got it on the streets of Toronto for under a hundred bucks."

Someone rattled the front door.

"Check it out," Runner said to Elmer and George. "If it's employees, tell them to wait." He addressed Fabriano. "Where's Sarah?"

Fabriano tightened his lips in determined defiance and said nothing.

Charlie reared back and dropped the baton on Fabriano's arm so hard the snap of bone echoed off the walls. Fabriano's shocked face, open mouth, and bulging eyes were the most comical reaction to an arm being broken that the Runner had ever seen. Charlie lunged in and covered Fabriano's mouth before he could scream in pain, his meaty hand enveloping the man's nose as well. Runner let Fabriano fidget under Charlie's hand for several seconds, then motioned him back when Fabriano was reduced to moaning.

"You'll die for this," Fabriano grunted between gasps of pain.

George came running back. "Looks like cops."

Runner glanced over his shoulder. "Cops? How? Nobody here would've called them." Through the thin sheers at the window, it almost looked like Parkman was outside trying to see in. "Shit. Okay, we're out of time. We need to leave now. Go back and tell them to give you two minutes. Tell them the key is in the back or something. Go." He patted George's shoulder, and the man was away.

"Last chance. Where have you idiots taken Sarah?"

"Fuck you." Fabriano's face had reddened again, and the sclera of his eyes had darkened. The man was furious and seemed driven by pain.

Charlie whacked the front of his knee with the baton in an address that resembled a golf swing. Fabriano's leg snapped outward and sideways. He went completely white.

"We need to leave," Runner said. He pulled the paper from his briefcase and set it on the table. "This says The Blade is back in town. I was willing to let things go, but you brought it to my doorstep." He leaned closer to Fabriano. "You should never have involved Sarah. She's an innocent. Because you trespassed against us, I trespass against you. The Toronto mafia is about to be decapitated. Literally."

Charlie stepped back as the Runner lifted the El Salvadorian over his head. Carmine Fabriano's eyes widened even more. He tried to put weight on his already swollen knee but only managed to grunt somewhere deep in his throat.

Something hard and metallic banged near the front door.

The Runner brought the blade down fast, slicing into and through the Italian's neck, cutting the carotid and nicking the inside of the spine near the brain stem. It came out the other side with a flicker of blood. By the time Runner finished the swing, blood pumped from Fabriano's neck in streams.

That banging again from the front.

Runner wiped the blade on the tablecloth, handed it to Elmer, grabbed the briefcase, and ordered his men to the van.

When he looked over his shoulder, Fabriano's head sat askew on his shoulders, still attached by the back of the neck.

Someone shouted at the front of the restaurant as the door opened from the outside.

"Hurry," Runner yelled as they dove inside the van.

George was already behind the wheel. The second the van's wheels screeched, Runner slammed the back doors. He watched the back door of Carmine's restaurant until they reached the end of the alley.

Holding on as George took the corner to the right, a man ran out the back door, looked the wrong way, then turned toward the van. A millisecond later, he was lost to sight. But Runner knew him. He knew the man's physique, his gait, his run. He knew the man's hairstyle and clothes.

The Runner would recognize his friend Parkman anywhere.

But what was Parkman doing at Il Forno Ristorante before they opened?

Chapter 17

PARKMAN HELD ONTO THE door handle as Casper had to slow for two red lights on the way to the restaurant. Driving erratically, Casper got them there without incident and parked behind a Cadillac. He killed the engine and smacked Parkman's arm.

"You ready for this?"

"If it means bringing Sarah home," Parkman said. "I'm ready for anything."

"You sure about this place?" Spencer asked.

"One hundred percent." Casper fiddled with the weapon in his lap. Parkman thought he recognized the make and model. "I have access to intel that led me to believe Sarah would be taken before she was taken." He glanced up and then back to his gun. "I just couldn't get here in time. Called you guys to pick her up, but there wasn't enough time."

"We called Aaron, but he had a lot working against him."

"Is that a Browning?" Parkman asked.

"It sure is." Casper held it up. "Semi-automatic, nine millimeter. I like that the hammer has to be cocked manually before the first shot." He said this as he admired the weapon, turning it left, then right in his hand. "Been in a lot of scrapes with this one."

"We going today?" Whitman asked. "Or are we going to sit here and see how long our dicks are?"

Casper adjusted the rearview mirror with his free hand. "You're right. Let's go."

The four of them exited the car simultaneously, weapons concealed. At the restaurant's front door, Casper pulled on the handle.

"It's locked." He put his face up to the glass and cupped his hands on both sides of his eyes. "There are people in there."

"Says here it doesn't open until eleven for lunch," Whitman said. "It's not even ten yet."

Parkman edged off to the side of the door to where it appeared the curtains on the inside were slightly open. Behind him, Casper yanked on the door again.

"Open up, police," he yelled.

Parkman cupped his hands to peer inside, but the glass was tinted. He could only make out slight movement by a light source near the back.

"I count two, maybe three men inside," he said. "But I can't distinguish their faces or even what they're wearing." He leaned in farther.

Someone inside approached the front. "I'll open the door in a minute," the guy yelled through the door. "The key is in the kitchen. Be right back."

Parkman returned to stand with the other men. "Something's not right."

"What is it?" Casper asked. "You saw something?"

Parkman shook his head. "Not like that. Just a feeling. Usually, these kinds of places have a thumb lock on the inside—fire regulations. He wouldn't need a key to open the door from the inside. How would everyone get out in a hurry if the place was about to blow? Something's just not right."

Parkman felt Casper's eyes on him a heartbeat longer, then Casper nodded. "Gentlemen, hands on weapons. We're going in." Casper yanked on the door and placed his mouth up against the crack. "Open up. Now!"

Parkman put an eye to the glass. "No one's coming."

"Stand back," Casper said.

He turned the Browning around in his hand, reared back, and smashed the tempered glass beside the deadbolt. It bounced off, the door unaffected. He hit it again. Then again, leaving nothing but a small mark where the butt of the gun made contact.

"Shit, anyone got anything better than this?"

They all shook their heads.

"I don't want to fire a bullet into the glass, nor do I want to shoot the deadbolt. We're too close to avoid small pieces of shrapnel, and even then, we could destroy the deadbolt and still be locked out." He smashed the glass again. "We have to find a better way."

"Want us to head around back?" Whitman asked.

"Sure."

Casper pulled his hand back and hit the glass so hard this time that it cracked.

"Guys," he yelled. "Come back."

Whitman and Spencer hadn't gone far. They started back toward them as Casper belted the glass again. The crack lengthened.

The next hit knocked a small chunk of glass loose. Parkman jumped sideways and looked between the curtains again.

"Nothing moving in there. Hit it like you mean it."

The next hit opened the glass to the size of a softball. Casper stuck his fingers inside to Parkman's consternation and clicked the thumb latch.

Casper shouldered it open and ran inside, the Browning front and center. Parkman entered behind him, with Whitman and Spencer taking up the rear. He almost stumbled over the bodies of three men sprawled on the floor to the side of the foyer. Parkman jogged toward the rear. He jerked back when he saw a man nearly decapitated. A few feet to his right was another man who had bled from a neck wound.

"Guys," he shouted. "Two more bodies over here."

Gun in hand, he placed his back to the wall beside the kitchen doors. After two deep breaths, he pivoted and burst through the doors, gun leveled in front of him. Casper came right behind him. The kitchen was empty unless someone was hiding in the freezer. The back door was wide open, drifting in the soft morning breeze. An engine revved outside the door in the alley. Parkman ran, gun down at his side.

He peeked out, saw no one, then ran outside. After looking one way, he turned and saw the taillight of a van before it disappeared down an adjoining street.

"Shit," he exclaimed.

Back inside the restaurant, he joined the other three by the decapitated body.

"You know this guy?" he asked.

"Carmine Fabriano," Casper said. "The man with the answers." He placed a hand on his forehead. "Shit. This guy reports directly to Falcone down at the docks. If anyone would know who took Sarah, it would've been Fabriano here."

"Guys?" Whitman said, holding a piece of paper up with a Kleenex covering his fingers. "Do you know anyone who goes by the name, The Blade?"

"The Blade?" Spencer said. "Yeah, that was the nickname the mafia gave some guy they went after years ago. They lost a lot of made men in that fight. An entire family was wiped out. Why?"

"Whoever did this left a calling card."

"Read it," Parkman said, thinking he'd heard something from Sarah once about Darwin being called The Blade.

"It says the days of organized crime in Toronto are over. The Blade is back in town. He's here to decapitate the heads of the 'Ndrangheta and won't stop until they're all dead." Whitman held it up for them to see. "He hand-wrote this part about how they wouldn't let it go, and now he was going to destroy them all."

"Shit," Spencer said. "A mafia war is all we need."

"No," Parkman said. "You're going to need a lot of body bags as well."

Casper turned and headed for the front door. "We need to get to the man next on our list before The Blade gets there and cuts off his head, too."

"We have to call this in," Spencer yelled.

"Fine, call it in." Casper stopped at the door. "From the car. We leave now."

Parkman started after Casper and Whitman fell in behind him. At the door, Whitman turned back.

"You coming?" he asked.

Spencer glanced around at the floor. He raised and lowered his hands in defeat and started after them.

"Shit. And I was supposed to be retiring from this shit."

Chapter 18

Sarah Roberts felt the sting without knowing what it was at first. The instant of calm was torn from her as someone slapped her cheek. She mumbled in her dreary state of mind to leave her be.

The slap came again. She opened her eyes, then closed them immediately as the small sliver of light that entered her head shot barbs of agony through her, a pounding of pain that pulsed with the beat of her heart.

Cohesive thoughts, connecting where she was and why she was there, seemed elusive. A man spoke to her. Someone else's voice emanated inside her head, but that voice didn't make any sense. The internal voice spoke gibberish, but somehow it felt more urgent than the one in her ears.

Another slap. Her patience tested, she rose from slumber in a fury, the headache spurring her on.

"Who da fuck?" she tried to shout, her eyes fluttering

open again.

"Wake up," the man yelled so close to her face his breath was a breeze on her cheek.

Something moved under her feet. It didn't make sense. Why would the floor be tilting to the right?

"Be quiet," she said. "Just shut up."

The man grabbed her hair and jerked her head back. The migraine masked anything she should have felt from his tight grip on her hair.

He leaned in close, his sweaty skin rubbing her temple and ear. "You're in no position to be telling me what to do," he whispered.

"You're talkin' gibberish 'n shit," she mumbled. Why was her tongue engorged, her mouth pasty and dry?

The man released her hair with a push. Her chin dropped and bounced once off her chest. She moaned, wanting to slip back into unconsciousness until the pain subsided. Her arms ached, too, her shoulders the most. It was like they were close to the heat of a fire—the joints were inflamed.

What the hell is happening?

"Just you and me in this room, baby," the man said. "No gibberish from me."

Sarah kept her eyes closed. The floor tilted to the left, then eased to the right. What could cause that? She couldn't solve the puzzle of the moving floor with her eyes closed, but she couldn't open them lest her head explode.

The gibberish started up again. She ignored it.

"You have to wake up and eat," the man said. "I can't believe I have to feed you like a fuckin' baby."

She shivered from the cold. The floor tilted the other way slightly. She eased to the right to counter it. A flex of her right arm didn't pull it closer to her body. Nor her left. Some of her position came to her consciousness, and she began to wake by degrees.

Her wrists were bound, arms extended outward, like wings. That explained the tightness in her arms and the agony in her shoulders. She was on her knees; her feet left unrestrained. No gag in her mouth, no blindfold. It didn't matter to these people if she saw them or used her feet to kick at them.

Apparently, they weren't worried about such things if her arms were bound as tight as they were.

Without any kind of warning, her head jerked back, and her body spasmed as cold water struck her face. She gasped, mouth open, and blinked the water out of her eyes.

"Rise and shine, baby girl," the man said.

Heart racing, Sarah fluttered her eyes until they were open enough to take in the room. Uncontrollably shivering now, she glared at the man as he set the empty bucket on the floor beside her. He was the same man from the airport. The one she'd called Semi-Automatic.

The room was a dull gray square. Large leather clasps, something she thought was used by those into bondage, enveloped her wrists. Attached to these thick clamps were chains that spanned five feet and were fastened to the wall in a large metal loop. Only a key in each lock would be able to free her.

She shook her head to fling the hair out of her eyes and realized her mistake immediately as the headache flared. Eyes closed tight to ward off the sting behind her face, she flexed her arms in a revolt against the situation she found herself in. What the hell happened? How could she be here with Vivian on her side? And who was that guy at the airport trying to tell her everything would be okay? How was this okay?

"What's your name?" she asked. "What do I call you?"

"Call me Vince."

He was busy doing something. She eased her eyes open again when the pain subsided enough. Vince was stirring something in a bowl on the other side of the small room.

A new irritation grew from her abdomen. Or maybe it wasn't new. Maybe it had always been there, and she was just now becoming aware of it. The warring sensations of a full bladder and an empty stomach, mixed with nerve-laden adrenaline coursing through her abdomen, felt toxic. She needed to urinate something fierce. Maybe the bucket would hold a dual purpose.

The fire in her arms was being reduced and pushed back by something altogether worse: numbness. She lifted one knee and tried to get a foot under her, but the pressure on the other knee became too great.

"Trying to stand?" Vince asked, watching her over his shoulder.

"Fuck you." She glared at him. "Fuck you for bringing me here and tying me up. You'll end up dead for this." She lunged his way, got pulled back by the restraints, and only succeeded in making a loud noise of aggression and chains clinking, then a subtle moan of pain as her shoulders complained.

He turned all the way around to face her, a wide grin on his face. "You're a peculiar one. You keep saying that I'll be dead. Like you can see my future."

"I can, asshole."

She planted her foot on the floor as it canted to the left. Then, doing her best to ignore the pain and her stretched limbs, she pushed up and planted the other foot. Now kneeling like a bird, arms outward, Sarah pushed up and tried to stand. For the most part, she was successful. Her legs didn't extend all the way, but the pressure was off her knees, and feeling began to course through her arms as they were slightly lower than before.

Vince moved closer, the bowl in his hands giving off a smell of caramelized onions and sautéed mushrooms. When he stopped in front of her, she could only stare at the bowl. A mixed vegetable dish. A stir fry. Her stomach seemed to move upward inside her like it wanted a piece of the dish and wasn't waiting for her slow mouth to acquire and chew the food.

The floor canted the other way, the chains that held her clinking in response.

She met his eyes. He wasn't smiling anymore. He had stopped stirring.

"Peculiar," he said again. "That's what I'd call you." He leaned back, released his right hand from the bowl, and drove a fist into her left cheek.

The blow knocked her off her feet, yanked her left arm to its limit, and she dropped back to her knees. She moaned involuntarily as pain flared in several places. It was the same cheek that was hit the night before.

The helplessness of the situation, the pain, and the humiliation bore a responsibility to hit back. She needed to strike back hard. It wasn't just an expected response but a desired one. It represented who she was and everything she was about.

She spoke around the coppery and bitter blood that pooled in her mouth.

"What drug did you give me?" she asked, hoping it wasn't heroin.

"Shut up." Vince leaned closer to her face. "That's why you're peculiar. You ask questions like you have a right to an answer. You tell me to go fuck myself like you're in charge here. Who the fuck are you, anyway?" Vince dropped to his knees. "You're a stupid little girl who got mixed up with the wrong people. And now you're my prisoner. Then, when this is over, I get to kill you. I get to watch the life leave those pretty little eyes."

He held up the spoon he'd been stirring the vegetables with.

"Here," he said. "Eat some of this. I need you at least walking on your own before the exchange."

She greedily clomped on the end of the spoon and pulled the broccoli and onions into her mouth. There was a new cut on the inside of her cheek and a sore, swollen area on the other cheek, but none of that mattered when compared to her hunger. She barely chewed before she swallowed the food and opened her mouth for more.

The floor tilted several times while Vince fed her. A short moment later and the bowl was empty. She licked her lips like a feline after a tasty meal and eyed him. The urge in her bladder wasn't abating, and nor would it until it got the release it wanted.

She was still dressed in the jeans and T-shirt she wore on the plane from Kelowna. She thought back to Officer Stephen Lee's office in Kelowna. The bomber's mother. The Realtor. It seemed ages ago, and yet it was only yesterday.

Vince picked up the bucket, wavered on his feet, and caught himself as the floor canted to the left, then turned to face her.

"What exchange?" she asked.

"The exchange where we give you back to that martial arts asshole for your other friend."

"My other friend?" She frowned. "Parkman?"

"You're a fuckin' retard. Why would we go to such lengths to grab you at an airport and risk so much just to get our hands on Parkman? Why not take him at the airport instead of you and be done with it?"

She thought about what he was saying. Something nagged at her. Why risk taking her? For her friend? What friend?

Awareness hit her like a strong punch to the gut.

Darwin Kostas.

Vince waited near the door, the bowl in his hands. "Seems to me like you've figured it out."

"What do you want with Darwin?" she asked, her voice calm now that she'd eaten. Even her headache was subsiding.

Vince walked back to stand in front of her. He kicked the bucket at her knees and regarded her with an expressionless face. Not a muscle moved to depict what he was feeling.

"That man, who you call a friend, did considerable damage to the families that run this city a few years back. We've been after him ever since. It's been a long chase. To the bosses, he's not just an enemy; he's our arch-rival or archenemy. No one in our extended family will sleep soundly until he and his wife are dead and buried."

"So, you went after me to bring him out of hiding?"

Vince nodded. "And once he sticks his head out of

hiding, we will do an exchange. You for him. Then you all die. Even your martial arts guy is marked for death. Later today, I burn his gym down. We will kill and destroy all of you until we get to Darwin."

"And you will fail."

He blinked, his pensive face broken by her confidence.

"Peculiar girl. How you talk so tough, yet you're so weak."

"Is it tough to speak the truth?" she asked. "Or is it simply the truth? Which in this case is hard for you to swallow."

He set the bowl on the floor. She waited for his blows, but they didn't come. Instead, he gripped her belt and undid it. Then he unclasped her jeans and lowered the zipper.

"What part of *kill Darwin and all his friends* is this?" she asked.

He met her gaze as his hands gripped the sides of her pants, then shoved them down, underwear and all. Sarah hung from the wrist cuffs with her jeans at her knees, completely exposed to him.

"Kick them off yourself," Vince said as he got to his feet and grabbed the empty bowl. "I'm sure you can manage."

She looked down at her exposed lower half, the bucket beside her, then back at Vince. "That's my toilet?" she asked, controlling her voice to not show an ounce of embarrassment.

He reached the door, his hand already on the knob before he looked back. "It's the bucket, or you go in your pants. Thought you'd want clean pants for the exchange. You don't leave this room until Darwin surfaces which could be days, maybe weeks."

"What if he doesn't surface?"

"You stay with us until he does."

"Where are we? Why does the floor move?" As she asked him, it came to her. "We're on a boat," she said, more to herself.

"Yes, you're on a boat. A cargo ship. We're anchored in Lake Ontario, far enough away from the Toronto shoreline that no one can see us." Vince opened the door, holding the empty bowl pressed to his stomach. He looked down at the small tuft of hair between her legs. "There are at least fifty armed men on this ship." Slowly, his eyes left her private area and rose to her chest, then her face. "No one would try to board us. We have all the proper papers, and according to the Canadians, this American cargo ship is merely awaiting a new manifest. And no one knows you're here." He looked back down at her vagina. "Pray Darwin surfaces fast. Since you will be with us for some time and then killed after the exchange, I would hate to see anything happen to that." He nodded toward her waist, his eyes never leaving it. "You never can tell who on a ship this large might come in the night for a little comfort." He met her eyes. "And with you tied up like that—it's almost an invitation. Who knows, we may have to form a line. You could do ten to twenty men per night." He met her gaze. "And there would be nothing you could do about it but scream. Out here, in the middle of the lake, no one would hear you. And screaming turns some of these guys on."

"Death comes to the man who tries. That man leaves this room a corpse. More truth for you to think on."

His smile flattened as he eased out the door. It closed softly. Then a bolt clicked into place.

Sarah released the air she'd been holding in a torrent. Her

body shivered in an all-over chill, her hair still wet from the water thrown in her face. Vince creeped her out hardcore. Unless they secured her legs, she would break the neck of any man that attempted to touch her. Knowing they wouldn't kill her until they got to Darwin, she would fight for her dignity.

In the meantime, she needed to get her pants low enough to hover over the bucket to pee and then figure a way to get them back up over her waist. Her arms subdued as they were, pants down, was a temptation to almost any man who knew he could get away with whatever he wanted. But that man didn't know Sarah.

Lifting her right foot, grunting with the pain in her arms, she began the arduous task of peeing in the bucket. It was then that she caught sight of the old man standing behind her. She stopped what she was doing and spun around enough to look at him. He wasn't looking at her.

"I thought I heard you earlier," she said. "You want to help me over here?" Entities couldn't help with physical matter. But knowing that wasn't any comfort. "Since you're of no help whatsoever, and all you do is try to comfort me with gestures of everything will be okay, can you leave now? I need to talk to Vivian, and you seem to be blocking that channel."

The man lowered his head, appeared to contemplate something, then hunched his shoulders, turned toward the wall, and walked through it like a mist through a screen door.

Sarah shivered. This extra sight was relatively new to her. Often these entities would appear as living and breathing human flesh to her naked eye. To know they were part of the other side, to know they existed on another plane, was freaky enough as it was. But to watch one disappear through a solid substance was like watching a special effect on a movie screen. CGI in real life.

"Shit, man," she muttered to herself as she fumbled with her jeans, goosebumps on her forearms.

"Vivian?" she called out to the small room as it tilted to one side. "Could use some help here."

The other side remained silent.

Chapter 19

Parkman's phone rang as Casper pulled up to Toronto's outer harbor. Several large ships were docked at the harbor, either unloading cargo or waiting to be loaded.

"Hello?" Parkman answered, not recognizing the number.

"Parkman. It's me, Aaron."

"How's the hand?"

"Better now. All bandaged up. Doctors took the knife out and cleaned things up. Should retain full use of the hand but not for a few months. Any news on Sarah?"

Casper turned off the car and got out. Whitman and Spencer exited the car to offer Parkman privacy.

"We just left a massacre."

"What?" Aaron blurted.

"Seven dead at an Italian restaurant on College Street in Little Italy."

"Restaurant on College Street? What?"

"The dead were four guards, two kitchen staff, and a man named Carmine Fabriano. Heard of him?"

"No."

"Ever heard of Martino Fermosa?"

"No. Why?"

"Marty and his wife Patricia were murdered sometime last night in their home. They're high up in Toronto's mafia chain."

"What the fuck is happening? How does any of that have anything to do with Sarah?"

Parkman watched Casper through the windshield of the car. He had gotten on his phone as well.

"Not sure, exactly. We're down at Toronto Harbor. Casper has intel on a couple of container ships called *The Santa Maria* and *The Carolina*. There might be a connection. A man named Lorenzo Falcone runs this part of town. Casper thinks he's involved somehow." Parkman paused for a moment, then, in a lower voice, said, "We might have an idea of what's going on, and it isn't good."

"Tell me. I'm ready for anything."

"It might involve Darwin."

"Darwin? How? He's one of us. He would never do anything to hurt Sarah."

"Darwin had a run-in with the mafia a few years back. The Blade, a moniker the mafia gave him, floated around for a while. When that ended in the death of dozens of Italian family members in Toronto, didn't Darwin move to Italy?"

"Italy is where Darwin and Rosina met Sarah originally. In Umbria."

"We suspect the bosses here in Toronto never forgot

Darwin and were always looking for him, biding their time. It's almost public knowledge that Sarah and Darwin have worked together."

"What are you saying? They kidnapped Sarah to get to Darwin?"

"That's my suspicion. Casper's too."

"Okay. That's fucked. They don't know who they're dealing with. Darwin will kill every one of them for that if Sarah doesn't first."

"That's what we're worried about. You don't think Darwin started with the Fermosas last night, do you? Could that be his handiwork?"

"You said the wife was killed, too?"

Casper got off his phone, faced Parkman, and waved a hand for him to come.

"Look, Aaron. I have to go. Where can I call you?"

"I had to borrow a phone. My cell died. I'll charge it and get back to you. I want in on this search. Benjamin's all fixed up, but he's heading back to the dojo to oversee renovations there. He doesn't want to put himself in the line of fire for a few weeks. Says he's tired of getting shot."

Parkman cleared his throat to suppress a laugh. "Sorry. Listen, how bad were his injuries?" he asked as he exited the car.

"He just needed stitches. He's up and walking around. It's fine, though. I need someone at the dojo. Daniel, Alex, and I want in with what you're doing. Tell us where to go."

"Take everyone to the dojo. Relax. Grab a bite to eat. Get some rest. As soon as we're done down here, I'll call. We'll meet up later on and brainstorm this."

"I'll wait at the dojo for your call then."

"Give me an hour at least. Possibly two."

"Done."

Parkman ended the call. It felt good to be doing something. To be mobilizing everyone into position. Sarah knew they were coming. It was only a matter of time until they found their way to her.

He followed Casper and the other two as they made their way to the largest ship moored at the dock. *The Santa Maria* stood out in bold letters on the ship's hull. Men milled about the area paying them little attention. It wasn't until they got close to the ship that one man noticed them, whistled loud enough to be heard by others, then dropped what he was doing and started toward them.

"*The Santa Maria*," Spencer whispered. "Lorenzo Falcone's ship. He also owns *The Carolina*." Parkman scanned the docks for another ship of the magnitude of *The Santa Maria* but couldn't see one. "*The Carolina* must have loaded up and left because it was here earlier," Spencer added, evidently thinking the same as Parkman. "This ship is one of several suspected of trafficking cocaine in and out of Toronto."

"Hold up," one of the men from *The Santa Maria* shouted at them, his hand outstretched. Five burly men, one holding a thick wrench, started their way. "You're gonna need a warrant to come any closer," the man said, a confident smile on his face.

"Looking for Lorenzo Falcone," Casper shouted over the wind that had picked up from off the water. "Know where I can find him?"

Seagulls squawked as they flew overhead, and the stench of dead fish wafted up from the sides of the dock.

"Got a warrant?" the man with the wrench asked.

The men stopped with no more than ten feet between them. Parkman moved until he stood beside Casper.

"Don't need a warrant to talk to a man," Parkman said. "We're not here to search anything." He waited a heartbeat, then added, "Yet."

"Never heard of anyone named Falcone." The man gestured back where they had come. "Look somewhere else."

Parkman and Casper didn't move. The ship's men stood watching them. No one broke the silence for at least a dozen seconds. Then Casper raised his hand, a business card at his fingertips.

"Fair enough," Casper said. "Tell Falcone we want to speak to him."

"If we ever heard of such a man, I assure you he would not want to speak to you."

Casper stepped forward. The five men tensed as a unit. "I assure you, Falcone will call me within the hour."

"And why would that be?"

"Because he will hear the news. People will talk. He will learn that Martino Fermosa and his wife Patricia are dead. If there were such a man as Falcone, he would also hear that Carmine Fabriano was decapitated. The only way for Falcone to keep his head is to call me." Casper was now close enough to the man to place the business card in his breast pocket, which he promptly did. "If Lorenzo Falcone wants to stay alive, he'll call. We're his only hope. You lot won't be enough for the man who's coming for him."

Casper started back toward the Ford. Parkman hesitated a moment, then followed behind Whitman and Spencer.

Back inside the car, Parkman asked, "You got new

information on the phone before we talked to those guys?"

Casper nodded, a hand on the steering wheel. He hadn't turned the car on yet. "The bodies have been found at the restaurant. A waiter and a cook showed up. They freaked out and ran down the street, leaving the front door wide open."

"Shit," Whitman said.

"Yeah, shit is right. A Citypulse News van happened by. They were due to interview a new business two doors from the Il Forno. They entered the crime scene, cameras rolling. It's all over the news now."

"What?" Parkman blurted. "They'll ruin that crime scene and jeopardize the investigation."

Casper looked at him sidelong. "Already done. The word hitting the street as we speak is a mafia war has started, and they're blaming the man from years ago."

"No way," Spencer said. "They can't know that fast."

Casper's hand tightened on the steering wheel. "They're saying it's the work of The Blade. He's back to finish what he started."

"That's all fine for Darwin, but what about Sarah? How do we get her back? How is she involved with all this?"

"That's what we'll ask Falcone when he calls." Casper keyed the Ford's engine and reversed out of the lot. "Until we hear from Falcone, I need a coffee and time to think. How about it, guys? You in? Coffee?"

"I need an extra-large," Parkman said. "I still haven't slept since we landed last night—" his phone's ringer cut him off. "One sec, guys."

Casper headed away from the docks as Parkman checked the number. He didn't recognize it.

"Aaron?" he answered. "Everything cool?"

"Not Aaron. It's Darwin."

Chapter 20

Curious George had driven the telephone van toward the lake and found a coffee shop where they could grab a beverage and clean up in the public bathroom. Charlie had two coffees, drinking the first like a refreshing Coke on a hot summer day. He nursed the second cup on the way out to the van.

"Next stop?" George asked from the driver's seat.

Darwin cleaned his blade and placed everything back inside the briefcase in the back of the van. Elmer twisted in the passenger seat to watch the Runner do his meticulous thing with the blade. Once deathly afraid of sharp and pointy things—to the level of irrational fear—Darwin handled them with extreme care and the respect a kayaker had for a class five river.

"We go to the docks," Darwin said.

"Lorenzo Falcone," Charlie added.

George nodded in the front seat. "Right. Then we visit Angelo Spinello. Then that's it."

Elmer turned back in his seat, a large coffee in hand. "That's what the contwact cawwed fow."

"Three men," Darwin said. He clasped the briefcase shut. "Three visits. Then you're out." He lifted his sleeve and read the time on his Tissot. "We should be done with this mission before sundown."

The van lurched forward, then eased into traffic heading south toward the waters of Lake Ontario. Charlie sat with his back to the rear doors, wiping his weapon down.

"Boss," he said under his breath. "Don't you need help tomorrow?" He jerked his head toward the men in the front seat.

"Not sure. Possibly."

"Why not, you ask? Why wait?"

"Track record."

Charlie's skull was bigger than an average man's. When Charlie frowned, his eyebrows dropped and pulled inward. His nose scrunched up, and his large mouth opened slightly. In some respects, it was comical. To an enemy, the image was frightening.

The van bounced over a bump, then jerked to a stop as someone cut George off. He muttered cuss words under his breath.

Darwin settled himself over the wheel well and set the briefcase at his feet. "They are building a track record." He gazed at Charlie. "After the Scarborough hit, when Spinello is gone, I will know then if they should help tomorrow. I have to count on them."

"And you think you can?"

"So far, yes, I *can* count on them. But I would hate to garner their commitment, and then they pussy out on the next job. Tomorrow is too important. I have a lot riding on it."

Charlie turned to look at Darwin. "If you don't commit them, it would be you and me."

Darwin glanced at his hands, then the briefcase. "I'm sure we'll manage." He met Charlie's gaze again. "You would never let me down."

"No, boss. Never."

Five minutes later, George turned the van to the right and stopped. Darwin had to grab the side to avoid falling off the wheel well.

"We've got company," George said. "You're not going to believe it."

"What?" Darwin asked.

"The guys from the restaurant."

"How couwd they get hewe so fast?" Elmer asked.

Darwin stared at the floor of the van for a moment, thoughts racing through his head. Could Parkman or Casper have a lead on him? Could they know his plans? Darwin faced Charlie's quizzical stare. He had to be thinking the same thing.

Darwin crawled forward and stared out the windshield at Parkman, Casper, Whitman, and Spencer as they talked to a group of dock workers.

"Shit," he muttered to himself. "How? Where are they getting their information?"

He retrieved his cell phone and sent an encrypted text to his wife, Rosina, explaining the situation. Could she discover what they know? How were they able to beat them to the next stop? Should he expect Casper and his team at the

Diavolo Club later?

"They're leaving, boss," Charlie said behind him.

He watched them head toward a Ford in the parking lot, then looked down at his phone and waited until they were leaving before he dialed Parkman.

Parkman answered right away. "Aaron? Everything cool?"

"Not Aaron. It's Darwin."

"Darwin?" Parkman said. "Where are you?"

"Looking for me?"

"No, no. Not that. Just, are you close? Sarah's been abducted."

"I know. I'm working on it."

Parkman paused for a moment. Through the phone, he listened as the sound of the car's engine slowed. Darwin watched the Ford's brake lights flare on, and then the vehicle stopped. "Working on it?" Parkman's door opened, and he got out of the car. He scanned the parking lot. "How?"

"I know who's taken Sarah. I know why they've taken Sarah. I'm the only one who can save her and stop this madness. You guys need to back off."

Even though Parkman was on the phone, Darwin watched as his hand gestured while he talked. "Whoa, Darwin. We can't back off. This is Sarah we're talking about. I want her found safe just as much as you."

"There's a difference."

"Yeah, what's that?" Parkman appeared to be staring right at the van.

George brought his palms up, facing out in a what-do-I-do gesture. Darwin motioned for him to keep the van where it was.

"They don't want Sarah."

"Then why do they have her—" Parkman placed a hand on his forehead. "They want you."

"And I'm going to give them me. But I have to make them angry first. I have to make them want to trade and feel they are out of options for that trade to be successful."

"So, you killed Fabriano at the restaurant." It wasn't a question.

Darwin pressed the phone into his ear, contemplating his words carefully. "I understand he had an accident."

"Unfortunate, yes."

Casper had exited the car and was walking around the front to stand beside Parkman.

"Where are you guys headed next?" Darwin asked. "Sarah's life will depend on your answer."

"If I didn't know you better," Parkman whispered into the phone. "That sounded like a threat. Then I'd start to think you were in on it somehow."

"I wasn't in on it, Parkman. But I'm responsible."

"Responsible?" Parkman asked as Whitman and Spencer surrounded him.

Darwin turned his attention to the men on the docks by a large container ship. From the van, he could make out the name: *The Santa Maria*. Several men had wandered out to watch Parkman talk on the phone.

"Yes. Responsible. This wouldn't have happened if I hadn't met Sarah. Or if these men didn't have such a hard-on for me."

"You can't own that. They did this. It's on them."

"But I have to own it. And I will end the mafia's reign in Toronto before I'm done with them."

"Rue the day and all that bravado shit." Parkman pulled the phone away from his ear, cupped it with his other hand, and then spoke to Casper. A second later, the phone was back at his ear. "Look, Darwin, come in. Talk to us. Tell us what you need. We can coordinate. We can help each other."

"If I told you I'd meet you downtown at the police station, would you go there and wait for me all day?"

"What are you asking?"

"I have something to do that'll bring Sarah home. I can't do it with friends close by." It was his turn to pull the phone away and cup it with his other hand. "Not you guys," he whispered to the three men in the van with him, then brought the phone to his ear again. "Someone could get hurt. Listen, Parkman, just go downtown. Wait for me. Keep your phone on. Let me bring Sarah home my way. It's the only way. By the looks of things at the docks, you guys aren't doing so hot today."

Parkman stared at the van again. He seemed to be thinking about Darwin's proposal. Then he said, "I can't make any promises." He moved away from the men behind him. "I trust you, Darwin. You've been a big part of Sarah's life, as I have. Which means I want in this fight as much as you do. Think what you're asking of me."

"I know what I'm asking. You are in this fight. I need you for the exchange. Sarah will need you when they give her back."

"And what makes you so sure they'll just give her back? They went to great lengths and risks to snatch her."

"Because they want me, not Sarah. She's bait on a hook. They took her because they knew I'd come for her. And they're right. But they don't know exactly what's coming."

"I can't let you do that—"

"Parkman. Just stall your men. I need three hours. Scratch that—Sarah needs three hours."

"One last question."

Darwin waited.

"Was that you last night at the Fermosas?"

"No."

Darwin pushed the end button. He tapped George on the shoulder.

"Reverse out of here. Then take us to Kingston Road in Scarborough. We need to visit the Diavolo Club. Maybe Spinello will be there. If not, I'm sure his truck will be. Let's move."

He watched Parkman and Casper as they talked. Several men from *The Santa Maria* started to make their way toward Casper's car. No one watched the retreating telephone van.

The men on the boat had no idea most of them would be dead within days. It was a comforting thought as Darwin leaned back against the interior wall of the van and began cleaning his gun.

He would reach out that night. The exchange could happen at dusk tomorrow. Sarah had better be alive and well, or every member of the mafia and their families and extended families in Toronto, Hamilton, and Montreal would be murdered by the end of the year. Darwin would see to it personally if it was the last thing he did.

Mass murder seemed to be the only answer when rooting out cockroaches.

Chapter 21

AARON RESTED HIS HEAD back as the traffic thickened and stopped over Yonge Street. Daniel had taken the Gardiner Expressway, an elevated highway slicing along the lower half of Toronto with concrete slabs, which meant they were parked above Yonge Street, bumper to bumper. Benjamin sat beside him, staring out the window, lost in thought. Alex took the front passenger seat. Talk was light, chit-chat nonexistent. Sarah was still gone, and they let it happen. The four of them had been responsible for her. Sure, they put up a good fight, but she was gone, nonetheless. They all owned her abduction to a level where it would appear they actually felt there was a degree of culpability. Aaron couldn't reason or argue them out of it. The group had been through crazy times in the past. They'd traveled to Greece to save Aaron's life once. They'd been shot, stabbed, and a cartel had taken Aaron's finger for Sarah. But now, some unknown assailant had Sarah, and the four of them were stuck in traffic.

Aaron closed his eyes and counted his breaths. One, inhale, two, exhale. Calm breathing. Think. Find a solution. Wait for Parkman to call back. Then, take action.

The world had gone insane. Nothing seemed to make sense anymore.

Traffic moved. The car edged forward. Aaron sat up, using his good hand on the door handle to watch through the windshield.

It would work out. It always did. Sarah had gotten herself out of worse scenarios.

Daniel cut into the far right lane, which seemed to be moving faster than the others. It was the one that left the Gardiner and dropped onto Lakeshore Road, which got them to Leslie Street. Two blocks from there, the new dojo was almost ready. Aaron had rented an old salsa dance studio. The owners had moved to a larger location and needed someone to sublet the place with an option to sign a new lease when the current one expired. Aaron jumped at the chance as the renovations were minor and something the four could handle independently. Students had called asking when the new place would be open.

Daniel got them onto Lakeshore Road and finely barreling toward Leslie. Minutes later, he parked behind the new dojo on Queen Street, near the intersection with Leslie.

"You guys want to take the rest of the day off," Aaron said, a statement more than a question. "There's no point in trying to get any work done right now. I'm waiting for a call back from Parkman. Once he knows more, we'll know more."

No one tried to leave the car. It was Daniel who turned

back to him first.

"We're all sorry, Aaron. It shouldn't have gone down like that."

Emotion welled up in him. He breathed in, gathered himself, then let the air out with a shake of his head.

"As much as your compassion moves me, this isn't anyone's fault. Those guys had plans we couldn't account for. They came more prepared. That's all. We'll find her. We got this."

Daniel nodded slightly. Benjamin nodded, too. Aaron couldn't see Alex in the front seat. He sat slumped down.

"We just want you to know we're there for you," Benjamin added.

"I've never doubted your commitment, guys. Never."

Alex used his shoulder to smash open the door. He flew from his seat and darted around the front of the car. Daniel and Benjamin opened their doors simultaneously.

"What the fuck?" Benjamin whispered under his breath.

Alex stopped at the back door of the dojo. He ran his hands along the seam, then along the top. After quickly inspecting his fingers, he dropped to the ground and tried to look under the door.

Aaron hopped out of the car, leaving his door open, and scurried over to Alex.

"What's up?" he asked, his voice low.

Alex didn't say a word. He pointed at fingerprints on the door a couple of inches above the knob.

"New," he whispered back.

Then he pointed at the lock. A small black piece of hard plastic or metal stuck out of the lock.

"What the fuck is that?" Aaron asked.

He almost touched it, but Alex smacked his hand away, then gestured outward and made a small air burst with his mouth.

Explosion.

Aaron's mouth dropped open. Someone had rigged the dojo to blow. Alex stepped away, staying close to the wall. He glanced over his shoulder as if he alone could hear something no one else could, blinked twice, then waved for the three of them to follow. A second later, he was running toward Leslie Street.

Aaron saw Alex's run as desperation and jolted into action, chasing after him. His bandaged hand ached as he pumped his arms to keep up, the fear of an explosion about to happen behind him. A glance over his shoulder assured him that Daniel had Benjamin. They weren't following Aaron, just moving the other way down the alley at a quick trot, putting distance between themselves and the building.

Alex rounded the corner, and Aaron followed, the throbbing in his hand increasing. On Queen Street, Alex turned again and headed for the front of the dojo. Aaron continued on his tail, feelings of sadness and remorse that he might lose this dojo, too. It wasn't even ready for students yet, and someone wanted to destroy it. Maybe that was a sign he wasn't cut out for this business. In the past several months, he'd tied up most of his savings, keeping his teachers in the black and paying for the renovations. If he lost this dojo, too, they might have to go get regular jobs, which was something he didn't want to think about.

Alex stopped at the dojo's front window. He eased around the lip of the sill and peeked inside. Aaron caught up, keeping his wounded hand above his heart at eye level, and peered inside, too. Nothing looked amiss. Not a single tool or work ladder had been moved. Even the small stereo they used with their iPhones for music while working sat untouched. The walls adjoining the comic book store to the left were bare where they had plans to replace the drywall due to mold. If Aaron didn't have Alex, he would've walked inside the dojo completely unaware.

Alex moved to the front door. He ran his fingers around the frame like he did at the backdoor. When he turned to Aaron, their eyes locked. He offered Aaron a subtle shake of his head. The place was wired to blow.

"Shit," Aaron muttered, his bandaged hand slightly above his shoulder, like he was waving a white flag. As that image entered his mind, he wondered if that was what he was doing. Throwing in the towel. One of these days, someone close to him, or he, would be killed. The way things were going, it was only a matter of time.

Alex grabbed his arm and led him to the front of the comic book outlet next door to the dojo. He released Aaron's arm, cracked his knuckles, and bobbed his head left and right to loosen his neck.

"We need to get inside," Alex said.

"No way. And blow the place up. Forget it."

"We need to go inside and appear at the windows. They're watching us right now."

Aaron started to look, but Alex's hand shot out and latched onto his jaw.

"Don't fucking look around," Alex said, barely moving his lips. "Two men in a BMW. Watching us. Several cars back." Alex moved back a few feet. "Call Daniel. Tell him to clear the hairdressers on that side of the dojo. Get everyone out of the building. Tell him they must use the back door. We'll clear this place."

"How are we getting inside the dojo?" Aaron asked as he retrieved his cell phone from his pocket. He leaned close to Alex and whispered, "They've rigged each access door to blow."

"I've got a plan. Call Daniel. Then meet me in here."

Alex disappeared inside the comic book store as Aaron dialed Daniel's cell. He didn't have to wait long for his friend to pick up the phone.

"Yeah," Daniel said, his voice broken from breathing hard. "What's going on? What's got Alex so spooked?"

Aaron faced the front display window of the comic book store. He used the reflection to scan the parked cars behind him. Moving from one empty car to the next, he turned slowly, waiting until his eyes lighted upon a vehicle with someone inside. The afternoon sun shone on the hood of a car over his left shoulder that appeared to have two people inside. Nothing more than a silhouette of their heads was discernible. They were definitely watching him, though. He could feel it on the back of his neck.

He let his gaze fall on the display inches from him. A *Superman DC Universe Rebirth, Son of Superman collector's edition,* was on display for just over twenty bucks. Also wrapped in plastic was a *Batman, I Am Gotham Volume One* for sixty bucks. These are just two of the hundreds of comic books that could be destroyed because someone wanted to blow up an empty store under renovation.

They didn't care about the building. They wanted to kill Aaron and anyone else with him. For what? To send a message? Something to hurt Sarah? Or Darwin?

How could murder be so easy for them?

"Aaron?" Daniel said, his breathing mostly back under control. "You still there?"

"Yeah, sorry. Listen, I need you to go to Salon One Hairstylists and get everyone outside and away from the building. You have to use their back door, though. The front's being watched. Two men in a BMW parked on the north side of Queen Street."

"Fuck." Daniel slammed something metallic on his end of the phone. "What's next, man?"

"I'm pissed, too. Listen, Alex has a plan. We do this, then end this shit forever."

"Okay, Benjamin's safe. I'll go to the salon now."

"Bring Benjamin."

"What?" Daniel nearly shouted into the phone. "Why? We're across the street and down a block. Hard work for a bandaged leg."

"We need him inside the building when it blows. The BMW guys need to think they got all of us."

"Now you're talking crazy shit. He won't like that." There was a pause. Then, "Wait a second, *I* don't like that."

"It's the only way. We have a plan. You'll be fine. Just empty the hairdresser's place and come on inside the comic book store using the back door." Alex popped his head out and waved for Aaron to come. "Gotta go. Meet us inside the comic book store two minutes ago."

He hung up and slipped the phone away, then followed Alex inside, hoping that when this was over, he'd survive the explosion and see Sarah again.

Would she ever forgive him for letting her get taken?

Chapter 22

A DIM LIGHT IN the corner of the steel room did nothing for her. It didn't offer comfort, warmth, or nourishment. No one had returned to feed her in however many hours she'd been shackled to the walls. The flop of her dry tongue reminded her of days when she drank too much whiskey—a morning after several whiskey shots could produce similar symptoms. The dry cottonmouth-like feeling that yearned for water to quench its desire. Cool, moist, cleansing water. The reason it was called a refreshment.

Sarah eased to her left, relieving pressure on that arm and applying pressure to the other. As much as exercise was important to keep her muscles ready for whatever was coming, the limited movement due to the restraints, the extension of her arms like she was trying to fly, exerted them, and inflamed her shoulders. Her hands had grown numb hours before and were now asleep. The feeling had disappeared from her fingertips, but she could still move them slightly.

She eased back to the right, keeping one leg up and the other down. She found swaying with the movement of the boat easier. The hunger pains in her stomach had subsided some. It was thirst that took over, making her crave bottled water. She'd be grateful if only her captors would produce a small serving of water.

The light in the room brightened. She raised her head and glanced around. The male entity from before had returned. He watched her with heavy eyes, which seemed weighed down with worry.

"What?" she asked. "What's got you looking so glum?"

She tilted her head as she moved position again, watching the man through half-lidded eyes.

The man twirled his hands in circles at shoulder height. He cupped the back of his right ear as if he was listening to something, then twirled his hands again.

"What the hell are you doing? I don't hear anything."

He did it again, this time cupping the other ear.

"A siren?" she asked. "You think you hear a siren?"

He stopped what he was doing, lowered his hands, then nodded.

"Why can you hear me, but I can't hear you?" Sarah stared up at the ceiling. "Hey Vivian, you getting any of this? 'Cause I sure would like to hear directly from you again. This riddle shit is irritating."

The man fell back into his routine. He made circular motions with his fingers, cupped his ears simultaneously, and then went back to twirling again.

"Who knew my life would be reduced to playing high-stakes charades with a dead man?" she asked out loud. "Are you telling me the police are coming?"

The man shook his head.

"Fire truck?"

He kept spinning his hands, mouth wide now like he was making the sound of a siren.

"Is it an ambulance you're referring to?"

The man stopped moving. He lowered his hands and backed away until he got to the stained wall. A moment later, he melted into the steel and disappeared. The wall became solid again, his shimmering image gone beyond it.

She barely had time to lower herself and close her eyes before the bolt in the door clicked and opened slightly. Whoever stood behind it peeked inside, then opened the door wider.

The man from the back seat of the SUV at the airport stepped inside her prison cell. It was the same man who had shot at her friends and stabbed Aaron's hand. At no more than five and a half feet, he seemed less formidable than his partner, Vince. He eased the door back, leaving it slightly ajar.

"Sarah, right?"

She stood and eased the restraints to their limits. The man was carrying a tin foil container with what looked like penne pasta in tomato sauce. Under his arm was a bottle of water.

He must've caught the hunger in her gaze because he set the water down in the far corner and laughed under his breath.

"This isn't for you, baby doll." He held up the pasta. "This is my lunch."

She glared at him. "Who would've thought that an innocent lunch could lead to murder. News at eleven."

He laughed again as he pulled the door open, retrieved a wooden chair from the corridor outside her dank prison, placed it a few feet in front of her, and then slammed the door shut. She made a mental note that he didn't lock the door.

"What's your name?" she asked. "Or should I call you what I want? I've got several ideas for names that'll suit you just fine floating around in my head."

"I'm sure you do. Call me Vito." He plopped down on the chair. "Everyone calls me Vito 'The Pun' Romano."

"Is that because you're punny, so to speak?"

Vito eased a fork from his jacket pocket and stirred the pasta. "That's exactly why they call me that." He took a large bite.

The smell overwhelmed her. She had to resist the urge to moan as he chewed the pasta. A display of weakness at this point only emboldened these kinds of people. She planted her feet firmly and stayed standing despite noticing a slight shake in her legs.

"Why are you here?" she asked.

His gaze fell on her jeans where the clasp wasn't done up. After urinating in the bucket at her feet when Vince left, she'd still had the strength to swing sideways and get her pants up to her hips using her hands, but the zipper and clasp had remained undone.

Vito took another bite of pasta and then set the container on the floor. He rose from the chair and produced a key from his pocket.

"I'm here to show you this," he said, his mouth still full

of food, a piece of tomato stuck between his front teeth. He used his tongue to swipe it away.

Could she faint from lack of food as the smell of the tomato sauce wafted toward her? If she were to find a way to kill Vito, could she reach the leftover pasta?

He moved closer. Her hunger raised emotions in her. Anger surfaced. How dare they starve her? For what purpose? To keep her weak? Docile?

Well, fuck that.

"This key unlocks those wrist restraints," Vito said.

His voice brought her back to the room. She studied his face. A short man who exuded a certain level of violence. She could feel that violence oozing off him.

Vito dropped the key into his front pocket. Before he got too close to her, he retreated and dropped back onto the chair, where he grabbed the container of pasta and began eating again.

"You know," he said between bites, "small minds are like concrete. They're all mixed up and permanently set."

"Is that one of your stupid puns?"

"You wanna hear a pun?" he asked, his face reflecting a child's excitement. "I've got dozens. Like, where does the white go when snow melts?"

"That's not a pun. That's just a dumb question."

"Wow, tough crowd tonight."

"Vito?"

He looked up, about to consume his last bite. "What?"

"Why are you here? I mean, really, why are you here?"

"Someone has to check in on you." He set the mostly empty container on the floor by the chair's leg and sat up straight. "Thought it'd best be me, as Vince is back in

Toronto at your boyfriend's martial arts gym."

Sarah didn't raise her head at the mention of Aaron. Only her eyes moved. She watched him, looked into his eyes, glaring at his smirk to see if he was telling the truth. It was in a moment like this when she missed Vivian. If only her sister would return and tell her what to do. It was so much better before the Denmark incident.

"What is he …" she swallowed. Harder than she intended to. "Doing there?"

"Kaboom!" Vito shouted.

Sarah jolted like she'd been hit, pain rippling up her arms and into her shoulders. A desperation overcame her. Locked away, she was too helpless. She needed to be out there, fighting, helping her friends stay alive.

She shook her head to clear it. Fatigue and a slight throbbing pain had weakened her body. Even if he let her go —which he wouldn't—could she get off the ship in her condition? Could she commandeer another vessel and get back to Toronto? How far out were they? She was helpless and knew it, which was one of the worst feelings she could ever possibly be expected to endure.

"Once Aaron and his stupid teachers are dead, we'll be in a better position to negotiate your release. An exchange. You for Darwin."

"You're wrong," Sarah said through a tight jaw. "It'll only make Darwin and his people more dangerous to the likes of you."

"Darwin more dangerous?" Vito mimicked her words in a feminine tone. "I highly doubt that." He got up and strode to her. "We leave messages for people, too." He came within an inch of her face. "We hurt who needs hurting, and that message is received." He leaned in another inch. She didn't flinch or pull away. The smell of the pasta on his breath was enticing, if only for a moment. "Aaron is nothing to us. His only use is in dying. Once he's dead, he no longer poses any threat. That shit he pulled off at the airport—well, let's just say he deserves what's coming to him." Vito jerked his head toward her. Their lips touched. He shot his tongue inside her mouth, their teeth connecting hard. Then he retreated and stepped back before she had a chance to clamp down on his tongue.

In the interest of getting him to do that again, she didn't spit his saliva out. She swallowed it without a grimace.

"I liked that," he said, wiping his lips. "We've got time." He checked his watch. "Several hours, really. You seem tied up at the moment. Maybe we should do a little more of that." He pointed at her open pants. "You also seem a little willing, leaving your jeans open like that." He met her eyes. "Inviting."

"Couldn't do them up." She tried to shrug, but the pain stopped her. "You know. Hands are busy."

"You know, in a nudist camp, men and women freely air their differences."

"That's not funny. Do you ever find that your humor annoys people?"

"The first day in the nudist colony is always the hardest." He didn't take his eyes off her. After a moment, he undid the top button of his shirt.

"Have you ever taken these to a convention? There's got to be a convention called Stupid Things People Say."

"Did you know the word listen has the same letters as the word silent?" He was on the fourth button. "I need to stop questioning myself. Right?"

His shirt unbuttoned, he eased it off his shoulders and set it on the wooden chair. Her mind raced through possibilities. One thing kept coming to her. Just one idea, but it was the one she detested the most.

"You know," Vito said. "I once told my doctor that I broke my leg in two places. He told me to stop going to those two places." He chuckled under his breath and shook his head back and forth a few times. "I kill myself." When he turned to face her, he unzipped his pants and reached inside to fondle himself.

She eased her foot to the left until it bumped the bucket holding her urine. She was ready for when he came for her. Her energy level had been boosted by adrenaline. Now that she had a plan and Aaron's life was at risk, she knew she could do what needed to be done. A glance up at her hands confirmed it was no use to her. She would have to do everything with her feet.

"Come closer," she whispered.

Vito moved closer, his right hand still rolling around inside his pants. He stopped two feet from her.

"When I take your pants off," he said. "I will enter you from behind. You will not fight me. If you do, there will be no trade with Darwin. We will let him think you're alive, but you won't be. Understood?"

Sarah nodded, preferring to keep her mouth closed in case she said something that would change his mind. She needed him closer.

"I'm going to approach you now to remove your pants. No bullshit, or I'll knock you out and fuck you anyway."

"What about kissing?" she asked. She needed him in

front of her. "We should at least do that, too."

He seemed to think about it for all of two seconds, then shook his head. "No. This is for my pleasure only. You're serving a purpose. That's it." He stepped closer, his hands extended. She prepared herself for what she had to do. "Now, let me take these pants off you."

A phone rang somewhere in the room. Vito stepped back and walked to the chair. Sarah breathed in and out, the adrenaline pumping fire into her veins. So close. She almost had him. So close.

"What?" Vito said into the phone. "Really." He glanced at Sarah. "They're all inside now?" He nodded as if the caller could see him, then he cupped the end of the phone and said to her, "Aaron and his three teachers are inside the gym. Vince wanted me to know they had twenty seconds to live." He uncovered the phone and nodded again. "Good. Do it. Call me when you're coming back to the ship." He paused. "What? Oh, I'm in the cafeteria. No, no, Sarah's fine. I checked in on her an hour ago." He held a finger to his lips for her to be quiet. She knew she'd never get out of this room by shouting to Vince for help. "Fine. Do it. See you when you get back." Vito hung up the phone.

"Looks like Aaron's gone." Vito set the phone on the chair. "Now this is a mercy fuck." He laughed. It came out as a whiny snort. "Or a sorry-for-your-loss fuck."

Even though she couldn't see or feel her hands, they tightened into fists. Vivian would never allow this travesty. After all they'd been through, how could she let this go on? How could Aaron, Alex, Daniel, and Benjamin be killed like that? For what? So that they could get to Darwin? Nothing made sense. The only thing she had to work with was her wits. The here and now. That was all, and that was what she would make damn good use of. Because she would fight until the day she died. And if Aaron and the rest of them were seriously gone, she would never stop killing Vito and his people until they killed her. Never.

Vito advanced, his hand back in his pants. A foot from her, his penis now extended and sticking out the zipper of his pants, he grabbed each side of her jeans and yanked downward.

As he stood back up, Sarah shot her head forward, bringing her forehead down on the top of Vito's nose with a sickening finality, the cartilage by the bridge of his nose breaking upon impact. She lurched back before he fell away from her and hopped off the floor to wrap her legs around his waist. He was close enough that her feet could lock together behind him.

He wailed as blood shot from his ruined nose. Like a spigot, the blood poured out and onto Sarah's stomach as she increased pressure on his waist. He pummeled her abdomen with his fists, but her tightened stomach muscles barely registered the blows. Driven by hunger and pain, driven by an absolute fury at what these people were doing to her and the people she loved, she tightened her scissor hold on Vito, her shoulders and wrists screaming in protest as she hung by her arms.

Vito's diaphragm was cut off, his ability to breathe severely limited, Vito's mouth gaped like a landed fish, and his arms grew weak at his sides. The blood from his shattered nose didn't slow, though. As she tightened to her limit, she watched his face. Blood had oozed into the corner of his eyes as his sclera turned red due to pressure building in his head.

Unable to breathe, lacking the energy to fight back, Vito looked about to succumb to her assault.

She noticed his right hand reaching behind him. He had to be going for something in his pocket. No amount of abdominal pressure would convince that hand to lie still.

She jerked him bodily toward her and drove her forehead into his face again. This time, she connected with the side of his cheek with the brow over her right eye.

His hand wasn't visible.

She jerked him in close again, using her only weapon, her forehead. After three consecutive hits, two in the ruined nose and one high on his cheekbone, Vito's eyes rolled back in his head.

At the second she was about to let him drop to the floor, he shuddered and opened his eyes again, seemingly alert.

Fighting for her life, a wildness came over her. A madness crept in. A place where sanity often couldn't be found. She sunk deep into this place, pulled from it, and yanked the enemy closer for one more vital injury.

Up close, she opened her mouth, clamped onto the tip of his nose, and bit down with a grunt. A piece came off and rolled around in her mouth. She spat it out and released Vito. He crumpled to the floor, his face a mess of blood and tissue. She stepped on his chest to keep him close. One swift kick would be all she needed to knock him back out if he tried to come to.

Without checking a mirror, Sarah was sure she didn't look much better. Her forehead throbbed, and blood would be pooled everywhere from hitting him so often, especially around her mouth from when she bit off the tip of his nose.

Her head spun momentarily, partly from lack of food but

also from the massive adrenaline rush and the constant panting.

She stepped on his waist and, with a quick shove, jammed his penis back inside his pants. As trivial as that one action was, she didn't want to attempt to extract the key from his pocket while that thing bounced around an inch from her toes.

Feeling gently for the key, she tried to nudge it to the pocket's opening. Even after getting the key, she dreaded what was involved in getting the key into the cuffs while both hands were suspended outward. With her hands numb and asleep, she wondered how she'd be able to use them.

Aaron had taught her to fight. He'd taught her how to fight in close quarters. What he didn't teach her was how to extract a key from someone's pocket using her toes.

It took her a frustrating minute to get the tip of the key stuck out. She then carefully clamped the end of the key between her big toe and the second toe and eased it out the rest of the way.

"There," she whispered to herself. "Got you, you bastard."

Vito stirred on the floor beside her. The blood leaving his face had slowed somewhat, but it still came.

The final test was upon her. Could she swing up and drop the key into her left hand? Would the right side of her body be able to sustain the weight and pressure needed to contort upward and sideways? She would need to suspend in the air horizontally for a quick moment, all her weight on that shoulder, that one wrist.

She tightened her toe's grip on the key, breathed in and out a couple of times, willing herself to endure the pain that was coming, and got prepared mentally. One shot was all she needed. Drop the key into her hand, insert it blindly into the lock, and turn it. With the left wrist unlocked, drop to the floor and walk to the right wrist restraint. She would drink the water bottle Vito had left in the corner, then leave the room and, ultimately, the boat. She could do it. If anyone could, she could.

One more breath. Then another.

Vito's phone rang. He stirred.

Sarah eased herself upward and to the left, then pushed off with her feet to suspend completely on the restraints, her wrists and shoulders feeling like she was being drawn and quartered.

A moan that slowly escalated into a cry of pain escaped her lips. She aimed and missed. Jumped again, her left hand open and scrambling for the key, but her foot couldn't get close enough. Could she dislocate her shoulder? Would it simply pop out of place?

Vito stirred below her again, with sounds like he was rousing. She jumped again but missed. Vito mumbled something. She shouted and tried again, this time getting much closer to her open palm. One more hop, putting an extra twist in her hips, and her foot hovered over her open left hand for the briefest of seconds. She spread her toes and fell back to the floor, the key gone.

She didn't feel it land in her palm.

Vito moaned something, his voice nasally.

"What?" she shouted at him. "Ahhh, fuck."

The exertion was too much, the pain in her right shoulder overwhelming. What strength she had was limited and running out. She placed a foot on Vito's throat.

"Don't." She leaned over to look down at him. "Say." She breathed in and out, hoping to quell the pain. "A fucking." She inhaled. "Word." A small amount of weight applied to his throat was enough to convince him to stay quiet. He spit blood out of his mouth. It rolled down the side of his cheek and disappeared in his ear.

The key. Where was it? She didn't hear it drop. She didn't feel it fall into her hand. Sarah searched the floor in a panic under her wrist. Did Vito see it fall and grab it?

"Where's the key?" she asked him.

He moaned and tried to roll away. She pushed down on his throat until his mouth opened and his tongue extended. He tried to look up at her, but she shoved her foot under his chin to keep his face pointed away.

When she tightened her hands into fists, something was in her left hand. She gasped in surprise and would have collapsed if she wasn't tied to the wall as she glimpsed the key safely in her left hand. She hadn't felt it land there because of how numb her hand was.

Applying her weight to the left, she turned the key in her fingers slowly and began the task of trying to insert it into the lock blind. The keyway was aimed toward the wall. She had no idea whether the ridges would be aimed upward or downward.

There was nothing else she could do but poke at the lock until, by a stroke of luck, the key slid home. She had subdued the enemy and stolen the key. She had gotten it miraculously into her hand. A quick turn, and she would be free. One more agonizing minute or one more hour.

Sarah lifted her foot off Vito's neck and turned her gaze on him. He wasn't moving. The blood coming from his nose had stopped. His eyes were open, but he wasn't seeing anything. She had kept her foot on his throat while she attempted the key insertion. Without realizing it, she'd leaned too far to the left and stood on his throat too long. Vito was dead.

"Fuck you, asshole." She spat on him. "You had it coming."

Bolstered by his death and the chance to escape, Sarah turned her attention to getting the key inside the lock. Tap, tap, tap. The tip of the key met resistance over and over. Deftly, she turned the key over in her hand and started again. Tap, tap, tap, breathing in and out, trying to stay calm as she was bound, suspended over a corpse.

Something gave way. The key went farther than previous attempts. She held her breath and applied pressure to the key. It slid in farther still. She raised her eyes upward, waited a heartbeat, then turned the key.

Something clicked.

The restraint snapped open, and her left wrist popped free. She fell to the floor, all the weight on her right shoulder dragging her toward that restraint as she dropped. Nothing short of being shot several times in the rotator cuff could equate to the pain that roared in her arm as the muscles stretched to their limits.

Wasting no time, she pushed herself up, kicked the cuff toward her, retrieved the key from the lock, then spun on the other restraint and unlocked it.

She was free, a dead captor at her feet.

Things were looking up.

She did up her pants first, then pounced on the water bottle in the corner. After drinking most of it, she used the last of it to wipe the blood from her face. A bump had risen on her forehead. She touched the tender spot without wincing.

Tingling sensations coursed through her arms and hands as things began to wake up.

She needed weapons. She needed off the ship. But first, she needed to warn Vince to leave Aaron out of this if it wasn't too late.

With Vito's phone in her hand, she dialed the last number that called Vito. Vince answered on the first ring.

"What do you need?" Vince asked, the wind from a lowered car window buffeting the speaker on the phone. "I'll be back in an hour or so. We're following our next target now. Looks like they're headed to the police station."

His job in Toronto was done. He was coming back to the ship. Could that mean Aaron was gone? His teachers were gone? The future dojo nothing but a memory? These men had kidnapped her and killed her friends. And for what? So they could get to Darwin? She couldn't fathom or compute the gravity of what was going on. All that rose inside was seething anger with no shutoff valve. Killing Vito didn't ease her or calm her. His death was only the start.

She gripped the phone tight. "I'm coming for you, Vincenzo," she said into the mouthpiece, her voice harsh, filled with malice. "You will die at my hands just as Vito did."

She pulled the phone away from her ear as she ended the call, the distant sound of Vince calling her name.

This would all be over soon, but before it ended, there would be a pile of bodies to clean up.

It seemed there was no other way to deal with people like

Vince and Vito or the men they worked for. Violence was the answer. After what they did to Aaron, she was fine with that.

She searched Vito's body for a weapon and came up with a knife similar to the one he'd stabbed Aaron with.

Armed with the knife and Vito's cell phone, Sarah edged into the corridor and started aft toward escape, toward freedom.

But most importantly, toward her destiny.

This was going to end, but it wasn't going to end well for them.

Chapter 23

AARON ENTERED THE COMIC book store. It was empty, the back door wide open to the alley. He caught up to Alex, who was shoving a display rack filled with pre-owned comics aside.

"Daniel's emptying the salon next door," he said, "then meeting us here. What's the plan?"

Alex pointed at the wall.

Aaron glanced at the wall, then back at Alex. "What? It's the adjoining wall to our dojo—" He stopped as he understood. On the other side of the thin partition between stores, the drywall in his soon-to-be-destroyed dojo had been stripped during renovations. A swift kick would give them access to their unit. "Shit, without motion detectors, anyone could've broken in this way."

Alex nodded, a knowing smile playing across his lips. With his knuckles, he tapped the wall several times in search of studs placed every eighteen inches. Aaron watched as Alex used his knuckle to mark the exact center between the two by fours. With several fast jabs, Alex dented the drywall on the comic book store side in a circular fashion. Then he moved away from the wall and motioned Aaron to do the same. Once in position, Alex took two quick steps toward the wall, jumped sideways with both feet extended, and kicked outward. A large hole opened, and Alex promptly disappeared into the next store.

"Hey," Aaron said as he ran to the hole. He stuck his head through and looked down at Alex on the floor. "Don't do that Jackie Chan stuff when the place is wired to blow." Alex sat up, brushing the drywall dust off his arms. Then he was on his feet and running toward the back. "Hey," Aaron called after him. "Relax until Daniel and Benjamin get here." But Aaron knew his warnings fell on deaf ears. Alex had his own way of processing the world—and gravity.

Aaron returned to the comic book store and peeked through a sale rack. The BMW was still out front. From his limited view, the passenger appeared on a cell phone.

He headed for the rear of the store. Before he got to the door, Daniel barged in with Benjamin, supported by his good leg.

"The salon is empty," Daniel said between breaths. "Where's Alex?"

Aaron pointed at the hole in the wall. "In there."

"In that hole?" Benjamin sputtered, out of breath from all the running. "What's he doing in there?"

Aaron shrugged. "He's got a plan to make the guys watching the place think we're dead."

"What plan?" Benjamin's voice let out a squeak. "I

sincerely hope it has nothing to do with guns."

"No guns," Daniel shook his head. "But he does want to blow us up."

"Oh," Benjamin said with an exaggerated bob of his head. "Then that's okay, then. Always wanted to be blown up —"

A whistle interrupted them. Aaron fixed his gaze on the hole in the drywall. Alex had stuck his head out. He pointed up at the ceiling.

"Move those boxy sale racks under the fourth ceiling tile from the wall." He gestured as he spoke. "The one with the water stain."

"What water stain?" Aaron asked, looking up.

"That one," Alex pointed again.

When Aaron followed Alex's finger, a small stain appeared on a white tile. As he watched, it grew larger.

"How did you do that?" he asked.

"Move those racks. Then get inside." Alex waved his hand. "Now. Hurry."

They rolled the racks in place, then scrambled toward the hole in the wall. Daniel and Aaron helped Benjamin through, then followed him inside their dojo, no one saying another word.

Alex had his back to the wall. He was edging toward the front of the empty unit. Tools were scattered throughout. Several saw horses were set up to hold cans of paint. The drywall delivered yesterday sat piled against the wall. A lot of money had been sunk into preparing the new location for the students registered at the other location. Would his insurance cover the damage?

In recent years, Aaron's dojo had grown in popularity

due to his affiliation with Sarah Roberts, whose exploits often made the front page of local newspapers. But what good would that be if there was never a building for him and his teachers to train those students?

Alex motioned them to the front of the store. With his heart in his throat, Aaron took Alex's direction and moved toward the front, hoping there wasn't a flaw in Alex's plan, whatever it was.

When the four men were huddled together near the front window, Alex eased away from them and peeked out from the corner.

"BMW still there. Passenger on the phone. I would guess we have less than one minute until this place is blown apart."

"What?" Benjamin nearly shouted. "Did I hear him right? Because if I did, why the fuck did we come in here?"

Alex pointed down the length of the wall. "See that ladder?"

Aaron nodded, followed by the others.

"Step to the window. All four of us. Make ourselves visible. Then ease back and run for the ladder."

"Where will you be?" Aaron asked.

"Ahead of you."

There wasn't time for humor. Alex wasn't being sarcastic. He literally would be ahead of them. If Aaron didn't know Alex was human, he'd think the bastard *could* fly.

"Ready?" Alex asked, three fingers raised.

"I can't climb a ladder with my leg like this," Benjamin said.

"You're going to have to," Aaron whispered. "I've only got one good fucking hand. So we're both fucked."

Alex stared out the front window. He lowered one finger.

"You go up the ladder first," Daniel said to Benjamin. "I'll push you up with my shoulder."

"How is Aaron going to climb with that hand?" Benjamin asked.

"Oh, I'll climb," Aaron said, holding his good hand up. "It's that or be blown up. Climbing'll be easy under those conditions."

Alex lowered a second finger.

Aaron took a deep breath. "Ready guys?"

Reluctantly, Daniel and Benjamin nodded.

Alex lowered his third and final finger. Benjamin stepped up to the window, peered out, then eased away as Daniel made himself visible to anyone watching outside. Aaron and Alex stood shoulder to shoulder until Alex tapped him on the back. Alex had a hammer in his hand. He intimated using it, smiled, and turned away.

Then he disappeared in a flash, running for the ladder. Benjamin was almost at it, limping closer as Daniel prodded him along. Aaron didn't need any further convincing of the potential danger of standing around inside a store wired to blow.

As Benjamin jumped to the second rung and began to climb, Alex lunged at the wall beside the ladder, jumped up, kicked off the wall, and landed on the ladder halfway up. It was like they had an agile monkey as a friend and confidant. Alex made the top of the ladder and disappeared into the dropped ceiling above the ceiling tiles of the comic book store before Benjamin was halfway up.

The roof in Aaron's unit was an easy twenty feet high with steel girders and support beams spanning the width. In each unit on either side, the stores had a dropped ceiling with white tiles suspended on thin metal strips. Alex meant to hide above the comic book store using the support beams to keep out of sight.

A brilliant idea.

Aaron got to the bottom of the ladder and started up behind Daniel. Alex's hands dropped over the edge and grabbed Benjamin when he checked to see how much farther they had to go. He hauled him up, then reached for Daniel.

Using his one good hand, breathing like a maniac starving for air in the panic of not knowing when the bombs would go off, Aaron ascended the ladder as fast as he could. With five rungs to go, only a pair of arms were visible at the top. Daniel and Benjamin were already over and out of sight.

That was when someone or something shook the back door. Aaron understood in the briefest of seconds that it wasn't a person at the back door. On the second to the last rung, four seconds away from the opening of the raised roof that would give them access above the comic book store and relative shelter from the blast, a concussive boom shook the base of the ladder, knocking it out from under him. He felt like he was floating for a moment. Then, another explosion shook everything below him, and the ladder completely disappeared.

Shrapnel, pieces of metal, wood, and drywall smashed into him from all sides. He covered his face with the large bandage on his wounded hand as he hung at the top of the wall, suspended in the open air.

Something had him, holding him in place, his shoulder aching under the stress. Then he was rising, being pulled toward the cavity in the ceiling. He chanced a look up and saw Daniel and Alex hauling him upward. His shoulder cleared the edge, then he rested his chest on the lip and kicked his feet over. He rolled in and away from the dojo until he rested along the roof's ledge.

Voices muttered below them.

Someone was in the comic book store. He faced Alex, who held a finger over his mouth to signal quiet. Aaron listened as Benjamin sat on a steel support beam eight feet away. Daniel stood on a beam two feet from him, and Alex remained on his haunches by Aaron's head.

The voices drew closer. One man said something about the dojo being destroyed. Aaron wanted to turn to the side and look back inside his place of business but decided against moving.

The men below were close enough to hear now. Aaron figured one was on a cell phone as he would talk, pause, and answer someone's question.

"Yes, we saw them all in the window." A pause. "No, both entrances were covered. They could not have exited their store or either store on either side." A pause. "That's right. We were out front. Ed and Mike just showed up. They watched the back. Two of them entered the back of the comic store, one limping. Ed said he almost shot the guy who was limping." The speaker laughed. "But there's no sign of them now. They were inside. No one could've survived that."

Aaron saw Benjamin's expression at the thought of almost being shot. He was clearly not impressed.

"No, sir." A pause. "There's no way they survived. The blast was so big, it smashed up the salon next door something terrible and blew a hole in the wall of the comic store." A pause. "Right. On our way. Back to the ship in just over an hour." A pause and the voice moved away. "Yes, sir. Thank you."

A moment later, the voices garbled by distance as the men left the store below them. Aaron looked from Alex to Daniel and finally to Benjamin. They had done it. Really, Alex had done it. But the dojo was gone, yet again. He brought his good hand to his forehead and rested it there. Should he even bother trying to own a dojo? Should he find another line of work, like training soldiers or cops how to fight? Certain companies offered lucrative contracts for those kinds of jobs. Maybe he should consider working with Darwin. He was always hiring mercenaries for one reason or another.

Alex climbed through the roof above the comic store's ceiling tiles until he stopped at an upturned empty water bottle. Alex pointed downward.

Of course. The stained tile was above the three display racks they'd moved with solid flat tops. The drop into the store below would be no more than six feet instead of a dozen.

Aaron grabbed a protruding piece of steel from one of the main beams to sit up. On his feet but bent over, he followed Daniel to where Alex waited. Once there, Alex wrapped his legs on a support beam and dangled upside down. With his hands-free, he gently eased the stained tile out of place and handed it to Daniel. Then Alex lowered his head slowly into the comic book store like Spider-Man would do.

He came back up and shook his head. "Store's empty."

As if gravity's rules didn't apply to him, Alex's legs released from the beam, and he dropped through the hole where the tile had sat moments before, no doubt landing on his feet.

"Who taught him all that shit?" Aaron asked. "Katas, sure. Black belt testing, no problem. That parkour, acrobatic, gymnastic shit, no way. It wasn't me."

Daniel shrugged. "YouTube, maybe." He moved closer to the hole to help Benjamin through. "I hear people can learn to dance *and* fight on YouTube."

"For fuck's sake," Aaron muttered to himself as the smell of smoke came to him. His dojo was burning. "Great. Fucking great."

Sirens roared in the distance as he descended through the ceiling tile. He needed to call Parkman. He needed him to know they were alive and not to worry. But he needed to learn who was running the operation to find Sarah because they had to include him in the hunt.

This shit was personal now. He wanted in. If they wouldn't let him, he'd do it his way.

Nothing would stop him from finding Sarah and making the assholes who took her pay for what they did to his place of business.

Nothing.

Chapter 24

PARKMAN LISTENED AS CASPER talked on the phone. Spencer had gone to deal with something in his office, and Whitman had gone for food. He was supposed to bring something back for Parkman.

He studied his phone, waiting for it to ring. Casper had asked his superior—Parkman had never thought of Casper as having a superior—if he could have several more men. They were now discussing the Patriot Act and how Casper could use it in Canada as he was an American, after all. Casper concluded that he would do what was necessary to secure Sarah's safety, regardless of what laws might stand in his way.

Parkman loved him for that. He loved how, throughout Sarah's long journey, she finally had law enforcement fighting for her. It was a good change and one Sarah would be happy with, considering she had come a long way regarding her opinion of the authorities. When he met her years before, Sarah hated cops. She wanted nothing to do with them. She didn't hate them in the sense that she wished them harm. It was more of a lack of trust. Several cops—Lincoln Cole, to name one—had abused their position and hurt Sarah tragically.

Now she worked with officers of the law and had grown to love working with people like Casper, Spencer, and Whitman, not to mention Parkman, a cop when Sarah met him.

Casper mumbled platitudes into the phone. The conversation was almost over. Parkman had overheard enough anyway. He wanted somewhere private to call Aaron back as he'd promised. Doing Darwin's bidding had been tough, but Parkman could do it. He'd convinced Casper to take them back to the police station to pool their resources before they continued to show up at known mafia hangouts and container ships. That meant no visit to the Diavolo Club in Scarborough, where Casper had wanted to go next.

Spencer had piped up from the back, agreeing with Parkman. He had calls to make and information to gather to discover if a mafia war was brewing.

A palpable relief set over Parkman as they drove toward the police station, Darwin's words echoing in his head.

I have something to do that'll bring Sarah home. Darwin had also said, *Just stall your men. I need three hours. Scratch that—Sarah needs three hours.*

Parkman checked his watch. It'd been one hour. Two more could become a challenge. He needed to call Aaron. Then, try to raise Darwin again to warn him if they were to head back out. He couldn't keep Casper inside the police station without good reason. Darwin would need to supply that reason if he wanted them to stay longer.

He grabbed his half-empty coffee cup and left Casper to his call in the small conference room. Passing several officers en route to the men's washroom, he checked the charge on his phone. Forty percent would be enough for a few more hours, but he'd need to locate somewhere to charge it before they went on the road again.

He slipped inside a men's room, dumped the paper coffee cup in the garbage, and checked under the door of the only stall. It was empty.

Without wasting a second, he dialed Aaron's number and waited as it rang. After seven rings, it went to voicemail. Parkman disconnected. His stomach dropped at the thought that something might have happened to him.

Parkman pulled up Darwin's number and was about to hit send when the bathroom door opened. Two plainclothes officers entered, both in suits and ties. As the first man pushed open the door, his jacket pulled away far enough to expose the shoulder holster and weapon.

Parkman slipped his phone into his back pocket and turned to the sink to wash his hands. The water flowing, his hands under it, the men muttered something to one another, like an inside joke, then closed the door. The man closest to the door coughed quite loudly. So loud it startled Parkman. Were they trying to get his attention?

He shook his hands to rid them of water, turned off the tap, and yanked a paper towel out of the holder. When he turned around, he saw why the second man had coughed. There was a thumb lock on the bathroom door. The man still had his hand on it, turned in the locked position. The cough was meant to suppress the sound of it clicking in place.

"How can I help you, gentlemen?" Parkman asked.

The man by the door was blond and wore a gray suit. The man before him wore a beige suit and sported an eighties feathered-at-the-sides haircut. He didn't recognize either man.

Eighties man rubbed his nose, a know-it-all smirk on his lips, snorted loudly, then turned his hand over. Blood caked his knuckles. From the look of it, fresh blood.

Something about the two men stirred a knot in Parkman's gut, and it wasn't just the blood. He'd been threatened by greater men in his time. Besides, what fear could they instill in a police station?

"You guys cops? Or do you always dress like that for your bathroom liaisons?"

Without hesitation, with no warning, the man standing in front of him shot his fist across the small space between them and connected with Parkman's jaw.

Parkman's head jerked back, and a low moan escaped his lips. He leaned away and covered his mouth. Before he looked back at his attacker, a foot filled his vision, hit his left cheek, and his knees gave way. Parkman dropped to the floor of the men's bathroom, one hand on his face, the other arm extended out to ward off another attack.

"What?" he tried to ask without opening his jaw too wide.

The eighties hairstyle man leaned close to Parkman's face and spit on him. If Parkman had a gun, he would have shot the man in the face, no questions asked, but Casper had taken the Smith & Wesson back when they got to the police station.

There were two of them. Both armed. And now he was injured. A sucker punch and a kick in the face. All in a good day's work.

"Fuck," Parkman mumbled. "You fucked up big time."

"Yeah?" Eighties Man said. "How's that?"

"You're in a fucking police station, asshole—"

This time, he was cut off by another punch to his face on the right cheek. Parkman's head snapped away, and just as fast, he spun around and drove a fist up into the man's crotch.

Eighties man doubled over, emitting a small squeak. To his credit, the man didn't fall. Bent over, he waddled to the side and leaned against the stall's wall.

Parkman got to his feet, spit blood into the sink, and faced the other man by the door.

A police issue Glock, a subcompact frame weapon issued to detectives, was in his hand, pointed at Parkman.

"Don't fucking move." The man gestured at his injured partner. "My man here wants to have a word with you."

"We already had our conversation. He doesn't seem to want to talk much now. Why don't you tell me why you two closet bummers came here to talk to me? A sucker punch?" he asked in a high-pitched voice. "Only a little sissy bitch sucker punches another man nowadays." He wiped blood from his lip. "You're probably both faeries looking for a rough date. Sorry, can't help you there. Head down to the Buddies in Bad Times Theatre. You can bone for biscuits there, fuckin' cock tools."

The other man with the gun pointed at his partner. Eighties Man was in the process of straightening up, his face beet red.

The pain in Parkman's face had numbed. He'd taken

sucker punches before. It wasn't so bad once you got past the initial shock of being hit so violently when you weren't expecting it.

He readied himself to throat-punch the man if he tried to hit or kick him again. The gunman wouldn't fire his weapon in the bathroom at a police station. A hundred cops would converge on the door. It was stupid of the blond idiot to think the gun was a serious threat.

"You've got a death wish," Eighties said, his jaw tight.

"Why were your knuckles bloody when you walked in?" Parkman asked, a dismal thought running through his mind. Whitman hadn't returned to the small conference room with food as he said he would. Could these guys have gotten to him?

"Your friend seemed to have no idea how to answer my questions." Eighties Hair was breathing better by the second. Standing straighter, too. "I can be persuasive—"

"No, you can't," Parkman interrupted. "But you can be an asshole. That much is for sure. Are you the husband, or is he? Who does who in the ass? Or do both of you dock cocks? Ya fucking pussies."

Parkman stepped toward Eighties Hair but was halted when Eighties withdrew his weapon.

"I should shoot you in the groin," Eighties said, spittle flying from his mouth. "We have a message for you. And we're not gay."

"Could've fooled me." Parkman was close enough to lean into the tip of the weapon. He pushed harder on it, then said, "A message, eh? You could've texted it to me. That's how normal folk pass messages back and forth." He shrugged. "Ever thought of that?"

Eighties Hair pushed Parkman backward with brute force until Parkman bumped into the counter, the gun forging a hole in Parkman's stomach. He angled his body slightly to the left so he wouldn't take a bullet in the spine if the weapon were fired by accident.

"Tell Darwin everyone's dead. Tell him we will continue killing people he knows until he surfaces. Then we'll go after his wife—"

"Who is dead?" Parkman had heard enough. He felt the color drain from his face. "Who is everyone?"

"Your little ballet boys. Those karate kids." That smirk was back on the man's face. "Karate gym blew up twenty minutes ago with Aaron and his asshole teachers inside. Vince did a great job with it." He jerked his head to the side, gesturing at his partner. "Show him the video." He eased off Parkman a notch.

It gave Parkman a chance to wipe a line of blood from his chin. Blondie still held the Glock in one hand and now had a cell phone in the other. A video began to play. Parkman recognized the dojo signage in the window. *Opening Soon* was displayed above the window. The camera was back far enough to see a comic book store beside the future dojo.

Something moved in the window of the gym. The camera zoomed in. Aaron and Alex were at the glass. He saw Daniel and Benjamin, too. Blondie was grinning so wide, it was like he'd just farted and was proud of himself. Parkman looked back at the camera. Seconds had gone by.

"Wait for it," Eighties said. "Wait for it."

The windows of the dojo shattered outward.

"We were stationed at the rear of the building," Blondie said.

"No one escaped," Eighties said.

Someone tried the men's door, then knocked.

"Almost done in here," Blondie shouted. "Come back in a minute."

A muffled male voice replied, "Thanks!"

Parkman felt dazed, like part of his mind turned off. Aaron dead? The teachers all gone? He wouldn't believe it—couldn't believe it. They don't randomly walk to the front window as a unit, show themselves off like that, and then wait to die. They did that to show the idiots in front of him that they were inside the building. Aaron must have figured out an escape route. Parkman was sure they had gotten out somehow.

"No one escaped," Eighties said again. "The salon to the right was partly destroyed, and the blast ripped a hole in the wall of the comic book store." He shook his head back and forth in a mock display of sadness. "They never had a chance."

"Whitman is in the dumpster out back," Eighties said. He raised the gun as a warning not to try anything.

What the fuck was happening? Who could systematically go about murdering and kidnapping everyone connected to Sarah? And for what? So Darwin would hear about it?

"What ..." Parkman tried to say. His face ached, his stomach hurt as it filled with dread, and his patience ran thin. "Is Whitman dead?"

Eighties offered him a half grin, then shrugged.

"Maybe. Not sure. Two bullet wounds." He exchanged a look with his partner. "Yeah, possibly. Hey, who knows." He leaned in close, the color returning to his face. "That's not too important. But what's really fucking important is that you take a message to your friend, Darwin Kostas."

On automaton, Parkman leaned back on the counter and waited for the message.

"Tell Darwin this is all his fault. Tell him he can stop the killing, even save your life, if he surrenders himself to us." Eighties moved closer until he was inches from Parkman's face, the gun still aimed at his stomach, leaning in on Parkman. "We'll even give that bitch Sarah back to him. Used up a little, but hey, what are stupid bitches for?"

Parkman spun sideways and out of the way so fast that the man's weight fell forward. By the time Eighties had righted himself, Parkman aimed his fist at the man's nose but missed and bounced his knuckles off the man's cheek. Before Eighties had time to react to the first punch, Parkman drove another fist toward the man's throat.

He shot forward, using his body weight to push the man off balance, and kept going toward the blond man, regardless of the gun aimed at him.

Something caught Parkman's right leg, and he was shoved off balance. He grabbed for the counter to correct himself while Eighties sprawled out on the floor below him. With his head down, it was impossible to see what the blond man was doing, but something connected with the back of Parkman's head in a deafening blow.

Darkness filled the edges of his vision. The ground came too quickly. Someone turned out the lights. He fought to turn them back on, but then a sledgehammer hit, and the lights remained off.

Chapter 25

Darwin watched the motel from across the street. The small twenty-room motel was attached to a bar called The Diavolo Club. All neatly packaged and run by one Angelo Spinello, or as his associates called him, Little Tony. Spinello was short, no taller than five feet, two inches. He was known as a scrapper in his early days. The information Darwin's wife gathered on the man was he'd been in and out of prison his whole life. Incarcerated by his eighteenth birthday, he ran things inside the Kingston Penitentiary, a couple of hours' drive from Toronto, midway to Montreal and Ottawa, which was all of the 'Ndrangheta's territory.

Because Spinello was so good at doing time, he was the fall guy for several crimes in his twenties and thirties, which kept men higher up in the organization free to roam. Little Tony didn't mind. His ship would come in one day. They'd promised him the Diavolo Club after a ten-year stint.

Spinello was now in his fifties and had served his time for the mafia. His days of wasting away in prison were over. Set up in the club and attached motel, filled with girls from every ethnic background to service Toronto's diverse tastes, Spinello had it good. Hundreds of men frequented the motel and club daily, and the authorities did nothing about it. Spinello paid his taxes along with several high-ranking officials. No one was to touch the Diavolo Motel. At least once a year, when a whore was used up, Little Tony arranged to have a *raid* on the motel. That girl got arrested, and the newspapers reported what the authorities told them in a press conference. Everything was all good at the Diavolo Club.

Darwin was amazed at how much Rosina could learn for him. She'd searched newspaper archives and matched dates of arrests and raids. Recorded the names reported in the papers and researched those people. Then she matched up the dates and names of which member of the police force gave the press release or who leaked information when she could find their name.

In the end, Rosina painted a picture of a horrid, decrepit animal of a man named Angelo Spinello, who made a living from human trafficking. Spinello thought himself untouchable. And in the end, maybe he really was untouchable because Darwin wasn't here for Spinello exactly. He was here for Spinello's shipment. It just so happened that Spinello knew where his shipment was, so Darwin was here to ask the man.

Through her electronic surveillance and encryption-breaking software, Rosina discovered that Spinello had a truck loaded with mattresses bound for Greece. Inside those crates, the mattresses were packed tight. And inside those mattresses were bags of vacuum-packed cocaine. The shipment was estimated at over ten million dollars' worth.

That was one of the reasons Darwin had been able to set up a meeting at the Il Forno Ristorante with Carmine Fabriano. Because they were already planning to send a container ship across the ocean and down into the Aegean Sea. Of course, Fabriano would want to entertain more money on the side. There would be room on the ship, so why not?

The second reason was Darwin figured Spinello would hold his truck back until Fabriano could confirm his meeting went well and everything checked out. Spinello wouldn't want to load his cocaine-filled beds onto a ship that was due to be raided if Fabriano's meeting turned out to be with Drug Enforcement Officers.

"What's the plan, boss?" George asked from the front seat.

"Pack as many weapons as you can. Keep them out of sight, though. We enter the premises. A group of men celebrating a stag. Charlie, you're getting married."

"I am?" Charlie asked.

"Of course not. But that's our story. Pick a girl, head to a room."

"I can do that," Elmer said.

"We're not to have sex with the girls."

Elmer's face dropped.

"You're to subdue them and gag them. I don't want any of the girls calling out. All the girls will be free to leave when this is over, so don't worry about a little force. At least they won't be violated anymore."

Darwin glanced down at his briefcase, idly wondering

what excuse he could use to allow him to bring it into the room with him. Would Spinello have security posted at random checkpoints throughout the building? If so, would they make him open it?

"I have to leave this here. And it's too risky to bring the blade inside."

"I want my baton, though," Charlie said.

Darwin nodded. "Once we have the girls subdued and we're all inside the building, call someone, anyone, into your room. Subdue them. There's four of us. That puts eight people out of the picture. Then, Elmer and George, I want you two to guard the exits at the ends of the hall. Leave the rest of the building to Charlie and me. Understood?"

"Guard the doors?" George said. "Don't let anyone in or out?"

Darwin nodded as he opened the briefcase and handed the collapsible baton to Charlie.

"No one in or out. Use your gun or knife to convince slow learners. I don't care who you kill as long as you save the girls. They've been through enough. And try not to kill any of the johns. Focus on Spinello's men if you *need* to kill someone. Our objective is Spinello. Once we have him, he'll take us to the truck with the merchandise." Darwin stashed two knives in their holsters inside his pant legs, then placed a small Beretta in the back of his pants. "We're done for the day once we nab that truck."

"What about tomorrow?" George asked. "Nothing for us?" He pointed at Elmer. "We done?"

"Possible job. That'll depend on how today goes. Now, suit up. Let's get in there before it's too late."

He slipped into a light jacket that concealed the gun at

the back of his pants. Then he watched the front of the Diavolo Club and Motel while his men got ready.

Damned Good was written in cursive about the small motel sign. Darwin surmised there would be a lot of people going to Hell at the Devil's Club this early evening.

"Ready, boss," Charlie said.

"Let's go."

Darwin slid the side door open, hopped out, waited for his three men to follow suit, then slammed the door closed. They started across the parking lot as a group toward the Diavolo Club.

It was his last stop to raise hell before making the exchange phone call. The last stop before Sarah was freed.

In that case, he reasoned it was his last chance as a free man to hurt the mafia as much as possible.

And that was what he intended to do. In spades.

Chapter 26

Someone splashed water on Parkman's face. He snapped awake, sputtered, and raised his hands to ward off his attackers.

"Hey, take it easy, buddy." Spencer.

Parkman lowered his arms.

"Easy." Casper's voice. "Raise your head slowly. Who did this to you?"

"No. Idea." He winced as the pain smarted. "Shit." The back of his head hurt more than his face.

"Possible concussion," Casper said. "I'll get you to medical."

"Can't," he muttered. "Have to get me up. Take me outside." He blinked rapidly, then tried to use the counter to get to his feet.

"Whoa, take it easy, man." Spencer grabbed him under the arms.

"Why do you need to go outside?" Casper asked.

Parkman was nearly standing, only bent a little at the waist. He closed his eyes as it all came back to him.

"Whitman," he said. "Get me outside. Find the dumpster."

He opened his eyes and stared into the mirror. Casper and Spencer exchanged a glance. Spencer shrugged.

"How do you know anything about Whitman?" Spencer asked.

"Attackers told me." Parkman turned around, using the counter for support, and started for the door. "Someone get me Advil."

Casper hovered close as they headed for the elevators. Parkman checked, but he wasn't bleeding anymore. His mouth felt like a carpet burn. Once inside the elevator, Casper turned to him.

"What can you tell us about your attackers?"

Parkman filled them in with as much detail as he could remember. Their descriptions meant nothing to Spencer, who worked in the building day and night. But then there were hundreds of men coming and going all day through the Toronto Police Services building. They could have been mafia enforcers with visitor passes.

Once outside the building, Spencer led them to the back, where the garbage trucks retrieved the large bins. There were three lined up side by side.

"Whitman," Parkman called out.

There was no response. Spencer grabbed the lid of the first one and opened it. He faced Parkman and shook his head. After opening the second and third bins, Spencer turned back to Parkman.

"Nothing. No sign of Whitman or blood. No sign of struggle anywhere."

"They said he was shot twice." Parkman looked up and down the alley, wondering if he had forgotten something they said. "He was in a dumpster out back." He turned back to Casper. "I didn't see sound suppressors on their weapons."

"They might have taken them off before meeting you in the john."

Spencer moved into the center of the alley, covered his eyes, and looked up at the police building. "If they shot him at the back of the police station, the risk of someone overhearing gunfire would be high." He faced Parkman. "Too high."

"Makes sense," Parkman said. "Then he's in another dumpster."

"You think we should be believing these guys?" Spencer asked.

Parkman shot past Spencer toward the bend in the back alley, his head clearing with the fresh air. "They had no reason to lie about this. They flaunted it."

Footsteps pounded close behind Parkman. At the next dumpster, he flipped the lid open. Nothing but leftover packaging, cans and bottles, and cardboard. A recycle bin.

A woman screamed from the direction they had just come. Parkman stopped so fast that he almost tripped over his own feet and started back.

The woman screamed again. It was coming from an offshoot of the alley behind the police building. Parkman headed that way with Casper and Spencer at his heels. As Parkman skidded around the corner, he knew they'd found Whitman.

A Chinese woman in a stained white apron stood beside two garbage bags behind her restaurant, the large green dumpster open five feet in front of her. She held a hand over her mouth as she slowly lowered to her knees.

Parkman headed for the bin with Casper at his side.

"Call an ambulance," Casper shouted back to Spencer. Then he overtook Parkman and got to the dumpster several seconds before him.

The look on Casper's face confirmed it. John Whitman, once known as Drake Bellamy, a close and dear friend of Sarah's, was inside the green garbage bin.

Parkman got there as Casper was climbing inside. When he looked in, Casper was checking Whitman's pulse. Blood had collected in large circles where two black holes gaped from his clothing. One near his shoulder, the other a little left of his belly button, slightly above the waist.

His face was a mask of wounds. They'd beat him first.

Of course.

Parkman had seen the man's knuckles. They were marked up, a mess of blood. Once they had beaten Whitman and shot him, he was thrown into the stench of a Chinese restaurant's dumpster.

The woman behind Parkman moaned loudly, then spoke in rapid Cantonese or Mandarin—he couldn't tell the difference. When he looked over his shoulder, several restaurant employees had stepped out to comfort her.

Parkman turned back to Casper.

"Getting a pulse?" he asked.

Casper met Parkman's gaze as Spencer ran up.

"Ambulance on its way," Spencer said. "Oh shit, man. Not Whitman."

"I had a hard time finding—" Casper swallowed hard. "I had difficulty locating his pulse, but I got one. He's alive. But just barely. He hasn't got long. Lost a lot of blood."

"I'll call them again," Spencer said, stepping away from the dumpster.

"Hang on, Whitman," Parkman shouted at his friend in the dumpster. "Stay with us, you bastard. Sarah needs you."

Moving away from the dumpster, he wiped his eyes clean, took a deep breath through injured lips, composed himself as much as could be expected at the moment, and then turned back to the dumpster, phone in hand. He snapped a photo of Whitman and then retreated to text it to Aaron's phone—if he was still alive—and to Darwin, wherever he was. After sending Aaron's text, he set up Darwin's. In the message to Darwin, Parkman explained briefly what had happened. He quickly typed that his bathroom attackers told him Aaron and his teachers were dead. They had shown Parkman a cell phone video of them inside the dojo before it blew up.

Most of their inner circle was dead, but Parkman and Darwin. And by taking Darwin's advice to divert Casper and Spencer, Whitman had been shot. There would be no more stalling. From now on, they were to work together or not at all. If Whitman died, it would be on Parkman's head because he had brought them here when Casper had wanted to visit that motel in Scarborough.

He hit send on Darwin's message. It was time to put up or shut up. Parkman was sick of the people he loved getting hurt. All the rules went out the window. Whatever would normally cause him restraint dissolved in an instant. All that mattered was getting Sarah from these people. How many members of the 'Ndrangheta had to die in that process didn't matter to him. They certainly didn't care about his life or the lives of his friends.

They had declared war on them—Sarah's crew.

It was a mafia war, after all. Just a different kind. Because it was one they'd lose.

Parkman clenched his fists at his sides and let a fit of anger out in a long scream that made the restaurant workers jump back. He punched the fence lining the alleyway, shouted again, the rage overwhelming in its ferocity, and then turned around to see if Casper needed any help.

A siren screamed somewhere in the distance.

Chapter 27

SARAH MADE IT THE length of the first hall before encountering a door. She hadn't thought of checking Vito's pockets for keys, but it didn't matter. The door was unlocked. She eased it open and peeked through the small crack. Beyond the door was another corridor. She started down it, Vito's knife gripped tight, the length of the blade parallel with her forearm.

The large ship canted to the left and then eased back. It lacked any kind of noise except the creaking of metal. The engines were off. No one walked above her. No voices could be heard. Didn't Vince say something about the ship being manned by fifty of his men? Was that a lie?

She approached a fork in the corridor and chose to go to the left. A sign said the kitchen was that way. If it was possible to eat something, she had to take that chance to ward off the shakes. Her hands and legs wobbled due to a lack of food and adrenaline withdrawal.

The door ahead sported a circular window. She eased up to it and peeked inside. A small kitchen. Two tables in the center of the room bolted to the floor. A bench seat lining the wall. Orange cushions on all the chairs. It was an odd color choice that made her think of seventies fashions.

The pain in her head seemed to be increasing, localized near her forehead. She certainly needed food. And if this ship was as abandoned as it appeared, she needed to find their medical supplies. They had to carry some form of headache medicine. Didn't seamen drink a lot on long voyages?

The kitchen door, too, was unlocked. Inside the small cafeteria, Sarah made her way toward the kitchen and found it abandoned. Inside a large silver fridge, she discovered scattered cartons of foodstuffs. She opened the first one she saw, her hunger spiking. Inside, she found tuna mixed with mayonnaise and tiny bits of celery. It was prepared and ready to make a sandwich, but she didn't bother to search for bread. She watched the entrance to the cafeteria as she dug into the container of tuna, swallowing it as fast as she could shovel it into her mouth.

When Vivian spoke to her, she almost dropped the container.

"What the fuck?" she said under her breath. Then, internally, *you could knock first. Let me know you're coming.*

I've been blocked—

No shit.

There's no time.

Sarah stopped chewing as she eased back into a corner of the kitchen.

What are you talking about? No time for what?

Don't escape.

Sarah shook her head slowly.

Excuse me? Why not?

The way out is to not escape.

"And that makes all the fucking sense in the world," Sarah said out loud, then commenced chewing. "I just killed a guy."

Eat. Drink. Stay in the kitchen. They will come for you.

What about Vito? He's dead.

It won't be an issue.

"Oh right, hey," she said a bit louder. "Thanks for killing him. Didn't really need that bad guy. We've got so many more." Her voice turned serious. "You do know that doesn't work for me. I'm leaving this ship."

No. You're not. Don't argue. We've made it this far. Trust me—

As abruptly as Vivian arrived, she disappeared.

"Great," Sarah mumbled, her mouth full of tuna. "Now what? Stick around this happening place? Fuck that."

Sarah exited the kitchen with her stomach showing signs she had eaten too much. After ten minutes of running through corridors, she found her way topside without encountering anyone. The sun dropped in the west, a solid reflection blindingly bright along the water's surface.

Vince had been right. They were aboard a large container ship anchored somewhere in Lake Ontario. Land was not visible in any direction. Even if she commandeered a lifeboat, she could not know which direction she should follow. If Vince was returning within an hour, he might encounter her along the way. Escape might be possible but highly unlikely.

She peeked over the railing. No one was visible below deck. If anyone was on this ship with her, they had to be on the bridge, and she wasn't about to storm the bridge with a knife and a cell phone. She had no idea how to take a ship like this into the harbor.

Maybe Vivian was right. She assured her it would be okay. The way out of this mess was to stay, Vivian had said. But if she were staying, it would be back in the kitchen. There had to be more food there. Maybe something to drink.

She hated the thought of giving up on her escape plans, but back in the kitchen, she found a large plastic container of spaghetti and meat sauce and began shoveling it into her mouth cold.

When she opened Vito's cell phone, the battery showed four percent.

"Shit," she mumbled to herself and tossed the phone aside.

She couldn't even call Parkman or Aaron to see if he was okay. At least her hands felt normal again. No residual effects from the restraints.

Once she'd eaten enough, she scrambled about the kitchen for something she could use as a weapon. When Vince came back, she wanted to be prepared. He would be angry about Vito. They were keeping her alive for the exchange so he wouldn't kill her. But he'd be pissed, and she needed to be ready if he tried anything.

In the cupboard next to the fridge, she found a corkscrew. She withdrew it and held it in her fist, the spiraled end sticking out through her fingers. Small and easy to hide. It would do.

Mouth lined with tomato sauce, she continued her search

of the kitchen. If Aaron were dead, she would murder Vince when he returned to the ship.

Something clanged on the other side of the room. She stopped rummaging in a drawer and dropped out of sight below the counter. The cafeteria door opened. Someone entered, whispering into a phone.

Sarah eased back under the counter, her back to the wall. She placed the corkscrew in her left hand, Vito's knife in her right, and waited.

"I understand," the man said. He had a heavy accent. Sounded Italian. "We're searching the ship now."

Sarah pulled her feet in and moved to the right, where the corner of the counter offered her more shelter.

"Yes, I'll have Guido weigh the body down and toss it overboard."

The voice drew closer.

Footsteps bounded into the kitchen from somewhere. "She in here?" someone else asked.

How did she not encounter anyone while roaming the ship? Where was everyone?

"I know that," the man talking into the phone seemed agitated. "You don't have to tell me. We'll find her." He paused, then said, "I have to go." The phone slapped down on the counter. "Shit," the man shouted. "This is a major fuckup."

"What's he saying?" the second voice asked.

"Find the girl, or we'll all have consequences to deal with."

"He said that?" The second voice sounded incredulous. "Really?"

"Not exactly like that. But he said there would be

consequences. Look, just find the girl. Keep her alive. Don't touch her. Don't fucking even look at her wrong. She's supposed to be ready for delivery, and now Vito has gone and fucked that all up."

Delivery? Where?

"Because Vito fucked up, even though Vincenzo warned everyone about how dangerous she could be, he's put us all at risk. Fuck him."

"What are you saying? Are you glad she killed him?"

Silence filled the kitchen. The men were probably only five feet from her on the other side of the counter, unable to see her unless they entered the fridge area.

"Something like that," he replied.

"Me too. Fuck Vito. He was an asshole anyway."

The man's voice drew near. He was coming in the back. His feet crossed in front of her. He stopped at the fridge and then froze.

"Hey, Mike."

"Yeah?"

"She's been in here."

"What?"

"She might still be here." His voice had dropped in volume.

Footsteps bounded toward the kitchen.

Shit!

The man by the fridge leaned down to look under the counter. Sarah lunged out and sliced at his ankle with the blade. It pierced his flesh above the sock line.

The man screamed as he dropped to the floor, blood pumping from his ankle.

The second man—Mike—came around the corner and

bent low. Their eyes met. He raised a gun.

"Out," was all he said.

The other man continued to scream, blood pooling on the floor.

"Help me, man. Shoot her. Call for help, man."

"Fuck you," Mike yelled. "I'm not killing her. That's a death sentence."

Sarah remained under the counter. Could she disarm Mike? Then what? Leave the ship? How? Maybe Vivian was right. Maybe she would wait for Vince to come back to *deliver* her, whatever that meant.

She crawled out, got to her knees, then stood to her full height. Mike eased back out of reach. As a sign of good faith, she set the knife and the corkscrew on the counter beside her and raised her hands.

"Unarmed," she said loud enough to be heard over the man screaming on the floor.

He had scrunched up in a ball, hands pressed tight on the open wound.

"Turn around," Mike ordered. "Gotta check that you don't have something else hidden."

Sarah obliged. She placed her hands on the counter and waited, her head turned to the side to watch Mike peripherally. There was a blur, a shadow moving too fast. She started to turn back, but then she was falling to the floor. Something had hit the back of her head. Someone turned off the lights. The man on the floor got quiet. Something was wrong, but she couldn't quite grasp what it was.

Then she was sleeping.

Chapter 28

Darwin stayed three steps ahead of his men until they reached the door. He was just touching the handle when his phone vibrated in his back pocket.

"One sec," he said, reaching in his pocket. "Go on in, guys. I'll join you in a second. Remember, Charlie's getting married. Look excited. Look pumped."

Elmer nodded. Charlie grunted something, and George opened the door to the front of the small motel.

Darwin turned away to type his code into his phone. A message from Parkman. He opened it.

A picture of someone bleeding. The person was lying on what looked like a pile of garbage. Darwin used his fingers to zoom in on the face.

John Whitman.

Darwin zoomed along the center of the photo. By the looks of the wounds, Whitman had been shot twice.

"Fuck," Darwin said under his breath.

He pulled out of the photo and read the text from Parkman. Whitman was dying. Aaron and his teachers were supposedly dead as well. Parkman typed that whatever was happening, it had to end. He was going to end this war on his terms.

"You're fucking right it has to end," Darwin said to himself, his jaw tight with fury. "Oh my fuck, am I going to end this." He stashed his phone back in his pocket and wiped away a tear that slipped from the corner of his eye. "It'll end on my terms, too."

He wiped at another tear at the thought that this was all his fault. Sure, he'd escaped the mafia's clutches years before, but popping up to help Sarah over the years had exposed him. They had gone after Sarah and her people to get to Darwin. Whitman shot? Aaron and the dojo boys dead? He didn't believe it. Refused to believe it.

Whatever happened now, he needed Spinello to give up the location of the cocaine-filled truck, and he needed Spinello to call in the exchange.

A life for a life.

A fair exchange.

Darwin scanned the parking lot. Traffic moved on Kingston Road, but the lot was quiet. Early evening at the whorehouse.

He entered the motel's front door, feeling an intense rage at the mafia and what they had done. His knuckles tingled with energy. He needed to punch something to release it. He wanted to burn the building down, get in the van, drive to every mafia-known hangout, and blow each one to hell.

They would all suffer for what they had done. In his

estimation, any member of the 'Ndrangheta was guilty by association.

His three mercenaries were talking to a big-breasted woman at the counter. She was dressed in a purple negligee with a black satin robe draped over her shoulders. Charlie was talking about securing four rooms for him and his friends for a one-hour session as per their prearranged plan to get inside.

Fuck the plan. The 'Ndrangheta would regret trying to call him out.

A barrel-chested man sat on a couch to his left in a small reception waiting area. The man dipped into a bag of Doritos between his legs, his attention fixed on the large TV screen where an image of Jenna Jameson's ass cheek tattoo was on full display, pumping up and down on someone's rod.

"We have four rooms," Charlie said. "It's booked."

"Would you all follow me, please," the girl said, the black robe flicking up as she walked.

Darwin hadn't moved from just inside the door. He stared a moment longer at the heavy man on the couch, then back to his men.

"Change of plans," he said.

His men faced Darwin and waited for their orders.

"George. Elmer. Go to each exit door on this floor at the end of the hallway as previously planned. Go now."

They bolted in opposite directions.

"Excuse me, sir," the woman called after them, her robe opening at the front as she turned. "You can't go that way."

Charlie moved closer to Darwin, ignoring the woman.

"What about me, boss?" Charlie asked.

The bag of Doritos hit the floor as the large man on the

couch got to his feet.

"Secure this door," Darwin said.

He faced the man by the couch.

"What's going on?" the man asked in a brusque voice. "Who the fuck are you?"

Darwin stepped closer to him. "What's your name?"

"None of your fucking business." A smile broke across his thin lips. Yellow Dorito powder crusted in the corners. "Whatever you're doing here will end with you not being able to feed yourself properly for a month."

"I highly doubt that." Behind him, he heard the distinctive sound of Charlie's collapsible baton extending. "Tell me where Spinello is," Darwin said.

"He doesn't do unexpected meetings with strangers." The man's hand slipped inside his jacket.

"I wasn't asking for a meeting. I'm asking for a location."

The woman moved behind the tiny reception desk and picked up the phone.

"Charlie."

"Yes, boss."

"Deal with her. No phones."

Charlie stomped away from the door.

"Where's Spinello?" Darwin asked. "Last chance. And take your hand out of your jacket."

Darwin eased the Beretta from the back of his pants. He pulled the silencer from his pocket and, with a couple of fast twists, affixed it to the Beretta behind his back.

Spinello's man came up with a cell phone in his palm.

"Drop the phone," Darwin ordered. The big guy typed something on the phone's screen. "Stop typing."

"Fuck you." The man punched the keys rapidly.

Darwin brought the Beretta around and aimed at the man's hands from one foot away. He squeezed the trigger as the man looked up. The bullet went through each hand, and the cell phone was lost to the air. A small hole opened in the wall beside the large TV that was now showing Jenna on her knees trying to finish off a husky male porn star.

The report from the gun was quiet, even in the confined space. The man screamed as he dropped to his knees, staring wide-eyed at his hands extended in front of him, blood rushing to his wrists. An expression of abject terror came over his face as if his hands had suddenly caught fire, and he couldn't figure out how to put them out.

"Spinello?" Darwin shouted. "Where is he?"

"Boss?" Charlie yelled from behind Darwin.

Darwin didn't turn around. He placed a foot on the man's shoulder and shoved him to the floor.

"What?" Darwin yelled back to Charlie.

"The girl knows about Spinello," Charlie said.

"She's not lying?"

"Claims to be telling the truth. Doesn't want to die."

"Then we don't need you," Darwin said to the man on the floor in front of him.

He aimed the weapon at the man's throat. "This is for Aaron." Darwin squeezed the trigger. The man's body jerked when the bullet entered his Adam's apple. Blood gurgled out of the wound. The man attempted to stifle the flow of blood with his hands, but it didn't work.

The woman screamed behind him. Something clamped down on her, cutting the scream off instantly.

The barrel-chested man turned his bulging eyes on

Darwin and glared at him as his life oozed out in a pool of crimson.

"Fuck you," Darwin said. "And all your organized crime asshole friends. You will all die. Any notion of the mafia is dead in Toronto. Darwin Kostas is back in town." He kicked the man in the ribs. "You fucks didn't learn the first time? That makes you stupid, and stupid people get a taste of Darwinism. Don't you idiots ever watch YouTube?" He kicked him again, his fury still rising. "This is for Sarah. This is for Whitman, Aaron, and anyone else you assholes have hurt."

"Boss?" Charlie called, cutting off Darwin.

Darwin wiped his forehead and turned around. He adjusted his shirt, stashed the gun away, and walked to the reception desk.

"You were saying?" Darwin addressed the girl on the floor.

She had dissolved into a ball, curled up on the floor. He looked down at her reddened, tear-streaked face. Her breast implants were so large that all he saw was her head and the two balloons acting as an umbrella for the rest of her body. They moved up and down with her quick breaths.

She pointed down the hall. "Spinello is"—she swallowed —"in room 110. He always visits when it's quiet."

"Who's with him?" Darwin asked.

"Alicia." The girl covered her face with her hands.

"That's it?" Darwin asked.

The girl nodded forcefully like she really meant it.

Darwin moved beside the counter and looked down the length of the hallway.

"He would've heard the screams," he said. "Why hasn't

he come out to investigate?"

The girl shrugged, sobs shaking her body. It wasn't every day she saw someone murdered.

Darwin counted five open doors along the corridor. An overweight man, clearly not Spinello, was trying to get his pants on as he ran to the exit door at the end of the hallway.

George, standing at the exit, met Darwin's eyes and shrugged. Should he let the man pass or hold him?

Darwin nodded. Let him go.

George opened the exit door and helped push the man outside. Then he shut and locked the door.

"Come with me, Charlie. Bring the girl in case she's lying. Let's go talk to Spinello."

Darwin started down the length of the corridor, his hand wrapped tight around the Beretta's grip. Charlie followed him, dragging the crying girl along by her arm. She stumbled a couple of times but stayed on her feet.

In front of room 110, Darwin put his back to the wall on one side of the door and nodded for Charlie to do the same on the other side. Charlie pushed the receptionist to the floor and ordered her to stay put.

Darwin used the handle of the Beretta to knock. "Open up, Spinello."

A car engine revved in the parking lot. The overweight man must have made it to his car and was high-tailing it out of the area. He'd probably never come back to Spinello's Diavolo Motel whorehouse.

Darwin knocked again.

"Open up, or I break it down," he yelled. After a moment of silence, he looked at the girl in the black robe on the floor. "You got a key for this room?"

She nodded. "Back at the"—she hiccupped—"counter."

"Get it."

Charlie helped the girl up and pushed her to run back to the counter.

"Last chance," Darwin shouted at the door.

The car leaving the parking lot came into view through the glass door. A four-door sedan. Darwin watched it turn left onto Kingston Road.

Seconds later, the girl returned with a key and slipped it into the knob. She turned it. The door opened a crack. Charlie kicked it open all the way.

Leading, Darwin entered the room, the Beretta gripped in both hands. No one in the bathroom. Bedroom empty, curtains drawn.

He swung back to the receptionist. "Where is he?"

"He came in with Alicia five minutes before you guys came in. I swear!"

The curtains moved. They billowed in the breeze.

Darwin ran over and yanked them back. The window had been opened. He stuck his head outside. Angelo Spinello was gone. He had escaped through the window.

The overweight man was in the parking lot by a pickup truck, still tying up his shirt, his attention fixed on the front of the motel.

"What kind of car does Spinello drive?" he shouted at the girl.

"I don't know. A Ford, I think. I don't know cars."

"Shit, let's go," Darwin shouted.

He texted Rosina as they ran the length of the hallway. He told her to get a lock on the signal of Spinello's phone as fast as she could. The asshole had slipped through Darwin's fingers.

They exited the motel and jumped in the van. This time, Darwin drove. He turned left on Kingston Road while waiting for Rosina to get back to him.

He punched the dashboard twice in frustration.

"Fuck," he screamed, then ran a red light.

Chapter 29

An ambulance careened around the corner of the alley and came to a stop beside the garbage bin. Parkman was impressed by how fast they arrived. He showed Whitman to the two male attendants. They nodded and went to work.

Parkman backed out of their way and moved closer to Casper, who was on the phone. Spencer paced by the back of the Chinese restaurant, mumbling something to himself. Parkman watched him, in touch with what Spencer had to be going through. He was supposed to retire soon. Spencer had planned to leave Whitman in the department with Spencer's caseload. Whitman had been Spencer's project. Bring Drake Bellamy back from the dead to go after the kind of people who tried to kill him in the first place. And now Bellamy/Whitman was bleeding out in a restaurant's dumpster in a downtown Toronto alley not a block from the police station.

Casper clicked off his call.

"Emergency crews have responded to an explosion on Queen Street. The video you saw of Aaron's dojo was accurate."

Parkman ran both hands through his wavy hair. "For fuck's sake." He looked skyward. The urge to fight back and kill those responsible was akin to how he felt when the Twin Towers were hit that Tuesday morning in September. He had turned to his partner on the force that day and said, "Give me a gun and line them up, and I will murder every single one of the people responsible."

He brought his attention back to Casper. Spencer had stopped pacing and stared at the ambulance attendants as they carefully lifted Whitman out of the dumpster on a collapsible stretcher.

"I'm going with him," Spencer said. He wavered on his feet, caught himself, and looked at Parkman. "If he dies …" Spencer wiped his face, then held his chin for a moment. "If he dies on the way to the hospital, he can't die alone."

"Go," Parkman said. "Stay in touch on your cell." He patted the back of Spencer's shoulder. "We got this. Take care of Whitman. When you're done, when you can get away, call. We'll meet up."

Spencer seemed lost, his thoughts far off as he moved toward the back of the ambulance. They had placed Whitman in the back and were hooking him up to something. Spencer jumped in the back and sat by Whitman's head. He nodded at Parkman and Casper before the driver shut the doors.

The ambulance pulled away, siren wailing. Parkman watched it until the vehicle turned a corner and disappeared. After a deep breath to collect himself, he faced Casper.

"What next? I mean, where do we go from here? No sign

or word from Sarah. Aaron and the dojo are gone. His teachers are presumed dead. Whitman and Spencer just left." Casper's face was deadpan, his eyes staring off at nothing. "Darwin is somewhere in Toronto on his own crusade. I mean, this is really fucked up."

Another siren wailed in the distance.

Casper blinked, then cleared his throat. "We go back in the police station and get someone working on video surveillance to identify those guys who attacked you in the bathroom. Then we arm ourselves and go to that last location I have in Scarborough. My sources also tell me to go to the Calto Social Club on Ellesmere. Marty Fermosa had connections there. After that, it's back to the harbor front where we'll hurt some of those seamen until one of them tells us where Lorenzo Falcone is." He placed a calming hand on Parkman's shoulder. "We rattle enough cages, we'll get somewhere. You in?"

"I'm fucking in. No question. Just get me armed."

The siren seemed to be getting closer. An ambulance came around the corner and rushed to stop in front of them. A woman and a man hopped out.

Parkman and Casper exchanged a worried look.

"We got a call about a shooting victim," the male driver said.

"In a dumpster," the female added.

A police car skidded around the corner behind the ambulance and came to a stop. Parkman's stomach dropped as he fumbled with his cell phone. He felt numb as he hit Spencer's number from his contacts. He moved away as Casper talked to the ambulance attendants and the two cops who had walked over. Spencer's phone rang twice, then clicked as someone answered.

"Yeah, Parkman?" Spencer said. "What's up?"

Relief swept through him. "You're okay?"

"Of course. Why? They're just giving a shot of something to Whitman now. The guy here says he's going to make it."

"There is a chance they're not real, Spencer," Parkman said. "The ambulance just arrived. Stop them from injecting anything into Whitman."

"What?" Spencer asked, his voice rising a pitch. "They're what? Say again."

"They may not be real ambulance guys. Get them to pull over—"

"Hey!" Spencer yelled into the phone. "What's happening to him?" There was the sound of movement, like a scuffle. "Parkman, Whitman's gone into cardiac arrest. He's convulsing—"

"It's whatever that guy just gave him," Parkman shouted into the phone. "Where are you?"

"I don't know. I can't see outside—"

Something crashed in Parkman's ear. More scuffling sounds. Spencer swore twice as something thunked loudly. The ambulance's siren was too loud to hear anything but a blanket of noise.

"Spencer!" Parkman screamed into the phone. "Answer me, dammit!"

Casper came to his side. In the phone, the siren turned off. He pressed the phone into his ear as the two police officers stood in front of him. Someone breathing heavily put the phone to his ear.

"Spencer?" Parkman asked. "That you?"

He waited a moment before a man said, "They're both dead."

Parkman took a steadying breath. He refused to believe it. How could they be dead? Whitman and Spencer? Gone? How did they not recognize the Paramedics as fakes?

"You and your little whore psychic will be dead soon, too. Soon enough, asshole."

The phone clicked off.

Parkman dropped to his knees. His phone clanged on the concrete beside him. He wailed at the loss of his friends as the pain tore him up inside, smacking at the pavement until his hand stung.

Chapter 30

THEY WERE FIVE MINUTES away from the Diavolo Motel when Darwin's phone rang. He clicked the speaker option.

"Rosina?" he shouted over the rev of the van's engine.

"I can't track him," she said. "Not fast enough. I've got a cell number here, but he's blocked it somehow. In all our research, all I have for this guy is the Diavolo Motel and Club on Kingston Road and his home address. But I can't guarantee that it's accurate. Also, I think his business is tied to a shipping company in Etobicoke."

"Shit." Darwin slapped the steering wheel twice. "Okay, give me the home address. We'll go there."

Rosina recited the address while Charlie wrote it down.

"Gotta go," Darwin said. "Will call you back." He clicked off the phone. "Where are we headed?" he asked. "Give me the address."

"Just go north on Victoria Park Avenue," Charlie said,

staring at his phone's GPS. "Then a right on Lynvalley Crescent."

In the van, doing his best not to attract police attention, Darwin drove as fast as he could and got to Lynvalley Crescent in seventeen minutes flat.

"We have to do this fast. In and out." Darwin parked the van two houses away from Spinello's. "We walk up to the house like we're his friends. We don't knock. Access the house using the side door. Once inside, we clear the house as fast as possible. He will probably be armed in whichever part of the house he's in. So don't get shot."

"Sounds reckless, boss," George said from the back seat. "But I'm curious if he's in there. I mean, why come home?"

"It is reckless," Darwin said. He turned off the van and glanced in the rearview mirror. "I won't lie to you. We have no choice but to go in hard. Spinello could be moving the truck. He could be calling for help. He could be doing a million other things, and we have to stop him. We've lost the element of surprise." He opened his door to get out, then stopped. "Any of you are welcome to wait in the car. I have no choice in the matter." He got out and shut the door.

As his door closed, Charlie's opened. He got out, followed by George and Elmer.

"We wif you, boss," Elmer said. "Aww, the way."

"All the way," George repeated.

The four men started toward 104 Lynvalley Crescent. Spinello lived in a plain, nondescript home. A one-level abode with small rectangular basement windows. White curtains decorated the front window. As they approached, Darwin studied the house for movement. Did a curtain move? Was the light turned on or off?

The driveway was empty. He didn't see the four-door sedan or a Ford parked close by. Two pickup trucks were parked across the street. A Jeep and a Kia were two houses down. Unless Spinello drove home and parked his car several blocks away, he wasn't in the house.

At the side door, Darwin turned to his men. "There's a chance he's not here." He checked his watch. "In and out in ten minutes. Then I call Rosina. She might have something for me."

Darwin motioned for Charlie, the tallest and strongest of the four men, to do the honors.

Charlie backed up, took two quick steps toward the door, then planted a foot hard beside the door handle and shoved his weight behind it. The door cracked and almost gave way.

Darwin grabbed his Beretta and aimed it skyward as Charlie kicked again. The door cracked loudly and swung open. Darwin spun around and entered the home first.

The side door offered four steps leading up to the main floor and about eight steps down to the basement. Riding an adrenaline high, he bounded up to the kitchen. Behind him, one of his men headed downstairs. Charlie disappeared down a hall to the back of the house, baton in his hand.

The living room was empty. At the front window, Darwin peeked out at the street from behind the white curtain. The streetlights were on as the sun was almost down now. Nothing was amiss. It was like no one had seen them. Unless someone had seen them and was calling the police from the confines of their own home, Darwin and his team were free to search Spinello's home.

"Clear," he heard from somewhere deep in the house.

He stepped away from the window.

"Clear," another man shouted.

Charlie came up the hallway, shaking his head. "Sorry, boss. He's not here."

"Figured that when I didn't see the car." He stopped at the doorway to the kitchen. "Does he have a home office?"

George came up beside him. Elmer followed.

"Not up here," Charlie said. He looked at the other two. "Anything downstairs?"

George nodded. "A second living room and bar down there. On the other side of that, there's a small room with a desk."

"That's got to be it." Darwin started for the stairs. "We're out of here in under a minute. Someone, watch the front."

He ran down the stairs to the back room office. Without regard for who might be in the backyard this time of night—likely no one—he flipped on the lights in the room.

Papers were piled all over the desk, scattered everywhere. The waste can overflowed, and boxes sat randomly on the floor. It was abundantly clear Spinello was not an organizer.

Darwin yanked open drawers, rifled through papers and ledgers, and then slammed them shut, one by one.

Nothing but bills of lading, contracts, and accounts receivables. Only if he were Spinello's accountant could he understand most of what he was looking at. Darwin had been in his mid-twenties when he began a life on the run. He hadn't paid taxes in years and traveled with fake passports. As far as he was concerned, his real name didn't exist anymore. One day, it wouldn't exist for the government either. Because of that, understanding the business of the paperwork in front of him wouldn't happen. He understood it fundamentally—everything came in and went out on paper—but he couldn't decipher how the documents would ever lead him to find Spinello.

He shoved everything off the desk with both arms in one swoop. Then he kicked the chair over and jumped up to stand on the desktop. Perched above the clutter of papers, he could see a common name and logo in orange on almost every document.

Universal Shipping. The U and the S were entwined to appear like the first letters of the United States.

He jumped off the desk and grabbed one of the documents. A bill of lading for a children's toy shipment out of Hamilton, Ontario. Another for a shipment of auto glass. Universal Shipping's address was in Etobicoke.

Rosina said Spinello was attached to a company in Etobicoke. The mattresses of cocaine were in a truck in Toronto somewhere, and Spinello was the only man who knew where. And he owned a shipping company.

Odds were Spinello was at his company's office.

Darwin folded the bill of lading and ran from Spinello's home office.

Back in the van, he performed a U-turn and explained to the men what he'd discovered and where they were headed. The offices and warehouse of a shipping company on Westside Drive in Etobicoke.

If he couldn't find Spinello, maybe he could locate the cocaine-filled truck instead.

He called Rosina and got her to research the company and offer them maps of the area and anything else she thought might help.

When he clicked the disconnect button, a text appeared.

"Get that," he said to Charlie. "Read it to me."

Charlie grabbed Darwin's phone and opened the text.

"It's from Parkman."

"Shit. What's it say?"

"Whitman and Spencer are confirmed dead."

"What!" Darwin shouted. The van swayed, then righted as Darwin re-gripped the wheel. "I thought he said Whitman got shot. He said nothing about Spencer."

Charlie shrugged like he was responsible for the message. "It says that right here, boss."

"Call him."

Charlie hit the number by the text. It rang twice on speakerphone before it was picked up.

"Parkman. It's Darwin."

"They're gone," Parkman's voice came through the speaker, weak and defeated. "They were fucking executed."

"What? How?" Darwin shouted. "They were just with you."

"An ambulance. They took them. Fake emergency team. Drove away, then killed them. A real ambulance showed up after."

"Shit, shit, shit," Darwin smacked the wheel so hard his hand stung. "They'll all burn in Hell for this," he yelled at the phone.

"Darwin?" Casper's voice.

Charlie held the phone closer to Darwin. "I'm here."

"Where are you?"

"Busy."

"You can't afford to be busy. If this involves you, I need intel."

"You'll get intel. I have one more thing to do. Then I'll

tell you everything."

"What are you doing?"

"Trying to keep Sarah alive."

"Are you with her?"

"If I were, I would tell you. And if I were, you'd be getting a call about a lot of dead bodies."

"What can we do to help?"

He liked that about Casper. Pushing Darwin would get him nowhere, and Casper knew that.

"Arrest every member of organized crime in the city. Make them sit on their hands. That'll slow their circles, their inner channels of communication."

"You know I can't do that."

"Then watch your back and stay the fuck alive. They can't be allowed to take out any more of us."

"You stay alive, too." Casper coughed into the phone. "Call me, Darwin. I'm your friend. I will work outside the law when needed. Call me, I can make shit happen. And Darwin, keep Sarah alive."

"I'm working on it."

Darwin pushed the gas pedal farther as his lower lip quivered. More dead. More dying. More yet to die.

He'd thought his plan would be hugely successful. It seemed easy and precise. Just that morning, while waiting on College Street at the Il Forno Ristorante, he thought it would all be done within a day's work. Sarah would be freed by that evening or tomorrow at the latest. But everything was fucked now. Aaron, his teachers, Spencer and Whitman, are all gone. Sarah was still gone, and Parkman was reduced to tears. Darwin still couldn't believe that Sarah's boyfriend was dead. It hadn't settled in yet.

While Darwin raced toward Etobicoke, hoping he was closer to finding the cocaine-filled truck and Spinello, he couldn't help but feel doubt. Doubt for his ideas, doubt for his plan, and doubt for Sarah's safety.

Maybe this was the end of an era. Strong Sarah, the girl with a unique talent to stay alive while listening to the dead, surrounded by capable colleagues, was trapped somewhere while an unknown enemy took her friends out individually.

Who they were as a unit, what they had become, was being torn apart and turned upside down. Could organized crime be that good? Or did they have help? Could someone, or a group of someones with vast resources, be aiding in the fight against Sarah's crew? Like rogue police officers?

He dismissed that thought out of hand because it was impossible. It had to be. There was no way the authorities were helping the mafia track their movements.

Or were they?

It would make a lot of sense if that were the case.

And didn't Parkman say he was attacked in the police station bathroom?

Wouldn't that be ironic after all the years of being a vigilante? That Sarah, who detested and distrusted the police in the beginning, had learned to not only trust them and help the authorities in several investigations, was being brought down by the very people she thought would be her ruin in the first place?

How could he kill members of the police force—providing they were involved—like he was doing with the mafia?

It couldn't be done. It just couldn't be. Darwin would become the most hunted man in history. He would end up dead for sure.

If any cops were involved, he would need proof.

That line of thinking could only get him in trouble.

He drowned out the external noise and drove on, turning his thoughts to Sarah and how he would handle the exchange.

Only that kept him sane. Anything else was enough to drive him mad.

Chapter 31

Sarah contemplated how thick her skull was. She had been hit in the head so many times since she was eighteen years old she wondered why she didn't have a permanent concussion. A persistent headache filled her every thought. On the bright side, she wasn't tied up in the room with Vito's dead body.

They had left her in the kitchen, handcuffed to a metal chair affixed to the floor in case of turbulent waters. Once the doors were locked, Vince's men felt it was safe to leave her alone. Normally, they'd be wrong, but in this case, they were right. Her headache was too intense to consider breaking free and running around the ship, getting nowhere. Resigned to being unable to leave the ship alone, she would sit like a good little girl and wait for Vince to return.

She'd only been out for a few minutes. Long enough for them to handcuff her to the chair and remove the man with the cut ankle. The uninjured guy returned to offer her water, checked her cuffs were secure, and then left the kitchen.

Vivian whispered something half an hour ago, but Sarah silenced her. She'd ordered her out of her head until the headache was gone. There was nothing she could do anyway, even if Vivian offered instructions.

The random dead visitors stayed away as well—a small blessing.

Sarah closed her eyes and lowered her head. When her chin rested on her chest, she focused inward, easing thoughts away and imagining her headache as a small red soccer ball. She'd read somewhere that a person could clear their headache by meditating on pictures.

In her mind's eye, she saw herself standing behind the soccer ball. The little red bastard of pain sat on the grassy field, acting like it didn't have a care in the world. She ran for the ball and kicked it hard. The soccer ball launched skyward. In her mind, it continued flying toward the heavens until it disappeared.

When she looked back down at the grass, the offending fucker was back. It was a smaller version of its predecessor but still as bright red.

She kicked that one until it disappeared. Then kicked the next. After several minutes of this, she opened her eyes and glanced around the kitchen.

To some degree, it had worked. Her headache had diminished in intensity. She smiled to herself, closed her eyes, and lowered her head again.

The door to the kitchen banged open. She flinched, the headache flaring again, sharp pains shooting up her wrists where the cuffs dug in.

"Take it easy," she shouted as Vince entered the kitchen. "For fuck's sake."

"Me?" He tapped his chest. "Take it easy?" Moving deeper into the kitchen, he neared her chair, his head shaking back and forth. "I think it's you who needs to take it easy." He placed a hand on her head, squeezed his fingers around a clump of hair, then pulled her head back. "You're a fiery bitch, ain't cha?"

The pain quickly rose to intense as she glared at him, teeth clenched to avoid shouting. She panted through her teeth, counting the seconds until he let go. It would take dozens of rounds of soccer to rid her of the headache now. Advil would definitely work faster.

"How the hell were you able to kill Vito and escape that room?" he asked. Thankfully, he released her hair. He moved away from her toward the fridge. "Vito was an asshole," he added, almost to himself. "If you hadn't done it, I'd have killed him myself."

She frowned at that comment. Weren't they working together?

Vince made it to the fridge and opened it. "Vito was supposed to feed you. That was it. Feed you and leave you alone."

Feed me?

"Keep you hydrated." Vince glanced at her over his arm, the one holding the fridge door open. "Our beef isn't with you, exactly." He looked away. "We're after your friend Darwin, and the people I work for will do anything to get to him." He grabbed something and shut the fridge. "Even kill you if that meant Darwin would come out of hiding." He had a see-through container of butter tarts and a bottle of water in his hand. "Shit, they'd kill a few dozen people to get to Darwin. But as long as he knows we have you and is willing to exchange himself for your safety, then nothing is supposed to happen to you."

Vince set the items on a table and pulled a chair up beside her. They hadn't secured her ankles, so he sat to her left side, out of her reach. He popped open the butter tarts container, grabbed one, and brought it to Sarah's lips.

She opened her mouth and bit off half of it with the first bite.

"Good girl. Need to give you strength for what you must endure when you leave here." He offered the rest. She chewed faster, swallowed, and then opened her mouth. Vince pushed the other half inside, wiping his hands on his jeans as she dealt with the mouth full of butter tart.

"I have several cell phone videos to show you," he said. "Then I have to prepare the boat to dock back in Toronto."

"We're heading back in?" she asked, the tart almost gone.

He nodded. "Under the cover of night."

"Why?"

Vince spun the cap off the water bottle and held it to her lips. She swallowed hungrily.

"Because Darwin will want to do an exchange. At least, we think so. So far, all he's done is murder several of our colleagues." He shrugged. "That's the nature of the business. Sometimes my people get complacent, they get lazy." He set the water bottle on the floor by his feet and reached for another butter tart. "Darwin's pissing off a lot of people. I can only imagine what his death will look like." He held the tart up close to her mouth. "It will be a long, arduous task of agony."

She clamped down on the tart and chewed with vigor. It was so good to eat. Butter tarts were always welcome. Thoughts of Darwin dying were not so welcome at all. Something in the way Vivian communicated to her earlier calmed her. Vince could spout his shit. Vince could talk tough while she was tied to the chair. But in the end, her team would win. Because wasn't that what this was all about? A war? A fight? Us against them?

Like that Pink Floyd song, *Us and Them*. Their side, our side, clear lines dividing who we are, fighting each other endlessly. It seems humans have this tendency to want to go to war. Even on this small scale. When it's all said and done, it is only round and round, as the song suggests. History repeating, fighting them while they're fighting us.

Sarah finished the last of her butter tart, drank from the offered bottle, and contemplated what it was all for. To stay alive? To kill them? And what, when they're dead, who was next? She had thought about it several times before, but would it ever end? Vince was just a face in a long line of faces. They blurred after a while into a mirage of images, alive once, dead now. Would she ever get to have children? Buy a house? Settle down? She thought not. Even at times, she refuted her own inner desire for those things and became angry with the world in her fight for what she thought was right.

She sighed, knowing this was it. This reality was her life. She excelled at it and would have to continue this life until someone got lucky and took her out. As long as they kept coming, she was left with no choice. A dose of *poor me* wouldn't solve a thing.

Vince got up and slid his chair away. "Now for the home movies."

"There's nothing you have to show me that I'll want to see." Sarah ran her tongue along her teeth in search of an errant crumb. "Just fuck off and come get me when we dock."

Vince ignored her while he tapped on his phone. "There," he said. "Have a look at this image."

He angled the cell phone her way. She saw a picture of Whitman's face, then looked away.

"How do you have a pic of John on your phone?"

Vince's grin was so big that his lips had paled. "A colleague of mine took this. After Whitman was killed."

"Bullshit." She kicked the chair to turn away from him. "I can be nice and mean at the same time. Fuck off and have a nice day."

"Not so clever, Sarah." Vince maneuvered in front of her again, camera angled down. "Here's a fancy shot of Spencer."

Spencer didn't look so good. His eyes open wide, blood running the length of his mouth. There was a gaping hole in his neck. It looked like something a large knife could do.

The butter tart in her stomach turned sour. She thought she'd throw it up if he had any more pictures to show her.

"I'm done with the pictures," he said to her relief. "But I do have a short video to show you."

She glared at him at the realization that Whitman and Spencer were dead. Would they Photoshop images to freak her out? Would they go to such lengths to offer her a short, sharp shock as it goes in the song?

Vince looked positively proud of himself. He started the

video and turned it toward her.

The front of Aaron's dojo was on the screen. She'd seen an image of it on Parkman's phone at the airport before boarding for Toronto.

"Why did you film—" She stopped talking when she saw her man in the window, very much alive. "Stop it, asshole. Cut the video." She looked away.

Vince grabbed her hair and jammed the phone in front of her.

"Watch it," he shouted.

All four martial artists stood in the window, then stepped back. Moments later, the glass blew outward as the dojo exploded.

With Aaron and his teachers still inside.

Vince stepped back as she tried to swallow and comprehend what she had just seen. It was impossible. It couldn't be.

She found it hard to breathe, yet her mouth hung open. A cold sweat broke out on the back of her neck as her muscles went rigid. She turned away from Vince and squeezed her eyes shut as if that could rid them of the vision she'd just taken in. Her breath caught, hitched, then caught again. She'd heard them say it but didn't think it would happen. She understood Aaron might be a target but hadn't fretted over it since Vivian said everything would work out.

If it were true, and Aaron was gone, everything she'd been working toward with him was gone. Whitman, Spencer, Aaron, and his three teachers are dead.

Impossible.

She felt cold on the inside. She wanted to draw her arms up and cover herself from the cruelty of it all but couldn't.

Her shock slowly turned to anger, then fury. How could they kill with such impunity? How could their callous group, their organization, attack, attack, and attack again without consequence?

She blinked rapidly, trying to focus on the world around her again. A kitchen. On a container ship. Vince moving away. By the door now. Laughing at her obvious distress. He loved this game. She zeroed in on him, an intensity that had nothing to do with her ability to see, hear, or feel the other side. This was Sarah, a woman, a human being, prepared to kill when given the chance. And then there was Vince, who knew it and kept his distance, at least for a little while.

The door closed as he left the kitchen, and she was alone again.

Now Sarah understood why her sister was gone, and none of the dead had returned to keep her company. The dead were emotionally bound to earth—they knew what was coming. They knew the intensity of Sarah's emotions after seeing her friends and Aaron killed.

"I'd stay the fuck away from me, too," she shouted to the empty kitchen, surprised by the sound of her own voice.

She wallowed in the pain and misery and said her goodbyes to Aaron. She would always love him and only him. And she would avenge his death, as well as Whitman's and Spencer's and the three teachers.

As many of Vince's colleagues would die as she could kill before she joined Aaron and her sister on the other side. She would blow up their container ship. She would close their businesses and never stop hunting them until they begged her to stop.

Because that's all there was left now. Kill until she was

killed.

Wasn't that what this was all about?
Us and them?

Chapter 32

The sun had dropped too low to offer any light as Darwin pulled onto Westside Drive in Etobicoke under the direction of streetlights.

"What's the pwan, boss?" Elmer asked.

"There is no plan," Darwin said. "Enter this warehouse any way you can and locate Spinello if he's here. If he isn't, find someone who can tell us where he is or how to get ahold of him." Darwin cracked his door open, then stopped. "This entire mission ends tonight if we don't find Spinello or that rig." He glanced over his shoulder at Charlie. "And stay alive. I don't want anyone else dying tonight. I've lost too many friends already."

Outside the van, he opened the back door. While the men joined him, he grabbed a packet of ammo and his El Salvadorian knife. He placed a baseball hat on his head.

"I'm going in the front offices," he told them as they

stocked up on ammo and weapons. He held his briefcase in his other hand. "You guys stay close to the bushes and make your way around the building. Enter anywhere. I don't care. Just get inside."

Darwin started away from the van with the sound suppressor still on his Beretta and tucked away in his waistband, the gravel crunching under his heels. Several rigs were parked on the lot near the back, and a couple of others were backed into bay doors of Universal Shipping's large, rectangular building. He heard a forklift moving around in the warehouse. Since this building was connected to Spinello, someone had to know how to find him.

As he neared the front door to the offices, he took a quick look back at the van. His men were all gone, lost to the shadows surrounding the property.

Darwin slowly entered Universal Shipping's offices. Something moved in the dark recess of the door to his left. Before he could react, the press of cold steel tapped his neck.

"Don't make a move," a husky voice whispered beside him. "You know, you're fucking certifiable coming here. I should put a bullet in your brain to let the madness free. Wouldn't that be delightful?"

"But you won't," Darwin said. "Because that would be too quick, and you want to make it last."

The sound of fabric twisting and being wrung tight beside him, and then a fist smashed into Darwin's side. He grunted and bent over but didn't lose his grip on the briefcase.

"What's in the case?" the man asked.

"Your girlfriend's panties. Wanna look?" Darwin flipped the case around to open it, but the gun pressed into his neck again, harder this time.

"Don't open it," the man said. He nudged him. "Move into the building."

Darwin did as he was told. To have an armed guard at a shipping company's front office at this late hour told Darwin that someone important was on the premises. Someone important like Spinello. Or maybe he hit the jackpot, and Lorenzo Falcone was there. Or Lombardi. As far as he got with his intel, it was Falcone's brainchild to snatch Sarah to force Darwin to surface. Although it could have been Lombardi as well.

Maybe they found success after all. Darwin had walked right into their hands.

The office held four large desks, two against each wall, and a receptionist's tiny counter. Two private office doors were on the right and two on the left. That could house a staff of eight to ten, not including a receptionist who would sit at the small desk by the front.

Darwin tried to turn to have a look at the man holding the gun on him. "Are you the receptionist?" he asked. "Here to welcome me?"

The man stepped in front of him. Not a single feature in the man was recognizable, even though Darwin had scoured the faces of members of the Toronto mafia for years.

"You're going to have a welcoming committee, all right. You just wait and see." The man shook his head. "Mr. Spinello," he called over his shoulder. "We have a visitor."

A toilet flushed behind the far door on the right. The door opened, and Angelo Spinello stepped out, tucking his shirt into his pants.

His eyes hardened when he saw Darwin. The expression

on his face changed to one of loathing, the top lip curling up, malice in his eyes.

"You bastard," Spinello whispered. "I've never wanted to murder someone so badly before. You bring out the worst in people."

"Either blow me a kiss or blow me away. But don't make me listen to your bullshit anymore. You're grown men acting like babies." He gestured toward the man with the gun. "Your receptionist needs to work on his manners."

Spinello smiled. It looked like he was trying to hold back a laugh.

"You've gotta be kidding me," Spinello said. "The mouth on this guy." Spinello reminded Darwin of Robert De Niro in *Midnight Run*. Same voice, the same lower mouth that drew down when he talked. "Where do you find guys like this anymore?" The goon beside Darwin shrugged. Spinello started toward Darwin. "The nerve of this guy." He laughed, short bursts between the sentences as he neared. Darwin braced himself.

"You must watch a lot of movies," Darwin said. "You know, to get the act down right. First, you're De Niro, now you're Christopher Walken in *True Romance*. When are you going to show me the real you?" Darwin leaned toward Spinello, who now stood two feet from him, a smug grin on his face. "I'll see the true Antonio Spinello when I'm torturing you, you slimy fuck." Darwin spoke with the most amount of contempt in his voice he could muster.

The sucker punch momentarily blinded him. Darwin hit the floor and smacked his head on the corner of a desk. It was the foot in the ribs that hurt most. The receptionist was having a great old time thinking Darwin was a human bean bag. Darwin would have to do something to stay conscious.

He rolled away, bumped a desk—Spinello's laughter had ratcheted to a madness level—felt another kick to the right hamstring that dislodged something, then swung the briefcase around at the offending shins. Miraculously, he had not let go of the briefcase. It connected with the receptionist's left shin with a solid thunk. The quick yelp told Darwin it was a solid hit. That and the assault on him died as suddenly as it started.

He fumbled with the briefcase, got one latch open, and then jerked at the sound of a gun firing nearby, the case tumbling from his hands.

Not feeling any impact, the weapon probably fired as a warning. Darwin twisted around to see who held the gun. Charlie stood over the body of the receptionist, his gun on Spinello. The smile on Spinello's face had disappeared.

Darwin gingerly got to his feet, his right hamstring pulsing in pain, and brushed the dirt and dust off his shirt. He touched the cut on his head where he'd hit the desk. A small amount of blood came away on his fingers.

"Meet *my* receptionist," Darwin said, pointing at the large seven-foot man. "He goes by the name Bruno, but for this little charade, he likes Charlie, as in Charlie Brown."

"Cute," Spinello said. "Do all of you have little nicknames from cartoons? What's yours? SpongeBob?"

"I'm the Road Runner." He wiped his forehead again. "Wile E. Coyote could never kill the Road Runner. You fucks should have learned that by now. And speaking of nicknames, what the fuck is *Little Tony*? You sound like you're advertising the size of your cock to the world. Antonio 'Little Tony' Spinello. Give me a break."

Spinello's nostrils flared, and a gleam of sweat broke out

on his forehead.

"Neither one of you will leave this building alive," Spinello said.

"Oh, on the contrary." Darwin raised a finger. "We will all leave alive, together. Because you're going to take me to the cocaine and then call Falcone or Lombardi or whoever has her and set up an exchange for Sarah."

Spinello's lips drew back in surprise, teeth bared. He blinked several times, then said, "Tell me, Mr. Kostas, or would you prefer Mr. Runner? Tell me, where do you get your information? Because it is faulty."

"Not faulty." Darwin raised a finger and wagged it back and forth. "Ten million in cocaine. Sitting on a truck. Bound for Falcone's ship. I know all about you and your dealings, Little Tony, or would you prefer Mr. Dysfunction?" Spinello jerked his head back. Darwin continued, "That is where you got your name, right? That's why you fuck your own girls at the Diavolo. Because you're so small, you can't get it up unless it's forced on a prostitute."

Darwin turned as a weapon fired in the warehouse somewhere. Then another. "We came this close," Darwin said, squeezing his finger and thumb together. "To nabbing you at the Diavolo." He shook his head. "A shame, really, we didn't catch you with your pants down."

"Whoever you have back there," Spinello pointed toward the warehouse. "They're being slaughtered. You both are next."

Charlie shook his head. "Not true." He switched gun hands, letting the other fall to the side. "We only saw two guards. Killed them both silently. The other six men were dock workers. Tied up in back."

"What's the gunplay then?" Darwin asked.

"Possibly another guard we missed."

"Or my reinforcements." Spinello looked proud of himself.

"Bullshit. You don't have any reinforcements coming. You didn't even know we would show up."

"True. But I needed extra men to move a shipment, knowing you were in town. I couldn't take a risk."

"Come on, Charlie. Bring Mr. Little to the back. Maybe George and Elmer need a hand." Darwin placed a hand on Charlie's large shoulder. "Wound him first. Pain is a fabulous motivator, wouldn't you say, Mr. Little?"

Charlie stepped into Spinello and elbowed him hard in the face before Spinello could get his hands up to block it. Charlie grabbed Spinello's left arm to stop him from falling to the floor.

"No trouble from you, capisce?" Charlie shouted over Spinello's whimpering. Blood seeped from his nose. Spinello's hands left his face and raised upward in surrender, still suspended by Charlie's grip, which looked vise-like as he yanked him toward the door to the back warehouse.

"Piece of advice," Darwin said to Spinello. "Do not anger my friend here. He's been known to paralyze an enemy with a punch. A *Little Tony* wouldn't last too long in the ring with this Charlie Brown."

At the door to the warehouse, Darwin wiped a slow line of blood off his forehead where it had started to trickle. Motioning for Charlie to stay back and keep Spinello to the side, Darwin opened the door and slid through. At first, the warehouse appeared empty.

He moved behind a stack of plastic-wrapped mattresses

piled ten high, a forklift parked on the other side of them. Charlie pushed Spinello in behind Darwin as he eased out to scan the warehouse. Along the back of the building, by a stack of loaded skids, a shadow ran between them. Based on the little he saw of the clothing, the man was definitely not one of theirs.

"Who's back there?" he whispered to Spinello.

"Fuck you."

"Tell me everything you can about who we're up against, or I will ask Charlie to break your wrist." He leaned in close to Spinello. "That'll be the start of what you're to endure for taking Sarah."

Spinello, his arm still held in Charlie's thick hand, was canted to the side. He moved his attention toward the wall and tightened his lips.

"Ahh, little baby doesn't want to talk." Darwin faced Charlie. "Break something."

Charlie put his gun away, then grabbed Spinello's left hand and forearm. The belief that Charlie would actually do it crossed Spinello's face. In protest, he barely opened his mouth before Charlie cranked the man's hand backward. He forced the arm up until something snapped inside.

Spinello screamed in pain, his face reddening instantly. The look on his face was pure shock.

When Charlie let go, the man's hand dangled at the wrist, a useless appendage. Spinello couldn't catch a breath, gasping and panting in pain, a high squeal emitting from his wide mouth.

Darwin turned to watch the warehouse. Nothing moved inside the building. He couldn't see anything moving outside through the few open bay doors.

"Shut him up," Darwin shouted.

Spinello's screams were instantly muffled by Charlie's large hand.

"Stay hidden," he told Charlie. "I'm going to see if our boys need help."

Darwin followed the line of mattresses until he came to a corner. Edging around, he saw that the mattresses continued to the wall, offering no way out but from the direction he had come.

But he could climb.

He slipped his gun away, then jammed his foot between the third and fourth mattresses. Grabbing the plastic that wrapped the ones near the top, he climbed. Halfway up, he jammed his other foot between two more mattresses, then rolled over the edge and eased onto the top mattress. Laying on his back, he studied the rafters. No gunmen hung suspended from them. After retrieving his weapon from the back of his pants, he moved slowly toward the edge of the plastic-covered pile of mattresses.

From twelve feet up, the warehouse looked as devoid of movement as before. Skids filled with juice boxes, plastic containers, and even car windshields with *Autoglass* written across the top of the wooden crate that held them littered the warehouse's concrete floor. But not a single man could be seen anywhere, yet gunfire randomly echoed throughout the building.

Like a hunter in the blind, Darwin stayed low and waited for his prey to expose themselves. He was rewarded when Elmer popped his head up from behind a forklift about thirty feet away. Darwin tried to focus on what Elmer was looking at as his man on the floor would better understand where the threat was coming from.

Elmer moved forward. It was easy to see the man was contemplating a run for cover behind a small stack of boxes. Darwin figured Elmer would make it as he saw no immediate threat anywhere. But just in case, he aimed his Beretta in Elmer's general direction.

Spinello cried out, but it was cut short as Charlie did something to him. Elmer paused another moment.

Someone walked out from behind a tall skid of computer parts. Darwin focused on the man, but the lighting wasn't good enough to see whether it was George.

A moment later, he knew it wasn't George as the man raised a gun and aimed it at Elmer.

Darwin adjusted his aim, held his breath, and squeezed the trigger. His distance came into question. The odds of hitting a target from forty feet away with a Beretta were slim. The only thing he had in his favor was the lack of wind inside the warehouse.

The weapon fired. The man behind Elmer jerked, then dropped from sight. Elmer spun around, gun drawn, then saw the man several feet behind him. He turned to where he thought the sound of a gun came from. Darwin waved. Elmer waved back and slipped his gun away.

"That was the wast one," he shouted. "Aww dead now."

"Absolutely?"

"Absowutewy."

Darwin climbed off the mattresses and started back to Charlie.

"Looks like they're all dead," he said to Charlie.

Spinello was curled in a corner, eyes shut.

"What'd you do to him?"

"He wouldn't shut up. Put him to sleep."

Elmer and George walked up. "Thanks fow that," Elmer said. "Saved my wife."

Darwin nodded. "All the dock workers dead, too?"

George shook his head. "We put five men in a truck near the back and locked the door."

"I owe you," Elmer said. "Saved my wife."

"Yeah, I got that." Darwin tapped Elmer's shoulder. "You'd have done the same. Don't worry about it. Now, we have to find that truck."

"It's here somewhere," George said.

"How do you know that?" Darwin asked.

"That much firepower to guard a warehouse shipping computers, car parts, and juice boxes." He shook his head. "No way."

"Good point." Darwin scratched his chin. "Elmer, George, fan out into the parking lot. Open all the trucks. Charlie will wake Spinello and ask him politely while I go talk to the dock workers. We'll find it if it's here."

He looked back at the stack of mattresses.

"Guys, wait up." George and Elmer stopped. Charlie looked over. "I think I found what we're looking for."

Chapter 33

AARON EASED BACK IN his chair and studied Alex's face.

"You're serious, aren't you?" Aaron asked.

Alex nodded, his face expressionless.

After the escape from the destroyed dojo, they wandered up Queen Street after deciding to leave the car behind. Whoever had been watching the building might discover the car gone later and suspect they were all very much alive. Several blocks away, the four of them had taken a TTC bus to Alex's small bachelor apartment, where he presented his idea.

They were in a situation like the days of Clive Baron, the British man who had killed Aaron's sister and then went after Aaron. The only way out of that mess was to murder Clive and his bodyguard. They achieved that in the middle of the night on top of a small mountain in Greece where an ancient prison sat in ruins. Aaron had barely made it out alive after being shot by Clive.

"He has a point," Daniel said. "They had every intention of killing us. I'm with Alex on this. We go in, and we go hard. Full-scale murder."

"Look, guys, I hear you, but murder is a prison sentence. We're not vigilantes like Sarah. We're not murderers. Yes, we've done it before, but as self-defense. Every time one of us has had to kill, it was to stay alive." He leaned forward, his elbows resting on his thighs. "I support that. I'd kill any day to save my own skin. But planning a murder," he shook his head, "with the actual intent of leaving this apartment dressed in those," he pointed at the black ninja suits, "bent on revenge?" He leaned back in his chair again. "Guys, that's premeditated. That's twenty-five years in the slammer."

"I know how it looks," Benjamin said. "But I think you need to consider it. For Sarah's sake. For our sake."

"For our sake? What does that even mean?" He grabbed the beer beside him and took a swig.

"Let's say this ends quickly, and Sarah's found and released or escapes. Let's say everyone walks away from this—"

"Will John Whitman walk away from this? You all saw Parkman's text."

"Just listen, man," Daniel said. He nodded at Benjamin to continue.

Aaron pulled on the beer bottle again as Benjamin started talking.

"How about this? Weeks go by. Everything's fine. We've all healed up. It's over. And then we wake to men in our houses, in our apartments."

"What men?" Aaron asked.

"Organized crime, hitmen, fixers, henchmen, goons. I don't know what they call them, but when this is over, I can assure you everyone in the mafia *won't* be dead. We were on their extermination list. When we're found alive, that doesn't negate their list." Benjamin turned his attention to Daniel, then Alex, pausing on each man's face for several seconds. "The mafia wanted us all dead. It almost worked. We would be dead right now if it weren't for Alex." He looked back at Aaron. "I say we attack them while they're weak and not wait for them to come in the still of the night."

"What makes them weak?" Aaron asked.

"They're scattered," Daniel cut in. "Dealing with the Sarah and Darwin issue. Their resources are spread out. And best of all, they think we're dead." He pointed at the black ninja suits Alex had pulled out of his closet. Suits they once wore to a Halloween party at Aaron's original dojo, a time before he knew Sarah. "No one will know what hit them when we show up in those."

"Okay, say I'm on board. Where do we hit them? We can't dress in those things and walk downtown on Yonge Street looking for Italian men who appear more mafia-like than others."

"I smell sarcasm," Alex said. "That disappoints me."

Aaron set his beer down and lowered his head, hands out pleadingly. "Look, I'm sorry, guys. It's just a lot has happened in the last few days." He raised his head and set his shoulders. "I'm all for being proactive. Let's call Parkman and see what he wants us to do. But ninja suits? Attack the mafia? Hurt them while they're weak?" He shook his head. "I'm just not buying into it."

The three teachers exchanged concerned glances.

"There's nothing we should do tonight," Daniel said. "That includes deciding what to do in the first place. Have a drink, have another. We sleep, then decide on our next play in the morning. Deal?"

"Seems fair," Aaron said. "As a team, decisions in the morning. Agreed?"

They all nodded.

"That means no outside contact. The world sleeps tonight, knowing we're dead and gone."

Everyone nodded again.

"Goes without saying," Benjamin said. "If they knew we were alive, we'd have to start worrying about another attempt on our lives, and I, for one, do not want to get shot again."

"I don't want to get shot either," Daniel yelled. He playfully shoved Benjamin.

Alex got up and left the room.

"He gonna be okay?" Aaron asked when Alex was out of earshot.

"Of course," Daniel said. "His heart was invested in the dojo. He loves us. He loves Sarah. For him, we've become his world, his family. He's like a caged lion who has the chance to eat his enemy, and he's being held back. You must remember, Alex has trained for this kind of thing his whole life. That's why he can do those flips and stunts that none of us taught him. He trained independently in several other styles like jujitsu and ninjutsu."

"I always wondered how he knew that extra shit," Aaron said idly, staring at the door Alex had left through.

"When you met Sarah," Benjamin said. "He got into it hardcore. Wanted to impress you."

Daniel nodded. "Wanted to save the world one day, and

now he has that chance. He has the chance to save you."

"To save the world?" Aaron said out loud, muttering the words as he thought about their impact.

"We're his world," Daniel added. "So yeah, this is Alex's chance to save the world. Think on these things while you sleep."

Aaron stared at Alex's closed bedroom door as he drank the rest of his beer. He knew his decision even before he fell asleep. He also knew it wouldn't change by the morning.

He would dress in a ninja suit and follow his *family* into war with the mafia. They would be liberated or killed as a unit. They had saved his life before, and he owed them the same call to action.

Calling Parkman for help could potentially leak that they weren't dead. Aaron had a better idea. Parkman had talked about two container ships down at the docks. *The Santa Maria* and *The Carolina*. Owned by some guy named Falcone, if he remembered correctly. They were involved somehow. Buck Schaffer's leads were rarely wrong. He would direct the teachers to board the ship and learn what they could of Sarah's abduction. One of the seamen would talk to them, or there would be a lot of broken bones to mend in the morning.

He would be there for his friends and family, even if it were unpleasant. Because, in the end, they weren't just family to him. They were his world as well.

Chapter 34

Darwin placed four fingers in his mouth and whistled as Charlie slapped Spinello's bloody face to wake him up.

"You'd think Spinello would've hid this shit in a truck, wouldn't you?" Darwin said, pointing at the mattresses. He knelt and examined the broken man lying at Charlie's feet. "You've done well, Charlie. I'm impressed. Only one broken hand so far."

Spinello opened his eyes and spat blood at Darwin, but it didn't reach him.

"Classy. Bet you never thought this day would come, eh? When an easy-going boy from Toronto took down the entire Toronto mafia. Twice."

"You will die trying," Spinello said, his words mumbled through several missing teeth.

Darwin glanced up at Charlie. The big man shrugged.

"He talks a lot of shit," Charlie said. "Figured it would

help him shut up."

"It's an improvement. Really, it is."

Spinello mumbled something.

"Try again."

"Buck boo," Spinello said, his lips swelling.

Darwin stood and looked down his nose at Spinello. "Have you ever heard of a man called The Harvester of Sorrow?"

Spinello's eyes widened as he looked at Darwin.

"He was a legend in your industry. You knew I was the one who killed him, right? This isn't news to you?"

Spinello nodded.

"And yet you taunt me."

Darwin thought he saw fear in Spinello's eyes for the first time since he'd met the man. The tables hadn't just turned. They'd been destroyed.

"George, Elmer. Head around to the front and ensure we're not surprised by anyone. We won't be long."

Both men headed away.

"Spinello. Where is Sarah?"

The man said nothing.

"Stand him up."

Charlie grabbed Spinello under the arms and lifted him like a ten-year-old.

"I warned you," Darwin whispered. He walked beside Spinello. "Hold his head," he said. When Darwin was slightly behind Spinello, he jumped up and came down with both feet on the side of Spinello's knee. It crumpled at an odd angle to the concrete floor, with Darwin's weight crashing down on the joint as Charlie released Spinello's head.

When Darwin stumbled off Spinello's leg, he couldn't

use it. It was certainly strained or dislocated. Not a sound came out of the mouth shaped like an O, but his eyes blinked rapidly.

Darwin withdrew his Beretta, aimed at the twisted knee, and fired twice.

"Just in case," he said. "Get him up and turned around."

Charlie did as he was told without pause.

"Use his belt to wrap a tourniquet."

Darwin kept the gun in his hand. Spinello whimpered, his face blanched in shock.

"Tell me who has Sarah. Maybe you'll walk away from this." He glanced at Spinello's leg. "Or crawl away. The point is you might still live. Just tell me who is responsible and where Sarah might be."

"Never," Spinello spat. "You for her. Exchange."

"I thought you'd say that, but we might be losing you," Darwin said. "If you faint, I'll wake you and shoot out the other knee." He grabbed Spinello's hair and yanked him to within an inch of his face. "Then I will shoot out each elbow. I will continue to torture you and keep you alive for as long as I can, just as your people did to me all those years ago. I no longer think of you or your people as human. You are an instrument for me to use until I get what I want." Darwin squeezed his fingers closed, yanking Spinello's head back farther. He clenched his teeth and shouted, "Do you understand!"

Spinello tried to nod. Darwin released him and stepped back.

"I'm going to ask each time before I shoot an appendage. There is something you must remember. A truck filled with cocaine can be replaced. Ten million dollars can be replaced.

Don't worry about your shipment. You, Little Buddy, cannot be replaced. You only have one life. Choose your answer wisely."

Darwin aimed his weapon at Spinello's other knee and looked him in the eye.

"Where is Sarah Roberts being held?"

Spinello appeared to nod.

"Yes?" Darwin said. "Ready to tell me?" He lowered the weapon.

Spinello nodded again. "On a container ship. On Lake Ontario. They will bring her to an exchange for you."

"Now that's more like it."

Darwin retrieved his El Salvadorian and sliced it into one of the mattresses. White powder flowed out over his hand.

"Holy shit," Darwin said. "It's brilliant what they did here. They hid the coke in mattresses, which were wrapped in plastic. That would help hide the smell from drug dogs." He glanced back at the crumpled form of Spinello. "Genius idea. Absolutely brilliant. Charlie, we need these loaded onto the nearest rig. Get George to help. Leave Elmer out front. I will take Spinello into the front offices to make our call. Can you do it in ten minutes, maybe fifteen?"

"Will try, boss."

"Remember the plan?"

Charlie nodded. "Of course."

"Get what you need from the van. When you're done, have George and Elmer come see me. They are free to leave. Just you and me, Charlie, I mean, Bruno. We can stop with the code names as Elmer and George are leaving us."

Bruno nodded. "Yes, boss." He turned away to head outside.

Darwin grabbed Spinello by the shoulders and dragged him toward the door to the front offices.

"You're losing a lot of blood," Darwin said between breaths. "Only serves to make you lighter." He laughed at his own humor and had to stop for a moment to collect himself.

Once the door was open, dragging Spinello got easier on the office's waxed tile floor.

Darwin managed to sidestep the body of the man Bruno had shot earlier on his way to the back office. He pulled Spinello all the way in and lifted him into the desk chair. Spinello cried out when his knee bent into the seated position. His broken hand must have bumped something. It swelled up like a cantaloupe.

"You're going to have to get that looked at," Darwin said. He felt nothing for the man. Not even pity.

Spinello clenched his eyes closed and gritted his teeth at the pain. Darwin waited for the man to pay attention to him. In the distance, forklifts whirred. That was good. The cocaine-filled mattresses were being loaded onto the trailer.

Spinello opened his eyes and glared at Darwin. "What do you want me to do?"

"Call Falcone. Tell him I'm coming in. It's over. No more attacks. No more fighting. Sarah Roberts for Darwin Kostas. A fair trade. I will meet him unarmed and without backup. No tricks. That would end this war, yes?"

"And if he doesn't go for that?"

"He will. If he doesn't, he's a dead man. Leaving me to roam these streets means every one of you bastards will die."

"I see your point."

"Tell him the ten million in cocaine is my insurance that Sarah is unharmed. She is to walk free of this and never be touched. If I get his word that she's unharmed and I see her walk to freedom, once I'm his captive, I will tell him where I've stashed the truck."

"He won't like"—Spinello winced in pain—"he won't like it. No guarantee on his end to get the truck."

"But he'll have me, and I will know where it is. Even I have limits to the amount of torture I can take."

"True. This is true. Each man has a limit."

"Call Falcone. Or we can discover what your limit is."

Spinello raised a hand. "I have reached my limit already. I will limp for the rest of my life now. I will make the call."

Spinello picked up the phone. He tapped in a number, and when he was finished, he faced Darwin.

"Ringing," he muttered.

Darwin wiped the sweat from his palm and re-gripped the weapon.

"Put it on speaker."

Spinello touched a button, and the ringing sound filled the room. A man said a tentative hello.

"Falcone?" Spinello asked.

"Who's this? Little Tony?"

"Yes."

"It doesn't sound like you."

"Lost a few teeth."

Darwin rolled his hand in circles, telling Spinello to get on with it.

"I have Darwin Kostas here." There was a sharp intake of breath on the other end of the line. "He wants to make a deal."

"No deal."

"You haven't heard what he's proposing."

"We've got Sarah. There's nothing left to deal with."

"He wants an even exchange. Him for Sarah."

Another sharp intake. Darwin felt this was all for show, and the exchange was exactly what Falcone wanted.

"He would do that? He would willingly become our prisoner? I don't believe it."

"Take me," Darwin said. "Release the girl."

"Let me think about it."

"There's no time to think about it," Darwin said. "I'm the one you're after. Carmine Fabriano is dead. Spinello will never walk right again. And all that in one day. Either make the deal, or I keep killing made men."

"Okay, you want to keep score. How's this then? I have Sarah Roberts. I've killed John Whitman and that cop friend of his, Spencer. I've also killed Sarah's boyfriend and his annoying teachers at that gay little ballet gym they ran. My men attacked Parkman in a *fucking* police station. I'm untouchable. So, tell me, what have you come to offer other than your pathetic self? Because I can get to you eventually. You're on the list."

"Ten million in cocaine. All of it stashed in mattresses. I've got the cocaine. Once Sarah walks away clean and unharmed, I will tell you where the cocaine is. That's the deal. Leave her out of it and get me and your coke back."

There was a long pause. Darwin waited patiently. Spinello grimaced in the chair, eyes shut tight.

"How do I know you'll keep your word?" Falcone said.

"You don't. How will I know Sarah will be unharmed?"

"You don't."

"So then, we have a deal?" Darwin raised the Beretta and pointed it at Spinello's face, waiting for the reply.

"Falcone?" Spinello said. "I need an answer. I'm recommending you take the deal."

"We have a deal," Falcone muttered as if the deal was hard to accept. Darwin was sure the exchange was the plan from the beginning. That was why he was hunting the cocaine like a hungry dog. He needed leverage to keep Sarah unharmed and to keep him alive the first night as their captive.

Darwin lowered the weapon. "We meet at ten tomorrow night. The exchange takes place on Toronto Island. Spinello told me Sarah's being held on a boat, so the island's perfect. I want you and your men to bring Sarah to the Avenue of the Island Bridge. Approach from the Toronto Island Park side. I will be on the Olympic Island side. Of course, if it's an outright ambush, I will not be alone, but I will cross the bridge alone at ten p.m. I expect Sarah to cross alone at the same time. Once we're over and I see Sarah leave with my colleagues on my side, I will be yours to do with as you please. And I will reveal the location of the coke. That is my deal."

"I will come myself," Falcone whispered into the phone. "I want to witness this last heroic act of Darwin Kostas."

"Do this deal, Falcone, or always look over your shoulder because I will come for you."

"Threats? At this late stage?" Falcone hung up the phone.

Darwin stared across the desk at Spinello. Their eyes met for a moment.

"Your use has been concluded."

Darwin raised the weapon and fired twice in quick succession. Both bullets entered Spinello's right cheek beside his reddened nose. The man tipped backward in the chair, arms windmilling, then slipped from the chair.

Darwin walked around the desk and checked Spinello's pulse. It was weak and fading, his face a mask of blood and bone chips, his body convulsing in the throes of death.

He waited, standing over Spinello, the desire to watch the man die changing something inside Darwin. He never hated anyone as much as he hated the members of organized crime at that moment. How they thought they were so elite. That they could ruin lives for their own selfish gain. That they could kill with impunity. Well, fuck them.

He waited until Spinello stopped breathing before he walked from the office.

When it was Falcone's turn to die, he would watch the life leave that man's eyes as well.

That one would be a greater pleasure. He was convinced of it.

Chapter 35

PARKMAN HAD BARELY SLEPT. The morning raced by in a dizzy fog. He'd had three large coffees and no food, and it was already mid-afternoon. The investigation had led them nowhere. Not a single thread of usable evidence emerged from the crime scenes at the Fermosas or the Ristorante on College Street.

He sat on a plush chair outside Casper's temporary office, elbows on his thighs, rubbing his face, trying to stay awake.

Spencer and Whitman's bodies had been found and delivered to a coroner, where autopsies were scheduled. How did it all get away from them? How could it be possible that Whitman and Spencer were dead? Sarah would be stunned and angry at their loss if she made it out of this alive. She'd known Whitman for so many years—even before she met Aaron.

A place in Scarborough called the Diavolo Motel had been hit by several someones wielding guns. Casper seemed to think that was Darwin's work.

It was such a clusterfuck that Casper had been on the phone all morning and afternoon coordinating resources, pulling in undercover cops, and gathering as much evidence on organized crime in the city as he could muster. Parkman shook his head and rested his face in his hands. How could it have gotten so far out of control? How could organized crime, on such a grand scale, be allowed to exist in the modern world with modern police forces and laws? It was an entity wholly and completely foreign to him.

According to Casper, they had a long history of using cafés and social clubs as meeting places and hangouts. Parkman learned that as recently as January 2016, they got hit hard in Toronto as the anti-organized crime unit raided Italian cafés across the Greater Toronto Area.

The 'Ndrangheta had grown to be the biggest criminal operation in Italy. La Cosa Nostra was quietly ousted as 'Ndrangheta grew to what they were today. Casper told him the Italian authorities refer to 'Ndrangheta as the *Liquid Mafia*—they filter into any hole and fill it.

The Fermosa hit was the only one baffling members of the anti-organized crime unit because mob hitmen usually avoid executing their targets in front of their wife and kids. In fact, killing the wife is the ultimate in disrespect. Therefore, they felt the Fermosa hit had to be an outside party, not an Italian one. Based on that, Casper had surmised it had altogether nothing to do with Sarah being taken.

Parkman got up from his chair and wandered to the small counter where the coffee maker was brewing another pot. His hands shook when he poured another large black coffee. Being aware that he needed food and more sleep wasn't enough motivation for him to attain those things. All he wanted was coffee and solutions. Solutions to the Sarah dilemma. Solutions to what the hell Darwin was up to and how it was all connected to the mafia in Toronto.

Without answers, the hope that they would locate Sarah and she would be unharmed was fleeting. Without answers, Parkman feared the worst. Like a jogger finding Sarah's body while on a morning run. Or a fisherman seeing her female form floating face down in Lake Ontario. Or worse still, Sarah completely disappearing and never located.

He sipped from his coffee and tried to block those thoughts from his mind. Lack of sleep and too much caffeine made him susceptible to intrusive thoughts. What would life be like without Sarah? He'd dedicated a large portion of the past several years working alongside Sarah. How mundane would his life become to head back to Santa Rosa and work as a private investigator following bored housewives or husbands to their next fling, all financed by angry spouses? He couldn't imagine how he would cope. Sure, he'd make decent money again, but for what? To live in a house, drive a car, pay taxes and interest to a bank for the rest of his life? What was that all about?

No, if something happened to Sarah, he would travel. He would see the world, find and redeem what he could of himself, and be the man Sarah expected him to be—the man he always wanted to be.

He opened drawers at the counter, rummaged inside, then slammed them shut. Toothpicks. He needed toothpicks to get through this. He'd been trying to quit. Hadn't had one in his mouth for some time, but now he needed one. Just one toothpick, and all would be well with the world for a short moment.

In the bottom cupboard, he found a cache. Once the package was torn apart, toothpicks cascaded to the floor around his feet. He grabbed several and jammed them in his back pocket, placing one at the edge of his lips. Without cleaning up the mess, Parkman retreated to the chair. His cell phone rang before he sat down.

"Yeah," he said into it without looking at who was calling.

"Parkman. Darwin here."

His face lit up. "Where are you? What's happening?"

"Where I am is not important. Where I will be is of utmost importance."

Parkman shook his head to clear it. He set the coffee on the floor and got to his feet.

"What are you talking about?" Parkman asked. He started to pace in front of the chair.

"Tonight. Toronto Island, by the Avenue of the Islands Bridge, Sarah will be freed from the mafia."

Parkman's mouth dropped open as relief swept through him. "You did"—he swallowed—"you did it?"

"Sort of. It still has to happen, but I've motivated the people involved to make this happen."

"Motivation?" Parkman wasn't sure what to say. A million things crossed his mind, but nothing was coming out right.

"Meet me on the Olympic Island side of the bridge just before ten this evening. At ten, I walk across the bridge by myself. Sarah will walk from the Toronto Island Park side.

We are to meet halfway, then Sarah comes to you."

"How can you guarantee they won't just kill her?" Parkman's caffeine-filled, sleep-deprived mind sorted through the trash and formulated the right thoughts.

A door opened along the corridor somewhere. He turned to see Casper walking his way.

"I have insurance," Darwin said. "They'll allow Sarah to come to you. Your job will be to get her safe and keep her safe until this is over."

"Once we have her, Sarah's safety won't be an issue. But what do you mean about it being over? Once we have Sarah, doesn't that conclude things?"

"Gee, thanks."

"What?"

"They'll still have me, Parkman. Wouldn't that mean it's not over? I'd like a chance to escape, too, if possible."

"Oh, right, of course. Sorry, just not thinking well. Couldn't sleep." Casper stood beside him, trying to listen in on the call. "Where will you be?"

"Wherever they take me. I have no idea."

Casper grabbed the phone from Parkman and hit the speaker option. "Darwin, it's Casper. You're on speaker."

"Casper."

"What are you talking about? You giving yourself to them?"

"Parkman can fill you in. Just be there for Sarah. She's going to need you guys."

Parkman leaned into the phone. "We'll be there. As much as I like what you're doing to negotiate Sarah's release, I don't like the sacrifice."

"You think I like it?" Darwin said, his voice a higher

pitch. "Look, guys, it's the only way. This is what they want. Let's give it to them."

Parkman watched Casper's face as he quickly deduced what Darwin was proposing.

"Let's wire you," Casper said. "We can track you. Break you out."

"They'll detect the wire. They'll be watching for that kind of stunt. No wire. No tracking devices. Nothing. I'm going in on my own. It's the only way to guarantee Sarah's safety and to end this once and for all." There was a pause on the other end of the line. "Too many people have died for this. Sarah will hate me for getting involved in her life when it's all over. She's lost so much this time around. I can never forgive myself."

"Look, Darwin," Parkman shouted into the phone. "This is not your fault. You had nothing to do with kidnapping her or killing Aaron, Whitman, and the others. And this isn't the answer to …" he waited a moment, frowned, then said, "Darwin? You there?"

Darwin had hung up.

"What did he say?" Casper asked. "Is there a meet set up?"

Parkman filled him in.

"Then we've got a lot to prepare for with only about," Casper pulled his sleeve back to read his watch, "six hours to go." He studied Parkman's face a moment. "You need sleep."

"I'll be fine," Parkman protested.

"Parkman," Casper placed his hands on Parkman's shoulders. "Listen to me. I need you. Sarah needs you. Four hours sleep, and then I'll brief you on where we're going and how we're doing it."

"I want some kind of lead on this."

"You got it." Casper raised his arms and stepped back. His foot bumped Parkman's coffee on the floor and knocked it over. He looked down. "You don't need that anyway." He turned his attention back to Parkman. "You're going to get some sleep and then report back to my office by eight tonight." He gave Parkman a stern glare. "That's an order. Sarah needs you, Parkman. Go to the back lounge and sleep on a couch. I'll tell them to guard the door so a repeat of yesterday's beating doesn't take place."

"Yeah? Thanks. That'd be great."

"You're pissed. You're sarcastic. That's okay. I like that. Get angry. Get in fighting mode. But first, sleep. Now go."

Parkman glanced down at the spilled coffee.

"Don't worry. I'll have someone clean that up. Just go."

Shoulders slumped, feeling dejected and exhausted but excited at the prospect of Sarah coming home, Parkman headed toward the lounge. Behind him, he heard Casper already on his phone calling for two police guards to meet Parkman at the lounge.

He would try to sleep. Then he would be ready to bring Sarah home. What he couldn't shake was that by his actions tonight, he was sending Darwin to certain torture and death.

To save Sarah, Darwin had to be sacrificed. It was unfair, unjust, and downright disgusting. His stomach did flips, knowing what Darwin was proposing.

If what Darwin said could be true, then one thing was for sure. Sarah would be coming back to them tonight. Darwin had mercenaries working for him. Darwin had ways to escape messes that no one else could fathom. Parkman had to believe that Darwin would have thought this through and that he wasn't merely sacrificing himself for Sarah.

Or maybe that was his plan all along?

Chapter 36

THEY HAD FED HER well that morning and even that afternoon. Her strength was up, but her back was aching from sitting so long. She needed movement. She needed to get on her feet and walk it off.

Vince promised her a big dinner, but then that would be it. He had told her he was taking her back into Toronto to release her in exchange for her friend, Darwin Kostas.

He worked away in the kitchen preparing her food.

"You can't do that," Sarah said to him. "Don't do the exchange. I won't let Darwin walk into certain death like that."

Vince looked sideways at her, then turned away and continued preparing something in the kitchen.

"You're in no position to tell us what we can and cannot do."

"What happens to Darwin?" The redundancy of the

question was maddening. She knew exactly what would happen to Darwin. He would be killed. Or tortured, then killed.

"You know exactly what'll happen to Darwin." Vince flipped something over. Sarah's limited view of the kitchen didn't let her see what he was cooking. From the smell, she assumed it was chicken. "The one stain on our collective family will be removed."

"Stain? You talk about Darwin like you spilled coffee on your pants."

Vince chuckled once, then stopped. He flipped something again, stirred a pot, set the ladles down, and turned to face her, one hand on his hip. "You are a tenacious woman. I like that." He studied her face. "What you did to Vito was a personal gift to me. I've often thought of killing that man. Now he's dead, and I don't have to cover it up with my bosses." The hand on his hip slipped off, and he absently began stirring a pot on the stove again. "Vito knew what happened at the Fermosa house." He shook his head. "Eventually, that might have come back to haunt me."

She waited for more. She wouldn't interrupt him if he were willing to talk this freely. It took several more minutes before he placed food onto plates and then came around the small kitchen to sit across from her and feed her. Chicken breast, Portobello mushroom sauce on pasta with asparagus. He wasn't kidding. The meal smelled amazing and looked better. She didn't have to worry about contaminants as Vince prepared the meal himself and ate his half from the same plate. Once the food was divided and they each had their own fork, it was bite for bite—he'd eat, feed her, then himself again.

After several servings, he stuck a piece of asparagus in his mouth and held it there, watching her face. "It's not Vito I have to worry about. It's his killer." He shoved the asparagus in his mouth and chewed. Using her fork, he twirled pasta onto it and brought it to her mouth.

"Why worry about me?" she asked, then opened her mouth to accept the pasta.

"You're going to come after us for taking Darwin. You won't let this go."

"It's not just Darwin," she said over the pasta in her mouth. "If that video you showed me wasn't doctored and Aaron and his teachers are truly dead, then you have to account for much more than Darwin."

He nodded. "That's what I mean. You won't let this die. With Vito, I could just shoot him in a back alley. You'd see that coming." He set the forks down. "So that leads me to the next question. What do I do with you?"

She shrugged. "You need me for the exchange. Do that. Then figure it out."

He crossed his arms on his chest and watched her through narrowed eyes. A grin thinned his lips.

He already has a plan, Vivian whispered in her head.

"About fucking time," Sarah said abruptly.

Vince jerked in his chair. "What was that?"

Sarah tried to cover her outburst. "It looked to me like you came up with a plan. I thought that was the appropriate response."

He nodded and uncrossed his arms, reaching for the forks again. "I think I might have. I'll fill you in on it later."

He has men who will be waiting for you after the exchange. But there's no need to worry.

Sarah took the proffered food Vince held up. She chewed, she swallowed. She ate what the enemy was willing to feed her. She needed her strength, her ability to fight back. She couldn't let them take Darwin, but she wasn't sure what to do about it yet. She wasn't a superhero with extra strength or powers of immortality. Sure, she had Vivian and, just recently, the ability to see random dead people, but when secured to a chair, she was still flesh and bone and had no choice but to wait it out.

If they delivered her bound and kept her locked up like a prisoner on death row, she'd be as useful as chopsticks in a sugar bowl.

Let the exchange happen, Vivian whispered. *Your time will come.*

Sarah nodded to the voice emanating inside her head, happy her sister was back. They ate the rest of the food in silence. Once Vince had cleared the table and placed the dishes in the sink, he walked to the door and stopped, hand on the knob. The ship canted to the side, leveled, and moved the other way.

Vince checked his watch. "It's after eight. I'll return soon so you can have a bathroom break, and then we'll take a boat into the harbor for the exchange." He met her eyes. "I can't say it's been a blast, but it's been good knowing you." He exited the kitchen and left Sarah to talk to Vivian.

Vivian told her about the hit on the Fermosa family—why it happened and how. She told her about the exchange and what that would look like.

But most importantly, Vivian filled her in on all the other details, some good, some bad. When she was finished whispering in Sarah's head, the door opened, and Vince entered the kitchen to take her to the bathroom.

She couldn't wipe the tears of joy from her face until he untied her hands. There was no doubt in her mind Vince mistook her tears for fear.

She couldn't care less.

Vince didn't have much longer to live, and Vivian just told her that Aaron and the teachers were alive and well and that she would see them after the exchange.

Chapter 37

THE FOUR OF THEM drove to Toronto harbor in black body suits, leaving the balaclavas aside for when they were out of the car.

"Everyone got everything?" Aaron asked. "You guys ready for this?"

Daniel nodded as he angled the car onto the loading dock's lot. *The Santa Maria* towered over a few smaller boats moored at the docks.

Aaron twisted in the car seat to look back at Alex and Benjamin. "You guys good?"

Alex offered him a slight nod. Benjamin lifted his weapon and clicked something on it.

"All good," Benjamin said.

"You know, carrying a gun isn't very ninja-like."

"Yeah, but I'm always the one who gets shot. I want to be able to shoot back."

The car slowed to a stop. Daniel set the emergency brake and turned in his seat. "Bullets can spray and hit unintended targets. Most times, a knife fight is more dangerous."

"True." Benjamin placed the gun in his waistband. "But it doesn't matter to me. I want to be able to return fire if I have to," he repeated.

"Only do it if you have to. Ninjutsu is about stealth, and guns aren't too stealthy."

"Don't have to tell me that. I've trained for years for a night like this." Benjamin's face turned defiant. "Hey, why's everyone harassing me about my choice of weapon? At least mine's more common than Alex's. He's carrying a fucking sword on his back."

"A Samurai 3000 Ninja, to be exact," Alex whispered.

"See?" Benjamin said. "Talk to him about that. The handle sticks up over his head."

"Alex is the only one of us who has trained with one of those for hundreds of hours," Aaron added. "He's going to carry what he wants, anyway."

"As I am," Benjamin said, arms crossed.

"It's fine. I wasn't saying you couldn't. Just that it was unbecoming. We're not like them—"

"You sure?"

Aaron waited a breath, nodded, and turned back around in his seat. "Everyone check their weapons. Twelve Senban hybrid stars, four combat throwing knives, and one blade ring." Each man in the vehicle whispered check as he read off the items. "Use all weapons at will, but remember to use your skills, which are just as lethal."

The sun had dropped enough that the shadows were long on the docks. They would wait until at least thirty minutes after nine and then head for *The Santa Maria.*

"Guys, gain access any way you want," Aaron added. "Whistle to get the attention of the others. And lastly, don't forget—none of these boys think we're alive. With these balaclavas, that notion won't change." He turned in his seat, addressing his three teachers. "Just like when you guys came to Greece to save me. Just like when we were dealing with the Enzo Cartel, this is full combat. This is what we have trained most of our lives for. But it's something bigger. We're here for answers. We're here to save Sarah. And we're here to hurt them. I'd venture away from killing if possible. Maim, injure, and incapacitate all you want, but only kill when necessary. I'd hate for any of us to be imprisoned after this when all we're doing is third-party self-defense, in my opinion. But our justice system sucks, so watch your back, leave no trace, get in, get out. We good?"

"Nice speech," Daniel said. "Yeah, we're good."

They donned their balaclavas.

"Lastly, remember, this is about Sarah. Someone on this boat knows where she is. It's our job to learn her location. Then we go and get her. Simple shit, right?"

"Yeah, simple," Benjamin said. "As simple as solving a Mensa catalog in a coma. We're entering into a major problem with extremely limited knowledge."

"I know. But Parkman said they couldn't get access to this ship. He said Casper believed the people on this ship were connected to Sarah's disappearance. She may actually be on board. That's good enough for me."

"Me too," Daniel echoed.

"Me too," Alex whispered.

Benjamin waited several moments, then said, "Me too."

"Okay, guys. Let's go get answers."

The four doors opened, and Aaron and his three teachers were lost to the shadows.

Chapter 38

Parkman sat on a park bench sipping a grande black coffee from Starbucks. They had woken him in the back lounge at the police station, piled him into a cruiser and then a small boat, and dumped him on Toronto Island five minutes ago. One of Casper's men shoved a coffee in Parkman's hand, and he dutifully began drinking it. More awake by the second, he faced Casper and gestured for him to talk.

"Tell me, what's happening?"

"We have a five-man team," Casper said. "They'll be hidden among these trees. Two of them will be acting as members of the public, simply walking by on the path on their side of the bridge."

"Worried about backing them up?" Parkman asked.

"We have backup on this side. The bridge they've chosen for the exchange isn't too big. My men from this side will easily be able to pick off assailants. They're trained marksmen."

"So, how is this supposed to play out?" Parkman couldn't stop drinking the coffee. He'd fallen asleep as Casper ordered but felt heavy since being awakened. When he awoke, a part of him wondered if everything had been a dream. Could Spencer and Whitman truly be dead? He wasn't sure about Aaron and the teachers as the fire department on-site at the Queen Street dojo hadn't found bodies in the wreckage yet. Witnesses from neighboring stores told an altogether different story than what the guys in the men's washroom at the police station had on video. Apparently, Aaron's boys coaxed the tenants of the stores on either side to leave the premises and move to safety. That meant they knew about the bombs. And if they knew, showing their faces in the front window was a ruse.

Casper felt the dojo boys would turn up at the right time. Multiple calls to Aaron's phone had proved fruitless.

Casper dropped onto the park bench beside Parkman, watching the other side of the bridge.

"There's not much to play out. We're assuming Darwin will be here by ten, about thirty minutes away, and the people who have Sarah will show up, too. The two of them will cross the bridge. Once they're side by side, my guys on this side of the bridge, who've already taken up lofty positions in these trees, will be able to fire on the mafia's position from over here."

"And Darwin and Sarah?"

"When guns start, Darwin will know to grab Sarah and run back our way."

"You're not going to brief him?" Parkman asked.

"I know a lot about Darwin. When the shit goes down,

he'll put Sarah first and cover her. He doesn't need to be *told* when to act and who to protect."

"I didn't mean it that way. He's planning on surrendering. He says he has a plan. Some kind of insurance guaranteeing Sarah's safety."

"Whatever he's got, this is the best plan. This guarantees Sarah's safety and his. They cross the bridge into our protection, and my shooters take out any resistance on that side."

Parkman faced Toronto and stared at the lights of downtown as he drank more coffee. It didn't sit right with him. Something was off in Casper's reasoning. Sure, Casper had been there for Sarah countless times, but no man was always right.

Casper had five men. Was that enough? Carmine Fabriano was dead. Someone had hit the Diavolo Club looking for Angelo Spinello. Parkman had to assume it was Darwin and his team of mercenaries, which meant Spinello was likely dead. The Fermosas had been killed. Of the big families in Toronto, only two prominent names stuck out. Lorenzo Falcone, the man in charge of the docks and making sure the 'Ndrangheta's shipments encountered no delays or issues, and Antonio Lombardi, the oldest man of the seven families. Even Mancuso Corrado, the owner of the Calto Social Club, is said to answer to Lombardi. A tight-woven band of families made up the elite in the organized crime world, and it all led back to Lombardi.

But no one had been able to locate Lombardi or Falcone in the past few days. They'd vanished from their local haunts and were probably orchestrating these events from some kind of bunker.

He drank the rest of the coffee and tossed the cup in the trash beside the bench. The evening was warm, with a soft breeze coming off Lake Ontario. Casper had stepped away to talk quietly into his cell phone. Parkman scanned the trees closest to the bridge. Three snipers were in position for the exchange somewhere in those trees, but he couldn't see a single one of them—as it should be.

He turned back toward the water at the sound of a boat approaching. His watch said 9:42 p.m. It was almost time. Sarah would be back in just over twenty minutes.

The small fishing boat eased to the shore, and the engine died. A man hopped off and started toward him. A minute later, Darwin stepped into view.

"Hey," he said. "We good? Ready to do this?"

Parkman got to his feet. "You don't have to do this. We can find another way."

Darwin moved in closer and placed a hand on Parkman's shoulder. "There is no other option, my friend. I know these people. It'll never end unless I do this."

Parkman tapped the hand on his shoulder. "It's admirable to see—"

"No," Darwin cut him off as Casper started their way. "It's not admirable. Don't confuse notions of honor with this. It is a requirement of me to give myself to these animals so that my friends can be freed from the rope I've tied about their necks by my actions. In the end, either kill every hornet in the nest or be stung to death. This is me dealing with the issue my way so no more harm comes to Sarah or anyone else I know, you included."

"You can rationalize it any way you want, Darwin, but I still see it as admirable."

Darwin stepped past Parkman without saying anything more. He stopped in front of Casper.

"I don't want any interruption," Darwin said. "It's vital their people take me."

"I don't have the same vision of how this will go down."

"I called you here for Sarah. Get her and clear the area. Everything else will work itself out."

"Whatever you say, Darwin."

Casper shot a glance at Parkman.

"Just stay back and keep Sarah safe. I'll handle Lombardi and Falcone."

"Is that who orchestrated all this?" Parkman asked.

Darwin turned back to him. "I have my suspicions, but I think this is all Lombardi. Falcone and Spinello went along with it. Fabriano may or may not have even known all the details."

"You have any weapons?" Casper asked.

"None," Darwin said, patting down his sides. "It would be a waste. They'd take them even before I got on their boat to leave this island."

"And no one is with you?" Casper prodded further.

Darwin shook his head. "No one. I'm alone." He wiped his nose and sniffled.

"Let me ask you a question," Casper said. "Was that you at the Diavolo Club?"

Darwin nodded like it was no big thing. "It was me. You'll find Spinello's body at Universal Shipping in Etobicoke. Investigating officers will find his home on Lynvalley Crescent open and waiting for your guys to go in and search his office. Been there, too. Anything else you want to know?"

Darwin's strength did not intimidate Casper. They were on the same team, and Parkman figured Casper just wanted to tie up loose ends as they might never see Darwin again.

"Yeah," Casper said. He ran a hand through his hair, then rubbed his ear. Parkman wondered if that was Casper's version of a nervous tic. He'd rarely seen Casper nervous. "The authorities will want to talk to you about what you've been up to today. I can't protect you on murder charges."

"Don't need protection."

"If some of these hardened detectives in Toronto decide to come after you … look, all I'm saying is I appreciate what you're doing for Sarah, but you're on your own with what you did to the mafia."

Darwin clenched his fists, then unclenched them. Parkman felt the tension in the air but had no desire to quell it.

"I think after what happened to Whitman and Spencer," Darwin started, his voice tight, clipped, "not too many detectives will spend a lot of energy hunting me down." He rubbed the back of his neck, then scratched his hairline. "You want to know what's hard for most people, Casper?"

"Tell me."

"Living off the grid."

"True. Basically impossible nowadays."

Darwin stepped closer to Casper. Casper stood his ground.

"I've been living off the grid for years. I find it easy. Even these mafia fucks couldn't find me with all their resources, and I've been living among them in Italy. That's why they have Sarah. They knew it was the only way to expose me."

"Why'd you do it? Why kill all their guys, then?"

"Because I wanted to hurt them before this exchange took place." Darwin pointed at the bridge. "They have taken so much from me and everything from Sarah." The emotion on his face told Parkman what he wanted to know. Darwin was a better man in so many ways. "They can't always walk away from their actions. They think they can, but they can't. I won't allow it. I chose to hit them hard. I wanted to make Lombardi invested in this exchange with extreme prejudice. I want him to hate me like no other adversary. That not only makes this exchange a reality, but it also ensures Sarah's safety. They'd never do anything to harm her knowing I'd voluntarily walk into their waiting arms if she's safely returned without a scratch. They've never had an enemy quite like me, and they need to destroy me, my name, and everything associated with me. But first, I have to walk across that bridge."

"Walking across that bridge seals your fate." Casper coughed into his hand as if the words were hard to say.

"I know what I'm doing." Darwin faced the bridge again.

Parkman moved around to stand in front of Darwin. He stared at Darwin's jeans and T-shirt, then searched in the man's eyes for sanity.

"Darwin, please, this is insane," Parkman said. "They'll torture and kill you before the sun rises in the morning."

"I'm sure they'll try." Darwin managed a smile.

"Why? Tell us, why are you doing this? There are other ways to get Sarah back from them."

"No, there aren't. This is necessary. Sometimes in life, you have to do what's necessary."

"You're talking about doing homework instead of

attending a party after school. Sure, sometimes you have to do what's necessary. But this isn't high school. This is your life, Darwin. Sarah wouldn't approve even though you're getting her out from under them."

Darwin met Parkman's eyes. In the dim light, Parkman saw a fortitude and determination on the man's face he'd never seen before on anyone's except maybe Sarah's.

"Pain is fleeting," Darwin muttered. "Torture is only effective if I let them think it is by screaming and shouting. Unless they paralyze me or dismember me, I'll heal. In the meantime, the wound of losing Sarah because of my actions would never heal. If they killed Sarah in my place, I couldn't live with it. And if I can't live with it, they would've killed me, too." Darwin edged closer to Parkman. "I don't see myself as noble. This isn't noble. It's suicidal. I know that and understand it. But there is no other way, like running into a burning house to locate your screaming wife. I have no choice. It has come to this, and I am ready." He turned his attention to Casper. "Neither one of you can talk me down. Now, let's get on with this, shall we?"

"It's your show," Casper said, gesturing toward the bridge. "For the record, I admire what you're doing. I've never met a man like you, Darwin. I respect that. And if this doesn't end well, I'll reach out to your wife and make sure she's taken care of."

"Both of us will," Parkman chimed in.

"I appreciate that, guys."

Parkman glanced back up at the trees, wiping at an errant tear. Casper's men were hidden so well that he couldn't see them. But none of that mattered. What mattered was their aim and if it would be true. He didn't want to lose Darwin, but he also didn't want to lose Sarah.

He fixed his eyes on the bridge. Sarah Roberts would walk across it for fifteen minutes or so, a free woman.

He sincerely hoped they didn't lose Darwin in the process, but hope was fleeting. Parkman had no doubt Darwin would spend the remaining hours of his life in incredible pain and leave this world a broken man.

If only there were another way.

Chapter 39

AARON LOST SIGHT OF his team before he reached the end of the dock. What surprised him was the lack of security around the vessel. On the deck of the boat, several feet above his head, he'd seen at least two men patrolling, pacing back and forth, staring off into the distance, but no one on the docks. Where was everyone? How could this vessel have so little security if they had rebuffed Parkman's and Casper's efforts to board?

If Sarah was being held here, the amount of security was no match to his four-man team.

At the far corner of the darkened dock, he quietly climbed onto a thick rope that bound the ship to the dock. He wrapped his legs around the rope, locked his ankles, and ascended the rope using his one good hand and the inside elbow of his bandaged hand. Without making a sound, he got to the boat and used his good hand to grab the edge above his head. Then he released his legs and swung sideways until his foot caught the rim of the boat's ledge. Easing over the rim, Aaron dropped onto the container ship's deck.

He retrieved a throwing star from the pouch at his waist and started forward, careful to stay in the darkest part of the deck. He slinked along the deck, a steel railing to his right. He'd been on the vessel three minutes before hearing the first grunt of pain. Up ahead, a set of stairs led to the deck below. He leaned out and looked down. One of the sentries was sprawled on the deck, his neck twisted at an odd angle. He wasn't moving.

Aaron got down the stairs and placed his back to the cold wall. Another grunt, this one louder, came from his left.

Where the fuck is everyone?

With his bandaged hand, he wasn't keen on too much fighting, but he still wanted to do his part.

"Aaron?" Alex called from somewhere above.

"Shit," he whispered out loud. "Why the hell is he shouting? We were supposed to whistle."

"Benjamin?" Alex called out.

Aaron moved away from the wall and looked up. "What?" he yelled back.

Alex stood two stories up, leaning over the railing. "Stay there. I'm coming down. Call the boys. We need to leave."

"Leave?" Aaron said to himself as he stepped back into the shadows.

Moments later, Alex materialized before him with a soft whoosh of air.

"Fuck, that scared me. I hate when you do that."

"We have to get to Toronto Island," Alex said, ignoring Aaron's comment.

"Toronto Island? Why?"

Daniel moved out of the shadows behind Alex.

"Daniel," Alex said without turning around. "Have you seen Benjamin?"

"Wait a second," Aaron said. "He walked up behind you, Alex. You're not inhuman. How did you know that was Daniel and not Benjamin, or one of the bad guys?"

"When I was coming down to you, I saw him. Recognized his shoulders. They're wider than Benjamin's. I know his walk, too. By the time I reached you, I figured he would be behind me less than eight seconds later."

"Oh. Okay, I see. Sometimes that shit gets to me. Like you're in some B movie and basically unstoppable."

"I am unstoppable. Now, listen. Sarah and Darwin are doing some kind of exchange on the island."

"An exchange?" Daniel asked. "For what?"

Alex turned to face him. "For each other. I talked to one of the men in the control room. The exchange is supposed to happen at ten tonight. We've got less than half an hour."

"Why didn't anyone call and tell us?" Daniel asked. "Wait, don't answer that. Everyone thinks we're dead."

Alex started away. "We have to find Benjamin and leave this boat."

Aaron ran to catch up, Daniel on his heels. "How are you proposing we get to the island in twenty to thirty minutes? We'd be late even if we drove over and tried to find a boat."

"We're taking one of the speed boats attached to this vessel." Alex held up a set of keys. "Courtesy of the man in the control room. He was willing to lose the boat after his leg and arm were broken."

"Holy shit," Aaron said. "You did good."

"Let's hurry, but be careful. We can't be sure we got everyone."

Alex led them down stairwells, along hallways, and down farther onto the flat part of the vessel where hundreds of containers were usually held.

"We're almost at our escape boat," Alex whispered. "No sign of Benjamin."

They stopped and stared back up at the navigation bridge. Aaron couldn't see anyone moving. The ship appeared deserted.

"Okay," Aaron said. "You two go. I'll stay behind and wait for Benjamin to surface. Once he does, we'll bring the car around." He set a hand on Alex's shoulder. "Go do something to bring Sarah home—"

A gun fired somewhere in front of them. They ducked as one. Aaron sprawled out flat while Alex rolled to the outer rim. Daniel disappeared behind him.

"What the fuck was that?" Aaron whispered.

"Hey, guys," Benjamin shouted from above them. "Got him." Heavy footsteps pounded down a set of stairs. "Fucker was tracking you three." Benjamin made it to their level and ran toward them. "I can't believe I nailed the bastard from one level up." He stopped in front of Aaron. Behind the black ninja balaclava, Aaron was sure Benjamin had a smile ear to ear. "See, this gun was a good idea."

Aaron started to get up. He glanced at Alex, but Alex was gone. Daniel stood up from behind a small white barricade.

"Where's Alex?" Benjamin asked. He stowed the gun away in his waistband. "He was here a minute ago."

Another weapon fired, the sound of ricochets filling the air.

"Get down," Aaron shouted.

Benjamin grunted and dropped to the deck like he'd lost his legs. Curse words issued out of his mouth as grunts.

Aaron crawled toward him and got up close. "You hit?"

"In the fuckin' leg. Above the ankle."

Aaron moved that way and gently touched the wound. There was enough light to see a gouge just above Benjamin's ankle.

He turned back to him. "You're barely hit. Nothing more than a few stitches to fix you up. You'll be fine."

"Why?" Benjamin asked. "Why me? Again?"

"Where's Alex?" Aaron asked Daniel.

Daniel shrugged.

Then Alex stepped into view. "He's dead. You can get up."

"What the fuck?" Benjamin said.

"You didn't hit him from up there," Alex said. "A handgun? From that distance? If you had hit him, it would've been one lucky shot. I went back to make sure he was dead. Sorry I didn't get there sooner. He got one off before I could snap his wrist and then his neck." Alex shrugged. "Hey, you didn't get shot, did you—"

"Don't say a fuckin' word," Benjamin grunted.

"Sorry, man." Alex got down on his haunches. "Everyone to the boat. We leave in half a minute."

"Where's the boat?" Aaron asked.

"Follow me."

Alex got up, walked to the side, and hopped into the darkness beyond. Aaron listened and waited. Seconds later, the water splashed as Alex entered Lake Ontario beside the container ship. He moved to the ledge and looked down. It had to be at least a fifty- to eighty-foot drop into the inky black water.

It was hard to see Alex in the water, but Aaron spotted him as he climbed aboard a speed boat moored against the side of the container ship. There had to be an easier way to get on board, but Alex was right; they didn't have time to navigate the lower sections of the container ship. The fastest way to the speed boat was gravity.

"Let's go, guys," he said. "Over the ledge."

"Not me," Benjamin protested.

"Daniel," Aaron ordered. "Help me with him."

The speed boat engine cranked on below them.

"Hey, fuck you guys. Don't throw me over."

"Well, you can't stay here. And we need someone to man the boat while we head in to help Parkman and Darwin."

"Yeah, but guys, I can't swim."

Aaron looked at Daniel, who shrugged. "Don't have any other options," Daniel said. "Just hold your breath. One of us'll grab you and haul you in the boat."

Benjamin tried to pull away, but his face scrunched in pain when he applied pressure to his injured ankle.

"Fuck, guys. I mean that."

They grabbed him under the arms, walked him to the railing, and threw him over without another word. Benjamin shouted something on the way down, but it was cut off when he hit the water.

Another gun fired somewhere behind them.

"Shit, go, go," Aaron yelled at Daniel, hopping up and over the ledge. More gunshots before he smacked into the water.

The breath knocked out of him upon impact, his body

seizing at the cold water's shocking contrast to the warm summer evening, he forced himself to struggle for the surface. The surface broke over his head in what seemed like minutes but was only seconds, and he gasped in life-saving air. Beside him, Daniel trod water, holding Benjamin's head up.

"Help me with him," Daniel pleaded.

Alex bent over the edge of the boat and grabbed Benjamin's arms. All four men were in the speed boat within seconds, and Alex jumped into the captain's chair. He revved the engine, and the back of the boat lowered in the water as the front rose and shot forward.

The sound of gunfire broke the quiet night behind them.

"Must've left some of them behind," Alex shouted over his shoulder.

"It was a big boat," Daniel yelled back. "It wasn't like we had a lot of time."

"Hey, Daniel," Aaron called to him over the wind. "Check Benjamin again. He might've gotten shot. Who knows, right? He's like a magnet for bullets."

"Fuck you, Aaron," Benjamin yelled. "Fuck all of you."

Aaron moved up to sit beside Alex. "You learn anything else from the guy on the boat?"

"Yeah, that we're too late."

"What? Why?"

"Earlier, there were six more men on the container ship."

"Where are they now?"

"On the island."

"Why?"

"They are there to kill Sarah and everyone who has arrived to take her to safety."

Aaron stared forward momentarily, then turned back to Alex, his gut churning in circles.

"But Parkman will be there. Casper, too. They'll have backup, won't they?"

"The exchange with Darwin is a setup. They're all supposed to die tonight, backup or no backup." Alex turned to him, then looked away. "That's why I'm in such a hurry."

Aaron looked at a small clock on the boat's dash: 9:55 p.m. They were ten minutes away.

They would miss the exchange.

Chapter 40

Sarah got off the small boat behind Vince and followed him to a park bench where half a dozen fully armed men had gathered. They had completely removed all her restraints and brought her fresh clothes. Slick black yoga pants and a black T-shirt. She felt more ready for the gym in her new clothes than participating in a deal with the mafia.

"What's this?" she asked, pointing at the weapons. "You don't need this kind of firepower."

"Shut up," Vince said. "It doesn't concern you."

He pulled out a small metal device, brought it to his mouth, and sucked on it. A puff of smoke escaped his mouth and rose above him.

"A vape? Really?" Sarah stepped around in front of him. "You're not worried it'll give away your position? You don't think Darwin will have men waiting on the other side of the bridge to pick you guys off?"

He stared at her a moment as several of the men around them snickered.

"Vito used to bother me about my cigarettes. Now I have you shitting on the vape." He turned away from her.

She looked across the bridge to the other side. "What time is it?" she asked.

Vince held his arm out, angled so Sarah could read the time.

"It's five to ten," she said. "Isn't the exchange at ten?"

Vince pulled on the vape, blew out smoke, and then nodded.

"What are we waiting for?" She leaned in close. "You're waiting until your men can scope out their side."

She punched his arm. The vape shot into the air. He swung around in surprise.

"This isn't going to be an even exchange, is it?" she yelled at him.

"Keep your voice down." He moved to within an inch of her face. "Yes, I have men who are here to cover us. You will be free to walk the bridge when they are in position. The delay has nothing to do with sabotaging the exchange and everything to do with making sure it goes right. Darwin was the one who picked this location, after all." He pulled back. "Did you consider that in your anger?"

She peeked through the trees to the other side of the bridge but couldn't make out how many people were over there, let alone who they were. This was all wrong on so many levels. She couldn't allow Darwin to sacrifice himself for her, but she also couldn't stay with these men. The only reason she was still alive—and treated so well—was because of their extreme desire to nab Darwin.

She studied each man surrounding them. They were fully equipped with Kevlar vests, weapons in holsters on their belt line, and bulky suit jackets covering other weapons underneath.

Vince wasn't taking any chances. All the odds were stacked in his favor. They were on an island, so she couldn't run away. She couldn't possibly fight them all.

There was nothing to do but wait this out. And antagonize Vince because he couldn't kill her. He couldn't even touch her this close to the exchange.

"Why did you take out Patricia?" she asked.

To his credit, Vince didn't flinch. He kept staring across the water at Toronto. His men spread out and created a perimeter of at least ten feet around them.

"Tell me," Sarah prodded. "Why kill Patricia Fermosa? Isn't that deemed highly disrespectful when the contract was only for her husband?"

With the information Vivian had supplied her when she was finishing her dinner on the boat, she had enough ammunition to piss off Vince for hours.

"Where'd you hear that?"

"Oh, fuck you. What a time waster. You were there. You know what happened in that house. You killed the husband and wife but forgot one thing."

Vince turned away from the lights of Toronto and sat on the bench. "You've got my attention. Go on. What did I forget?"

"Their kid."

Vince seemed to think about that a moment. His eyes drifted down, then to the side. A moment later, he jerked his head toward her.

"How do you know? Who told you?"

"Their kid heard the shots and watched you and Vito walk out to your vehicle to leave." Sarah let out a derisive cluck of her tongue. "Fucking amateur night at the mafia execution. You were even holding your arm."

Vince shot up from the bench and grabbed her T-shirt in both fists, shoving her backward a couple of feet.

"Who the *fuck* do you think you're talking to?"

"A dead man—"

"Let her go, Vincenzo," a man shouted behind Sarah.

Vince held on a moment longer, then released her. She took a step to gain her balance, then turned to see who ordered Vince to release her.

A tall, heavy-set man approached with a batch of his own men in suit jackets. Each man held a semi-automatic rifle.

"What's with the Colt AR-15s?" Sarah asked. "You expecting a war?"

"Someone shut the girl up, but do it gently."

"What the fuck—" A hand clamped over Sarah's mouth, and an arm wrapped around her abdomen. She was locked in a partial bear hug, forcing air over the man's hand to breathe.

"Everything in place?" the new man asked.

"Yes, sir, Mr. Lombardi," Vince said. "Just waiting on the all-clear from my men on their side of the bridge."

Lombardi nodded.

Sarah stopped fidgeting to listen. The hands holding her loosened some, but not enough to break free.

"Good. I'll be over here. Make sure when Sarah makes it to the other side, Darwin is brought to me. No mistakes. I want this bastard to myself."

"Of course, Mr. Lombardi. You got it."

Lombardi turned to Sarah. "When this is over, and Darwin is nothing but a memory, maybe I'll come find you. We can finish what we started here today. How does that sound to you?" Lombardi nodded at the man holding her. The hand over her mouth pulled away.

Sarah gathered saliva and spit at Lombardi. It fell short.

"Fuck you," she rasped. "You spineless piece of shit."

Lombardi yanked a handkerchief from his pocket and dabbed at his jacket where he thought some spit had hit him.

"What are ya gonna do?" he said to his men, a smile playing across his lips. "Take it easy, little girl. We'll have you home to mommy real soon." He lowered the handkerchief. "Then we'll come over to your house for a little visit, eh? Maybe I'll stay the night and fuck you with a butcher knife." His hand came up so fast that she didn't see it until it was too late. The slap was loud in the still night, jerking her head sideways. The sting was worse than being punched. "Fuck you, little cunt. Don't forget, I own this city and everyone in it."

Her left eye watered. "You sure? Do you own the city? If so, why kidnap a little girl like me to get to Darwin? Big man you are."

"Get her outta my sight."

Arms jerked her sideways and half carried her a dozen feet until the hand clamped over her mouth again.

She studied the terrain. How deep was the water under the bridge? Once she met Darwin, could they jump in and get away as whoever was on Darwin's side of the bridge covered for them?

Lombardi said the name Fermosa. She went limp in the man's arms, hoping he'd stop struggling so she could hear better.

"I have confirmed that Marty and Patricia were not a contract hit," Lombardi was saying. "Darwin killed them, too. With Fabriano and Spinello gone, Darwin has a lot to answer for."

Sarah moved to look at the two mobsters talking. She saw Vince's face clearly. He was watching her, knowing she knew he'd killed the Fermosas. That was on him, not Darwin.

Vince raised his hand and used his finger and thumb to pantomime a gun aimed at her. He lowered his thumb and jerked his finger back. The message was clear. She would be dead if she raised an objection about the Fermosas.

Lombardi and Vince talked in hushed tones after that as she watched three men conversing on the other side of the bridge. If she wasn't mistaken, she could've sworn it was Parkman, Casper, and Darwin.

That's all they have? Against this veritable army?

Once they met on the bridge and passed one another, what would stop Lombardi's men from opening fire on them all?

Darwin's team had to have firepower hidden somewhere. They just had to.

Lombardi raised his voice, ordering his men to disperse and take up position.

The time for options was over.

The time to walk the bridge was upon them.

Chapter 41

WHEN THEY NEARED TORONTO Island, Alex killed the boat's engine. The foursome sprawled on the floor of the boat as it rode the forward momentum into the island's shore.

Aaron knew the area well. Alex had skirted by the Royal Canadian Yacht Club Island and came into the Olympic Island from the side. According to the man Alex had spoken with back on the container ship—who had sworn he was telling the truth—Darwin was supposed to cross the Avenue of the Islands Bridge from the Olympic Island side at ten that night. They were coming in on the island's far side—about 400 yards from the bridge where the exchange was to take place—seven minutes late.

But they had two things going for them. One, no one expected the dead men from the dojo bombing to come to life at the exchange. The second thing was they hadn't heard any weapon fire yet. Aaron believed no gunfire was a good sign.

Three of them hopped off the boat, leaving Benjamin behind with his handgun to guard the shore and prepare the craft in case a quick escape was needed.

Aaron followed Alex and Daniel into the trees and away from the shore until he lost sight of them in the shadows. Minutes later, the empty Avenue of the Islands Bridge appeared in the distance.

At this late hour, the island was vacant. Using the trees as coverage, he slinked along, getting as close to the bridge as possible, as fast as possible. Could the man Alex talked to have lied to him? What if Sarah was on the other side of Toronto, and all this was a waste of time?

He didn't think so. Alex could be quite persuasive.

Fifty yards from the base of the bridge, Aaron stopped. At the sight of movement on the other side of the water, he dropped to the ground and stared. A man stood to the other side of the bridge in shadows, moving slightly. He seemed larger than normal, but with only the silhouette to go by, there wasn't enough light for Aaron to see why. He waited, watching.

A male voice rose in the distance. Someone was barking orders. His stomach felt heavy with lead as the man stepped from the shadows. But it wasn't one man. It was two people.

He had been restraining Sarah.

At the sight of her, promise and hope swept over him.

She moved away from the man. She was dressed all in black, making it hard to see her. Sarah's blond hair gave her away. She strode to the access of the bridge and stopped. Aaron rolled slowly, careful to be silent, until he leaned into the base of a tree. With a full view of the bridge now, he saw Darwin had walked to the access point on this side of the bridge.

They were going to do it. An exchange. A life for a life.

This is fucking insane.

Darwin was sacrificing himself for Sarah. Aaron's eyes welled up. There wasn't a single person he knew, outside of maybe Parkman or himself, who would do such a thing for Sarah. They all knew how important she was. Seeing her again, in the flesh, on the other side of the bridge, caused an urge in him to protect her, to shield her. But this was Sarah Roberts. If someone were going to protect anyone, it would be her.

He watched them both as they stood on opposite sides, staring at each other. Sarah appeared to be talking to a man on her side, which stalled the exchange.

Averting his eyes, he took in as much of the surrounding area as possible. Two men stood a dozen feet behind Darwin, watching him. From Aaron's vantage point, he was sure it was Casper and Parkman.

He rolled onto his side and looked behind his friends, following the shoreline to the area where Benjamin waited in their speedboat, but didn't see another soul.

Where was everybody? What if the mob on the other side released Sarah and then opened fire, killing everyone on this side of the bridge?

Something wasn't right. Parkman wouldn't have come without some form of backup.

The trees?

After a quick glance to see Sarah and Darwin still hadn't moved, Aaron rolled onto his back and looked up into the tree above him. The tree's branches and leaves were too dark. Nothing to see whatsoever.

He closed his eyes and waited until they adjusted to the dark. Someone shouted something from the bridge area.

He opened his eyes slowly, studying the tree above for any line that might be off, any irregular shape.

A click of a weapon sounded above him. The impulse to move, roll away, and run caused him to jerk. In his suit, it would be next to impossible for anyone to see him. Whoever was in the tree above him had a weapon, and they were preparing to use it.

But on whom? Darwin or Sarah? Or both?

And wasn't this an equal exchange? As much as he didn't want to lose Darwin, he selfishly wanted Sarah back. If the shooter above him were to cut Sarah down, he would be lost forever.

Without Sarah, there was no future.

He curled into a ball, rolled onto his feet, and placed his back to the tree. A soft breeze came in off the water, rustling the leaves above. He hopped up and clung to a branch with his one good hand.

Deftly, he curled his body again and placed his feet on the branch. Seconds later, he sat up on the branch and glanced over at the bridge.

Sarah had started across with Darwin coming from the other side. The exchange was happening now. Whoever was in the tree above him had their orders, and those orders involved a weapon. He couldn't think of any result that satisfied him by leaving the man alone in the tree to follow those orders.

Without wasting another thought, Aaron glanced above him, saw the next branch he intended to use, and ascended higher into the tree, intent on pushing the gunman out of his hiding spot.

He just hoped he wasn't making a mistake.

Chapter 42

WHEN LOMBARDI'S MAN RELEASED her, she stepped away from him, wiping the sweat of his hand off her mouth. Lombardi's armed men had taken up positions in spots hidden from her view. Only Lombardi, Vince, and herself were visible on their side of the bridge.

On the other side, Parkman, Casper, and Darwin waited.

"I'm not walking across," she said. "This isn't right. You're going to kill Darwin as soon as he sets foot on this side."

Lombardi crossed the concrete path and moved to within feet of her.

"Sarah, I have no beef with you. I don't like you, but I have no beef with you." His hands never stopped gesturing as he spoke. "It's not your fault you have no idea how to pick friends." Lombardi snuck a look across the bridge at Darwin, then turned back to Sarah. "This isn't about you. He did this.

And as much as you care about him, you must walk across that bridge, or everyone will die. There are weapons trained on you. You're only alive because that man is willing to cross this bridge."

She stared at Parkman and Casper as they stared back. What did they have planned? Where was Vivian? Any assurance from anyone on her side would help her place one foot in front of the other and cross the bridge.

Of course, she didn't want to die. But she also didn't want to live with Darwin's murder on her head because she didn't do something to stop it.

Whisper the Fermosa details to him, Vivian said abruptly.

Is that all you have for me? How about, Hey Sarah, Darwin will live? What about, Hey Sarah, walking across that bridge is the best thing for you?

Vivian ignored Sarah's pleas and filled her in as she waited by the bridge, with Lombardi not three feet to her left.

"The Fermosa hit wasn't Darwin," she said, slightly above a whisper.

"Excuse me?" Lombardi leaned in closer.

Sarah walked to the edge of the bridge, which put her closer to Lombardi. Darwin did the same. They stared across the span at each other. She wished she had something to lean on as her knees grew weak.

"The Fermosa hit wasn't Darwin," she repeated.

Lombardi matched her whisper as he replied. "And how would you know something like that?"

"You know who I am, don't you?" She didn't let her eyes leave Darwin.

"Of course I do. A low-life vigilante. You're not much

from where I'm standing, but hey, perceptions can be off some, yes?"

"Mancuso Corrado ordered Vincenzo Balzano from the Calto Social Club to execute Marty Fermosa because of a lousy bet. Corrado felt it would be cheaper to pay Vince ten grand than fulfill the bet he lost and pay Martino two hundred grand. The board didn't sanction it, as you already know. Vince took his new recruit, the late Vito Romano, with him."

"Bullshit. This is no time for brownie points. The games are over." His shoes scuffed the pavement as he pivoted and turned to walk away.

"Not bullshit. Talk to your associates at the club on Ellesmere. And Lombardi?"

Without turning away from Darwin, she heard him stop. After a moment, he said, "What?"

"Vince took out Patricia for fun. Fact check. You'll be able to confirm with Corrado—he would never lie to you."

Lombardi hesitated, then stepped back over to her. He lifted his lapel and spoke into it.

"Whatever happens tonight on this bridge, the girl walks free," he ordered. "I need confirmation from each team member."

Lombardi stood close enough to Sarah that she heard several men click their confirmation into their devices wherever they were.

"Goodbye, Sarah. You have won yourself a reprieve. But we will meet again as it seems you know more about me than I expected. That needs to change. I might want to meet up in a week or two and discuss this further."

"I agree. Let's have dinner sometime."

She stepped onto the bridge. Behind her, as Lombardi rejoined Vince, she heard him ask, "What was that all about?"

"A failed attempt to negotiate for Darwin's life."

"Fat chance."

"That's what I told her."

Sarah took another step. Then another. She was finally coming home from the airport. But in doing so, Darwin was leaving.

He started across the bridge toward her. Parkman and Casper eased back into the shadows of a tree.

They were about to do the impossible. How could she let him finish his walk across? How could she voluntarily allow him to kill himself?

She wouldn't do it. She couldn't.

When they stopped halfway, she would hug him. Then, throw him over the railing and into the water. Let the men on the surface fight it out.

She had spent her adult life saving strangers. When it came to friends, she would give her life to save them.

Just as Darwin was attempting to do for her.

Chapter 43

DARWIN MOVED TO WHERE the path ended, and the bridge started. He struggled with his emotions when he saw Sarah. He was relieved to see she looked fantastic. Walking across the bridge would be hard for him. He knew what he was walking into. But he could only imagine what Sarah was going through. This walk represented everything she was against. She saved lives. She fought for the underdog. She would risk herself a thousand times over for a stranger. What Darwin's enemy was asking of her was simply too much. He knew that going in and understood Sarah enough to know that she would never complete the walk across the bridge without some form of insurance.

The best time to deal with an objection is before it happens. He had planned to deal with Sarah *before* she tried to save him. To get in front of Sarah, he would have to thwart her. It was the only way.

He waited patiently, watching her on the other side of the bridge talking to Lombardi, the man who needed a coffin more than anyone else present. Lombardi had orchestrated everything. He was the man who located Darwin by taking Sarah.

Darwin and Rosina had hacked into enough of the Toronto mafia's devices over the previous years to catch random chatter between the families. They narrowed down Sarah's name and where the information was coming from. To get to Darwin, take Sarah Roberts.

Well, it worked.

What they didn't account for was Darwin would come with baggage. Ten million in cocaine worth. Stolen from the halfwits who were taking him.

They wanted a game of whispers, a game of death, and that was exactly what he would offer them.

Sarah started toward him with a tentative step. He matched her, step for step. He remained human throughout the process, as frightened as any man may be. But he learned long ago that when faced with a threat, attack the person making it, eliminating the threat immediately. Living with something over his head was no way to live. He couldn't eliminate every single member of the mafia in every city on the planet, but what he could do was start with the ones interested in threatening him or his way of life. That meant Lombardi, Spinello, Corrado, Fabriano, Vincenzo Balzano, and many more had to go.

They were ten feet apart. Lombardi had moved back from the mouth of the bridge to the shadows. A breeze kicked up, ruffling Darwin's hair and cooling the sweat in his shirt.

They took another step. Grateful he wasn't tearing up, he

moved forward again. As if in a slow-motion romance movie, they walked toward each other across the span of the bridge under the light of the moon. To an outsider unaware of the life and death game being played out on the Avenue of the Islands Bridge, this would be a great video for YouTube.

Four feet apart, he saw the gleam in her eyes, and he nearly broke down.

"I'm so sorry, Sarah," he whispered.

"Not your fault."

"None of this would've happened if you didn't know me."

"I'm a better person for knowing you, Darwin."

They stopped walking a foot apart.

"Don't," he said.

"Don't what?"

"Make me cry before I walk to their side."

"Why, Darwin? Tell me why you arranged this?"

"Your freedom."

"Not good enough. I can't walk away knowing they're going to kill you."

"Thanks for reminding me."

"Darwin, turn around and run."

"I can't."

"What's the hold-up?" Lombardi yelled.

"Saying goodbye," Sarah shouted back. "Fuck off."

"Make it quick."

They stared at each other. "I can't let you do this," she said.

"You have to. They'll cut us down before we make a break for it. I saw half a dozen men or more, fully armed, on their side."

A tear streaked down Sarah's cheek. "I refuse to allow someone to dictate their terms to us. Let's take our chances and jump."

"No, Sarah. This is the only way." He closed the gap between them and placed his hands on her shoulders. "Can they hear me? Listening devices? You wearing a wire?"

She shook her head. "Not that I'm aware of."

He brought her into him and hugged her tight. "I'm so sorry this happened to you." She rested her head on his shoulder. "I'll make them pay before this is over."

"How?" came her muffled reply.

"I've got insurance."

She hugged him tighter, her feminine arms as strong as any man's.

"What kind of insurance?"

"Meet me at that huge truck stop just north of the city on Highway 400 at five in the morning. That gas station and restaurant place. It's got a Tim Horton's and a hamburger joint. You'll understand everything then."

Her grip on his rib cage lessened briefly. "How are you able to dictate terms to them? What have you got up your sleeve?"

"Just be there."

He tried to release her, but she tightened her grip. It suddenly dawned on him that she would do something, some trick to thwart the exchange.

"Sarah? Don't."

Then her arms let go. Her legs let go as well, and she fell to the pavement. Her eyes rolled back in her head, and she was out. He felt for a pulse. It was strong and pumping.

"Let's go," Lombardi yelled. "Enough with the games.

We gave her back as promised."

"What happened?" Parkman shouted from the other side.

"Not sure," Darwin shouted back. "She just passed out."

Then Casper said the one word that got Darwin to his feet.

"Vivian."

Of course. Vivian intervened to stop Sarah from whatever it was she was going to do. It all became clear to Darwin. His plan would work. Vivian believed in it. Whatever she'd told Sarah so far hadn't convinced her to go against her nature, who she was on the inside, so Vivian had to take over.

Imagine that, a woman in a battle with herself on the inside, where one entity had the power to knock the other one out at will.

Darwin kissed his fingers and tapped Sarah's cheek.

"I hope to see you soon, my dear friend," Darwin whispered. "Thank you for your sacrifice. And Vivian, if you can hear me, take care of her for me."

He stepped away from Sarah and started toward his mortal enemy. Lombardi materialized from the shadows, followed by Vince.

"Where's Vito?" Darwin asked. "Lurking around here somewhere?"

"Vito's dead," Vince said. "Courtesy of that bitch you just knocked out. She has hers coming one day."

"Vincenzo," Lombardi snapped. "We had an arrangement. Safe passage for Sarah has been guaranteed."

"It's fine, Lombardi. Once I'm dead, all bets are off. I know how this works."

Lombardi nodded at Vince, who produced white plastic

ties for Darwin's wrists. Once his wrists were secured, he turned back to look at the bridge. Vince patted him down while Lombardi's driver hopped out of the vehicle with a wand and ran it up and down Darwin's body.

"He's clean," the driver said, then disappeared back inside the SUV.

On the bridge, Parkman had run to Sarah's side. He was attempting to lift her onto his shoulder.

Lombardi moved toward the SUV.

"There's the matter of my truck filled with cocaine," Lombardi said. "I'm assuming you're willing to give that back now."

"On the condition that you use one bullet when the time comes."

Lombardi snapped around. He looked shocked and offended that he might miss the chance to torture the mafia's most hunted and hated enemy.

"That wasn't the arrangement. The rig for Sarah's safe passage. You arranged the deal yourself when you called me from Spinello's warehouse before you killed him."

"Arrangements can change." Darwin shrugged. "You still get me. You get your murder. I'm just trying to buy a little dignity here."

"Get him in the vehicle. We'll discuss this at the warehouse."

Vince opened the back door and shoved Darwin inside. Before closing the door, Lombardi spoke into his lapel.

"Execute all of them. Including the girl. Do it now."

"Noooo!" Darwin shouted as he shouldered the door back open.

Vince grabbed him around the neck and held him back.

Lombardi smiled down at Darwin. "Arrangements can change. I still get my murder. And now a little dignity. How about that, eh?"

Gunfire erupted on the other side of the bridge. Parkman jerked and spasmed, then dropped from sight.

Darwin screamed.

Chapter 44

AARON HAD CLIMBED THE tree with stealth, his wounded hand throbbing with the effort. He kept it close to his chest, ignoring the pain and hoping it wasn't bleeding under the bandages.

Within a minute of moving upward, navigating the tree's limbs above his head, he had put himself directly behind the man who had taken up residence in the tree. The man, dressed in black, held a sniper rifle aimed at the bridge. He was so focused on his target, staring through the eye of the scope on top of the rifle, that he wasn't paying any attention around him. Of course, he wouldn't have expected a man dressed in a ninja suit to be stalking him in the tree's branches.

Positioned carefully, balanced on strong branches, Aaron's good hand ready to shove the man from his post, he waited. As it was, he had no idea if this man was with

Parkman and Casper—his best guess—or aligned with the guys on the other side of the bridge, and he wasn't about to ask him. That would ruin the element of surprise.

Leaves blocked most of his view, but he could see sections of the bridge. Darwin and Sarah had met and spoken briefly. They hugged. Then Sarah fell to the pavement. He leaned forward, intent on watching what was going to happen next. From his vantage point, Aaron was one foot from the backside of the man holding the rifle. It was only a matter of time before the man turned around and saw him. But he waited. Friend or foe, he had to wait. Killing or maiming one of Casper's men wouldn't go over too well.

Darwin moved away from Sarah, leaving her alone on the bridge. Aaron lowered his head to see better. Parkman was running to Sarah's aid. The men meeting Darwin placed something on his wrists, spoke to him momentarily, and shoved him toward a waiting SUV.

SUV? On an island?

Aaron watched. He waited. Maybe everything would play out smoothly. He finally decided that the man sitting a foot away had to be Casper's man covering the area in case the mafia double-crossed them.

Parkman lifted Sarah onto his shoulder.

A soft thump sounded to Aaron's right, at least fifteen to twenty feet away. It sounded like someone had jumped and landed on the ground hard. The gunman lifted his head from the rifle's scope and turned that way. Aaron didn't move. He didn't even breathe.

The gunman listened to something coming through his earpiece.

"Roger that," he whispered.

He placed his eye back to the scope and aimed his weapon.

He's going to shoot. He's going to fucking shoot.

Aaron lowered his head to find the sight line of the weapon to discover what the man aimed. He could've sworn the gun was aimed at Parkman.

Planting his feet firmly, the inside of his elbow clinging to the branch above his head, he pulled out his combat knife, flipped it into position, and raised it above the back of the man's neck.

The man's rifle spit a bullet. Aaron jerked at the sound. Wide-eyed, he saw Parkman jolt upon impact and drop to the pavement beside Sarah.

Shocked that he'd waited too long, Aaron stabbed downward with his knife, slicing into the back of the man's neck. He unlocked his elbow from the branch over his head and dropped his weight onto the sniper's back, his knife hand still sawing deeper into the flesh until he hit bone, at which point he added more muscle to the task.

The man became epileptic below him, slipping sideways, the rifle forgotten. At one point, in Aaron's blind rage to maim the sniper who shot Parkman, the man slipped from under him, dropped five feet, careened off branches, and continued downward to the ground below.

Aaron slowed his hand as it cut into a branch, his mouth wide, staring back at the bridge.

More gunfire erupted. Another thump from a tree to his left. And then another.

The SUV carrying Darwin squealed away into the night.

Then all hell broke loose.

Chapter 45

PARKMAN FELT THE IMPACT and dropped to the ground to cover Sarah. The bullet had to have come from a high-powered rifle from the trees behind him. Casper's men were up there. Could the mafia have bought any of them? Or could Lombardi have already planted his men on their side of the bridge before they arrived?

The back of his ribcage ached where the bullet hit the thin Kevlar vest Casper had made him wear. He was eternally grateful for the things Casper made him do.

Gunfire erupted above his head. Bullets volleyed across the water. A police siren screamed in the distance.

He lifted Sarah's legs and pushed them against the railing. Then he pushed her arms and shoulders deeper into the shadows. To cover her vital organs from a stray bullet, he laid across her, the vest strategically in place.

Within a minute, the gunfire died down and then stopped.

Someone yelled in pain. Someone else shouted something in Italian.

He wasn't leaving Sarah until Casper gave him the all-clear.

Sarah stirred below him. "Huh," she muttered. "What happened?"

"You fainted," Parkman whispered.

"What?" Her eyes shot open. "Fainted? Parkman, get up."

"In a second. There's gunfire. Not sure if it's over—"

"All clear, Parkman," Casper yelled to him.

He eased off her. "Sounds like it's over."

"I didn't faint. That was Vivian. She knocked me out."

"You sound angry about that."

She glared at him. "I was about to shove Darwin into the water with me. We'd swim to safety."

"That look in your eye," he said. "Didn't think I'd see that on our reunion. You look mad enough to fight a grizzly."

She shook her head. "Sorry, just seriously pissed that Vivian would do that."

"There's another plan. Something bigger than us." He sat back against the railing gingerly. "Vivian probably knows."

"Where's Darwin?"

"He left with Lombardi."

Sarah got to her feet and brushed herself off. "Vivian just signed his death warrant. No way they keep him alive. Not Darwin Kostas. Not even if he thinks he has some kind of insurance on them."

Parkman used the railing to get up, his rib cage protesting where the bullet impacted. Casper ran up to them.

"Sarah, so good to see you."

"Casper."

"Physically? You okay? Need a paramedic?"

She shook her head.

"Appreciate you looking out for me," Parkman said.

"Oh, right," Casper faced him. "Parkman, shit, sorry about that. Happy you had the vest, though."

"Yeah, me too."

"Come." Casper led them off the bridge as police boats approached the island.

Several men stood around an unlit fire pit. More than the number of men Casper and Parkman had come with. As he drew closer, he saw the three extra men dressed in black, head to toe. He recognized their builds and almost shouted with joy.

"Aaron, Daniel, Alex," he said, singing their names.

Aaron pulled his balaclava back and patted Parkman's shoulder as he walked around him to hug Sarah.

"So happy you're back," Aaron said, relief coursing through him as he squeezed her.

Sarah relaxed in his arms. "I want to be happy it's over, but I can't. Not at Darwin's expense." She pulled away and looked from Parkman to the boys and Casper. "They showed me a video of the dojo—"

"Alex figured out what they were up to," Aaron said, glancing at Alex. "We showed ourselves at the window, then bolted for a ladder, climbed into the roof, and dropped down into the comic book store after the bombs blew. Not a scratch."

Sarah and Aaron embraced again. Idly, Parkman watched the authorities securing their vessels and start toward them.

Finally, Sarah pulled away from Aaron. "We have to get

Darwin back."

Casper nodded. "I know. We will. First, it was a chase to find you. Now we're chasing Darwin. I've got a dozen people working on it."

"What happened over here?" she asked. "Who shot at us."

"They did," Daniel said, pointing.

A dozen feet away, six men lay sprawled out, limbs askew.

"They dead?" Parkman asked.

"Quite," Alex said.

"Lombardi's men," Casper said. "Planted hours ago to execute us all after the exchange. We didn't see them. If it wasn't for these three," he pointed at Aaron, Alex, and Daniel, "we'd all be dead."

Daniel shrugged. "We heard you guys had trouble at the docks. Parkman mentioned something about it to Aaron before the dojo blew up. So, we thought we'd board *The Santa Maria*. It was empty but for a few guards. One of them told Alex about this exchange. So here we are."

"Alex took out four of them even before they had a chance to shoot," Aaron said, patting Alex on the shoulder.

"Great job. Stellar, really, but we need to leave," Casper said. "We have a police escort back to Toronto. We can regroup at the police station and decide where to go from there."

"We've got our own boat," Aaron said.

"I'm going with Aaron," Sarah added.

Casper hesitated a moment, then clapped his hands and said, "Okay, fine. Did I mention I'm happy to see you boys alive?"

Aaron nodded.

"What a crazy twist of events," Casper continued. "We thought you were dead, but here you are, in the flesh, saving *our* asses." He looked down at the ground and shook his head. When he looked back, he stared at Aaron. "I'm usually pretty good at covering my ass in the field." He jerked a thumb at the line of dead bodies. "So, thanks for that."

Sarah murmured her thanks, and Parkman smacked Aaron on the shoulder.

"Shit, man, without you guys." He left the rest hanging.

"Great," Casper said. "Now that that's out of the way, we have a good idea where they will take Darwin. My team will start there."

"And I have a good idea where Darwin will be tomorrow at five in the morning," Sarah said.

Parkman stepped closer. "Where?"

"Aaron, take me off this island."

"With pleasure."

"Casper, I'll call to fill you in. Do what you want between now and three a.m., but be ready for my call. I'll need an assault team ready to go to a location just north of the city by four. Can that be done?"

"One hundred percent. We'll be ready. I know better than to press you for details."

Sarah nodded. "Thank you. Too tired to fight right now, anyway." She turned sideways. "Parkman, come with us, okay?"

Parkman nodded. "Of course."

Aaron started away. Daniel and Alex moved out to the sides to flank the group as Parkman and Sarah followed them. Police officers swarmed the area by the bridge, coming in off their boats. Casper's voice traveled to Parkman across the shore as he began to direct clean-up efforts.

Minutes later, Aaron pointed at a speed boat floating by the shore. Benjamin stood near the front of it, waving.

Once everyone was on the boat, Daniel pushed it into the water and climbed on board. Alex fired it up and steered them into open water.

They had just watched their best friend willingly sacrifice himself for the safety of their Sarah. Parkman understood innately that this meant every single soul on the boat around him was prepared to do whatever it took to bring Darwin home.

There was nothing more noble than what Darwin did for Sarah.

Except maybe putting their lives on the line for the man who saved her.

Chapter 46

Darwin recognized the warehouse immediately. Lombardi had chosen Universal Shipping, Angelo Spinello's business, as the secluded warehouse to take him to. Spinello was probably still cooling in his office, the first signs of rigor mortis setting in.

Nothing remarkable had happened on the drive over from the shore where the small ferry had dropped them off. What should've happened was the police boats were supposed to stop the ferry and arrest everyone on board except Darwin. But they didn't. In fact, it was several members of the Gang in Blue, as Sarah called them, who guided Lombardi's SUV off the ferry and offered his vehicle a free pass to clear the area.

When Darwin had asked how he could achieve such status, Vince told him to shut up.

Darwin learned a lot at that moment. Even if he'd called

out for help, even if he'd managed to attack and fight the men in the SUV, the authorities were working for Lombardi —at least the ones who aided in their exit of the downtown core.

Now, far away from any commotion, on a dead-end street in Etobicoke, pulling up to an empty warehouse, Darwin began to fear for his life. He had no means of escape, and only ten million in cocaine keeping him alive.

How ironic because sometimes cocaine kills people. Darwin was sure he'd make the night *because* of the cocaine. Although, once it was recovered, his life would be forfeited.

The driver, a wide-shouldered man, spun the wheel and eased the SUV up to the front office section of the building. Lombardi hopped out, Vince followed, then the driver. Darwin sat alone in the back seat, his wrists cuffed.

The three men conversed quietly among themselves, then dispersed. Vince opened the side door to let Darwin out as Lombardi and the driver headed into the building.

"Out," Vince said.

Darwin lowered his head and slid across the seat. He swung his legs out and hopped down. Vince shoved him toward the warehouse. Darwin stepped twice, slowed to regain his balance, then started toward the building. He ascended the steps and waited for Vince. After a moment, Vince opened the door and gestured inside. "Go."

Darwin was led through the offices and into the back warehouse where a pile of mattresses filled with cocaine had once sat. Bruno had done a great job clearing them out.

Lombardi stood by a steel chair near the side corner of the building. It had been placed quite close to the exact bay door where they'd loaded the cocaine-filled mattresses onto the trailer. The driver had removed his suit jacket and put on a plastic apron.

"That's it?" Darwin asked. "Just you guys?"

Vince shoved him again, this time so hard he stumbled toward the chair and regained his balance in front of it.

"Sit," Lombardi said.

His stomach dropped. Nothing about the next five to ten hours was going to be pleasant. But it was preferable to leaving Sarah with these men.

He eased onto the chair. The driver moved behind him and secured his hands. Then he did the same to his ankles.

"Why shoot Parkman?" Darwin asked. "Why double-cross me? You got what you wanted. We both know you'll get the location of the cocaine out of me. So why go back on the arrangement?"

Lombardi pulled out a nail file and went to work on his index finger as the driver continued to secure Darwin to the chair. Vince disappeared around the corner and came back with two folding chairs. He placed one down for Lombardi and then sat in the other himself.

"We never had an *arrangement*," Lombardi said, the last word coming out in a deeper voice. "You killed friends of mine years ago. Now you've killed more friends of mine. In fact, a friend of mine is sitting in the other room, dead because of you." He meticulously moved the nail file back and forth across the baby finger on his left hand. "When we are finished with our business," the file stopped moving as Lombardi looked up, "and you are dismembered and strewn about the city dump in pieces, I will go after every single man, woman, and child involved in your life." He slipped the file into a breast pocket and leaned toward Darwin, his elbows resting on his thighs. "That includes Sarah Roberts. That man, Parkman, and his colleague with the American government, Buck. They'll all have an accident."

The driver finished securing Darwin to the chair. He tried to shrug, but the restraints were too tight. He craned his neck to look at what the driver had done and was surprised to see straps on his upper arms and thighs that appeared to be attached to nothing.

"This isn't working," Darwin said. "Release me from this chair. Offer me a beer and maybe some take-out pizza. That might help me decide to tell you where the cocaine is." He shook his head and flexed his hands. "This, nope. Not very friendly."

Vince chortled under his breath. A sharp look from Lombardi cut him short.

"You're a comedian?" Lombardi asked. "You don't have much faith in us. Every man has a limit. We'll find yours."

The sound of electricity zapped behind Darwin, and a cold sensation passed through him.

"What are these straps for?" he asked. But then it dawned on him. "Tourniquets," he whispered.

"That's right, tourniquets," Vince said in a brusque tone.

He got another look from Lombardi.

"I can't have you bleeding out," Lombardi said. "Not before you tell me what I need to know."

Another zap of electricity behind him.

Lombardi pulled out the nail file again and started to work on his other hand. "We're at the dead end of our street. Only the birds in the rafters will hear your screams in this corner of the building." The file zipped back and forth. "By morning, it'll all be over." He stopped the file and met

Darwin's gaze. "When the workers in neighboring buildings come to work in the morning with their cup of coffee and bagged lunch, you'll be nothing but a memory."

"That's interesting," Darwin said, using all the willpower he could muster to stay composed. "I see things completely different."

The nail file stopped. "How's that?"

"I see all of you dead by morning, not me. Then I'll go after the rest of the 'Ndrangheta until none of you exist anymore." A nervous laugh escaped his lips. "Just accept it, we see things differently."

The driver came around to stand in front of Darwin, his arms dangling at his sides, hands empty.

The rage on Lombardi's face, mixed with the color that rose to his cheeks, told Darwin that he'd gotten under the man's skin.

"Where's the cocaine?" Lombardi asked.

"Untie me. Order pizza."

Lombardi nodded at the driver, who stepped closer, pulled back his arm, and swung.

The pain was incredible, much more than anticipated. Darwin swung his head back around, blood oozing from the wound. He glared at the driver's hand: brass knuckles.

No wonder it felt like a fucking train hit me.

"Where's the cocaine?" Lombardi asked.

"Pizza, asshole." Darwin spit out blood.

"Hit him again, but be careful not to break his jaw. I need him to be able to talk until this is over."

Another punch in the same spot. Darwin wondered why the chair didn't fall over but then figured they'd bolted it to the floor for this purpose. He couldn't see the legs of the chair when he looked down.

Stains on the concrete floor surrounded the chair.

Blood?

They'd used this chair before. Others were tortured in this exact spot.

He raised his head, spit out more blood, and used his tongue to feel around his teeth. All intact.

"Don't worry about your teeth," Lombardi said. "You won't have any soon enough." He smacked Vince's arm. "Get me the pliers in Spinello's desk." Vince bolted from his chair and headed for the front.

Lombardi faced Darwin, a crooked grin on his face.

"For the third time, where is my cocaine?"

"You guys are thick," Darwin said, trying not to mumble the words as his cheek swelled. "Order pizza, then we'll talk."

Lombardi checked his watch. "It's early. We've got all night. Hit him again."

The fist came in high this time, and Darwin was knocked unconscious.

Chapter 47

Once back on shore, Aaron led them to their vehicle, and Parkman called a taxi as they wouldn't all fit in one car.

Sarah let them handle everything as she moved to the side and tried to reach out to Vivian. She asked a dozen questions in her head, going crazy with the notion that Darwin was a captive of the mafia. She blamed Vivian for that because of her interference. It was on her to fix this.

Where was Darwin? Could they get him out? What's going to happen at five in the morning at the truck stop north of Toronto?

The taxi pulled up, and they agreed to meet at the Marriott Hotel on Highway 400 north of the city, a five-minute drive to the gas station rendezvous where Darwin told her to be in just over six hours.

Vivian remained quiet. What was more maddening was that Sarah wasn't seeing dead people, so Vivian's silence was on purpose. She stayed mute for a reason that Sarah was supposed to trust. If she'd learned anything over the years, it was to trust Vivian implicitly, but that was thinning some. Sarah wanted action, and she wanted answers. Hearing nothing in her head offered her no hope of finding Darwin.

Half an hour later, the two vehicles pulled into the Marriott's parking lot. Parkman paid the taxi driver, then they headed to check in.

The clerk eyed them suspiciously. Parkman's chest bulked out with the Kevlar. Sarah was dressed in black, and behind her were four men in black suits. At least the dojo boys had removed their balaclavas. Benjamin was still limping from the bullet wound, and blood had crusted up on his new one.

"What's going on?" the clerk asked, probably wondering if he should call the police.

"Costume party," Sarah said. "We need two rooms. Preferably on the same floor and close to each other."

The clerk did a double take, then accessed his computer and used a finger to scroll down the screen. He assigned them rooms 307 and 309. Once their keycards were issued and Parkman paid for both rooms with his credit card, they started toward the elevator.

Upstairs, inside the rooms, Aaron and Sarah took 307 and bade goodnight to the others. They were to meet at three-thirty in the lobby. Sarah would call Casper and have a couple of cars brought around.

She flopped down on her bed and covered her eyes with her forearm.

"You okay?" Aaron asked.

"No."

"Did they hurt you?"

"No. Well, one tried."

"What happened?" His voice took on a hard edge.

"I had to kill him."

"What? That's it. You just killed him?"

She pulled her arm away and looked around for Aaron. He was sitting in the corner chair.

"There will be retribution," Sarah said. "Once they've dealt with Darwin, they'll come after us. They had a plan to kill us at the exchange. Even Rosina is no longer safe. We have to reach out to her and get her on the move. There's no telling what they'll learn from Darwin before they kill him." She felt the tears rise to the surface. "How could he do that for me?" she asked. "Why?"

"He was always selfless," Aaron said. "He could've stayed off the radar in Italy and still be there right now. Instead, he wanted to help us, help you. It's not his fault, nor is it ours. It just is."

She covered her eyes again, wiping them periodically.

"I'll never be able to face Rosina."

In the five minutes of silence between them, Sarah detected a presence moving close. She felt it on her skin as if it inhabited the room. She opened her eyes but was still alone with Aaron in the hotel room on the third floor.

"You okay?" he asked.

"Yeah, just felt something. That's all."

She waited, then a distant voice echoed in her head. A man's voice.

She glanced around the room quickly. She could see the dead sometimes but never hear them except for gibberish. Maybe if she listened well enough, she could hear them as clearly as Vivian. Could that be why Vivian was so quiet? To make room for others to offer advice and knowledge of the future? Things she wasn't aware of?

Arabella came through to her.

"Arabella?" Sarah said, repeating the word. "That mean anything to you?" she asked Aaron.

"Not that I can think of. Why?"

"One second." She held up a finger for him to wait.

She closed her eyes and focused inward. The presence drew closer.

Arabella Fermosa ...

"Arabella Fermosa," Sarah said.

"You might want to call Casper," Aaron offered.

The voice moved to her inner ear and whispered the rest.

Rattled by hearing someone else's voice in her head in the spot Vivian usually occupied, Sarah lunged across the bed and snatched up the phone.

"What's going on?" Aaron asked.

"Listen when I talk on the phone so I don't have to say it twice."

He came around the bed to stand beside her.

She dialed Casper's number. He answered on the first ring. Voices and commotion resonated from wherever he was.

"Casper, it's Sarah."

"Okay, hold on. Let me move away from these guys."

The noise eased down, then was gone.

"Okay, shoot," Casper said. "I'm in the men's room. No one's here."

"Where is Arabella Fermosa?" Sarah asked. Instantly, Vivian filled in the rest for Sarah.

"Not sure. Why?"

"I just heard from"—she stopped, then said—"my sister. I need a location."

"She didn't tell you?" he asked. "Okay, sorry. Last I heard, once her parents were found dead, she was brought in and interviewed about what she might have gone through. Then, some uncle picked her up. She could be anywhere now, and wherever she is, I'm sure she's asleep."

"Casper, I need you to listen to me." Sarah pushed the phone into her ear, her lips pressing into it as she spoke. "I was told saving Darwin's life will come down to a short window of opportunity. Don't ask what that means because I don't know. But what I do know is that Arabella will make the difference—"

"Make the difference to what?"

"Darwin's life."

"Meaning you need me to find her and pick her up?"

"Yes. We need Arabella to be at the gas station for the meeting."

"Is that where Darwin will be?"

"I can't be sure. That's where he told me to meet him, so I'm assuming so."

"When did he say this?"

"When we talked on that bridge. Before I passed out. You need to find Arabella and bring her to that meeting."

"Sarah, I can't do that."

Her hand tightened on the phone. "Why not?"

"She's only twelve years old. I can't trade her for Darwin. I can't negotiate with a twelve-year-old—"

"That's not what this is. We need Arabella to talk to Lombardi."

"Talk to Lombardi? About what?"

"I have no idea. All I know is that Arabella and Darwin both live through this if that girl is at the meet with Lombardi."

"Then what? They talk, and Darwin lives? I don't get it."

"We give Arabella to Lombardi. She leaves with him. That's how it needs to work."

"Impossible. It still sounds like an exchange. I can't yank her from her warm bed at one or two in the morning, drive her to a gas station, and give her to the city's biggest mob boss. Especially after her parents were killed in a mob hit. If it was a mob hit, then Lombardi's behind it. We'd be no better than them. They'd have *me* on kidnapping charges because you're using the girl to negotiate release terms for Darwin."

"No. Lombardi isn't behind the Fermosa hit. And I'm not trading a kid for Darwin. You have to fucking trust me on this one." She fought to maintain control of her voice. Darwin's life depended on it. "For some reason, the girl is on our side. Casper, just do it. Find Arabella and bring her to the gas station. Trust me, everything will work out if you do that."

"I can't, Sarah. I'm sorry. I won't do it. Find another way."

"Then Darwin will die."

"I trust you, Sarah. Just find another way."

"This is it, Casper. This is the only way. Do it, or Darwin's life is over."

"Sarah, I'm sorry, but there's no way I'm going to—"

She hung up the phone.

Aaron wrapped his arms around her, and she clung to him.

"Do you think he'll do it?" Aaron asked.

"No. If there were any other way to do it on our own, I would. Only Casper has the resources to locate Arabella in such a short time." She looked up at the ceiling. "Unless someone up there wants to tell me where Arabella is?"

"Let's try and get a little sleep."

Sarah shook her head. "I can't. I need time to think. I'm going down to get a coffee and think in the lobby. If Vivian tells me where Arabella is, I'll need to be ready to go get her."

"Then I'm coming, too. There's no way I'm letting you out of my sight until Darwin's home safe."

She glanced at him. "Darwin isn't coming home ever again if we don't find Arabella."

"Then let's hope to hell we do."

Chapter 48

DARWIN TRIED TO REMEMBER how many times he'd passed out but lost count after four. The violence had started hours ago, and they were still at it. Most of his body was numb with shock now. Even if they released him, he couldn't walk away. He might be able to crawl.

Lombardi wanted his ten million in cocaine. He professed to keep Darwin alive—at least until that cocaine was returned intact. He said nothing about how much pain Darwin would endure until then.

He overheard Lombardi talking to the driver about others arriving. They were bringing adrenaline shots to keep him from passing out. That sounded like a fabulous time. He couldn't wait to be awake for all the beatings, not just some of them. Lombardi said a nail gun and a blow torch were coming.

He hoped whoever was coming could wait long enough

for him to set the five in the morning meeting he'd told Sarah about. It would keep Sarah safe and give him the best chance at escape.

They woke him minutes ago and left him to stew in his juices. They'd removed five teeth so far. He'd been electrocuted several times and even thought his heart had stopped once. One eye was swollen shut, and he could barely move his mouth.

The driver had to stop using his hands to inflict abuse, so he'd turned to his tools. A sharp blade—the kind Darwin would've gone insane to see years ago when he suffered from *aichmophobia*, an irrational fear of sharp and pointy objects —was drawn along the skin on his legs and arms. The driver did this part slowly, watching as Darwin's skin separated under the slight pressure of the blade. Blood oozed out, only to be dampened by a grease-stained rag and then duct-taped.

The threat of losing fingers and toes was next. The madman leader of the Toronto mafia had fashioned himself after Columbian drug lords. He wanted to torture Darwin to the edge of his last breath. The idea that Lombardi wanted to cut the tops of Darwin's eyelids off so he couldn't ever close his eyes was madness. Lombardi said he would force Darwin to watch everything until the end, keeping him alive for days on adrenaline shots. Lombardi had even ordered the driver to start a fire. They would use a flame to cauterize the nasty wounds when fingers and toes—eventually limbs—were removed. Darwin could never be allowed to bleed out. That would be a travesty.

Only a week in the hospital would fix him now. While there, he figured a thousand stitches and a dental surgeon would be required, but even after all that, this Humpty

Dumpty would not be able to be put back together again—at least not to the way he was. Especially not if they began removing his extremities. At best, if he could live through this, his body would be littered with scars for the rest of his life.

Lombardi stepped into view. He'd changed into a white wife-beater and torn jeans.

"I still need that beer," Darwin mumbled, barely moving his lips. Red-coated saliva oozed from his mouth. "Wait, make that a whiskey. A double."

"You're really something," Lombardi said. "Still defiant."

"I don't trust you. I reveal the location of your cocaine, and you kill me."

"Reveal or don't reveal; you're dead regardless."

"Motivate me to talk, then," Darwin said. "Negotiate something. Allow me to die with the dignity of a deal."

"Okay, how about this?" Lombardi looked up and left as he thought about something. He glanced at the driver, who was steadily building the fire ten feet away. A moment later, his attention turned back to Darwin. "Tell me where my cocaine is, and I'll offer you not only a reprieve from the pain but your death will not be prolonged. You have my word. It'll be quick."

"I want two more things."

"Two? You're asking for a lot, a man in your position." Lombardi leaned forward and rubbed his face. "I'm waiting to hear these ridiculous demands."

"One, I want a handful of Advil and a glass of water. Then that whiskey I asked for."

Lombardi shrugged. "Fine. Tell me where my cocaine is,

and I will give you that."

"Number two, I want—"

"Two?" Lombardi cut in. "I thought that was two. Pills and whiskey."

Darwin shook his head, then winced. "No," he said, his voice strained in agony. "The pain relief was the first one. Water for the Advil, and whiskey is for pain." He sucked in a large breath of air, then exhaled slowly. "The second thing I want is to come with you to retrieve the trailer."

Lombardi shook his head and sat back in his chair, crossing one leg onto the other. "No fucking way. You don't leave this warehouse. Absolutely not. In fact," he uncrossed his legs and leaned toward Darwin again, "I have four more men coming here to help. They'll be here in," he glanced at his cell phone, "five minutes."

"Then no deal. I die, and you're out ten million bucks. Needlessly, I might add."

"Fuck you, Darwin. You'll tell me. Lose a finger, fine; keep your mouth shut. Lose a hand, we'll see. Have your leg cut off at the knee while still alive, and then each eyeball removed and left dangling on your cheek, no," he waved a finger back and forth, "you'll tell me what I want to know."

"I won't live through that. You know it, and I know it."

"Then tell me where my product is, and I will guarantee this stops. I will offer you pain relief and will not kill you until I have confirmed the trailer has my mattresses in it. That's the best deal you'll get."

"I'll think on it."

Lombardi got up so fast the chair fell over. "You'll think on it?" He leaned in close to Darwin. "There's no time left. It's almost three in the morning. Don't you see Waldo there is prepping the fire? I have four more men coming because Waldo's fists are wrecked." Lombardi's spit coated Darwin's swollen eye. "The last hours of your life will be agony, and you'll *think about it*." He shouted the last three words. "Fuck you, Darwin. Deal's off."

Lombardi stomped away.

"Hey," Darwin called after him. "Where's the driver?"

Lombardi shot a glance over his shoulder. "What?" he asked, his face reddened in anger.

"Get it? Where's the driver? His name's Waldo. So, like, where's Waldo?"

Lombardi turned around and crossed his arms, head tilted to the side slightly.

"You're joking at a time like this?"

"Just struck me as funny." He blinked his one good eye, trying to clear it of blood to see Lombardi better. "I didn't know the driver's name until now."

"When this is done, I will use bleach on the floor below your chair. My people are stained by your existence. My country, my men, our legacy is stained by your presence. I will not have my warehouse stained by you as well."

"You want your cocaine, asshole?"

"The deal's off. You had your chance."

"New deal. Same terms, but leave me here then. I'm dead either way. Stop the torture and get me Advil and whiskey. I'll talk then."

Lombardi seemed to think on it. He glanced at Waldo, who returned his gaze, the fire already rising high enough for their purpose.

A door opened to Lombardi's right. More men entered the warehouse.

"Falcone," Lombardi said. "So glad you could come."

They embraced.

Vincenzo Balzano stepped in behind Falcone, and then three other tough-looking men formed a semi-circle behind Falcone.

"This him?" Falcone asked.

Lombardi nodded. "I think we just made a deal."

"A deal?" Falcone said. "What kind of deal?"

Lombardi filled them in.

Falcone faced Darwin. "I say if the man wants to designate how he dies and when, we should let him, providing he doesn't lie about the location of the cocaine."

"Agreed." Lombardi tapped Vince on the shoulder. "Go into Spinello's office and find Advil. Bring a glass of water and find Spinello's stash of whiskey. I think it's in the bottom drawer of his desk. Sometimes he just has Grappa, but bring the whiskey if it's there."

"You're really doing a deal with this guy?" Vince asked.

Lombardi glared at him, and Vince pivoted on his heels and headed toward the front offices.

The men conversed in whispers until Vince returned. Waldo was instructed to undo Darwin's right arm so he could drink on his own.

"You've been offered a generous reprieve," Falcone said moments later.

Lombardi righted the chair he'd knocked over earlier, then sat facing Darwin. Falcone sat on the other chair.

He had the attention of everyone in the warehouse.

Darwin cleared his throat. "I have your word nothing happens to me until you retrieve your trailer with the cocaine and return to the warehouse?"

Lombardi nodded. Seconds later, Falcone nodded.

"Everyone agrees," Lombardi said. "Vince? Waldo?"

They both concurred.

"Your rig will be delivered to a gas station just north of the city at five in the morning sharp. It's the one with the sign Mini-Max painted red on the side. It's two short trailers, making up one long one. Two random drivers I hired to drop the truck will drive the rig. They will park it and walk away. They will arrive at the gas station in the Mini-Max truck and drive to the rear, where all the rigs sit when drivers rest. You said it's after three in the morning. My guys will be there in less than two hours. They're expecting to see me."

"That's why you wanted to come?" Lombardi said. "What's to stop us from shooting them and taking the rig?"

"Nothing. They would die. But that's not on me. You changed the deal. I wanted to come."

"Okay, let's go." Lombardi got to his feet. "You do know what happens to you if you're lying?"

"The same thing if I told the truth. I die."

"There's a subtle difference, in which I'm sure you're well versed. Dying can be quick. You'll learn the slow way if you're sending us on a wild goose chase." Lombardi moved away from him. "Everyone, come with me. Vince and Waldo, you two stay and make sure nothing happens to him."

"You're going?" Vince asked. "Falcone, too? Isn't that a risk? What if this is a setup?"

"It isn't a setup. Darwin still dies. No one knows he's here. They can't arrest me for gassing up."

Lombardi approached the warehouse door with Falcone and his men trailing him.

"Everyone, lose your cell phones. We can't risk anyone

tracking us." They all pulled out their cells and placed them on a steel shelf beside the door. "Vince, I have a throw-away phone if I need to call you. And Vince? Waldo? We have an arrangement. Don't touch Darwin until I return. Understood?"

Vince and Waldo nodded.

Darwin sipped his whiskey.

"Speak, man," Lombardi shouted.

Both men voiced their understanding.

Lombardi and his crew disappeared out the door.

Darwin sipped his whiskey. It tasted better already.

Chapter 49

SARAH DOWNED THREE COFFEES and a sandwich the front desk clerk grabbed from the back kitchen before she headed back to their room around three a.m. Aaron had stopped at one coffee.

They woke the boys and got everyone outside just as the clock edged past four. Aaron called a taxi for him, Sarah, and Parkman while the three boys jumped in Aaron's car and left the hotel's parking lot.

"Does anything we'll do this morning bring Darwin home?" Parkman asked between yawns.

"I have no idea," Sarah said. "Odds are a lot better if Casper got Arabella."

The taxi came ten minutes later. They headed north on Highway 400. At the gas station, the three of them entered the main building, where several restaurants were already open for the early morning traffic.

Sarah headed in for another coffee. Parkman joined her. Aaron headed for the men's room.

The clock on the wall said it was 4:44 a.m.

Her stomach churned, and her heart palpitated. Maybe she didn't need any more coffee.

She ordered a large and waited for Parkman at the side exit. After regrouping, the trio headed outside and into the back area, where a dozen rigs were parked at an angle parallel to each other.

"No sign of Casper or his men," Parkman said.

"No sign of Darwin, either," Sarah added.

"We sure we have the right place?" Aaron asked.

"Absolutely." Sarah sipped her coffee and watched the access road. "They'll be here."

Five minutes later, two black SUVs pulled up to the curb where they were standing. The back door of the first one opened, and Casper stepped out.

"Sarah, I'm warning you on this one," he said. "You'd better be right."

"I am," she said without hesitation.

Casper walked to the rear SUV and opened its back door. A little girl hopped out, her hair done up in one long ponytail. She saw Sarah and tried to smile. Her half-lidded, sleepy eyes told Sarah that Arabella had been asleep on the ride over.

Casper walked Arabella to them as several of his men got out of the SUVs.

"What's the plan here?" Casper asked.

"I don't think Darwin is coming," Sarah said. "I have a feeling he wanted to, but things changed somehow. I'm not being told how. All I know is Parkman is to walk Arabella to a truck that will park there," she pointed to an empty spot, "in less than five minutes. Lombardi is waiting. He will speak to her, and they leave. That's it."

"You have any other guarantees regarding Darwin?" Casper asked.

Sarah shook her head, then looked down at Arabella. "Hi, sweetie. You look tired."

"I am," she said, her voice soft and sleepy.

"It won't be long now, and then you can go home."

"I heard Uncle Lombardi's name. Is he coming to pick me up?"

Sarah and Casper exchanged a glance. "Yes, your uncle should be along shortly. I just need you to do something for us."

"What's that?"

"I need you to describe the men you saw leaving your house that night."

Arabella angled her head to look up at Sarah. "Is that why the police asked me to come with them? Am I part of the investigation?"

"Something like that, yes. Uncle Lombardi wants to know who hurt your parents. Since you saw the men, you can tell him, right? Can you do that for us?"

She nodded, her head bobbing up and down.

Casper moved away. "Sarah, can I talk to you for a moment?"

Sarah nodded, then addressed Parkman. "You'll walk her to Lombardi?"

"Of course," he said without hesitation. He took Arabella's hand and moved a couple of feet away.

Sarah eased closer to Casper. "What?"

"I went to a lot of effort getting her here. If something happens to that girl while in my care, it'll be my career."

"Nothing will happen to her."

"You're sure?"

She met his eyes. "Why all the questions? Of course, I'm sure. I don't lie. I don't bluff. If I weren't sure, I'd tell you the risk involved. Regarding her safety, there is no doubt in my mind. She's a child. I wouldn't put her in harm's way to save Darwin, and Darwin would understand that." She gave Casper's shoulder a soft jab. "Why would Lombardi hurt family? He sees Arabella as family. What's important is what she saw that night, and Lombardi needs to hear it."

"And this'll help Darwin in some way?"

Sarah nodded as she drank more coffee.

"How?"

"That I don't know."

"But you're sure about the other—"

"Casper, seriously."

"Okay."

"It's not all about you or your career."

"I'm not making it about me. I'm prioritizing that little girl. I need to make sure she's safe. There are repercussions if something happens to her. Damage of the collateral kind."

"Nothing will happen to her." A truck's engine revved behind them. "Go, that's got to be the truck. Do what you and your men have to do, but get out of sight."

Everyone scattered but Parkman and Arabella. Aaron hopped in one of the SUVs as they pulled away from the curb. Casper and Sarah fell back into the shadows of the building. To a random observer, Parkman stood with a little girl on the curb, possibly waiting for a ride.

A truck pulling two small trailers eased into the spot Sarah had pointed at moments before. The truck stopped, and the engine died. Two men opened the doors and hopped out.

The screech of a car's tires came from the access road. Another black SUV, similar to Casper's vehicles, raced up and stopped behind the rig.

Parkman took his cue and started toward the back of the rig.

"I don't like this idea at all," Casper whispered to Sarah. "For the record."

"Me either," Sarah whispered.

Casper shot a glance at her, but she ignored him.

They could barely hear the voices at the back of the rig. Parkman wasn't there yet. He seemed to be holding back, keeping Arabella out of the picture for some reason.

Sarah moved closer along the wall of the building. Then she ran a short distance until she was hidden behind a truck parked beside the one that had just shown up. Casper was not far behind, a gun in his hand.

She motioned for him to put it away. He did as he was told.

The sound of the doors opening on the back of the rig was loud.

"Where is it?" a man shouted.

"Where's what?" someone else said.

More car doors opened.

Arabella sounded like she was crying.

"We were told to deliver this rig and walk away," a man said. "We were paid a thousand dollars each." The driver and his passenger entered Sarah's view, their hands above their heads. "We have no beef with you."

Sarah peeked around the side of the trailer. Parkman still held Arabella's hand. Two men in leather jackets stood close to the driver and the passenger of the rig that had just arrived. Lombardi and another man were moving closer. They whispered something to one another, talking quietly to themselves.

The driver and passenger watched the new arrivals, looked at each other, then turned and ran into the darkness behind another truck.

"Nothing in the truck," Lombardi said.

"Sorry, boss," one of the leather-jacketed men said. "Nothing."

Parkman and Arabella stepped out of the shadows. Everyone turned at the intrusion. The men in leather jackets pulled out weapons and then lowered them when they saw the child.

"And you are?" Lombardi asked.

"Delivery guy."

"Oh," Lombardi said, watching Arabella. "How's that?"

"This little girl is related to you. I was told to reunite family."

"By whom?"

Parkman didn't answer.

Lombardi started toward Arabella. His men fanned out, searching around like an imminent threat was upon them.

"We'll take Arabella with us, but you're coming, too."

"No, that's not part of the deal," Parkman said.

"There's no choice in the matter," Lombardi said. He pulled a weapon out from his jacket. "Now get in that vehicle."

Sarah stepped into the open. "He stays," she yelled from

twenty feet.

Lombardi glared at her. "You?"

Only seven hours had passed since they had parted company on Toronto Island.

Casper moved out to stand behind Sarah.

A man dressed all in black slinked along until he reached the front of Lombardi's SUV, then leaped out and snatched the gun from Lombardi's hand. He flipped it around and aimed it at Lombardi less than a foot away. Behind him, Falcone—the name popped into her head from somewhere—was subdued just as fast, his right arm twisted over his shoulder, making him stand as if he was leaning backward.

The leather men looked confused about what to do, so they stood stock still, waiting for an order from Lombardi.

"What's this?" Lombardi asked. "Am I being arrested?"

"You are not being detained," Sarah said. "You are being warned."

Falcone was released. He adjusted his jacket and stood with his legs apart. Any chance he had at being macho had vanished, though.

"A warning?" Lombardi asked.

"You can be gotten to. You're not so big that I can't get to you. We are delivering Arabella back unharmed. Just remember how easy it was to get her. No one is safe in the city you claim is yours. Not you. Not your family."

"That includes you, Sarah Roberts."

She sipped from her coffee cup as if they were discussing the weather or something more mundane than who would kill who first.

"So we take Arabella and just leave?" Lombardi asked.

"Just leave," Sarah said.

"You can't let them leave," Casper whispered. "They've got Darwin."

She grunted at him in derision.

Lombardi held Arabella by the hand. He opened the rear door for her and then climbed in. Falcone climbed in, then his men hopped in the front, and the SUV quickly sped past Sarah and Casper.

"That's it?" Casper said, his voice taking on a higher pitch. "That was the master plan."

"Take it easy. We just saved Darwin's life."

"What?" he shouted. "How? Tell me how?"

Sarah shrugged, the coffee once again at her lips. "I have no idea. I just know."

"Sarah, you are maddening sometimes."

"And then some." She swallowed more of the beverage, her insides roiling worse. "You think I like this?"

Everyone converged on the two of them.

"Thanks for that," Parkman said.

"Couldn't let them take you."

"What's next?" Aaron asked her.

"We all pile in Casper's vehicles and follow Lombardi to Darwin." She looked at Casper. "But we should stay a mile back at least."

"How are we going to follow them from a mile back?" Daniel asked.

"Casper planted a tracking device in Arabella's shoes," Sarah said. "We can hear inside their vehicle as well. Lombardi would never suspect her, and he didn't even know she'd be here, so he hasn't checked her—and he won't."

"How did you know?" Casper asked, the hint of a smile on his lips.

"Really?" Sarah drank more coffee, then decided she was done with it. "Are you actually asking me how I know? Or can we stop wasting each other's time and go follow the bad guys and bring Darwin home?"

Chapter 50

SEVERAL TIMES SINCE LOMBARDI left the warehouse, Darwin asked the time. The Advil and whiskey had calmed things down for him. Despite the throbbing pain, he was starting to feel better by at least thirty percent. He would leave the warehouse intact if Vince and Waldo did as Lombardi instructed and left him alone. The last he heard from Vince, it was 4:32 a.m.

He decided to wait five more minutes, then start talking.

The fire had died down. Wood from broken pallets and skids rested in a pile beside the fire, but Waldo had disappeared up front.

He counted how many men were on the premises. According to Lombardi, one man guarded the front gate, and Vince and Waldo were inside. That was fortuitous. The fact that Lombardi brought him to Spinello's warehouse was also extremely lucky. Darwin had no idea where Lombardi would take him, but Spinello's warehouse was exactly where he would want to be. If Darwin were anywhere else, he would have had to be brought here for his plan to work, and it didn't seem that Lombardi was interested in taking Darwin anywhere.

"Hey," he shouted. "Hey," he tried again, louder.

No one responded. They were both in the front offices.

"Hey!" he tried even louder, then winced at the pain that shot through his jaw.

A door opened. Vince came around the corner.

"What do you want, asshole?"

"I want to confess."

"I'm not a priest. This isn't a confessional." Vince turned back toward the front offices. "Confess at the gates of Hell," he added over his shoulder.

"Wait," Darwin said, but Vince disappeared behind the wall. The door opened again.

"The cocaine is here," Darwin shouted, despite the pain.

The door didn't close right away. He could see around the corner, but he figured Vince was standing in the doorway, trying to decide what to do.

The door closed. Vince materialized again.

"What did you say?" Vince asked.

"The cocaine. It's here. Been here the whole time."

Vince placed his hands on his hips, his smile so wide his teeth showed through, yellow and stained.

"You're fucking kidding me."

"No."

"You're a piece of work. You lied to my boss and made him drive to that gas station for nothing." He shook his head. "You're in for a world of hurt. Beyond all of your wildest dreams." Vince moved closer. "So tell me, where is it then?"

Darwin jerked his head behind him. "In that trailer at the door just behind me. It's been here all along. We loaded it onto that trailer and left it. My men were waiting for my call to move it wherever I needed, but I didn't get the chance to call."

"You're fucking joking, right?"

"Nope. Open the door. You'll see."

Vince jogged back to the front offices and returned seconds later with Waldo.

"Asshole here says the coke is in that trailer," Vince told Waldo.

"Could be some kind of setup," Waldo said.

"That's why you're going to open the trailer." Vince withdrew his weapon and held it pointed down. "I'll cover you if anything happens."

Waldo looked from Darwin to Vince, then back to Darwin.

"It's not wired to blow?" Waldo asked.

Darwin shook his head slightly. "Not wired. I just want this to end. It was wrong to piss off Lombardi further. I'm done with this game. Open the trailer. Take your coke. Just kill me fast when Lombardi gets back."

"Oh, you'll die all right," Vince said.

Waldo opened the warehouse door and checked the back of the rig. There was no lock, so he flipped the latch and eased the door upward.

Vince howled when he first saw the mattresses piled high in the back of the trailer. Waldo pushed the door to the top and stepped inside. Vince moved closer.

"Holy shit, man. You weren't joking. Hey Waldo, how

does it look? Is that the shit?"

"This is it. Lombardi's going to be pissed it was here the whole time."

"I'll call and tell him." Vince pulled out his phone and dialed a number.

Darwin waited until Lombardi's phone rang on the steel shelf by the door. He wasn't prepared to remind Vince that Lombardi left his cell phone behind.

Vince looked over his shoulder, then remembered.

"Shit." He walked over and slapped Darwin on the shoulder. "It's over, Darwin. It's finally over for you. Even in your last act on this planet, you managed to piss off the one man who already wants you dead. Well done."

Vince moved away to stand by Waldo. "Let's unload this thing; surprise Lombardi when he gets back. I know he had it on Spinello's floor for a reason." He laughed to himself. "Won't he be royally pissed and happy simultaneously?"

Within minutes, both Waldo and Vince began the task of lifting the mattresses out, one after the other, piling them eight deep along the outer wall of the warehouse. Darwin monitored the time in his head, hoping they'd finish before Lombardi got back.

He watched for ten minutes, worrying they wouldn't get done in time, watching as they made their way, mattress by mattress.

Then Vince's cell phone rang. He answered it quickly and ran toward Darwin, speaking fast in unintelligible tones.

"Yes," he said, getting closer. "Of course. Here, let me put you on speakerphone for Darwin to hear."

Vince hit a button, and Lombardi's voice boomed over the little phone.

"The trailer was empty." Lombardi sounded like he was in a rage. "Vince tells me everything is at the warehouse, and they're unloading it now."

"Sorry about that," Darwin said. "Must've slipped my mind."

"Take me off speaker phone," Lombardi ordered.

Vince hit a button and moved away from Darwin. "Right, I understand." Then, "Yes, sir. Will do." Vince disconnected the call. He whistled loudly, a large grin on his face. "I've never heard that man as pissed as he is right now. Man, do you have a death wish, or what?"

"Come help me here," Waldo said. "Getting tired already."

"One sec," Vince said. He leaned down in front of Darwin. "You know, I'll never forget you. I don't think we'll ever have an opponent quite like you ever again."

"Vince," Waldo called.

"Coming. Fuck." Vince left to help with the mattresses.

It wouldn't be long now before they reached the last stack, which wasn't a stack at all. Sitting nearest the front of the trailer, inside a wooden crate that once held auto glass, was a large friend of his about to ruin the party. Two mattresses were stacked on the crate to shield it from view. Within minutes, Waldo and Vince would remove the last mattress. It would move sideways, revealing his hiding spot, and then Bruno would simply aim, fire, and kill both men.

Darwin would be untied, and together, they would wait for Lombardi to walk through the warehouse doors so this nightmare could end.

He blinked to clear his one good eye and stared along the length of the trailer. Three more piles of mattresses in

Bruno's way. Just three more, maybe five minutes. Perhaps less.

Vince stopped what he was doing and slapped Waldo on the shoulder.

"I think this calls for a drink."

No! Keep emptying the fucking trailer.

"Yeah, I'm done," Waldo said. "The boss can use those other guys to finish this when they return."

The two men walked out of the trailer and past Darwin.

"You guys aren't done," Darwin said, unsure what he could possibly say to convince them to continue. He certainly didn't want to be a sitting duck when Lombardi returned.

"Someone else can finish," Vince said. "We're not dock workers."

They disappeared around the corner and headed toward the front offices.

"Shit. Shit. Shit."

He looked inside the trailer. Too many mattresses are still on top and in the way of Bruno. As strong as that man was, hidden in a crate for roughly twelve hours was probably maddening on his limbs.

Tied up tight, Darwin had no choice but to wait for the mattresses to be removed. The gamble he had made to get Sarah away from these men was large, the bets all in. Lombardi would walk through the warehouse door at any minute. Darwin's Trojan Horse was stalled for the moment. It wasn't going to work until more mattresses were removed. Perhaps he should've thought of something else, although it was too late for second-guessing. This was happening now, and he could do nothing about it.

All he had left was time.

And there wasn't much of that at all.

Sweat from his brow mixed with blood and slipped into his eye. He closed it and hoped he'd see his wife again.

Chapter 51

THEY ALL LISTENED TO the conversation inside Lombardi's SUV as Casper's driver raced them back into Toronto using GPS to track and follow the signal planted on Arabella. Lombardi's vehicle traveled south on the 400 and then west on the 407. Staying close to two miles back, Sarah stared at the screen in the dash of Casper's vehicle, where a red dot showed Lombardi now heading south on the 427.

"I think I know the man who did that," Lombardi was saying.

Arabella had just described Vito and Vince to a tee. She'd remembered hair color and clothing. When she said the taller one had a minor arm wound, Lombardi had to know it was Vince.

"I have to make a call," Lombardi said.

Sarah and Casper exchanged a look as they waited to hear Lombardi's side of the conversation.

He talked to someone, then was put on to Darwin, reporting that the trailer was empty. They couldn't hear the caller speak but knew by what Lombardi said that a certain amount of something valuable to Lombardi was recovered.

Whomever Lombardi called, he went on to tell that person to leave Darwin alone until he got there. He wanted to kill him himself.

Casper recorded everything coming through the speakers.

Parkman rested a hand on Sarah's shoulders. "We're right behind them. We'll get there in time."

"Drive faster," she said. "Once Lombardi arrives to wherever he's going, Darwin won't have much time."

"We'll get there in time," Casper said. "And Arabella's presence will save Darwin's life. You said so yourself."

Sarah stared out the window as the sky lightened in the east. She watched the traffic race by as Casper's SUV drove past the airport where it all began, heading farther south toward Etobicoke.

So much had happened since landing from Kelowna. The small amount of time she'd had with Aaron wasn't enough. She was too tired, exhausted, and emotionally spent to be any kind of girlfriend to him. It seems life was getting busier with age.

Which led her to thoughts of retirement again. Maybe it was time. They had enough money to start a business together. They had enough friends and resources to set things up. Parkman could reclaim his life and get so busy in his private detective business that he'd left alone for a long time.

Maybe it was time to put away the psychic abilities and raise a family.

She tightened her grip on Aaron's hand that she hadn't

realized she was holding. He turned to her, his eyes asking if she was okay.

She smiled and rested her head on his shoulder.

She would talk to him when this was over. They could make a plan. Go away. Change their names. Live a life of obscurity. Would he be okay with that? Would he want that?

Today, save Darwin. Tomorrow, retire.

It was time, and Sarah felt ready.

The life of a vigilante either stopped voluntarily or at the end of a knife or barrel of a gun. The luck she had had over the years would run out one day. Better to stop and make a life while she still had the chance.

She wrapped an arm over Aaron's shoulders. She would tell him tomorrow, and a new adventure would begin.

Perhaps one with baby bottles, diapers, and strollers.

And a wedding.

Sarah smiled to herself. She was so ready for that life.

Chapter 52

DOORS OPENED AND CLOSED somewhere in the warehouse. Darwin raised his head as Lombardi stepped inside, holding the hand of a girl about twelve or thirteen years old.

Lombardi angled the little girl so she didn't have a direct sightline to Darwin, then glared at him. After the man took in the initial pile of mattresses, he knelt to whisper to the little girl. She nodded twice, then rubbed her eyes.

Darwin had no idea who the girl was or why Lombardi would bring her to a place like this. What if Bruno broke free and weapons fire was exchanged? It would be a tragedy if the little girl were killed in the crossfire.

Lombardi handed her to Falcone.

"Waldo?" Lombardi called out. "Vince?"

When Lombardi yelled the driver's name, Darwin considered some Where's Waldo jokes but kept them to himself. He probably had minutes to live and didn't want to muddy his thinking with humor.

Lombardi removed a weapon from his jacket and hid it behind his leg. What the hell was he doing? His attention wasn't on Darwin yet.

The familiar sound of the door swinging open from the front offices was louder this time as Vince and Waldo entered the warehouse.

"You see what we did?" Vince shouted. "Look at that!"

They came into view. Darwin could've sworn they'd tasted Spinello's private stash of alcohol while waiting for their boss to return.

Why was Lombardi hiding a gun from Vince and Waldo? And come to think of it, why was Lombardi even back at the warehouse? Darwin had told Sarah about the gas station on Highway 400. Wouldn't she have done something to Lombardi to find out where Darwin was?

As Vince and Waldo entered the warehouse, Darwin barely noticed the girl move behind Falcone's leg. Lombardi got down on his haunches beside the girl.

"Is this the man you saw?" he asked her, loud enough for Darwin to hear.

The girl nodded.

Lombardi stood and looked at Falcone.

"What's going on?" Vince asked.

Falcone walked the girl toward the front offices while Lombardi circled Waldo and Vince.

"Waldo," Lombardi said. "Step aside. Go tend that dying fire."

As Waldo moved toward the remnants of the fire, all sense of a smile gone from his face, the side warehouse door opened, and the two men who'd left with Lombardi earlier entered.

Lombardi raised his weapon at Vince. The men by the door did the same.

"Pull your weapons out, Vincenzo," Lombardi said. "On the ground. Now."

"What's going on?" Vince said. His voice took on a pleading that made Darwin smile. Was this Sarah's doing? What had she done? "C'mon man, this is me, Vincenzo Balzano. We go way back."

"Who ordered the hit on the Fermosas?" Lombardi asked.

Realization dawned on Vince's face. "That was their daughter?" His voice cracked. "Shit man, that wasn't me—"

"It wasn't? Then how come Arabella described you and Vito to a tee? Huh? Explain that."

"I was there," Vince's nod reminded Darwin of Arabella's, childlike and overdone, "but it wasn't me. Vito did them, man."

"Weapons out," Lombardi said. "I won't tell you again."

Vince stole a look at Darwin. "What about him? We have to finish him off."

"In good time." Lombardi fired his weapon. Vince's foot flew out from under him, and he stumbled to the floor.

With a gentle nod to the muscle by the door, they dove on Vince, yanked his gun out, then retreated to the door.

Vince squealed like the worn brakes on a slow-moving train. A high-pitched sound emitted from his mouth.

"Who ordered the hit on the Fermosas?" Lombardi shouted over Vince's wailing. "I won't ask again."

He received no response as Vince tried to get to his good foot, stumbled, then righted himself and hopped a couple of feet away.

Lombardi shot him again. This time in the other leg. Vince dropped to the warehouse floor, the squealing almost over. It came out more like a high-pitched moan now—like a grunting pig.

"Darwin did it," Vince managed to say. "It was all Darwin."

"Lying to me now? Arabella fingered you for the hit. You were ordered by Mancuso Corrado to execute Marty Fermosa, weren't you? You took Vito with you and enjoyed killing a little too much. The wife wasn't supposed to be hit. Why'd you kill the wife?"

Vince rolled over and put his hands up. "Okay, okay," he said, pleading, sounding breathless. "You're right. I'm sorry, man. It happened so fast. I got shot in the arm—"

"I know. Arabella saw you holding your arm when you left her house."

"Patricia was an accident. Vito did that, and now he's dead for it."

"Dead? Sarah Roberts killed him when he tried to rape her."

"See, man. That's the kind of guy he was."

Lombardi turned his attention to the muscle by the door. "I want his arms broken first. Do it now."

"Nooo," Vince yelled as Lombardi's men moved in on him.

Vince tried to scramble away. One of the men flipped him onto his stomach, wrenched his arm back, and Vince screamed louder. The man placed a knee at Vince's elbow and jerked the arm backward with tremendous force, like breaking a piece of wood at a campfire. Vince's arm snapped like a thick branch.

Darwin's stomach protested. He swallowed to keep things down.

The other man held Vince's contorting shape secure on the floor as they grabbed his other arm and repeated the process. Vince's arms flopped beside him on the warehouse's concrete floor, as useless as if they were made of jelly.

His moans had deepened, his breathing oozing as a raspy, guttural grumble.

Lombardi motioned to a set of three concrete steps beside Vince. "Put him on the steps, stomach on the floor."

The men did as they were told.

"Open his mouth like he's going to eat one of the steps."

Half conscious, Vince barely made a sound as the men set his face on a step. Darwin blinked rapidly to maintain a clear vision of what they were doing to Vince. When something moved beside him, he glanced around to see what it was. A mattress slipped off the top of the pile in the rear of the trailer.

Bruno!

Another mattress moved.

Hurry up, my friend. I need you out here.

He turned back to Lombardi. Vince was sprawled on the concrete floor, his head up, his mouth open as far as it could go. He looked like he was about to bite an extremely large hamburger. Lips drawn to their limit, his lower teeth rested on the vertical side of the step and his upper teeth on the horizontal side.

This did not bode well for Vincenzo Balzano.

Lombardi moved behind Vince and walked along his body, stepping just outside either arm until he stood directly above the back of Vince's head.

Darwin suddenly knew exactly what Lombardi planned but couldn't look away. The mafia boss looked down at the man who had betrayed him by killing someone he knew. Blood oozed from Vince's two leg wounds, but Darwin didn't think that mattered in light of what would happen to him.

"This is for the disrespect," Lombardi said. "You work for me. You do contracts for me. You do not take on an unsanctioned contract. Especially one that harms my friends." He wiped his nose. "They were like family to me."

Lombardi jumped and came down, at least two hundred pounds of him, on the back of Vince's head and neck.

Vince's mouth broke open as his head bounced off the stairs. The neck appeared to be dislocated from the spine as it came to rest at an odd angle. Vince's lower jaw dangled like the broken face of a ventriloquist's puppet. His body sagged to the side. Small bits of white had shot out of Vince's mouth, and his teeth shattered. Darwin tried to comprehend the violence he'd just witnessed and knew it would never leave him.

He had never seen a man's face so ruined. There was no way Vince could ever eat with that mouth again if he lived. The man's skull was completely deformed. Darwin focused on keeping his stomach from clenching and sending whatever was in it upward.

A gun fired outside the building. Then another.

"Go," Lombardi yelled. "Check that out."

He retrieved his weapon, aimed it at Vince's face, and fired it three times rapidly. Darwin looked away as what was left of Vince's face fell apart at the seams, his skull a broken mess of bone fragments and bloody flesh.

The men had disappeared out the door.

Lombardi turned to Darwin. "Now it's your turn."

Chapter 53

Halfway up Westside Drive, Casper ordered his driver to the shoulder.

"What's going on?" Sarah asked.

"Before the exchange with you on the island, Darwin said something about Spinello's home and business. He said we'd find Spinello's body at Universal Shipping in Etobicoke."

Sarah looked through the windshield. The sign on the gate up ahead said *Universal Shipping.*

"So that's where they're keeping Darwin."

Casper pointed at the red dot on the screen. "That's where Arabella is. They must've taken her somewhere quiet. We can't hear anything anymore."

"We need inside," Parkman said. "Fast."

"Arabella's presence was supposed to give Darwin precious seconds, if not minutes, to save his life," Sarah said.

"But I agree with Parkman. We need inside."

"Wait," Casper blurted. "Pull back."

The driver put the vehicle in reverse and started backward, then spun the vehicle around.

"Drive until the gate is out of our sight line."

"What's going on?" Aaron asked.

"Movement by the gate," Casper said. "Someone was watching us."

Westside Drive turned to the north, and Universal Shipping's gate disappeared in their rearview mirror.

"Let us out," Alex said. "We'll get inside."

"How?" Casper said.

"All you need is a will. Once you have that, the *how* will reveal itself."

"Is that some Buddha or Tao shit?"

"Tony Robbins."

"Oh," was all Casper said.

The doors opened, and the dojo boys exited, leaving Parkman, Sarah, Casper, and his driver.

"Now what?" Casper asked.

"Call for backup," Sarah said. "Get every cop and emergency task force member you can to converge on this warehouse. Give me a gun, and I'll see you when this is done."

Casper ordered the driver to stay with the SUV and to call for backup. He jumped out and handed Sarah a weapon.

"You know how to use this?"

She slipped it into her pants. "Any other questions?" She started away, not waiting for an answer. She made a beeline for the side fence using the shadows beside the road. Parkman stayed low, moving behind her. Casper disappeared on the other side of the road.

With everyone advancing on Universal Shipping from different angles, she was convinced they'd gain access before something dire happened.

A weapon fired from inside the building.

Sarah picked up her speed, worried Darwin had been shot. At the tall fence, too high to scale, she stopped to catch her breath. Parkman was right beside her. Overcast skies above kept the sun's light to a minimum, but as the sky brightened, they lost their ability to hide.

A weapon fired inside the warehouse again.

"I'm going in," Sarah said. "Even if I have to bulldoze my way past those sentries at the gate. We need to get to Darwin."

"You're sure he's in there?" Parkman asked.

"You're starting to sound like Casper. Of course, he's in there."

"Okay, I'm with you. Let's do this."

Sarah started along the length of the fence toward the access gate, Casper's weapon held in front of her, each step taken carefully to avoid creating unnecessary noise. Near the end of the fence where an arm like at a parking garage would admit vehicular traffic, she slowed. She held up a hand for Parkman to do the same. Someone was on the other side of the wall, gravel crunching under their feet. The person edged closer to the opening. Then closer.

A gun fired, and she jumped. Then another weapon fired closer to her.

The person on the other side of the fence dropped beside the gate. She looked around to see who had fired a weapon. Casper came out of hiding from the other side of the road.

"He was getting too close to you," Casper said in hushed tones as he jogged over to them. He shrugged. "Didn't like it."

"Thanks," she mouthed back in a whisper. "What was that second shot? You?"

He shook his head. "His weapon as he fell." He shrugged. "Reflexes?"

Sarah ducked under the arm at the gate. The two men followed her. They dropped to their haunches and put their backs to the fence wall. Sarah scanned the parking area and loading docks. Nothing moved. Something caught her eye on the roof of the warehouse. Like a shadow moving.

Alex? Daniel, maybe? She didn't think Aaron would've climbed to the roof with his injured hand.

A door opened along the warehouse wall. Two large men exited the building, weapons in their hands.

Sarah lifted hers. Casper lifted his.

Together, they blasted away at the men. Then someone was firing at them from the front offices, the loud pinging of several bullets hitting the wall over their heads. Sarah, Casper, and Parkman lay flat until the bullets stopped.

It was over as fast as it had started. She peeked out from under her arm, furious they were being shot at in the open. It was stupid and reckless, but Darwin needed them.

The two men who had exited the warehouse were on the ground, two black-clad figures standing over them.

Alex, Daniel?

The man who came out from the front of the building had stopped firing as someone dressed in black had landed on his shoulders from the roof.

Another weapon fired inside the warehouse.

Sarah jumped to her feet and ran for the warehouse door. Parkman and Casper were close behind. The dojo boys were already at the door, about to rip it open.

She saw Aaron leave the man by the front office's steps and run inside. With the six of them—*where's Benjamin?*—Darwin would have a fighting chance.

If Darwin was still alive, she meant to keep it that way.

Chapter 54

Darwin watched Lombardi as he locked the door to the outside, slipping a heavy steel bolt into place. The mob boss crossed the warehouse floor toward him, his gait strong and determined.

Hurry up, Bruno!

After witnessing what happened to Vince, he offered Lombardi the most stoic face he could muster. Darwin held his chin high, the whiskey helping him feel bolder than he might have otherwise.

Someone banged on the warehouse door as Lombardi reared back and prepared to smash Darwin's face with the butt of the weapon.

But Lombardi had been out of the warehouse for a couple of hours. He had forgotten that Darwin was served a glass of whiskey, and his right hand was freed to drink on his own.

In Lombardi's rage, he didn't see Darwin's right hand at his side, hanging loosely. When Lombardi began his downward swing with the weapon in his hand, Darwin brought his right hand up and clamped onto Lombardi's wrist, twisting it backward.

The gun dropped from his hand. Lombardi fought to get loose. He brought his other hand around and punched Darwin in the cheek.

Darwin redoubled his efforts, adding his own rage into the grip of his fingers, bending Lombardi's wrist back as far as he could.

Another mattress dropped behind him. Bruno was almost free. More banging on the warehouse door. A weapon fired. Then again. Someone was trying to shoot their way inside.

Lombardi panicked. He punched Darwin twice, then tried to pull away with renewed vigor.

Another gun fired outside. Steel protested as someone wrenched on the warehouse door.

Another mattress fell. Bruno shouted something, but Darwin didn't catch it over Lombardi's grunts and moans as he struggled to free his wrist.

In a last-ditch attempt, as Darwin's strength waned, Lombardi kicked Darwin in the chest and yanked himself free.

A weapon fired behind Darwin.

Bruno was free of the mattress-covered crate.

Wide-eyed, Lombardi left his gun on the floor beside Darwin as he whirled around and ran toward the front offices.

The side door of the warehouse finally smashed open, and several figures barged in, guns waving.

"Sarah," Darwin called, but his voice was too weak to

carry to her.

The front door shut and bolted, the sound resonating throughout the warehouse.

Then Bruno was beside him.

"Sorry, boss," he said, working on Darwin's restraints. "The gunfire woke me. I fell asleep. It's nighttime, and those mattresses are heavy. Boss, there were a lot of them—"

"Just get me out of here."

"Right."

Sarah ran over to him, her face a mask of anguish. "I'm so sorry, Darwin." She covered her mouth with a hand. "What have they done to you?"

"It would've been much worse if you hadn't shown up."

His legs were free, and Bruno was just pulling his left hand free.

"Can you walk?" Sarah asked.

"Don't think so," he said. "Bruno?"

Bruno leaned down on one knee. He gently placed an arm under Darwin's knees, then slipped his other arm behind Darwin's shoulders and stood. Carrying Darwin like a baby, Bruno waited for direction.

"Lombardi ran to the front offices," Darwin said. "He can't leave this building alive."

Casper and Parkman started that way. Sarah followed, and Bruno took up the rear. At the door, Sarah put a hand on Darwin's arm.

"I'm so sorry," she said to him. "They beat you and cut you. Holy shit …" She gasped and caught her breath.

"Just get Lombardi. I can heal later."

Casper fired into the door leading to the front of the building as sirens wailed in the distance. Arabella screamed from the other side of the door.

Casper shouted for her to get out of the way and fired again, pulverizing the lock—it shot right out of the door. Then he shouldered it, but the door stayed in place.

He tried again. The door didn't budge.

"There has to be a bar or something across the door on the other side," Casper said. "I don't think we can get in this way."

A weapon fired on the other side of the door. Arabella screamed again.

Darwin turned around to see what the guys dressed in black were up to, but they were gone. He looked for Sarah—she was gone, too.

Chapter 55

A voice told Sarah what to do even before Casper shot into the door. The voice in her head—or voices—seemed to be there just when she needed them the most.

She exited the warehouse door, sprinted along the side of the building until she reached the front, and ran up the stairs two at a time, mindful not to step on the man still sprawled out unconscious. Once inside the first glass door of the front offices of Universal Shipping, she had to open another glass door, but this one was locked.

Sirens screamed closer. Backup was on the way. There was no way Lombardi was leaving the building on his own. He would be in custody or a body bag.

Inside, she saw him. Lombardi held Arabella by the hair. She followed Lombardi's gaze to a desk in the corner. Aaron hid behind it, pinned down by random shots from Lombardi.

She aimed her weapon low and to the side, then fired into

the glass. It shattered inward. She dropped low and prepared to dive inside.

Lombardi jerked toward her and fired his weapon madly, waving it left and right. Then he backed into an office and disappeared, dragging the crying Arabella with him.

Sarah, panting like a wild animal, her heart skipping beats in her chest, dove inside the building, slid on several shards of glass that sliced into her skin, then rolled toward Aaron's hiding spot.

She got behind the desk beside Aaron, ignoring the blood smear she had left behind. Arabella continued to cry.

"You hit?" she asked.

Aaron shook his head. "You?" He looked at the blood on Sarah.

"Glass."

"What are you planning?" he asked.

"To kill him."

"Good plan."

Arabella continued to cry. They heard nothing from Lombardi.

"How?" Aaron asked.

"No idea." She checked her gun. "Shit. One bullet left."

"That's all you have?"

She held the weapon close to her chest and looked skyward. The emergency task force would show up if they could hold Lombardi off long enough.

But she didn't want to. She wasn't a *murderer* in the true sense. She didn't desire to kill people by any stretch. Even the bomber of Kelowna, a self-proclaimed Satanist, lived because she didn't kill him when she had the chance.

But Lombardi was a different case altogether. A man like

him had money. He had connections. His time in prison—what little time he did get—would be comfortable. He would still pull the strings from the inside. As long as Lombardi lived, they would have to watch over their shoulders and sleep with one eye open.

Emergency vehicles pulled up out front. Arabella's crying simmered down a bit.

"What's he doing?" Aaron asked.

"Waiting out the authorities. His big-shot lawyers will have him out by tomorrow."

"No way," Aaron said.

"No fucking way," Sarah echoed.

She edged out from behind the desk, the gun extended in front of her, both hands steadying it.

"Lombardi," she called. "It's over. Come on out."

"Fuck you, Sarah. I step out; you shoot me."

"Not with Arabella in your hands. Come out and leave your weapon on the floor."

Something thumped above her. She adjusted her aim upward.

"Sarah," Aaron said. "Don't shoot." He pointed at the ceiling tiles. "That's Alex. Keep Lombardi talking so Alex can zone in on his position."

Sarah nodded and retook her aim on the doorway of the office Lombardi hid inside.

"Let the girl go, Lombardi. We both know you're not going to kill her."

"Then you don't know me very well."

Arabella stepped into view. First her shoulder, then her whole body. The tough mobster held Arabella's hair in one hand, the gun in the other, placed against her temple. He peeked around the edge.

"Drop your gun, Sarah."

Outside, noises of car doors closing and people grunting orders came to her through the broken glass. Her hands were slick with sweat, and blood still oozed from her cuts. She blinked salty water out of her right eye.

"The place is surrounded, Lombardi. There's nowhere for you to go. You're willing to add the murder of the young girl to your list of charges?"

"I let her go; you kill me. I'm looking to walk out of this building, my body still intact."

"Oh, like how you left Darwin still intact? Fuck you. Just let the girl go."

A ceiling tile dropped in the office behind Lombardi. Sarah caught sight of the corner of it as it fell from above.

Lombardi jumped at the sound and moved out of the office. He wrapped an arm around Arabella and drew her close to his chest, then fired back inside the office several times.

If Alex had just fallen from the ceiling above, Lombardi's bullets would've hit him unless he found cover.

Sarah's finger squeezed the trigger in rage, but she couldn't fire her only bullet. If it hit Arabella, she would never be able to live with herself.

Lombardi, out in the open, swung his gun hand to Sarah.

"Drop it, Sarah. Do it now. Or I fire at you and then kill Arabella."

"Okay," she shouted. "Hold on." She had to think, but there was no time. Not a single voice echoed in her head. She was in this position because of them, and now they were silent. *Thanks so fucking much.*

Aaron stood up from behind the desk. "Take me," he said. "Leave the girl and take me as your hostage."

Lombardi moved his gun toward Aaron and fired, then swung it back to Sarah before she had a chance to take proper aim. Arabella screamed when the gun went off. Aaron twisted violently sideways as Lombardi's bullet hit him, then dropped back below the desk.

"Sarah," Lombardi shouted. "Last chance to throw your weapon aside."

Tears clouded her vision. She couldn't shoot straight now, even if she wanted to. It was over. Whitman and Spencer were dead. Darwin would take weeks to heal and be scarred for life. Aaron was shot down five feet to her right, and she only had one bullet in the gun she couldn't fire for fear of hitting Arabella.

Nothing was left to do but lower her weapon and dive for cover.

Her right hand numbed.

Just like she'd done countless times in the past, Vivian was taking over. Sarah's aim was true and accurate when Vivian held the weapon. Celestial eyes had proven infallible in the past.

"Sarah!" Lombardi screamed.

She closed her eyes as Vivian took over her other hand and arm. She didn't even have to hold them up anymore.

A ceiling tile fell from above again. There was a heavy thud, a grunt, and then a moment later, Sarah's weapon discharged its final bullet.

Arabella screamed.

The door behind Sarah burst inward. Another weapon fired nearby. She fought to open her eyes under Vivian's cloud. At least a dozen men in SWAT gear burst into the front offices of Universal Shipping.

Vivian took a stronger hold of Sarah. She felt herself falling until she stopped moving and lay sprawled on the floor, Aaron's face beside hers.

Then Vivian blessedly turned the nightmare off and took Sarah's consciousness away from her.

Chapter 56

ONE WEEK LATER ...

Sarah eased the hospital door open and stepped inside. Casper and Parkman were seated on a small couch against the wall. Aaron stood at the window, massive white bandages wrapped around his bullet wound. Doctors said he was lucky. Missed all vital organs. Entered a meaty part of his shoulder and exited cleanly. Nothing but a scar would be left behind to add to his other bullet wounds. How many times could a man be shot before one of the bullets counted? She'd punched him in his good arm and swore that if he got shot again, she'd surely kill him.

In the other corner of Darwin's hospital room, Daniel, Alex, and Benjamin sat on small wooden chairs the nurses had brought in for this meeting.

"Everyone's here," Casper said.

Sarah moved across the room to stand beside Aaron. Everyone was still dressed in black. Officers from around the country had attended Spencer's and Whitman's funerals. Security had been extremely tight as word on the street was the 'Ndrangheta had its head cut off, and members of the seven families vied for street control and territory amongst themselves. Some sought vengeance for Lombardi's death.

Add to that the deaths of Falcone, who never regained consciousness and died in the hospital, Spinello, and Fabriano, and the entire organization was in upheaval.

Sarah's last bullet had found success that morning in the front offices of Universal Shipping. Vivian had fired Sarah's weapon. The bullet struck Lombardi between his eyes. His aim off, Lombardi's weapon fired once more before he dropped it.

Alex had lost his balance and fallen in the office Lombardi had been cowering in. He bounced off the top of a desk, and by the time Lombardi fired back into the office, Alex had dropped behind the desk without being hit by any of Lombardi's bullets.

Just as Sarah had felt Vivian taking over, Benjamin dropped from the ceiling, bad leg and all, right beside Lombardi, knocking the man off balance. Arabella screamed and jerked away from Lombardi as he swung his gun around to shoot Benjamin. Sarah's gun had fired, and Lombardi was dead before a paramedic entered the building.

Arabella was removed and taken into foster care. She would get a new name and life, far away from any men associated with organized crime.

Other than Darwin's wounds, Aaron was the only one who took a bullet, to Benjamin's delight. Not that he was happy Aaron got shot—quite the opposite. He was just happy it wasn't him again. The tables had turned.

Sarah still couldn't get over Darwin's careful planning of the robbery of cocaine and his decision to return it to Lombardi with Bruno inside. He had gambled with his life, hoping Lombardi wouldn't maim or kill him until the coke was returned. His plan to stall Lombardi and have the truck unloaded almost worked. However, without Arabella showing up and fingering Vincenzo for a crime against the family, which held Lombardi up long enough to stop inflicting damage on him, Darwin would've probably died in that warehouse.

It was all reckless and insane. But it was the lengths her friends were willing to go to protect her, and she was eternally grateful for all of them.

Her eyes puffy after crying at Whitman's and Spencer's funeral, she sat by Aaron in the corner of the hospital room and waited until she had their attention.

"Darwin, the doctor says you can leave tomorrow," she said.

"And I need all of you to escort me to the airport so I can get the hell out of here." Sarah heard the humor in his voice. He didn't want to leave his friends but enjoyed his life off the radar. "I need to get back to Rosina. She's worried sick."

Bruno walked in and crossed his meaty arms, then leaned against the wall by the door.

Sarah waited for the door to shut. "Glad you could come, Bruno."

The big man nodded at her and offered a half smile. Then it was gone, his mouth a thin line again.

"I called you here today to let you know I'm retiring."

Several gasps emitted around the room. "Too many years, too many close calls." She looked down at her fingers resting in her lap. "And now Whitman is gone, even though I will always remember him as Drake Bellamy." She looked up and found Parkman. "Remember the crypt in Montone, Italy? That church where those assholes put you up on the cross, and Rosalie's team came in and got you down?"

Parkman nodded. "How could I ever forget?"

She glanced at the faces around the room. "That was all before this. Back in those days, it was just Parkman and me. The first time I heard the name Drake Bellamy was in that crypt. He was supposed to be killed at a baseball game in Toronto. I found a way to stop it, and Spencer helped." A sob escaped her lips. "I'm sorry. Give me a second."

She blew her nose, balled up the Kleenex, then took a deep breath.

"It's been a long journey and one I'm blessed to have been on. I've had outside help," she looked at Parkman, "but Rosalie died on that trip to Europe. Rod Howley was killed shortly after that. Esmerelda and Dolan, dead." She wiped a tear. "I met a relative with similar abilities in Vegas, and he was killed in Toronto. Cops have been murdered along the way, and I'm still standing. I guess what I'm saying is so many people have come and gone, and I wouldn't be able to live with myself if any of you in this room were ever killed because of a job I'm doing. As far as I'm concerned, we just buried Whitman and Spencer, the last two friends I'm willing to lose."

Aaron placed a hand on her shoulder.

"So, I'm retiring," she continued. "I talked to Vivian and told her everything. Told her to stop giving me prophecies of any kind. No more future stuff. Only sisterly things." A giggle came out. "I mean, if she wants to tell me what dress to buy, we're good. I can still shop with my sister. I like that."

A couple of them laughed, some didn't.

"What are you going to do?" Casper asked.

"Take Aaron on a vacation. Drive somewhere. See the country." She shrugged. "I always wanted to go back to Europe as a tourist. Who knows where life will take us? Maybe we'll even settle down. I'm going to be twenty-seven soon." Aaron turned to her, and their eyes met. "Maybe we'll start a family."

Parkman clapped his hands once, twice, then stopped. "I like that idea."

"What about you, Parkman?" she asked.

"Santa Rosa bound. Check-in on your parents and dust my office. Check messages. See if I can detect it privately and make a little cash. Drink a little bit. Catch up on some reading."

"I know the boys are eager to continue renovating the dojo. Once the fire department clears it, you guys are going back in, right?"

Alex nodded. Daniel nodded.

"It won't be the same without you, Aaron," Benjamin said. "But we'll manage."

"I'll be back," Aaron said, mimicking Arnold Schwarzenegger. "We won't be gone long. A couple of months, maybe."

Sarah nodded. "Not much is changing other than no more vigilantism and no more of my friends dying needlessly."

"Or getting shot," Benjamin added. "Kinda sick of that."

No one laughed.

"That sum it up?" Casper asked.

"Yes, it does."

He pulled out his cell phone. "Gotta make a call." He started for the door. "I'll be back in a few minutes to say goodbye." He brushed past Bruno and was out the door.

The room remained quiet for several moments, everyone lost in their thoughts.

Then Vivian spoke.

"What?" Sarah said.

They all looked at her.

You can retire. That's fine. But something's coming you can't avoid.

"Like what?" she asked out loud. "Vivian," she said by way of explanation.

A betrayal.

"Betrayal? By whom?" She glanced around the room. Darwin was trying to sit up. Aaron moved around her to stand in front. Parkman edged closer.

This runs deep. Too deep for me to see everything yet. Go on vacation. Get out of Toronto. But hurry. Someone is planning something against you.

"Planning what?"

Oh, shit—

"What, Vivian?" Sarah shouted.

Sarah. I'm so sorry. There's nothing I can do. Go, get out of Toronto. We'll talk more soon. I'll guide you ...

"Vivian, what did you see?" Her insides became heavy with worry and fear. "Vivian, talk to me."

I see you and Aaron.

"And?"

The betrayal is devastating. It ruins you.

"How so?" Everyone had made a semi-circle around her. "Vivian, how does it ruin me?"

Sarah Roberts no longer exists because of it.

Then Vivian was gone. A poof in her consciousness, then nothing. The conversation was over.

She stumbled, lightheaded. Arms grabbed her and held her up.

"What was that all about?" Aaron asked.

Sarah found her voice and looked up at the faces surrounding her. Casper pushed the door open and stepped back inside.

"What'd I miss?" he asked.

"I guess I'm not retiring."

"What?" Aaron said. "Why not? What did she say?"

Sarah met his strong gaze and looked deep into him. "Vivian said I'm going to be betrayed."

"Tell us who and how we can fix it."

"She doesn't know. It's too personal. Something about me. Which has always blocked her to some degree."

"Then we wait, and we watch. We can be careful."

A tear slipped past her lid. "Vivian said that Sarah Roberts no longer exists because of the betrayal."

"Exists?" Aaron blurted out. "So, you don't die, then? Sarah Roberts doesn't exist. That could just mean you're living with an alias. If you were going to die, wouldn't she say that?"

"I don't know, Aaron, I don't know. But whoever will betray me, and how they do it, will be quite costly. We need to leave town right away."

"Is that what Vivian said to do?" Parkman asked.

Sarah turned to him and nodded. "She said to leave immediately."

"Then let's go. We'll escort you out of the hospital. You and Aaron can pack up, and we'll drive you out of Toronto. We'll head to Ottawa or Montreal."

Sarah nodded. "We need to leave, Aaron."

Once their goodbyes were done, Sarah turned back at the door.

"Darwin, get well. Make it home. After what you did for me, I couldn't deal with it if something happened to you."

"I'll be fine, Sarah. Just get out of town and stay alive." He blinked once, then jolted in bed. "Shit."

"What?"

"Back when we entered that warehouse looking for Spinello, my men rounded up some of his dockworkers and placed them in a truck in the back of the warehouse lot. I don't recall anyone letting them out."

"Oh well. It's been a week. Not much we can do now." She smiled at him.

He offered a warm smile back.

She let the door close as she started down the hallway escorted by her entourage of men.

Stay alive? How, when her sister saw her death clear as day. Vivian had whispered two words to her: The Betrayal.

Afterword

DEAR READER,

Indulge me. Let me tell you a quick little story about a hole in the wall and a robbery. If you've read the Sarah Roberts Series and all the Afterwords, you might have heard some of this before, but not all of it.

Back in the late eighties and early nineties, I wanted to be a cop. My dad was a cop, and I excelled in law class in high school. The day I turned eighteen and could work as a security guard, I applied and got the job. I wanted everything law enforcement-related on my future résumé.

With that security company—the same one with the Toronto airport contract where we met Unibrow and his colleagues in this novel—I got promoted to patrol supervisor and worked as their dispatcher for a while. Finally, before leaving that company several years into it, I was promoted to a private investigator. I was licensed and would take jobs that included working undercover at a factory, following a wife on Tuesday nights because her husband thought she was cheating, and following a high school teacher for several reasons, one being infidelity.

Those were the days. I absolutely loved chasing people, following them, parking in such a way as to use my mirrors to watch them, and writing reports. In my opinion, I was cut out for the work. If that spouse were cheating, I'd not only find out, I'd have it on tape or camera as I'm very aggressive when I want something.

Ultimately, my efforts did not lead to a career in the police force. For several reasons, but the main one was my back. I broke my back when I was eleven years old. My lower back muscles would often give out when encountering too much stress. It still does to this day—maybe once every three to five years. Back in my late teens and early twenties, my back would pop out monthly. I'd fall to my knees and have difficulty walking for several days after.

After several years in the gym, doing yoga, and strengthening my core, this issue has been mostly erased from my life.

Since my dreams of being a police officer had vanished, I ended up in a retail career. I owned several stores for nearly twenty years while writing novels and short stories. (One of my stores is still open and making decent money—my ex-wife runs it.) In 2010, I left retail life and became a full-time writer, and here we are.

Now that that's out of the way, I want to tell you about a store I ran in Burlington, Ontario, on Upper Middle Road in 1992. I lived in Hamilton, Ontario, at the time. I ran six stores in those days: three in Hamilton, two in Burlington, and one in Stoney Creek. They were all within a half-hour drive of each other.

One night, my pager (remember pagers?) went off at two in the morning. An alarm had sounded at my Upper Middle store in Burlington. The police were already on their way to the location and requested the key holder's presence.

I bolted out of bed, dressed, hopped in my Camaro, and raced to the store, about a twenty-minute drive in the morning.

The police were already there when I arrived. Once the store was open, they entered, cleared it, and then I followed and surveyed the damage.

My store had sensors on the entry points—the doors—and motion sensors. When we got inside, several thousand dollars worth of merchandise and a lot of money from the safe were gone.

In that strip mall, the unit beside the store was empty, under renovation, and without an alarm system, as there was nothing in there to steal.

The wall between my store and the empty unit was thin. Just like the wall Alex broke between the dojo under renovation and the comic book store. That's where that idea came from. In my store, the thief had entered the empty unit beside mine, walked midway down the length of the store, and smashed a hole in the wall. The motion sensors picked him up as soon as the culprit crawled into my store. He dashed about, grabbing as much as he could, and disappeared out the back door, which set off that sensor.

The thief was later caught and arrested. Here's why: He was an employee.

True story.

This guy had been robbed before (he concocted a story to cover the truth) when he was working a Sunday night shift, and the safe was full of the weekend cash. That robbery was him as well. He later confessed during an interrogation to both robberies.

The first robbery always bothered me. That employee (I still remember his name but won't print it here) repeated his first robbery story word for word as he'd memorized it. Something didn't sit right with me, but I had to let it go. I wasn't the investigating officer, after all.

When the police examined the hole in my store's wall (the second robbery at the same store), they asked me if I suspected anyone. Had anything weird happened lately? Had the store had any unusual customers and so on and so on?

I told them I suspected my employee had lied about the first robbery. He was the only one that came to mind when the police asked if I suspected anyone. Otherwise, this would have to be labeled a random hit.

They picked up the employee and drilled him for hours downtown. When these guys interrogate you, they talk as if they think you've done it to sweat you. I've been interrogated for a robbery (another story for another Afterword one day), and it was hardcore.

Anyway, the employee confessed to everything and was charged.

One night, about a month later, that employee came back to the store and asked to speak to me. I stepped outside, prepared to listen to what he had to say. Instead of angst, he apologized for his actions and then attempted to justify them by saying that his mother was ill and he needed the money.

Ready for this: he was studying to be a lawyer one day.

I'm not kidding.

I wanted to share that story so you could see where the hole in the comic book store idea came from in chapter twenty-three.

Now, on to other things …

In chapter fourteen, Darwin sits outside Fabriano's Il Forno Ristorante, thinking about Toronto and how much he loves it. When you read the beginning of that chapter, you're reading mostly my words.

I grew up in Toronto and the surrounding area. In the late '80s, I shopped at the World's Biggest Bookstore and the Sam the Record Man store. I remember when Mel Lastman called in the army to clear the snow. Growing up, I went to dozens of concerts in Toronto, from AC/DC and Cheap Trick to Peter Gabriel and Bruce Springsteen, Foreigner, Richard Marx, Phil Collins, and Heart, to name a few. I have stories that are heartwarming and others that are tragic about Toronto. That's one of the reasons I visit it so often in my novels—it's a city that's so dear to me. I look back on those days with fondness and miss that city.

I love it so much I own a book called *Toronto* by Allan Levine. It's a biography of a city. A biography? Of a city? What? Really?

Yes, and I love it!

That said, I think this sums up our nineteenth journey in Sarah's life. Book twenty, *The Betrayal*, is next. That one will be a life-changing experience for many of the characters in Sarah's life. Then watch for book twenty-one, *Sarah's Return*. (You might ask yourself, why does she have to return? You'll know why once you read *The Betrayal*—no spoilers here, though. Sorry).

Thank you for reading. First and foremost, thank you. Without you, the reader, where would we be?

Special thanks to my editing team, starting with Robb Grindstaff. What a scholar and a gentleman. And a special thanks to my beta readers—they find the smallest errors that everyone else seems to miss in each manuscript. Without them, this novel, or any other I write, would not be whole.

I may write the words, but it takes a village to create a novel ready for the marketplace.

I'd like to send a special thanks to my cover designer, who is always there when I need him and makes changes within minutes, so thanks, Daniel Johnsen. (Daniel of the dojo boys was named after him. They look the same, too. Alex and Benjamin are his brothers in real life.)

That's it for another journey. I sincerely hope you enjoyed this edition and look forward to *The Betrayal.*

Be well. Take care of yourself and each other.

And get caught reading.

Jonas Saul

About Jonas Saul

Jonas Saul is the bestselling author of the Sarah Roberts Series—more than two million sold!—and has written and published over sixty thrillers. After acquiring an agent, he signed several deals in Los Angeles, with MadRiver Pictures optioning his Sarah Roberts Series— over forty books!—(currently in development).

Jonas has often outranked Stephen King and Dean

Koontz on Amazon over the past decade. He's regularly invited to be a guest speaker, teacher, or workshop presenter at international writing conferences and film festivals worldwide. He hosts an annual writer's retreat in Greece, where he currently lives. He focuses his teaching on how to get tension and emotion in every scene, on every page, how he made it as a creator/writer, the path to success in this business, and the pitfalls to avoid. He also hosts a reading retreat in Greece with guest authors, yoga retreats, and hiking retreats. Visit the Imagine Greece Retreats website at www.imaginegreeceretreats.com, or email him directly to discuss an opportunity to join one of the retreats at jonas@imaginegreeceretreats.com.

Jonas is also a professional freelance editor. He works for several publishers and does private editing for clients, with many testimonials on his website at www.imaginepress.org, which details each author's response to Jonas's editing skills. Email Jonas directly for an editing quote at editor@imaginepress.org.

To book Jonas for a speaking engagement at a writer's conference/festival, to have him on your jury at a film festival, or even to say hello, email Jonas directly at jonassaul@icloud.com.

For updates on releases, hit the "Follow" button on Amazon or Bookbub, and join Jonas on Facebook, where he's most active.

Contact Jonas Saul

Linktree: Find me here

Email: jonassaul@icloud.com